HOOKER

J.L. PERRY

To Jeanette,
Brock sends
his love.

[signature] x

hachette
AUSTRALIA

WARNING—this book contains sexual content, coarse language and some violence. It is recommended for persons over the age of 18.

This is a work of fiction. Names, characters, places and incidents are the product of the author's imagination. Any resemblance to the actual events, locales, or persons, living or dead, is entirely coincidental.

⌐⌐ hachette
AUSTRALIA
Published in Australia and New Zealand in 2016
by Hachette Australia
(an imprint of Hachette Australia Pty Limited)
Level 17, 207 Kent Street, Sydney NSW 2000
www.hachette.com.au

10 9 8 7 6 5 4 3 2 1

National Library of Australia
Cataloguing-in-Publication data:

Perry, J. L., 1972– author.
Hooker/JL Perry.

ISBN 978 0 7336 3584 7 (pbk)

Romance fiction.

A823.4

Cover design by Soxsational Cover Art, www.facebook.com/SoxsationalCoverArt
Cover image by Svetlana Fedoseeva/Adobe Stock
Typeset in Perpetua by Kirby Jones

FSC
www.fsc.org
MIX
Paper from
responsible sources
FSC® C009448

Printed in Australia by Griffin Press, Adelaide, an Accredited ISO AS/NZS 4001:2004 Environmental Management Systems printer The paper this book is printed on is certified against the Forest Stewardship Council® Standards. Griffin Press holds FSC chain of custody certification SGS-COC-005088. FSC promotes environmentally responsible, socially beneficial and economically viable management of the world's forests.

This book is dedicated to my dad,
my hero ...

BOOKS BY J.L. PERRY

Destiny Series

My Destiny
My Forever
Damaged — Jacinta's Story
Against All Odds — Angel's Story

Standalone Reads

Bastard
Luckiest Bastard — The Novella
Jax (coming soon)
Nineteen Letters (coming soon)

It doesn't matter where you've come from,
or where you've been.
Love is extraordinary. It has the power to heal.
When you find the one you're destined to be with,
the missing part of your soul,
dreams will come true, and the magic will happen.

PROLOGUE

The Past ...

JADE

I'm cursed. Or so I've always thought.

But I think things are finally looking up for me. I can't believe I've finally been adopted after all this time. For the past eleven years of my life, I've been shifted from one horrible foster home to the next. Today is the day my life changes for the better. Now I'm going to have everything I've ever wished for.

A real home.

A real family.

My adversity started the moment I came into this world. My mother haemorrhaged and died giving birth to me—at least that's what I've been told. That alone can come with catastrophic consequences for a child, but that was only the beginning of what was in store for me. Her death started a chain of events that would devastate me. Losing his wife and being left to care for a newborn turned out to be too much for my father. A few months after I was born, he gave me up. That's how I became a ward of the state.

Over the years, I've been inappropriately touched, mentally and physically abused, and almost sent to the brink of starvation by one incredibly cruel family I was unlucky enough to be placed with. Sure, not all foster homes are bad. I did, on many occasions, get placed with nice families. The trouble with foster care is it's only temporary. And those nicer homes never lasted. Young as I was, it never took long to distinguish between families who fostered because they cared, and those who did it solely for the money.

The things I've been through in my short life would've broken even the strongest of characters, but not me. As the years passed and I realised nothing and no one could change my situation, that no one was going to ride in on a beautiful white stallion and save me from the miserable predicament I was in, I began to use my experiences to my advantage. Every hardship only served to strengthen my will to survive. And if my life has taught me anything, it's that things aren't always as they seem.

As we pull up to the front gates of my new home, I'm sure my jade green eyes are wide with disbelief. I pinch myself on the arm just to make sure I'm not dreaming. This place is huge—like, a mansion. My gaze traces the large initials moulded into the black wrought iron gates, as they slowly open. I wonder what 'MM' stands for?

The long driveway leads towards a large white house. This place looks like something you'd see in the movies. I still can't believe I'm going to be living here. I can't contain the excitement that courses through my body as I bounce up and down on my seat. I've been told that jade is supposed to be a symbol of luck. It's even been said to guard against accidents and misfortune. I never believed that. Look at the life I've led up to now.

2

Maybe I'm wrong.

Maybe it's actually true.

Maybe jade really is lucky.

When the car finally comes to a stop at the entrance to the house, the excitement vanishes as the fear takes over. This always happens when I arrive somewhere new. It's probably because I never know what lies behind those doors. Some of the terrible places I lived in over the years flash through my mind.

Please let this be one of the good ones.

'Are you ready to go inside?' Cheryl, my social worker, asks.

She must see the uncertainty in my eyes because she reaches across the seat, taking my hand in hers.

'It's okay to be frightened, Jade,' she says in a reassuring voice. 'I understand this'll be hard for you, but Melody handpicked you out of all the other children in the orphanage. She can see how special you are, just like I can.'

I feel a smile tug at my lips. Cheryl has always been kind to me.

When she lets go of my hand and exits the car, I do the same. After opening the trunk, she passes me my worn brown suitcase. The handle is broken so I tuck it under my arm. It and the few clothes it contains are my only possessions in this world. I treasure them.

After we climb the front steps and stop at the large wooden door, I notice the same initials that were on the front gate carved into the rich wood. When Cheryl raises her hand to knock, I take a large breath and square my shoulders. I'm a big girl now, I can do this.

An elderly man answers a short time later. He's dressed in a suit. His eyes rake over Cheryl before landing on me. He

3

has a look of disgust on his face. I don't think I'm going to like him much.

'My name is Cheryl, I'm with the Department of Community Services. This is Jade.'

He looks down at her outstretched hand, but doesn't take hold. 'M is expecting you,' is all he says, stepping aside so we can enter. He seems mean. It brings all my worries back.

That thought gets pushed to the side when we enter the grand foyer. 'Wow,' I breathe as my eyes try to take it all in. I've never seen anything like this before. I still can't believe this is going to be my new home.

'This way, please,' the mean man says after clearing his throat. We follow him into a large room to the side of the main entrance. 'The child is here, ma'am.'

'Welcome, my dear,' Melody says, rising from her desk and coming to stand in front of me. She has a pleasant smile on her face, which makes me feel better. She was really nice to me the first time I met her in Cheryl's office. I hope she's nice all the time.

'Thank you,' I whisper, bowing my head.

Cheryl stays for a short time, but when she finally prepares to leave and says her goodbyes, my stomach churns and the butterflies return. I'm going to miss seeing her. I'm suddenly feeling unsure again about being left on my own in this big house.

Standing by the window, I feel sad as I watch her drive away. A short time later, Melody returns from seeing Cheryl to the door, and offers to escort me to my new bedroom. Scooping my bag off the floor and tucking it under my arm, I trail behind her. Silently, I count the white marble steps on the staircase as I go. When we reach the landing, she leads me down the long hallway until we come to a stop outside one of the doors. I can't believe my eyes when she opens it to reveal the beauty within. My heart rate picks up the moment I step inside.

'Wow. Is this really my room? Like, forever?' I ask in disbelief, because I really can't believe it.

'Yes,' she replies.

It's so beautiful. Too beautiful for words. I'm so excited; I have to try hard to hold in my squeal. My bed is so big. It has a pretty pink cover and white lace canopy over the top. I have my very own princess bed. I take everything in as I slowly spin in a circle. I'm a princess, and my new home is a castle.

I can't believe I'm rich.

Boy, I'd love to rub this in Ruby's face if I could. She's one of the mean girls from the orphanage. She was always horrible to me. She used to tip water on my mattress and then tell everyone I peed myself. *Lying cow.*

I gently place my suitcase on top of the covers of my new bed.

'Get that filthy thing off there!' Melody screeches, making me jump with fright. Quickly picking it back up, I clutch it to my chest before hesitantly turning to face her.

'I'm sorry,' I whisper, bowing my head again.

'Come with me,' she snaps as she walks towards the white door on the other side of the room.

My heart starts to race. I hope she's not going to lock me in the cupboard. At one of the foster homes I stayed in a few years ago, I'd get locked in a cupboard for hours sometimes. It was so dark and scary.

I release the nervous breath I'm holding when she opens the door. It leads to a large white bathroom. 'Give me that bag and take off your clothes,' she orders.

I'm frozen with fright.

'Take off your clothes, Jade.'

Her voice is stern so I do as I'm told. My hands are shaking as I undo the buttons on my favourite pink dress.

'Everything,' she adds when I'm down to my underwear. Once I remove my undies, I use both my hands to cover my private parts. Her face screws up as she picks my things off the floor with two fingers, like I have cooties or something. 'I want you to take a bath and get dressed in your new clothes. When you're done, come downstairs for lunch. You'll find everything you need in the chest of drawers next to your bed.'

'Where are you taking my things?' I ask in a quiet voice.

'These rags? They're going in the trash, where they belong. You won't be needing them anymore.' With that she turns, leaving me alone.

No! Not my most treasured possessions. I successfully manage to fight back the tears that threaten to fall. Over the years I've become a master at it. Crying only seemed to get me in more trouble.

*

As upset as I was at the time, my measly possessions were soon forgotten as the weeks and months passed. I now had a wardrobe full of beautiful clothes and shoes. There were even pretty bows for me to wear in my hair. Life here was good.

M placed me into one of the most exclusive all-girl schools in the country. I'd attended over twenty different public schools in the previous five years. Although I was bright, I was behind on my school work because I'd been shuffled around so much. M hired private tutors to help me catch up. That's what

I call her. I found out the initials MM stood for Miss Melody, but she prefers just plain M.

It would be another seven years before I'd find out the true meaning behind those initials.

M sent me to elocution lessons. I thought there was nothing wrong with the way I spoke, but she disagreed. Apparently talking like you have a plum in your mouth is the way people communicate in her circle. To be honest, at the time I was just grateful she seemed to care. Boy, were those thoughts misguided. It was all just part of her devious, masterful plan.

On weekends, I attended one of the finest finishing schools money could buy. She said I wasn't refined enough for a lady. Newsflash, I ain't no lady. Well, I wasn't at the time. I was an eleven-year-old girl who, due to her past, was tough and street smart. Over the next few years though, that's exactly what I became. *A lady.*

Once I hit fourteen, I was given my own personal trainer to help me stay in shape. M's words, not mine. There was nothing wrong with my body. I was tall and slim with curves in all the right places. Despite all my misfortunes, I was lucky enough to be blessed with the most amazing genetics.

As I grew older, M enforced strict rules. She forbade me to have a boyfriend. Like, threatened to go ninja on my arse if I even went near a boy. I honestly thought she was looking out for me, so I did exactly as she requested. I was only a child after all, so I didn't really care, or know any better. Boys weren't high on my agenda at the time.

I was about sixteen when M confessed why she'd handpicked me from the orphanage. 'You're exquisite, my dear. You have the face and body of a goddess. Those eyes, *breathtaking*. The moment I saw you I knew you were the one. My men are going to be clawing to get their hands on you.'

I had no idea what she meant by her 'men'. Unfortunately, I'd find out soon enough.

I'm not going to lie, I was confused and hurt to think she'd chosen me solely on my looks. Appearance was everything to her, so it shouldn't have surprised me. I was continually scolded if I hadn't dressed to her high standards, or acted accordingly.

As long as I played by her rules, I had everything handed to me on a silver platter, the finest designer clothes and vacations all over the world, but my new home lacked love and affection just like the others. Looking back now, I suppose you can't miss something you've never really known. Sure, M treated me well, but there were times she made me feel more like an object than an actual human being.

It wasn't until my eighteenth birthday that I discovered the real reason M had been putting so much time, effort and money into making me so refined, so perfect. As it turns out, she wasn't as generous as I thought. *She was grooming me*. With all my experience, I should've known nothing in life comes for free, and the day had come when I'd have to pay M back. Every single cent she'd invested in me, and more.

It was also the day I found out the first M in MM didn't stand for Miss at all, but Madam. Madam Melody. Monster Melody would be better suited. Madam Melody owned the most exclusive, high-class escort agency in the country. I became her protégé. Her new meal ticket.

'I've put a lot of time and money into you, my dear,' were her exact words. 'It's now time for you to repay that debt. You will be coming to work for me.' The tone in which she spoke told me this wasn't up for negotiation. 'With your exquisite beauty, that body, and your sweet persona, Jade, you're going to make me a lot of money. Make us both a lot of money.'

A week after my birthday, her long awaited plan came to fruition. I was set up in my own luxurious apartment, and began the training that would ultimately make me her number one girl.

Six months later, I was ready to embark on my new life as a high-class escort—a hooker, for lack of a better word. She made me sign a contract, binding me to her for the next seven years; one year of service for every year I'd lived with her. Initially I was devastated. After reading the contract, I felt sick. Physically sick. It hurt to think all the nice things she'd done for me weren't because she cared. It was obvious I was just a commodity for her sick and twisted plan. This was why I'd been forbidden to associate with the opposite sex. She needed to guarantee my virtue would remain intact. That way she could sell me off to the highest bidder like a piece of meat.

My contract stated fifty percent of all my earnings were to go to M. Repayment for all she'd outlaid getting me ready for this role. She was my carer, my guardian. There shouldn't have been any need for repayment. I felt trapped. I had no money and nowhere else to go. Sure, I'd had a good education and would eventually find employment, but if I fled, I'd be forced to live on the streets. She had manipulated me into thinking I owed her, and that what she was doing was for the best.

The only positive thing I could see in this situation was the kind of money on offer, as it would give me the opportunity to set myself up for life. A chance to start fresh, once M released me. To live my life the way I've always wanted to live it. A chance to be free from all the horrors of my past.

My first night on the job was the worst. That first sexual encounter will haunt me forever. *For-fucking-ever.* The night I lost my virginity to a disgusting client. He was a short, stocky, balding, middle-aged, perverted pig of a man. He was the highest bidder for my innocence.

The day before, M had paraded me around in front of all the potential suitors, wearing only skimpy white lace underwear, a garter belt and stockings. It was humiliating, and so degrading. Once they'd had their fill of ogling me, she made me leave the room so the bidding could begin.

Two hundred thousand dollars was the amount he paid to strip me of my virtue, and all my self-worth. I only know that because one hundred thousand dollars was deposited into my bank account the next day. My cut. Knowing what I know now, I wouldn't relive that night for all the money in the world. *No fucking way.*

Over the years though, I've learnt to deal with my situation. The life of a high-class escort isn't all glitz and glamour. There've been times when I've struggled with what I'm expected to do, with the person I've become. Like, really struggled. I remember thinking to myself I'd rather die than do it again. What little respect I'd still had for M was gone. It was replaced with hate. With contempt. How could she do this to me?

As much as I hated it, however, in the grand scheme of things, it was a walk in the park compared to most of my childhood.

I only had two more years of my sentence to serve, and then I'd be free. I'd finally accepted this was my destiny, my fate. This is who I was meant to be. For the interim anyway. Or so I thought.

I had no idea that I'd soon be faced with a situation where I'd break all the rules. M would've spit kittens if she ever found out I'd betrayed her trust. Yet she betrayed me in the worst possible way. She should've been the one person who looked out for my welfare, not the one to throw me to the lions.

It clearly states in my contract that I'm not allowed to have any contact with a man outside of my work. That meant no boyfriends and definitely no casual sex. I had no qualms about that clause—because of what I've been forced into doing, I kind of hate men anyway. Well, I had no qualms until I met Brock Weston. After my encounter with Mr Weston, my life would never be the same.

One night of passion with a sinfully hot, charming and charismatic stranger would change everything.

Would change me.

CHAPTER ONE

'How are you feeling tonight, ma'am?' Rupert asks when he opens the back door of the limousine for me.

'Fine thanks, Rupert,' I reply, my eyes meeting his as I smile. It's what I always tell him, even if I'm not okay. I love how he always asks though. He's been my saviour since he came to work for M.

I was sixteen when Rupert arrived. At first I was wary of him: some of M's henchmen are creepy or just plain thugs. Once I got to know Rupert though, I soon realised he was one of the good ones. He's a lovely man, and sincere.

It took him a few years to work his way up the ranks and gain M's trust, but once he did, he was assigned to me permanently. Rupert's been looking after me for five years now. Truthfully, I was over the moon about it. He's always been kind. In my opinion he's far too nice to work for someone like her, but I guess she pays well. Of course I didn't tell M how happy I was— she's a spiteful bitch. She would've used the knowledge against me if she knew I was fond of him. She's a master manipulator.

Rupert's controlled by M just as much as I am, but from the very beginning, he's always looked out for me. I'm not

13

sure if I would've survived this long without him. Especially after that awful first night.

*

Rupert escorts me up to the penthouse suite. It's the room M reserves for her best clients. I'm on the verge of throwing up when we reach the door. I'd been thrust into the arms of strangers for as long as I can remember, but never in my life have I felt so much despair. So utterly helpless.

Although it's against the rules for him to stay, Rupert can see my apprehension—my entire body is trembling. The pained look on his handsome, aging face, tells me he is just as troubled by my circumstances as I am. I'm not used to people giving a shit about me, but it's quite obvious he does. It surprises and soothes me all at once. Reassuringly, he promises me he'll be waiting right outside the door. It gives me the confidence I need to enter the room. Without Rupert, I'm not sure I would've been able to go through with it.

When I see the man who awaits me, bile rises to my throat, and all the hairs on the back of my neck stand on end. Great, the creepy one. The one who'd been licking his lips the whole time M had me on display the day before. Just having his eyes on me makes me feel dirty. Out of the twenty or so men M had invited to bid on me, he was the one I'd prayed I wouldn't get. Of course, fate being the bitch it is, it was him. *I knew I was fucking cursed.*

As I stand in the foyer of the penthouse suite, the creep rubs his grubby little hands together as his beady eyes travel over my body. It literally makes me shudder.

'Undress,' he commands.

I'd spent the previous six months training, being taught the art of seduction, but in this moment, everything is forgotten. All I want is to get this over with as fast as possible. Just being in his presence repulses me.

The moment I'm naked, he instructs me to go into the bedroom and lie on the bed. *I can do this*, I chant in my head as I make my way down the hallway, *I can do this.*

Once I've laid down, I fix my gaze firmly on the ceiling above me. I can't bring myself to make eye contact with him. I will my mind to transport me anywhere but here. I hear him shuffling around the room, but my eyes remain glued on the ceiling. *I can do this*, I encourage myself. In a few hours, hopefully sooner, this will all be over.

He stands beside the bed, looking down at me. Out of the corner of my eye I can see him undressing. Quickly, I snap my eyes shut. *I can do this ... I can do this.*

My eyes spring open when I feel something drop beside me on the bed—a black bag, similar to the one I use when I go to the gym. I don't want to see what's inside, so my eyes hastily move back to the ceiling. I hear the sound of the zipper over the erratic beating of my heart, before he grabs hold of my wrist.

'This will ensure you stay exactly where I want you,' he says.

I still can't bring myself to look at him. The moment I feel the cool metal against my skin though, I can no longer look away.

'What are you doing?' I ask. The fear in my voice almost makes it unrecognisable. I want to scream, but I can't. M had pre-warned me that this man had paid a lot of money to spend time with me. She forbade me from protesting against any of his demands. She insisted I was to give him anything he wanted. I hated her even more for putting me in this position.

'Making sure you can't move,' is his reply as he quickly fastens the handcuff around my wrist before securing it to the bed. Instinctively, my arm tugged from its position. I'm trapped. He moves to the other side of the bed while my heart thumps furiously against my ribcage. *I can do this … I can do this*. My chanting is kind of moot by this point—this was going ahead whether I wanted it to or not.

Soon, both arms and legs are tightly fastened to the bed posts. He has me spread out like a starfish. Bile rises in my throat again as he licks his lips and admires his handiwork.

'Now that's a sight,' he murmurs as he bends down and retrieves his phone from the bag. *Click … click … click*, is all I hear as he snaps shots of me from different positions. Tears sting my eyes, but I will them away. *I can do this*. But in that moment I know I *can't* do this, and it's too late.

When he's done, he kneels on the mattress, making the bed dip. As his face comes towards mine, my eyes hastily close again. His wet mouth presses sickeningly against my lips briefly as his hands palm my breasts.

'Your tits are perfect. By the feel of them, I'd say real too,' he whispers in his creepy voice as he roughly squeezes the one he was holding, sending pain radiating through me. 'Open that pretty mouth of yours,' he demands as his finger traces a line across my lips. 'I'm looking forward to fucking it later.'

Instinctively, my mouth clamps tightly shut.

'Open your fucking mouth,' he sneers as his hand comes to rest around my throat. This time I do as I am told. My repulsion is quickly replaced again by fear.

I gasp for air as he shoves something soft into my mouth. A gag. Panic fills me. Why is he gagging me? What is he going to do? My nostrils flare as I inhale a large breath through my nose as his revolting body comes to rest over mine. I squirm as his chubby little fingers trail a line up my inner thigh, then *boom*. I let out a groan of pain as he forcefully shoves a finger inside me. I'm not turned on in the slightest, and it hurts like hell.

'You like that don't you, you filthy slut?'

I clamp my eyes shut, trying to hide the tears I can no longer hold in. Images of that sick bastard from one of the foster homes I'd been in years ago flash through my mind. He used to put his hands down my pants and touch me when nobody else was around.

'Mmm, you taste delicious. Just like I knew you would,' the creepy guy breathes as he places the finger that had been inside me into his mouth.

My stomach turns as he opens the foil packet beside him, rolling a condom onto his stumpy little dick. Thank Christ for small mercies. M had made me watch porno after porno in preparation for my new career. She'd given me a running commentary, even made me take notes. Although this is the first penis I've seen in real life, I know it's small compared to the ones I'd seen in the movies.

'I'm gonna fuck you now. They say your first stays with you forever. I like the thought of you thinking about me for years to come.'

A muffled whimper escapes as I try to close my legs, but it's an impossibility. The metal of the cuffs cuts into my skin as I frantically tug on my restraints while he settles himself between my thighs. He's right about one thing, I'll never forget this night. *Never.*

His fingers reach between us as he circles my clit, but it does nothing for my libido. Nothing this man could do would arouse me. Nothing. He's a turn-off, not a turn-on …

repulsive. I cry out in pain as he forcefully pushes himself inside me. I try to think of the ocean, of rolling meadows, anything to escape this moment, but nothing works.

He's making horrible grunting sounds as he continues to thrust inside me, over and over again. I'm in agony. It hurts so much more than I thought it would. Anna, one of M's girls, warned me the first time would hurt, but I didn't expect the pain to be this severe. The girls in the pornos always look like they're enjoying the sex. Maybe they're just good actors.

'You're so tight. I'm not sure I can last much longer. Your cunt feels amazing. So fucking good.'

His words turn my stomach. I pray he can't last much longer, because I just want this to be over. My natural instincts are to thrash around and try to get him off me, but I stay perfectly still. Moving only makes the pain worse.

'I need to see my cum on your pretty face.'

With that statement, my eyes spring open again. Unfortunately, just in time to see him rip off his condom and move his body towards my face. My hands tug on the handcuffs around my wrists as my head thrashes from side to side, but there's no escaping. I watch in horror as he strokes himself a few times before his body starts to tremble and a feral sound escapes him as he ejaculates all over my face.

That image ... that sound ... those feelings ... will haunt me forever.

I start to choke on the gag as the vomit rises to my mouth. My tears are falling freely now as he hops off me and retrieves his phone again. *Click ... click ... click.*

'I'm gonna enjoy looking at these later.'

After placing the phone beside the bed, he removes the gag and unfastens the handcuffs. 'You were worth every cent.

I'm looking forward to having you again. Go clean yourself up and get back here,' he says, dismissing me with his hand.

Now's my chance to escape. There will be no more—that I'm sure of. I'd rather die than let this man touch me again. I won't survive it.

Scrambling off the bed, I crawl across the carpet trying to put some distance between us. He comes up behind me, slapping me hard on the arse.

'I'm gonna fuck this too before the night is out.'

Like hell he is. A whimpering sound escapes me as I push myself off the floor and onto my feet. My legs threaten to give way as I make a hasty retreat out of the bedroom towards my clothes, still sitting in a pile in the foyer. Gathering them in my trembling hands, I dress as fast as humanly possible.

'You need to loosen up if you're going to make it in this game, sweetheart,' he calls out from the bedroom. His words are all a blur. All I want to do is get away from him as fast as I can. I don't even allow myself time to get cleaned up. His filth is still all over me.

Within minutes I'm flinging the door open. My eyes land on Rupert, pacing the corridor. Unease is etched on his face as he approaches me.

I break down the moment I collapse in his open arms.

'What the fuck did he do to you?' His anger is apparent in his voice. No words are needed when he makes eye contact with me. The evidence is there for all to see. 'I'm gonna kill him,' he says as he manoeuvres me to the wall, gently encouraging me to sit.

I'm not sure how long he's in there, but when he returns, he scoops me into his arms and carries me to the lift. I feel safe with Rupert. Once inside, he places me on my feet and retrieves a handkerchief from the breast pocket of his jacket. I notice blood on his knuckles as he cleans up my face as best he can. When the handkerchief in his hand moves to wipe the cum out of my long dark hair, humiliation floods me.

Rupert almost blows a gasket when we arrive back at my apartment. He sends me to the bathroom to get cleaned up while he calls M and demands she come straight over.

The first words out of her mouth when she sees me are, 'Grow the fuck up, Jade.' This woman doesn't have an ounce of compassion in her. But I can't go through a situation like that again. I just can't.

I'm a complete mess and flat-out refuse to continue working for her. I don't care if she sues me. In that moment I don't care what she does, I'm adamant I'm not going back, even though I know that isn't an option.

M sends Rupert away. The look he gives me as he leaves tells me I'm about to pay for fleeing my first job. Reaching out, she roughly grabs my hair and pulls me to my feet. 'You ever pull a stunt like this again,' she snarls in my face, 'I'll fucking kill you.'

I know it isn't an idle threat. M means every word. I've seen with my own eyes exactly what this woman is capable of.

*

So here I am, twenty-three years old, and still turning tricks for a woman I'm terrified of. A woman I loathe. Trapped in a world I can't escape.

After that first terrible night, M made me an exclusive escort. She couldn't risk me displeasing one of her clients in that way again. Now I have twenty regular clients—that's all.

I only work four nights a week, unless a special request comes up, but that doesn't happen very often. M showed me some kindness through all of this, though, by allowing me to set some limits, including the age of my clients: forty-five is my cut off, as well as no photographs, no kissing, no bondage, no bodily fluids on my face, and no anal. *Definitely no anal.* That part of my anatomy is off limits. No ifs or buts. No pun intended.

Not all of my men expect sex; some just require companionship or dates for charity events and functions. I love those clients the most. At the end of the day though, my men pay big dollars for me, so I make sure they get their money's worth, one way or another.

CHAPTER TWO

BROCK

My leather office chair creaks when I lean back into it as Natalie from accounting wraps her lips around my cock, bringing it to life. To my father's disgust, I've had sexual liaisons with most of the women who work here. Well, the single, hot and age appropriate ones, anyway. I only do it to piss my father off. I don't need to pick up at work; I can have anyone I want. I'm yet to come across a woman who can say no to me.

My head snaps up when the office door flies open. Shit. I told Amy, my secretary, I didn't want to be disturbed.

'You can't go in there, Clarissa.' I hear the panic in Amy's voice when she calls out from the reception area. Fucking Clarissa. What the hell does she want?

Natalie's lips loosen as she draws her head back. Placing my hand on top of her hair, I hold her firmly in place. She's always been a good sport, plus she's under my desk and out of sight. If anything, the blowjob will help me get through this unwanted conversation with Clarissa.

Clarissa gives Amy a dirty look before slamming the door in her face. I wish I could stop her coming here, but I know my father wouldn't hear of it. She's the precious only daughter of one of his oldest friends.

'What do you want, Clarissa?'

'Oh, that's a really nice way to talk to your fiancée.'

Fiancée? Not this shit again. 'I'm not your fucking fiancé, Clarissa.'

'I beg to differ. I've just come from a visit with your father. He still wants us to get married,' she says smugly, coming to sit on the corner of my desk. Let him fucking marry her. All my life that prick has tried to control me.

My angry eyes meet hers. She's beautiful, I'll give her that, but that's where my compliments end, because she has an ugly heart. At school, she was known as the ice queen. It suited her perfectly, and that voice. It's like nails on a damn blackboard. I can't stand being around her for more than a few minutes, so the thought of being married to her—no fucking way. Not happening.

'I'm not marrying you, so give it a rest, will you? My father has no say in who I marry.'

She folds her arms over her chest and pouts as crocodile tears appear in her eyes. Pinching the bridge of my nose, I have to suppress an eye roll. Who's she trying to kid? I've known this woman for most of my life and she doesn't have a sympathetic bone in her body. I've seen her work this bullshit with her father. She can turn her tears on and off like a damn tap. 'You can cut the hurt act too. That shit won't work on me.'

Natalie's lips curve into a smile around my cock as a muffled giggle escapes her. It sends a vibration down the length of my shaft. Clearing my throat, I loosen my tie.

Clarissa stands. 'I want my damn engagement ring, Brock,' she says, stamping her foot like a child.

23

Christ, I think I'm gonna blow. Shit, not now.

Being the head of a global security company, I'm trained to stay cool under any situation, but I'm not sure I'm going to be able to pull it off this time. 'You'll be waiting an awfully long time, sweetheart, because I have no intentions of ever marrying y—' Fuck. Here it comes. My hands fist in my short dark hair as I tilt my head towards the ceiling. 'Sweet Jesus,' I groan as my orgasm shoots through me.

'Brock. Are you okay?'

I can hear the concern in Clarissa's voice as she hastily makes her way around to my side of the desk. I hear her gasp when she sees my pants around my thighs and Natalie on her knees under the desk. My cock is still in her mouth. I have to hold back a laugh when Natalie gives her a little wave.

'How could you? This shit is going to stop when we're married. Do you hear me?' Clarissa screams, turning on her heel and running for the door. Natalie and I both burst out laughing when it slams closed behind her.

I push my chair back and stand to pull my pants up. Holding my hand out, I help Natalie to her feet.

'Well that was awkward,' she says, making me chuckle.

*

Hours later, my office door flies open again. The floor to ceiling windows behind me rattle as the handle hits the adjoining wall with a loud bang. Christ, doesn't anyone know how to knock anymore? My head snaps up in annoyance. Great, my father. He only ever comes in here when he's pissed and wants to rant. My guess is Clarissa went home and had a little cry to Daddy.

'Have a seat, Father,' I say sarcastically as he sits in the chair opposite me without waiting for an invitation.

'I want her name. I'll fire her immediately.'

'I have no idea what you're talking about,' I say as I settle back into my chair and casually fold my arms behind my head.

'Don't play coy with me, young man. This is a business, not a damn whorehouse.'

'You'd know all about that,' I mumble under my breath. My father's been seeing whores behind my mother's back for as long as I've been old enough to know better. Does he think I'm stupid? At least I don't have to pay women to have sex with me.

'What's that supposed to mean?'

'Exactly that. If you weren't married to my mother, I wouldn't give a shit about what you do, but the fact remains you are.' The disdain in my voice doesn't go unnoticed as I watch him squirm in his chair.

'Don't turn this around on me. I want her name, and I want it now.'

I have to repress my smile when I notice his face turning red. 'You can't fire someone who doesn't work here.'

'What do you mean she doesn't work here? Who was she then?'

'She works at the coffee shop across the street,' I lie, because I don't want Natalie to lose her job. She's a single mother and needs the money. 'You should go there some time. They give great service.' I don't know why I get pleasure out of getting under his skin, but I do. Maybe it's because I don't like him. Not a nice thing to say about your father, I know, but I lost all respect for him years ago.

'There's nothing funny about this,' he yells, slamming his hand down on the desk. 'Why I thought you could run a multimillion dollar enterprise, I'll never know. You're as useless as your fag of a brother.'

My knuckles turn white as my hands clamp onto either side of the desk in an effort not to wring his fucking neck. I lean towards him. 'I'm doing a hell of a lot better than you did when you were in charge. This business has grown by fifty-seven percent in the two years since I've taken control, and it continues to grow daily.'

My father leans back in his chair, clearing his throat. He has no reply to that because he knows I'm right. Nobody could run this business as well as I do. Nobody.

After looking down at my Rolex watch, I lean across the desk and push the intercom. 'Amy, can you tell my driver I'm ready to leave, please.' I stand and grab my jacket off the back of the chair. This conversation is over.

'If you'll excuse me, I have a plane to catch.'

*

JADE

I can't contain the excitement that courses through me as Rupert packs the last of my suitcases into the trunk of the limousine. This is my favourite time of the year: my one-week holiday. It's the only time off I get, so I look forward to it. No M, no clients, no rules. Well, the rules are still there, but she's not around to enforce them. M insists Rupert accompany me everywhere, but I'm okay with that. He lurks in the shadows mostly, letting me enjoy my free time.

My flight to New York leaves in just over three hours, but we need to stop by M's place for my final inspection. I hate that she controls me like this. Two more years, I keep telling myself. Two more years.

While I make my way into the house, Rupert unloads the bags from the car so she can go through them. She insists that because I'm on show twenty-four-seven, she needs to inspect what I've packed and make sure it's up to her standards. I'm forbidden to wear jeans, shorts, yoga pants, sweats, tees; things of that nature. I must dress and act like a lady at all times. I'm a fucking prostitute, for god's sake. I get paid to have sex with men. There's nothing ladylike about what I do for a living.

She is clueless to the fact that Rupert lets me pack my casual attire—the clothes I usually wear in my down time when I'm locked away in my apartment and away from her prying eyes—into his suitcase. She never looks inside it. I presume she thinks, like the rest of her staff, he does exactly as she instructs.

'Jade my dear,' she says when I enter the parlour. She's dressed to the hilt as usual. I'm guessing M would be in her mid-fifties, but she's had a lot of work done over the years, so it's really hard to say for sure. She looks great for her age. I've never seen her looking anything but perfect. Her blonde hair is always styled meticulously in a short bob. I wouldn't be surprised if she sleeps with a full face of makeup. The permanent scowl on her face, though, detracts from her beauty. She smiles rarely, unless it's an evil one. Her dark eyes are totally devoid of any sparkle.

Her gaze travels the length of my body. I'm wearing a tailored white pants suit, a large red handbag and matching red heels. There's a hint of red lace from my camisole peeking from underneath my buttoned-up jacket. My long thick brown hair is styled in loose waves—I had my personal hairdresser stop by my apartment this morning. My makeup is applied to perfection.

'Turn around.' Her finger does a twirl.

When I pass muster, she gives me the usual air kiss on each cheek. That's about the limit of her affection. I move to the side as Rupert lifts my suitcases onto the table one at a time, opening them so she can look inside. God forbid she has to bend over. She moves the contents around, checking everything.

After five years I have this down pat. I know the things she classes as suitable, so I always pack accordingly. The first few years she scolded me and removed half of the items. I'll never make that mistake again. That's when Rupert came up with his masterful plan of stashing my casual attire in his bag. He really is my saviour.

Once the inspection is complete, I remove my shoes and walk over to the scales that are placed by the window. She weighs me daily. 'Good,' she says with a nod as she looks down at the numbers displayed between my big toes. She walks over to the desk to retrieve a large white envelope from the top drawer. It contains my meal plan for the week. Like I said, she controls everything. 'Follow it,' she demands shoving it in my hand. 'I expect you to be on your best behaviour, Jade,' she says as she leaves the room. No 'safe travels'. No 'enjoy your holiday'. No nothing.

Rupert smirks when I roll my eyes at her retreating back. I shouldn't let her coldness get to me, but it does. There's a part of me that wants her to care, to give a shit.

Once we arrive at Sydney Airport, Rupert takes our luggage to the check-in counter. I head to the newsagency to buy a magazine to read while we wait for our flight. We still have just over two hours before our plane takes off.

After picking up a few magazines off the rack, I go to the counter. Maybe a Snickers bar? M doesn't let me eat junk food, but I sneak some in occasionally. Snickers bars are my favourite. With the amount of hours I work out at the gym to stay in shape, I know I'll have this baby burnt off in no time.

After paying for my purchases, I open the chocolate bar and take a bite. Rupert knows I'm not allowed to eat these, but he'll keep my secret. There've been a few occasions over the years when I've had a shitty day, and I've climbed into the limousine to find a Snickers bar sitting on the back seat. He does that to cheer me up.

I flick through one of the magazines in my hand, taking another bite of my chocolate, and walk back to the check-in counter.

Boom. I crash into something solid. My gaze goes to the floor where my chocolate and magazines now lay. Shit. I was enjoying that. A pair of shiny black men's dress shoes stand beside my poor unfortunate chocolate bar. A delicious manly scent surrounds me, invading all my senses. Nope, not a wall. My gaze travels up his expensive grey suit pants, past the matching tailored jacket and baby blue shirt and tie, until I reach the face of an angel.

I swallow nervously. He's stunning. Absolutely breathtaking. He has big brown eyes and perfectly chiselled features. Can a man be beautiful? Because goddamn, he is.

'I'm sorry,' he says in a deep, dreamy voice.

Closing my eyes briefly, I try to compose myself. I can't seem to find the words to answer him, so I eventually just smile instead.

'You have a ...' His hand moves towards my mouth, skimming over my bottom lip. I'm frozen. Never has a man

29

affected me like this. Why can't my clients look like him? Sure most are far from what you'd call ugly, but damn.

Pulling his hand back, he holds his finger up for me to see. Even his hands are perfect. I imagine what it would feel like to have hands like that caress my body. The thought sends a shiver down my spine. But it soon vanishes when I notice the small piece of chocolate sitting on the tip of his finger. I'm immediately consumed with humiliation. My eyes widen and my mouth gapes when he places his finger in his mouth, sucking the chocolate off.

'Delicious.'

Holy hotness. I have an urge to clench my thighs together as a warm, tingling feeling spreads through my body. Far out. How could such a small gesture make me feel like that? I'm not used to being turned on. My job is more about me pleasing my clients, not the other way around.

Our eyes remained locked for what feels like an eternity. Our little staring contest is broken when I hear a voice beside me. Rupert. Shit. Mr Delicious looks from me to Rupert before bending to retrieve my magazines and chocolate bar from the floor. He clears his throat when he sees the page I'd been reading.

'Looks like someone isn't doing his job properly,' is all he says, before placing them in my hands and briskly walking away.

I look down at the bold heading of the article. TEN WAYS TO ENSURE AN ORGASM DURING SEX. I feel my face flush as I give Rupert an awkward grin.

His tongue briefly dashes across his front teeth. Pointing at my mouth, he says, 'You have chocolate on your teeth.'

Of course I do, and I smiled at Mr Delicious.

Somebody kill me now.

CHAPTER THREE

BROCK

He has to be her father. Surely. She's far too beautiful to be with someone twice her age. Unless she's a gold digger and he's her sugar daddy, but I didn't get that impression about her, even though our encounter was fleeting. Come to think of it, I didn't even get her name.

She could have anyone she wants—even me. She's just my type.

Appearance wise, I'd say she's just like all the other rich girls I know. I've been surrounded by her kind all my life. Meticulously dressed in her designer clothes, groomed to perfection. Spoilt and extremely high maintenance. In saying that though, she had one distinct difference: her sheer beauty far outweighs all of them put together. I can't remember the last time I was so overcome just by the look of a woman. Don't get me started on those exquisite eyes of hers, or those lips. I've never seen eyes that shade of green before. It took every ounce of strength I had not to pull her into my arms and lick that chocolate off with my tongue.

But there was something else, something endearing about her. An innocence. I chuckle to myself when I think of the chunk of chocolate that was on her front tooth. Utterly adorable.

Pushing all thoughts of her out of my mind, I take a seat in the member's lounge. No point thinking about another man's woman. That's not how I roll. I hate that my father is a cheating son of a bitch. I swore to myself when I was growing up that I'd never follow in his footsteps.

Pulling my laptop out of its leather case, I boot it up. I still have a while to wait until the plane leaves, so I have time to check my emails and catch up on some work.

'Can I get you something to drink, sir?'

A waitress is standing in front of me. 'Scotch on the rocks please.' I reach into my pocket to retrieve my World Elite Mastercard. After the day I've had, I need a stiff drink. When the waitress walks away, I scan the room. I freeze when I find a pair of familiar, beautiful, jade green eyes. I feel my lips curve up at the corners. Snickers is sitting a few metres away, staring straight back at me. Quickly lowering her head, she looks down at her lap before picking up one of the magazines and holding it open in front of her, concealing her pretty face. I can't hold back my laugh when I notice the magazine is up the wrong way. If she's trying to look inconspicuous, she's failing miserably. I wish I knew her name. Referring to her as Snickers seems juvenile, but for now it's the best I've got.

I continue to stare at the upside-down cover for a few minutes, but to no avail. She refuses to look my way again. At the very least she's lightened my mood with her antics. I really should go over and introduce myself. Then I remember the gentleman she was with earlier.

But he's not seated near her. It only takes a few seconds to spot him. He's standing against the wall a few metres away from Snickers. His steely eyes are trained on me, his expression giving off a clear warning: *Keep your distance.*

Who is this man? Maybe he's her minder, or bodyguard. If so, who is this woman? She could be a famous model. She definitely has the looks. Once upon a time I would've known who she was. I probably would've bedded her as well. I've been out of the loop for far too long running my father's company.

I look away from the man, and back to Snickers. She's peeping at me over the top of the magazine. At least she's turned it up the right way now. I chuckle when she quickly hides behind it again.

The waitress returns with my drink and credit card sitting on a small black tray. 'Thank you,' I say with an appreciative smile as I reach for them.

'Any time, handsome,' she replies with a wink as she bends, revealing a glimpse of her cleavage. Pulling a small piece of paper out of her bra, she hands it to me. 'Look me up next time you're in town.'

I'm used to women throwing themselves at me. Believe me, it gets old fast. For once I'd like someone to look past my physical appearance, or my bank account, for that matter. There's a lot more to me than good looks and money.

Settling back into my chair, I savour the burn of the fine malt whisky as it slides down the back of my throat. My eyes are again fixed on Snickers over the brim of my glass. She's still hiding behind that bloody magazine, so I use this time to check out the rest of her.

I glimpse a hint of red lace underneath her white jacket. It makes my cock stir. She's got a fine rack on her. By the size of them, I'm guessing they're fake. My gaze moves down her long, lean legs. Damn she's sexy. I'd love to see her wearing

J.L. PERRY

nothing but those sexy-as-fuck red heels. Christ. Why did I let my mind go there? Adjusting my crotch, I close the laptop. My work can wait. Looking at her is far more entertaining.

*

'First call for flight 607 to New York. We are now boarding all first-class passengers travelling on flight 607 to New York. Please make your way to departure gate 39.'

That's my flight.

As I'm packing my laptop back into the leather case, from the corner of my eye I see Snickers stand. Interesting. I decide to stay seated, so I can watch her leave. My eyes meet hers briefly. When she gives me a shy smile, I reciprocate with a wink. My lips curve up when I see her eyes widen and her face flush red. I love her timidity. The women I'm used to aren't backwards in coming forwards, that's for sure. They're not afraid to go after what they want.

Once she passes me, my gaze moves down her long dark hair before landing on her arse. Fuck me, what an arse. The intoxicating swing of her hips has me hypnotised. And those legs. They go on for days. I'd love nothing more than to have them wrapped around me.

A loud grunt beside me breaks me from my trance. When I look up, I meet the hardened eyes of her gentleman friend as he follows closely behind her. He takes a step to the right, blocking my view as he walks. *Prick*.

I wait a few more minutes before going to the departure gate. I find myself hoping that she's seated near me in first class. It will make for an interesting flight. That's if her shadow doesn't interfere.

After handing my boarding pass to the flight attendant, I make my way along the corridor. 'Welcome aboard, Mr Weston,' another flight attendant says as I enter the plane. Snickers is the first person I see when I round the corner. Her eyes are closed. When I get closer I notice she has earbuds in her ears and her perfectly manicured fingers are tapping on the armrest to the beat of the music.

Her shadow is sitting beside her and gives me a dirty look as I pass. What's his problem? His attitude is really starting to get under my skin. I'm seated two rows behind Snickers, but on the opposite aisle. After I stow my laptop in the overhead compartment, I take my seat. I can only see part of her shoulder and her hand from here. Such a shame. I could easily spend the next twenty-one hours admiring her beauty.

I watch the leggy blonde flight attendant make her way down the aisle. She's a real looker. If Snickers wasn't sitting only a few feet away I'd be all over that. The thought actually surprises me. I've never let another woman get in the way of what I've wanted in the past. Never.

I listen intently when the attendant approaches Snickers. 'Good afternoon, Miss Davis ... Mr Henderson,' she says with a pleasant smile. 'I'm Clara, your attendant, for the duration of the flight. Could I get you something to drink while we wait for the other passengers to board?'

When I hear the word 'Miss' I'm smiling again. Fuck, what is this woman doing to me? I'd prefer a first name, but Miss Davis is better than Snickers, I guess.

Clara makes her way down the rest of the aisle before stopping in front of me. 'Mr Weston,' she says, and gives me the same spiel she gave the other passengers.

'I'll have a scotch on the rocks, please. Do you have any Snickers bars?'

Her face screws up slightly at my question. 'I can check for you, sir.'

She returns a few minutes later with my drink and the chocolate, placing them on my tray in front of me. 'You're in luck.'

'Actually, the chocolate is for Miss Davis. Could you give it to her for me, please?'

Clara gives me a sceptical look when I point to where Miss Davis is sitting.

'Are you friends?' she asks.

'Yes.' It's an untruth, but I'll gladly be her friend if she wants that. Friends with benefits, that is.

I'm actually feeling nervous when Clara walks towards her. *I never get fucking nervous.*

'Excuse me, Miss Davis, Mr Weston asked me to give this to you.' She takes the chocolate bar from Clara then swings around in her seat. Her surprised eyes lock with mine and her face turns a sweet shade of pink before it breaks into the most beautiful smile. It literally takes my breath away. Seeing her smile at me like that makes my heartbeat accelerate.

When I notice her clutch the chocolate to her chest, my smile grows. For some reason, her gesture touches me. How can such a small act make her so happy? Maybe she isn't a spoilt little rich girl.

'Thank you,' she mouths.

'You're welcome,' I mouth back, wishing I was that chocolate bar, wanting her luscious mouth on me. More. Than. Anything. This woman has bewitched me.

CHAPTER FOUR

JADE

Rupert escorts me to my suite when we reach the hotel. I'm dead on my feet. We left Sydney at 4 pm Wednesday. With the time difference between both countries it was 7 pm New York time, yet still Wednesday, after our twenty-one-hour journey. I hate those long-haul flights. I haven't slept in over twenty-four hours because I have trouble sleeping on planes.

We wait together in my room until the bags arrive, so we can unload my casual clothes out of his suitcase before Rupert makes his way to his own suite next door. M likes him to be as close as possible. I'm surprised she doesn't make us bunk together so he can monitor my every move.

After retrieving my silk nightgown, I head to the bathroom. I can unpack in the morning. All I want to do now is shower and climb into bed. I'm exhausted.

The second my head hits the pillow my thoughts drift to Mr Delicious. I lost sight of him once we disembarked. I can't tell you how disappointed that made me. This attraction I feel for him is foreign to me. Given my experience with men, I've yet to come across one who has made me feel anything remotely close to this. Maybe with a bit of luck, I'll run into him in the streets of New York. On the other hand though, maybe it's better if I don't. No point wishing for something that can never be.

I still have the Snickers bar he gave me in my handbag. I couldn't bring myself to eat it. No man, apart from Rupert, has ever done anything so sweet for me. To him, it may have been an insignificant joke. To me, it meant everything.

*

I'm jolted from my sleep when I hear a knock at the door. Looking at the clock beside the bed, I see it's 10.20 am. Guilt floods me. I never sleep this late. I'm not allowed too, is more like it. M makes sure I'm up and at the gym by six every morning. Seven days a week. There's no reprieve from her demands. Even on my days off I have to put up with her bullshit.

I reach for the pink silk dressing gown that matches the silk nightie I'm wearing. Rubbing my eyes, I go to the door, where I'm greeted by Rupert's cheerful face as he holds a takeaway coffee cup up to me.

'You missed breakfast, so I thought you might like this,' he says. 'You have your appointment with José at 11.30, remember? You'll need to get ready if we're going to make it across town on time.'

'Shit. I forgot that was today.' I always visit José when I'm in New York. He designs the most exquisite lingerie. His pieces are sought after worldwide. He caters exclusively to the rich and famous. When I called to tell him I'd be coming to New York, he said he'd design some special pieces for me. In my line of work, lingerie is important; M makes all her girls keep a spreadsheet on what we wear and with whom. We're forbidden to wear the same garments with each client more than once.

'I've organised a car to pick us up at eleven. I'll meet you down in the foyer.'

'Thank you. I'll be ready in time.'

He nods his head approvingly before heading towards his suite.

'Oh, and thank you for the coffee.'

'You're welcome.'

*

After my fitting with José, I leave with fifteen new pieces. I know M will be pleased with my purchases. Rupert and I stop for lunch on our way back to the hotel. Since I missed breakfast, I'm starved.

We wander the streets of New York after lunch, doing a little more retail therapy. I love this city. The people. The atmosphere. *Everything*. Once Rupert's hands were overloaded with bags, I decided it was time to head back to the hotel. Poor Rupert. He never complains though.

Since I missed my gym session this morning, I need to rectify that. God forbid I went home carrying any extra weight, I'd be punished for sure. Last year I remember M confiscating Anna's passport because she'd come back from vacation one kilo heavier than when she'd left. I'd be devastated if M took my passport away. Travelling was the only thing I had to look forward to and I alternate my holiday time between New York and Paris. My two favourite cities in the world.

The only places I can escape from my wretched life.

*

BROCK

I spent the better part of the day at our New York office going over the presentation and contracts for my big meeting tomorrow. If I can secure this multimillion-dollar deal, it will place Weston Global in the top five security firms in the world. My father always said it was unattainable, so I'll get great pleasure in proving him wrong.

My phone rings in my pocket. Pulling it out, I see Josh's number flashing on the screen. 'Hey, bro,' I answer. Joshua is five years younger than me and we weren't close growing up—for the most part I thought of him as my annoying little brother. That all changed six years ago. I had no idea Josh was homosexual until the day he came out. Sure, looking back now the signs were all there, but I was so wrapped up in my own life I was oblivious to them. His announcement came as a shock, but he is my brother and I love him regardless of his sexuality. Our parents though, that's a whole other story.

Our father was the worst, but our mother didn't even try to defend her son. Her behaviour was inexcusable. Father is a tyrant, so in a way I can understand why Mum didn't speak up, but I can't forgive her for standing by while Father kicked Josh out of the house and wiped him from their lives as though he never existed. He's their flesh and blood. Their son. That should've been enough. He was only seventeen.

I had long since moved out, so I took him in without hesitation. He had no job, no money, nowhere else to go. I was twenty-three and already working for my father, learning the ropes so I could one day take over. When I wasn't at the office, I was partying and screwing around. But things slowed down once I had to start caring for Josh. Well, to an extent. I slowed down on the partying, but the screwing around not so much. It was my vice, my only release.

Josh stayed with me until he turned twenty. After finishing his education, he opted to enrol in a two-year, full-time hospitality course. His dream was to one day own a bar. Of course I was going to make sure that happened, and the day he graduated, I handed him the keys to his very own establishment. I'd not only purchased the building, I'd made sure it was fully equipped with everything he needed, including an upstairs living area. But I was sad to see him go—I'd gotten used to having him around.

I was there for the grand opening, but haven't been back since. Not because I don't support him—we still talk on the phone daily, and meet up for dinner and drinks a few nights a week. But, after that night, I refused to set foot in that place again.

I'm in no way homophobic and I should've known going in what to expect. What I wasn't prepared for was all the advances. I had men offering to buy me drinks, asking me to dance, and when one guy groped my arse, I had to control the urge to knock him out. Josh thought it was hilarious. I, on the other hand, didn't.

In the past few years, he's built the place up into one of the most exclusive gay bars in Sydney. I'm proud of how far he's come.

'How's New York treating you?' he asks. 'Did you secure the big deal yet?'

'The meeting's tomorrow.'

'Well, I hope it's successful. I'd love to see the look on our father's face if you can do something he never could.' His comment makes me chuckle. It's the main reason I've worked so hard on this. Is it wrong that I get great pleasure out of sticking it to my father? Because I do. 'Listen, the reason I'm calling, I have a friend who's seeking a new security firm to look after his construction sites. He's a developer. He wants to set up a meeting with you when you're back in town. It's a big job, and yours if you want it. This guy is loaded.'

'Text me his number and I'll give him a call. I'll be flying home Sunday night.'

'Great,' he replies. 'Good luck tomorrow, and let me know how it goes.'

'Thanks. I will.'

'Try not to break any hearts while you're in the Big Apple,' he adds with a laugh, before ending the call. My brother knows me well.

I head straight to the downstairs bar when I arrive back at the hotel. I'm feeling a little on edge about my meeting tomorrow. My father will never let me live it down if I can't pull this off. It's my chance to prove to him that I'm a better man than he is, even though I already know I am.

My father is unscrupulous, to say the least. He's a liar, a bully, a cheat and just an all-round prick. Compared to him, I'm a fucking saint. I'm honest to a fault and always keep my word. Sure, I sleep around, but I've never cheated. Every woman I've ever been with knows exactly what she's getting into—I make sure of it. I'm not the commitment type. That's why I've remained single my whole life.

I'm not sure I have it in me to commit to one woman. I'm not sure if I'd even want to. My parents haven't exactly been the best role models and I like my life just the way it is. It would take someone pretty special to make me even consider settling down. I'm yet to meet anyone who's come close to making me entertain that idea.

Removing my tie and shoving it into the pocket of my suit jacket, I loosen the top few buttons of my shirt and take a seat in a corner booth. I'm not in the mood for any company. I just need a few stiff drinks to help me relax. Something to help me sleep.

While waiting for the waitress to bring me my drink, I scan the room. That's when I see her. Fucking Snickers is sitting at the bar just a few metres away. Is it a mirage? I rub my eyes. Nope, it's her. I can't believe my luck. She must be staying in this hotel as well.

I was consumed with disappointment when I'd lost sight of her at the airport. I'd turned my phone back on after disembarking, only to be flooded by messages. It only took a glance at my phone for her to get away.

I'm out of the booth in a flash and heading towards her before my brain even registers what it's doing. Fate has brought us together again, and this is an opportunity I'm not about to pass up.

No fucking way.

CHAPTER FIVE

JADE

After hitting the private gym in the hotel for a few hours, I hung around in my room, relaxing and watching the food channel. I have a passion for cooking, have had for as long as I can remember. When I'm in my apartment, I'll sit in front of the television for hours, taking notes and jotting down recipes.

Maybe my love of cooking came from the lack of food I sometimes had growing up. Maybe it was from the praise I'd occasionally received when I cooked for the families I stayed with. I really can't say. All I know is that I love it. I'm in my element when I'm in the kitchen, creating things.

I'd like to open a small restaurant when I'm finally free from M. One that serves only the finest, most exquisite desserts. I have a real sweet tooth, and desserts are what I like to cook. I begged M a few years ago to let me enrol in a part-time course that was being held by a local well-known pastry chef, but of course the answer was a flat-out no. It would've been a dream come true to learn from one of the best. Her refusal really upset me. I should be allowed to do whatever I want in my free time.

By 5 pm, I'm showered and dressed in a pair of dark skinny jeans, a sleeveless lemon blouse and a pair of matching lemon ballet flats. My long hair is pulled into a ponytail. My face is totally free of makeup. Although I don't think there's anything wrong with it, I know M would have a coronary if she saw me looking like this, especially in public. This is the real me, the person I'm yearning to become again.

After texting Rupert, he meets me in the corridor and we head towards the lifts. Tonight I've opted to have a small wood-fired pizza in the hotel bar downstairs. The pizzas in New York are the best I've ever tasted. I do this every time I come here. I'll do some extra time in the gym tomorrow to compensate.

I take a seat at the bar while Rupert moves to the opposite side. He stays close enough to keep an eye on me, but far enough away to give me space. If it was anyone other than him, I know this constant minding would piss me off, but I enjoy having him around.

'So we meet again,' someone whispers in my ear, making me jump. Without even looking I know who it is. I'd recognise that dreamy voice anywhere. Mr Delicious.

Swinging around, I look up. His handsome face is mere inches away. His delectable cologne invades my senses. I can't even put into words how happy I am to see him again. He's been on my mind all day. I even found myself looking for him as I walked the streets of New York.

'So we do,' I reply with a smile as my heart starts to race.

'Would you like to join me for a drink?' he asks, gesturing to a booth by the wall. My eyes immediately dart to Rupert. I can't hide my grin when he gives me a little nod. I've always known that I was fond of him, but in this moment I think I actually love him.

'Sure. That would be nice.' Butterflies dance in my stomach as I stand and follow him to the table. I have no idea what I'm going to say to him. Over time I've learnt to put on an act when I'm with my clients. I become a different person. I ooze confidence. But this is real life, I'm not on the job now. This is Mr Delicious. I'm not sure if I can pull this off.

When he holds out his hand, offering me a seat, I smile to myself at his gentlemanly ways. Once I'm seated, I rub my sweaty palms down the front of my jeans. I can't remember the last time I felt this nervous.

He takes the seat opposite me, looking at me with those stunning chocolate eyes, and smiles beautifully. 'Hi.'

'Hi.'

We sit there staring at each other for a long time. It's like neither of us can actually believe we're here together.

Eventually he speaks. 'Are you going to tell me your name this time? Or will you forever be known to me as Snickers?'

I can't help but laugh. He's cute, I'll give him that. 'Jade,' I say, holding my hand out to him across the table.

'Brock. Brock Weston,' he replies, taking my hand in his.

A tingly feeling shoots up my arm once his fingers wrap around mine. That's never happened to me before, but I like the feelings he ignites within me. I'm pleased that he doesn't let go of my hand too quickly. His warm skin feels wonderful against mine.

'Nice name,' I tell him. 'It suits you. I thought I was going to have to refer to you as Mr Delicious for the rest of my life.' I feel my cheeks flush when I realise I just said that out loud. I hadn't meant too.

His face lights up. 'You think I'm delicious?' he asks.

Quickly removing my hand from his grasp, I look away and clear my throat as my fingers twirl around my ponytail.

He leans across the table, invading my space. 'For the record,' he whispers as his warm breath hits my skin. 'I think you're delicious as well.'

A nervous laugh escapes me as my eyes shoot up to meet his. He spoke those words with such sincerity. Excitement courses through me as I replay his words in my mind. *He thinks I'm delicious.*

Thankfully, the waitress approaches the table, breaking the awkwardness. 'Your scotch, sir,' she says before turning her attention to me. 'Can I get you something to drink, miss?'

'I'll have a beer, please.'

Brock looks surprised by my request, but beer and pizza are the perfect combination. I have a client whose name is Theo. He's my favourite out of all my men. He's gay, so never expects anything from me of a sexual nature—I'm his ruse, his fake girlfriend. He hires me in the hope of fooling the world into believing he's actually straight. He has this silly notion that it will affect his business. It saddens me that he feels he has to hide who he really is. He has a beautiful heart. His sexuality shouldn't be an issue. Mostly I accompany him to functions, or I'm his date for dinner parties, but there's been a few times when he's just needed a friend or a shoulder to cry on. Like him, I know what keeping a secret feels like. It can be hard. On those occasions, when it all gets a bit much for him, we sit around, talking, eating pizza and drinking beer. He's the closest thing to a friend that I've got. I adore him.

'Make that two beers,' Brock cuts in as he pushes his scotch aside, smiling at me. When the waitress walks away, he gives me a quizzical look. 'I wouldn't have picked you for a beer drinker.'

I shrug. I'm not sure how to reply. 'I don't drink it much, I'm not really allowed to.'

'What? What do you mean you're not really allowed too?'

I sigh at my slip up. Why did I tell him that?

'By him?' he asks, flicking his head in Rupert's direction.

'No. Rupert's pretty cool. He lets me do a lot things I'm not supposed to.'

'Huh,' Brock says, raising one of his eyebrows, like he doesn't believe me. 'Well, by who? Your parents?'

'You could say that.' It's not really a lie. M is technically my parent.

His brow furrows at my answer before a sympathetic look crosses his face. 'So while the cat's away, the mice will play,' he jokes.

'I guess.'

'I like you,' he says, reaching for my hand and giving it a squeeze.

'I like you too.' It's the truth, I do. His words touch my heart. I've only ever had a handful of people in my life show me kindness.

'So, what brings you to New York?' I ask, trying to steer the conversation away from me. Talking about my life puts me in dangerous territory. I'd hate to say anything that may incriminate me.

'Business. You?'

'Holiday.'

After that, we fall into easy conversation, while we wait for our drinks. I'm still stunned that we are actually here together. Happy, but stunned.

'Have you eaten?' I ask Brock when the waitress returns.

'No, I haven't. Why, are you hungry?'

'I came down here to grab a pizza. They're to die for. I get one every time I'm in New York.'

'You drink beer and eat pizza?' I can hear the amazement in his voice. Doesn't everyone? Well, normal people, anyway. I think I'd pass out from shock if I ever saw M doing it.

Instead of replying, I nod my head.

'Wow. I definitely had you pegged wrong.'

His statement puzzles me. How did he have me pegged? I don't ask him to elaborate.

*

As the old saying goes, time flies when you're having fun. Looking down at my phone, I see it's just after eleven. My gaze moves to Rupert. The poor thing has been sitting at the bar waiting for me for six hours. This job must get boring for him.

After giving him a smile that hopefully conveys my apologies, I turn my attention back to Brock. 'It's getting late,' I say, disappointment in my voice. 'I probably should get going.' I've had the best time. Probably the best time I've ever had in my life. I know I'm going to look back on tonight with fondness for years to come. We talked and laughed about anything and everything. Though nothing too deep. He did ask a few personal questions over the course of the night, but when he could see I wasn't forthcoming with information, he didn't pry any further.

I hate that it has to come to an end, but it does. My life doesn't permit this type of evening.

'I suppose you're right,' Brock says. He sounds just as disappointed as I am. 'Can I see you tomorrow?'

My heart sinks and I look down at the table. I'd like nothing more than to spend time with him, but it's not an option. Rupert has risked everything, letting this go as far as it has.

'I'm sorry, but I can't.' My heart hurts when his face drops. I hate myself for even uttering those words. My gaze darts back to Rupert, just as Brock stands abruptly. My first thought is that he's going to walk away, and panic rises in me. Instead, to my horror, he heads in Rupert's direction. I cover my eyes with my hands, because I don't want to witness what's about to happen.

Minutes pass and Brock doesn't return. Curiosity gets the better of me, so I sneak a peek through my fingertips. I'm surprised when I see Brock and Rupert talking calmly. I kind of expected them to be rolling around on the ground, fighting.

Brock pulls a business card from his pocket and hands it to Rupert. Then, to my amazement, they smile and shake hands. Wow. That wasn't how I expected this to go down. I remove my hands from my face when Brock turns and walks back to our table.

I grab the hand he offers when he's standing beside me, and let him help me out of my seat. He places a soft kiss on my knuckles. As innocent as the gesture is, it sends desire surging through me. No man has ever made me feel like this. I want to feel his lips all over me.

'I'll pick you up at four,' he says as a beautiful, triumphant smile spreads across his face. Looking around him, my eyes meet Rupert and he gives me another nod. Excitement shoots through me. I'm going to get to see him again.

'Okay,' I breathe, trying to contain my eagerness.

'Wear something comfortable.'

'Okay.'

'Goodnight, Jade.'

'Goodnight, Brock.' When his face inches forwards, for a split second I think he's going to kiss me. Surprisingly, I truly want that, but he doesn't.

'Dream of me,' he whispers instead. His warm breath dances over my skin, making it pebble with goose bumps. He drops my hand and turns towards the exit. I stay fixed to the spot.

I'll most certainly be dreaming of you, Mr Weston. That you can be sure of.

CHAPTER SIX

BROCK

I headed into the office early, having hardly slept a wink because I couldn't get Jade out of my mind. I was eager for 4 pm to roll around so I could spend more time with her. Last night I didn't want our time in the bar to end. I found her nothing like I'd expected. Utterly charming would be the first phrase to spring to mind. Then: absolutely mesmerising. Not only funny and incredibly smart, Jade has the face of a goddess, and a sinful body that I'm just itching to get my hands on. No woman has ever been able to capture my attention like this. There's something about her that makes my heart accelerate whenever she's near. It's a strange yet pleasant sensation. I find myself craving that feeling, which is a total mind fuck.

Never in my life have I looked forward to seeing someone as much as I am her. This will be the closest to an actual date I've ever come. Sure, I've been out with other women—I rarely go to functions unaccompanied—but my main reason for doing that is so I don't get stuck with damn Clarissa as my date. No, this is the first time I've ever asked a woman out for the sheer reason of wanting to be near her. Jade evokes something deep inside me. I can't quite put it into words, but I'm drawn to her.

Despite my distraction, I was able to keep my head in the game long enough to secure the new contract. The moment they signed on the dotted line and left my office, you can be sure as shit my first act was to ring my father and rub it in his goddamn face.

Tonight will be a double celebration. I managed to pull off something my father doubted I could ever do, but more importantly, I'll be spending time with the woman who appears to have captivated my heart.

*

The nerves kick in as I fasten my Rolex around my wrist. I've dressed casually for our date, black jeans and a grey shirt. At a glance, Jade appears to be the type of girl who likes to dine in fancy restaurants, but last night proved me wrong. She's obviously from immaculate breeding, but on the other hand, she's extremely down to earth. Sophistication rolls off her yet she has a playful innocence I find endearing. She was extremely closed off whenever we touched on anything personal, but in fairness to her, I am a stranger. I'm hoping today she opens up to me. I want to know everything about her.

I've made no reservations or real plans for this evening. I'm going to play it by ear. Her bodyguard seems to be her constant shadow, and that tells me Jade doesn't get to experience much of a life on her own, so tonight is about her. I'm willing to do anything that will make her happy.

When Jade said she couldn't see me again, I was crushed. I had to at least try to change her mind. I couldn't let that be the end of us. So I was pleasantly surprised when I approached Rupert—I wasn't expecting things to go over so well. It's quite obvious he cares for her. He was hesitant at first, but after I explained who I was and where I worked, he seemed to let his guard down slightly. I was relieved that he'd heard of our company. Even though my father is a prick, Weston Global has a very good reputation. We pride ourselves on our integrity.

He softened when I explained that all I wanted was to spend some time with her, and that my intentions were honourable. I promised to have her home at a reasonable hour, and assured him I'd treat her with nothing but respect. I've never had to beg to spend time with a woman before, but Jade is worth it. I'd stoop to any level to see her.

I roll my shoulders when I reach her room, trying my best to calm myself before knocking. My breath catches the second she opens the door. The smile that lights up her face is like a sucker punch right to my chest. 'Hi,' I say, trying my best to remain composed as I shove my hands into the pockets of my jeans. I have the urge to pull her into my arms and kiss her, but I don't want to scare her off before we've even left the hotel.

'Hi. Come in.' She moves aside so I can enter. She has that same little lip-biting thing going on that drove me crazy last night. I want to bite those luscious lips of hers too. Doesn't she realise having me in her room is dangerous? The sinful things I'd like to do to her ...

'I just have to grab my phone and we're good to go.' Her sweet fragrance envelops me as she breezes past.

My eyes are glued to her delicious arse as she walks across the room and shoves the phone into her back pocket. *Lucky phone.* She's wearing a pair of faded denim jeans that hug her luscious body perfectly, showcasing her sexy long legs. She's teamed them with a tight white singlet that accentuates her beautiful tits. There's a pair of white Converse sneakers on her feet and her long dark hair is loose. I'm itching to run my fingers through it.

She pulls a thin white cardigan from the wardrobe. When she slides her arms into it, I can see a hint of lace underneath her singlet. It makes my cock twitch. Fuck, she's sexy. It's going to be hard to keep my hands to myself.

'Ready.' She's smiling as she joins me. I shove my hands in my pockets again, so I'm not tempted to pull her into my arms, because, by Christ, I am.

'You look beautiful,' I say.

'Thank you,' she replies as the loveliest shade of pink rises to her cheeks.

Fuck, I'm a goner.

*

JADE

We fall into easy conversation as we head down Seventh Avenue. Words can't express how happy I am to be here with him. So far, I've only ever seen Brock in a suit. Casually dressed Brock leaves me with no words. He's even more delicious than I imagined. So tall, so manly—so perfect. His body is lean yet muscular. He's every woman's dream.

He's my dream.

I have no idea where we're heading, but I don't care. I'd sit at a damn bus stop with him for the rest of the night, as long as we're together. I'll forever be grateful to Rupert for allowing this. All he said to me earlier was, 'Be careful, call me if you need me, and for Christ's sake, have fun. If anyone deserves it, it's you.' I think he was taken aback when I threw my arms around him.

As we cross the street, Brock takes my hand, lacing our fingers together. It sends my heart into a flutter. I look at our locked hands, then back at his face.

'You don't want me to hold your hand?' he asks.

'Of course. I like it. Nobody's ever held my hand before.'

My reply stops him in his tracks. 'What do you mean, nobody's ever held your hand?'

Now I feel stupid. I cast my face downwards.

'Hey,' he says, placing his finger under my chin, tilting my face up to his. 'Haven't you ever been with a man before?'

I shrug. 'Sure.' My gaze moves back down to the pavement. 'It's just none of them have ever held my hand.'

'Well, they're fucking idiots,' he says, giving my hand a squeeze before starting to walk again. I'm relieved he doesn't pry any further.

Eventually we reach our destination: Central Park. I love this place. I come down here often when I'm in New York. 'It's too early to eat, so I thought we could hire a buggy and do a tour of the park,' he says. My smile widens when he points to the line of buggies along the sidewalk. I've always wanted to ride in one of them. 'Is that okay?'

'Perfect,' I reply. He tugs on my hand as we make our way towards the group of men near the three-wheeled bicycles with a long bench seat positioned behind the driver.

'We'd like to hire one,' Brock says to the first man we come across.

'Sure. It's eighty dollars for a ride around half the park, or one hundred and fifty dollars for the full guided tour.'

Brock doesn't hesitate. He pulls out two one-hundred-dollar bills and hands them over. After the man stashes them into the black leather pouch that's fastened around his waist, he starts to count out the change. Brock holds up his hand.

'You can keep the change as long as you take your time on the tour.'

'Thank you,' the man says.

Grabbing my hand again, Brock helps me onto the bench seat before joining me. The second he's settled, he laces our fingers together. It sends tingles running through my body. Who knew something as simple as holding hands could make my body feel so alive?

Brock and I stare at each other, grinning, as the driver sets the buggy in motion. I vaguely hear him talking as we travel. He points out where scenes in certain movies were made, but neither of us is really listening, we're too focused on each other. Usually, I'm uncomfortable being stared at, but I'm surprisingly at ease under Brock's watchful gaze.

A few of the things the driver says register, but my eyes don't move from Brock's even once. 'This is the fountain where the opening of the *Friends* sitcom was filmed.' I also hear him mention Marilyn Monroe, but I missed the rest of what he said. 'The Kennedys lived over there.' My eyes still can't seem to move from Brock. 'In those apartments across the street was where John Lennon and Yoko Ono once lived. Just on the sidewalk below is where he was shot. The memorial was moved over here to the park because of the large number of visitors to the site, making it a traffic hazard.'

Even though the driver did as instructed and took things slowly, the tour came to an end far too quickly. I sigh with disappointment and Brock asks, 'Do you want to go around again?'

'I'd like that.'

Letting go of my hand, he pulls out his wallet. He hands the driver another two hundred dollars. 'Can you do another lap? No need for the commentary this time.'

'Thank you,' I say when his eyes meet mine again.

'You're welcome.' He gently strokes my cheek with the back of his fingers and his touch sends a shiver running down my spine. He's so tender with me. My breath hitches when his face moves closer and he does something I've been hoping he'd do since our time together last night. He kisses me. A long, lingering kiss that sends currents of electricity shooting through every last nerve in my body.

My first ever kiss.

I'm surprised by how disappointed I am when he pulls away.

'I'm sorry,' he whispers, 'but I've been dying to do that from the moment you crashed into me at the airport.'

His words make me smile. He drapes his arm around me, pulling my body in closer. When I rest my head on his shoulder, he places a soft kiss on my hair and my heart melts. I pray this day will never end.

CHAPTER SEVEN

JADE

I'm so overcome with sadness when we reach the door of my suite that I actually think I might cry. My time with Brock today was magical. He gave me a taste of what my life might be like once I'm free from M.

After our second ride around the park came to an end, we walked the streets of New York hand in hand, talking and laughing. Later, Brock took me to one of his favourite restaurants. He ordered a bottle of wine for us to have with dinner. I opted for a chicken salad, while he ordered a steak that was the size of my head. I couldn't hold in my laugh when the waitress placed it in front of him. It looked delicious, though. M doesn't let me eat red meat.

He talked about his business, and his brother. There was no mention of his parents. I didn't divulge much about my life; there's really nothing I can say without giving it all away. I thought I'd pretty much come to terms with being a hooker, but being with Brock makes me see that's not the case. Just thinking about him finding out who I really am, and what I really do, fills me with shame.

I did confess one thing: I told him about my love of cooking, and how I was hoping to one day open my own restaurant. That was a huge step for me. I've never spoken of my hopes or dreams before.

'I was hoping tonight would never end,' Brock says, reaching for my hands. 'I promised Rupert that I'd have you back in the hotel by midnight, and I'm a man of my word.'

'I don't want it to end either,' I reply as tears sting my eyes. Letting go of my hands, Brock runs his fingertips tenderly over my hair before tucking some strands behind my ear. His eyes are locked with mine, and there's something about the way he looks at me that makes my pulse quicken.

'I'm captivated by you, Miss Davis.'

Before I have a chance to reply, his lips are on mine. Sliding his hands around my waist, he pulls my body flush with his. This kiss is so much more than the peck he gave me at the park, and when I open my mouth slightly, he deepens it. My arms slide around his neck, holding on tightly as my legs threaten to give out. I've never been kissed like this before, but I just follow his lead in the hope I can pull it off. Besides, I've watched enough pornos in my time to know how it's done.

This kiss is sweet and hot—is it possible to orgasm just from a kiss? Because, by God, this man has me so turned on. I'm certainly no stranger to orgasms, though I've never had one with any of my sexual encounters in the past. It's my job to please them, not the other way around. What I have learnt over time, however, is how to turn myself on. Some of the men who require sex seem to like it when I touch myself in front of them. I, on the other hand, only do it to get wet. I don't ever want to experience the pain of my first time with that pig of a man again.

My body's natural instincts take over. When I slide my tongue into Brock's mouth, he groans, pulling me even closer. I feel his erection pressed up against my stomach, which only turns me on even more. I start to wonder what he'd feel like inside me. For me, sex has never been enjoyable, but with Brock, I get a feeling it would be different. Very different.

We're both breathless by the time the kiss ends. I'm not sure how long we make out in the corridor, because time seems to have stood still. I'm no longer aware of my surroundings. Brock rests his forehead against mine and mutters one word, 'Wow.' That's an understatement. Kissing is a hard limit for me, but not with him. I could kiss him forever.

'I'd invite you in,' I say, once I'm able to string two words together, 'but Rupert is staying in the room next door.'

'Come back to my suite then. I'm not ready to let you go yet. To be honest, I'm not sure I'll ever be ready.'

His words both melt and break my heart. I don't want to let him go either, but I know I don't have a choice. It just makes me hate M even more. I'm still bound to her for two more years. A few weeks ago, it didn't feel like a long time— now it feels like an eternity.

'Okay,' I reply. I'm taking a huge risk, but if tonight's going to be the end of us, then I want to experience it all. He'll forever remain the first man to hold my hand. My first kiss. I want him to be the only person I've ever wanted inside me. The first person I've had sex with, without being paid or forced. I wish there had never been any other man but him. Sadly, that ship sailed years ago.

'Really?' His whole face lights up with surprise. I nod.

He grasps my hand in his and leads me back to the lifts before I can change my mind, which I know I won't. I want this night with him more than I've ever wanted anything in my life.

Once we're inside the lift, he presses the button that takes us to the fiftieth floor. He must be staying in the penthouse suite. The moment the doors close, he backs me up against the wall, caging me in. Threading my fingers into his dark hair, I pull his mouth to mine.

His hands glide down the sides of my body, before coming to rest on my arse. He lifts me and I wrap my legs around his waist. We're so lost in each other, it takes a few seconds for us to realise the lift has stopped.

Stepping back, he carries me towards his suite. He balances me up against the wall while he fishes in his pocket for his room key. Using his shoulder to push the door open, he carries me inside and closes the door with his foot.

His lips are locked with mine before my back even touches the wall. He pushes my hair back as his lips trail a path down my neck. 'I've never wanted anyone as much as I want you right now,' he breathes against my skin.

'Take me. I'm all yours.' I'm surprised at how liberating it is to say those words. They're something I never thought I'd say willingly. The men in my life have only ever taken, whether it was offered to them or not.

'Jesus,' he groans as he pulls the cardigan I'm wearing down my arms. 'Your skin is so soft.' His lips trail along my collar bone. I need this singlet gone. I want his lips all over me. Reaching for the hem, I tug my top up and over my head, revealing my white lace bra.

Brock looks at my chest. Usually the way I'm ogled by my clients repulses me, but in this moment, the look of appreciation I see on Brock's face makes me feel beautiful, not dirty.

Shifting my back slightly off the wall, he runs his hands up the length of my spine so he can unclasp my bra. 'You're fucking perfect,' he says when it drops to the ground.

Unwrapping my legs from around his waist, I stand. My fingers work their way down his shirt as I undo the buttons. I need to feel his skin against mine. My hands move up to his shoulders and down his arms as I peel the fabric away, letting it fall to the ground.

I drink him in, marvelling at his chest and his ripped abs. He's even more beautiful than I imagined. 'You're perfect too,' I say as my fingertips run down his body before hooking into the front of his jeans. Using my thumb, I flip the button open before sliding down the zip. I want to give him something back. I want to thank him for everything he's given me today.

When I fall to my knees, Brock growls. I pull his jeans down around his thighs. His large erection bulges from inside his black boxer briefs. My tongue trails a line along his skin, just above the band.

'Jesus, Jade,' he breathes as his hands fist in my hair. I'm going to give him a blowjob that he'll never forget. Over time, I've become a master at it. When I learnt that men love a good blowjob just as much, if not more than, sex, I watched every porno I could find on the subject until I had it down to a fine art. If I could do it well enough, there was a chance I wouldn't have to sleep with them. Somehow sucking a man's cock didn't seem as personal as having them inside me did.

If I couldn't escape my wretched life, I needed to find a way to make it at least bearable.

*

BROCK

Jade seems sweet and innocent, yet she can suck cock like a damn pro. I don't even want to know how she learnt to do this. Just the mere thought of it sets off a raging jealousy inside of me. That's a feeling I'm not accustomed to and I don't like it. In just a few short days, this woman has managed to turn my whole fucking world upside down.

A minute or so in, and already I'm gonna blow. As much as I'd like too, I can't bring myself to come in her pretty mouth. Reluctantly I pull away, placing my hands under her arms and pulling her to her feet.

'I wasn't finished,' she says as her brow furrows. Without giving her a chance to mutter another word, my lips crash into hers. My fingers immediately go to work on her jeans. Once they're undone, she takes over, pulling them down her incredibly long legs.

I step out of my jeans and underwear before scooping her into my arms. 'My turn,' I whisper as I cross the room and gently lay her on the bed. Seeing her sprawled out like that, wearing nothing but a tiny pair of white lace panties, is a sight, I can tell you. She literally takes my breath away. Does this woman even realise how spectacularly beautiful she is?

Out of the corner of my eye, I spot the red tie I wore to the office earlier today slung over the back of the chair. I've never felt compelled to tie a woman up before, but for some reason with Jade, I do. I'd like to have her tied to my bed permanently if I could. That thought shocks me. It usually doesn't take long for me to lose interest, but I get the feeling that won't be happening any time soon with Jade.

Kneeling beside her, I place my lips on hers briefly before I grab hold of her arms, pulling them above her head. The moment I wrap the tie around her dainty wrists, I see fear flash across her face before her eyes clamp shut.

'Shit, Jade,' I say, quickly removing the tie. 'Are you okay?'

When her eyes spring open I see tears glistening them. Fuck. Placing my hands on her shoulders, I pull her towards me, wrapping her in my arms. I can feel her body trembling as I hold her.

What the fuck just happened?

'I'm sorry,' I whisper. I don't know what else to say. Me and my bright fucking ideas. I hold her until she stops shaking before leaning back on my haunches to make eye contact with her. 'What's this all about?'

'Nothing. I'm okay,' she answers.

Like hell it was nothing. My mind is swimming with all kinds of fucked-up scenarios. Something's happened to her in the past to make her act this way, and I intend to find out.

'Please.' She holds her wrists out in front of her, but there's no fucking way I'm going there again. I throw the tie across the bed.

'Please Brock,' she pleads. 'I need this.'

'Why did you look so scared when I tied your wrists? Has somebody hurt you?' It's the only logical explanation I can think of. She shakes her head vigorously as her bottom lip starts to quiver. She can shake her head all she fucking wants, but I know the answer is yes. Rage boils inside me at the thought of someone hurting her. 'Talk to me,' I plead as my hands tenderly cup her face. My eyes search hers, looking for answers, but I find none.

A small smile tugs at her lips as she pulls my mouth down to hers. She can avoid this conversation all she wants, but I'm not letting it go.

When she pulls out of the kiss a few minutes later, she reaches across the bed for the discarded tie, before lying back down. The pleading look on her face as she holds it up to me has me crumbling immediately. I have a feeling I'm going to have a hard time denying this woman anything.

'Are you sure?' I ask.

After giving me a reassuring smile, she moves her hands above her head. I watch her carefully as I bind her wrists again. I'm having huge reservations about doing this now. Any sign of a freak-out and I'm done. I refuse to be a part of anything that's going to make her feel uncomfortable.

'I trust you,' she says.

I like that she trusts me. I hope she knows I'd never intentionally do anything to hurt her. She remains calm as I finish tying her wrists before securing them to the bed head.

'Are you okay?'

'I'm perfect,' she replies.

'If at any time that changes, just say the word and I'll untie you immediately.' When she nods, I smile before kissing her.

Pulling my mouth from hers, I kiss a trail across her jaw and down her neck. My hand skims over her toned stomach before palming one of her breasts in my hand. She has the most amazing tits. I'd presumed they were fake, but I've felt enough in my life to know these aren't. This pleases me to no end.

She pushes her head further into the pillow and moans when I roll her hardened nipple between my fingers before replacing them with my tongue. She moans again the moment

I suck the taut peak into my mouth as her chest pushes towards my face. I love how responsive she is to my touch.

When my lips eventually find hers again, my hand glides down her skin until my fingers are dancing over the lace of her panties. I smile to myself when she opens her legs for me and I run my hand between her thighs. The dampness I feel through the fabric makes my cock throb. I need to touch her, I need to taste her, but more than anything, I need to be buried balls deep inside her heaven.

Grabbing the lace, I tear it easily from her body as my eyes drink her in. She's even more beautiful than I imagined. Her hips raise towards my hand as my fingers glide over her perfectly manicured pussy and she whimpers when my thumb circles her clit. I slide one of my fingers effortlessly inside her. I love how ready she is for me. She's perfect. Everything about this woman is damn perfect.

Kissing my way over her abdomen, I don't stop until I'm settled between her thighs. Then I push her legs towards her torso, opening her up for me. I need to see her.

'You're beautiful,' I whisper as my mouth bears down on her magnificent pussy. She tastes sweet, just like I knew she would.

'Brock,' she whimpers, tugging on her restraints. I love hearing her say my name like that. I want to hear her scream it when I make her come. 'I need to touch you.' That will have to wait. I'm not stopping until she comes all over my face.

Moments later, her body starts to tremble and her head thrashes from side to side, and I know she's close.

'Yes, that's it. Come for me, beautiful,' I demand against her sensitive flesh.

'Oh, Brock,' she screams as her orgasm takes hold. That's what I wanted to hear.

Making my way back up her delicious body, I kiss her as my hands go to work at untying her from the bedhead. I'm craving her touch. The second she's free, her hands fist in my hair as she pulls my lips closer to hers.

'Thank you,' she whispers into my mouth, and her words touch my heart for some reason. I'm not sure if she's thanking me for untying her, or for the incredible orgasm I just gave her. Either way, I feel like I'm the one who should be saying thank you.

Reaching across the bed, I open the bedside drawer to retrieve the box of condoms I know will be in there. Staying in the penthouse suite comes with perks. It was one of the requests I made the first time I stayed here a few years ago. I've noticed every time since, the suite is always stocked with my preferences: my favourite scotch; the kind of snacks I like to eat; even right down to the brand of shampoo I use.

Leaning back on my haunches, I tear open the foil packet with my teeth. Jade's exquisite green eyes follow my every move.

'Are you okay?' I ask once I'm settled between her legs again. I'm dying to be inside her, but I'm still concerned about her little freak-out earlier.

'I'm wonderful,' she replies, tenderly stoking the side of my face. 'I'm more than wonderful.' Her sweet words make me smile. This woman is something else.

Lining myself up with her opening, I take one more glance at her face to make sure she really is all right. I'd hate to do anything she's not ready for. She's smiling when she pulls my face forwards. Resting my forehead on hers, I gaze into her eyes as the head of my cock slides inside her.

'Sweet Jesus,' I groan the second I push all the way in.

'Brock,' she whispers as her eyes drift closed. Hearing her utter my name so sweetly touches a place deep inside me.

'Look at me, beautiful. I need you to see who's making you feel like this ... who's giving you pleasure.'

A smile spreads across her face as her eyes flutter open. 'Nobody could ever make me feel the things that you do, Brock. Nobody.'

Normally if another woman said that to me, I'd freak the fuck out. If anything, Jade's words set off the caveman inside me. I want to be the only person to make her feel like this. I don't want anyone touching her.

She's mine.

*

JADE

Tonight Brock's given me more than he'll ever know. He's shown me how beautiful sex can be when it's with the right person. Tonight I'm not a hooker—I'm just plain old Jade, a woman. What a wonderful feeling that is.

With every thrust he brings me higher and higher. I never knew it could feel like this. I guess those girls in the pornos aren't faking it after all. Rolling onto his back, he brings me with him so I'm now straddling his waist. God, he feels so good.

Placing my hands on his shoulders for leverage, I move my hips in a circular motion as pure ecstasy consumes my body.

'Jade,' he breathes. Slightly lifting his torso off the bed, he sucks my nipple into his mouth. It sends pleasure shooting down to my core. 'Christ, you feel amazing. I can't seem to get enough of you.' He sits up and I wrap my legs around him as his arms encircle my waist, bringing me even closer. 'You intoxicate me, Miss Davis,' he whispers against my skin.

That's all I need to send me over the edge again. Wrapping my arms firmly around his neck, I throw my head back and moan as the most intense orgasm rockets through me. Within seconds, I feel his body shudder and I know he's coming undone too.

'Sweet Jesus,' he groans as his mouth finds mine. We're both breathless, but neither of us move. I don't want to break the connection I have with him. I wish we could stay like this forever.

Brock Weston has managed to cleanse me of all my previous sins.

CHAPTER EIGHT

JADE

'Jade. Wake up, sweetheart,' I hear as someone peppers tiny kisses all over my face. Opening one eye, I see Brock smiling down at me. It's a wonderful sight to wake up to.

'Good morning, beautiful.'

'Morning,' I groan as my arms slide around his neck. I'm aching in places I didn't even know existed. I feel like I've been hit by a bus.

'As much as I hate the thought of kicking you out of my bed, it's just after six, and I promised I'd have you back in your room before Rupert wakes.'

I sigh. I'm not ready for this to end.

Brock places a soft kiss on my lips before helping me sit up. 'I've ordered us some breakfast. Maybe we can have a quick shower together while we wait for it to arrive?' He stands and extends his hand out to me.

'You're amazing.'

I don't know what feels better, the warm water beating down on my sore and weary muscles, or Brock's strong hands as he washes me. Nobody has ever washed me before. There's something so erotic, yet beautiful, about it. I'm not used to this attentiveness, but it's something I could easily get used to.

'You have the most incredible skin,' he says as his mouth trails kisses down my neck and his hands cup my breasts.

'I'll never forget the time we've spent together.'

'Neither will I,' he says with a grin. 'You say that like it's so final. I don't want this to be the end of us, Jade. I want to see you again. Not just here in New York, but once we're back in Sydney as well.'

Tears sting my eyes at his words. *If only.* I wish that more than anything, but I know it's impossible. Fisting my hands in his hair, I bring his mouth down to mine. I want to savour every second we still have. I don't want to ruin it by telling him I can't see him anymore.

He backs me up against the tiles and deepens the kiss. As tender as I'm feeling, I need to have that connection with him one more time. Lifting my leg, I slip it around his waist. He growls into my mouth as he lifts my other leg off the ground and hooks it over his hip before sliding inside me.

'I don't think I'll ever get my fill of you,' he breathes as he withdraws to the tip before pushing all the way back in. I know I'll never get my fill of him either.

Brock insists on walking me back to my room after breakfast. He had a mini freak-out when he realised we hadn't used protection in the shower. 'I've never done anything so careless before. I'm so sorry, Jade.'

He calmed down once I assured him I was on birth control. Although all my clients *must* use protection, M made me have a hormone implant inserted in my arm as a safeguard against pregnancy. Neither Brock nor I have ever had unprotected sex before, so I knew we were both safe in that department as well.

We ate breakfast wrapped only in our towels. He sat me on his lap and fed me. It was the sweetest moment I'd ever experienced. My heart felt heavy when it was time to get dressed and leave. I tried my best to hide that from him.

'My panties,' I'd said when I gathered up my clothes that were still sitting in a pile just inside the door.

'I ruined them when I ripped them off that luscious body of yours, remember?'

'But where are they?'

'They may have found their way into my suitcase,' he told me with a devious smile. 'I guess they decided they wanted to come home with me.'

His brazenness made me laugh. Then I scooped his black boxers off the floor.

'I guess these are coming home with me then.' When he playfully wrestled me to the ground trying to snatch them out of my hand, I laughed until I could hardly breathe. In the end he let me keep them anyway.

'I'll be at the office for most of the morning,' he says when we reach my suite, pulling me into his arms. 'Can we do lunch when I get back?'

'When Rupert wakes, I'll ask him,' I reply. 'Thank you for taking me on the most wonderful date. I'll never forget it.'

'It's only the beginning of what lies ahead for us, Jade.'

I close my eyes and fight back the tears when his lips meet mine.

The beginning of the end.

*

The moment I enter my room, I flop face first onto the bed, and let the tears finally fall. I'm not sure how long I lay there, but I'm eventually pulled back into reality by a knock on my door. Rupert.

Flinging the door open, I fall into his arms. I'm reminded of the last time I'd done this, but this time my heart was breaking for totally different reasons.

Placing his hands on my shoulder, he gently pushes me back. 'What did he do to you?' he asks. The rage is clear on his face.

'Nothing,' I assure him. 'It was wonderful—he was wonderful.'

'Then why all the tears?'

'Because you know as well as I do that nothing can ever come of this.'

'Oh, Jade,' he says, pulling me into his chest. 'I'm sorry I put you in this position.'

'Don't be. Without you, I never would've experienced the most magical night of my life. I just hate that this has to be the end of us.'

'I wish I could get you away from M,' he whispers as his embrace tightens. I love him for saying that. 'I hate that she has this control on your life.'

He holds me until the tears stop. 'Can you call M and tell her I'm sick or something? I need to go home, Rupert. If I stay here any longer, I'm not sure if I'll be able to walk away with my heart intact.'

'Are you sure?'

I nod because I can't bring myself to utter the words. This isn't what I want to do, it's what I have to do, and that knowledge makes my heart shatter into a million tiny pieces.

CHAPTER NINE

BROCK

I'm usually meticulous when it comes to my company. This morning though, I find myself skimming and rushing through everything so I can hurry back to the hotel—back to Jade. This woman has wormed her way under my skin and, surprisingly, I'm not worried about it in the slightest. I actually welcome it. I want to continue seeing her. I want to see where this leads.

There's something special about her, and I'd be a damn fool to let her go.

Excitement flows through me when the driver stops outside the hotel and I have an unfamiliar bounce in my step as I head into the lobby. The woman behind the front desk gives me a flirtatious smile as I pass. She's pretty, but has nothing on my Jade.

'Mr Weston,' she calls out as I pass, heading to the lifts. I turn. She better not hand me her number. Coming around from behind the desk, she says, 'I forgot, I have a note for you. Miss Davis left it at reception for you earlier.'

'Thank you,' I say, taking the envelope from her. I smile when I see 'Brock' neatly written on the front. Sliding it into my pocket, I head for the lift again.

I stupidly forgot to get Jade's phone number this morning. My common sense seems to elude me when I'm in her presence. Our lunch plans are still up in the air, so I'm gathering the note has something to do with that. Rupert's been pretty obliging about us being together, so I'm confident he won't stand in her way today.

When the doors to the lift close, I press my floor number. I want to get changed out of my suit before I go and see her. I slide the envelope out of my pocket, smiling like a damn fool as I open it.

My heart drops when I read what it says.

My Dearest Brock,
I'm sorry. I'll never forget you.
Jade.

She's kissed the page underneath her name. It's the same shade of red lipstick she was wearing the day she ran into me at the airport. My fingertip skims lightly over the imprint of her lips before I press the number of the floor she's staying on. When the doors finally open, I find myself practically running towards her room. Rupert must've said no to her having lunch with me today. He can deny her all he wants, but I'm not giving her up without a fight.

A hotel cleaning cart is sitting in the corridor and the door to her suite is open. I enter without knocking. I can still smell Jade's sweet scent, lingering in the room.

'Can I help you, sir?' the cleaning lady asks.

'I'm looking for Miss Davis. The lady who's staying in this room.'

'I'm sorry, she checked out earlier this morning.'

My head starts to spin as I try to wrap my mind around what she's just said. 'What about the man staying in the room next door?'

'He checked out as well. I've just finished cleaning that room.'

I screw the letter in my hand into a ball, and clutch it to my chest. This can't be happening. She wouldn't just walk away from me like this. Or would she? I exhale a deflated breath as my shoulders slump. A crushing pain, like nothing I've ever felt before, settles in my chest.

She's gone.

*

I spend the rest of the day locked away in my suite, a vast array of emotions running through me: shock, hurt, rage, confusion, despair. After leaving Jade's room, I'd headed back down to the reception desk. I needed to make sure she wasn't staying somewhere else in the hotel. I then tried calling all the other hotels in New York, to see if there was a Jade Davis staying there. That's when I broke out the bottle of scotch—I needed to be numb.

I pull the crumpled piece of paper out of my pocket, smoothing it out with my hand. I read it over and over, but the words won't sink in.

I try to make sense of what I'm feeling. Maybe it's only because I'd never felt the sting of rejection before. But even I know that's a lie. My feelings for Jade run deep— her disappearance was a shock to my soul. That fact is only cemented when I lay on the bed.

The scent of her still clings to the bedding, and like the pathetic pussy she's now made of me, I clutch her pillow to my chest and don't let go until I eventually pass out.

CHAPTER TEN

BROCK

To say I've had a crappy fortnight would be an understatement. I'm still consumed with thoughts of Jade, and I hate myself for that. Part of me wants to forget I ever met her, the other part of me knows that's never going to happen.

What I had with her was special. It was like nothing I'd known with any other woman. I honestly thought she felt that too. Maybe it was just wishful thinking on my part.

'Mr Weston,' Amy says through the intercom. 'Theo James, your 3 pm, is here.'

'Thanks, Amy. Send him in.'

Amy knocks once and pauses briefly before opening the door. I'm not sure why she does that. Maybe it's because she caught me buried balls deep inside Renee, my father's secretary, last year. I had her bent over my desk as I gave it to her from behind. It was awkward all around, I guess, but it didn't stop me from finishing what I started. It took Amy a good week or two to make eye contact with me again. I chuckle to myself as I stand. I'm lucky she's a good sport because she's a great secretary. I'd be lost without her.

'Mr Weston,' Theo says when he approaches my desk.

'Mr James.' I extend my hand to him. 'Call me Brock.'

'Theo.'

'Take a seat,' I say.

'Thank you.'

'So, I believe you're a friend of my brother's.'

'I am,' he says. 'I frequent his bar.'

'Good,' I reply, leaning back in my chair. 'I believe you're in need of some security for your development sites.'

'Yes. The current company I'm using seems to be falling short. I have a range of expensive equipment and building supplies that remain onsite when the builders knock off. In the past few months the incidence of theft has risen dramatically.'

'Well, that's something we can definitely help you with.' The majority of our dealings are corporate based, but we can easily accommodate Theo's request.

We spend the next hour or so going over the layout of his sites, including all the finer details. When he's satisfied with my suggestions, the meeting comes to an end.

'I look forward to working with you, Theo,' I say when he stands. 'I'll have Amy draw up an appraisal, and then we can discuss this further. If you have any questions in the meantime, just call.'

'I appreciate you agreeing to take this on.'

'Any friend of Joshua's is a friend of mine.'

He smiles. 'Listen. I'm having a party at my home next weekend. I'd love it if you could come. Some of my investors will be attending, as well as my board members. I think it will ease their minds if I can introduce you to them, and explain what your company has planned. These thefts are proving to be quite costly. Everyone's a little on edge.'

'That's understandable. Give all the details to Amy on your way out. She can pencil it into the diary.'

'Thank you. I will.'

After making a few notes, I page Amy into my office. 'Could you type up a proposal for Mr James, please?'

'Of course,' she says, taking the folder out of my hands.

'I have that charity function tonight, so I'm going to head home early. Can you organise for my driver to meet me downstairs in thirty minutes?'

*

'I'll have a scotch on the rocks,' I tell the waitress when I take a seat at the bar. This is the first time I'm flying solo at one of these events. I didn't have it in me to bring a date. There's been no one since Jade.

I've tried to forget her, but I haven't been successful. I know in my line of business I could easily track her down, but I decided against it; I need to keep what little dignity I have left. She knows my name and I told her where I worked. If she wanted to find me she could, but it's fucking obvious she doesn't. I'd be lying if I said I wasn't hurt by that.

I'm pathetic.

Fuck her. This shit stops today. Brock Weston doesn't pine over women, and he sure as hell doesn't chase after a piece of arse either.

Keep telling yourself that, buddy.

'So, you decided to leave your whores at home tonight.' I don't even need to look to see who it is. That annoying voice gives it away.

'Fuck off, Clarissa. I'm not in the mood for your bullshit tonight.' I hear her gasp beside me and a satisfied smirk forms on my lips. I'm not usually this harsh with her, but she picked the wrong night to be a bitch.

'What's up your arse?' she says, taking the stool beside me. I choose to ignore her. 'Looks like someone isn't getting enough. If that's the case, you know I'd be more than happy to help you out.'

Her hand comes to rest on my crotch, but I instantly remove it. That's one place my cock will never go.

'Thanks, but no thanks.' I grab my drink off the bar and walk away.

I'm sure my dry spell is partly responsible for my rotten mood. I've never gone this long without sex before. That's only a very small part of my problem, though. A certain green-eyed brunette who ran from me just when I was getting to know her is the real reason. And I can't seem to wrap my head around it.

I make my way towards our table. My mother is sitting there on her own. Figures. My father's probably casing the room, looking for his next lay. My heart goes out to her, because although I hate the weak person he's turned her into, she's my mother and I love her regardless. She's been to hell and back, being married to that prick. Why she puts up with his shit and continues to stand by him, I'll never know. Maybe that saying, love is blind, has a ring of truth to it.

'Brock,' she says. Her face lights up when I bend down and kiss her cheek.

'Mother. How are you?' I barely have anything to do with her nowadays. Ever since Josh came to live with me, things have been strained. I'm not comfortable with our situation, but my parents' actions towards my brother were inexcusable.

'I'm good, sweetheart. How's your brother?'

The question instantly gets my back up. It's the first thing she always asks me. I usually say, 'He's doing really well,' but tonight I'm in no mood for this bullshit.

'Why don't you ask him yourself?' I try to hide the venom in my voice, but fail miserably. She bows her head and doesn't reply. It's obvious she still cares for Josh, so why she lets my father dictate to her confuses me. I wish she'd stand up to him. This whole mess is tearing both Josh and our mother apart. Our father, on the other hand, is too wrapped up in himself to care.

I sigh before downing my drink in one gulp. Everyone seems to be getting on my nerves tonight. I think I might fake a headache and blow this godforsaken joint.

CHAPTER ELEVEN

JADE

Yes. I do an inner fist pump when I receive my working schedule for the next few days. My lucky streak continues. Through some grace of God, in the three weeks since returning from New York, I've been fortunate enough to only be assigned to those of my clients who don't expect sex. I've given a few blowjobs, but that's it. I know it can't last, but every day that passes where I don't have to give my body unwillingly to a stranger is a blessing in my eyes.

I still belonged to Mr Weston—for the interim at least.

I've struggled since returning, but I've been trying my best to put Brock out of my mind. Do I miss him? Hell yes. Do I regret walking away from him? Of course I do. But I learnt at a very young age there's no point wishing for something you know you can never have. Memories are forever, though, and I'll treasure the time we shared. Nothing and nobody can take them from me.

Sadly, a memory is all it will ever be. If M were to find out what I've done, there's no telling what she'd do. She already suspects something's up—she made Rupert take me straight to the house the day I flew home from New York. Of course she wasn't concerned that I'd cut my vacation short because I was ill, she just wanted to make sure it wasn't going to affect my ability to work.

I was physically and emotionally exhausted when we landed, but grateful that Rupert allowed time for me to fix myself up before we got into the car. No amount of makeup could cover the bags under my eyes, but I did the best I could.

'Leave us,' M had snapped when we entered the house, flicking her hand at Rupert. I could already tell by her tone that she wasn't in a good mood. Nothing unusual for her. Like me, Rupert did as he was told. I wasn't even worried about what was to come when I'd followed her into the parlour. I felt numb.

'What is this all about?' she asked, abruptly turning to face me, the permanent scowl she wears prominent.

'I was feeling unwell in New York, so I decided to come home.'

'Have you seen a doctor?'

'No. I think it's just a bug. I'll be okay.'

'You better be,' she snarled. 'Get on the scales.'

Removing my shoes, I did as she requested. I knew I hadn't been following my meal plan, but I didn't really care. I was over this. Over my life. Over M. On a positive note, I hadn't been able to bring myself to eat on the flight home, so maybe that would be enough to get me over the line.

I wasn't paying attention to the numbers on the scale, so when her hand connected with my face, hard, it knocked me off balance. It hurt like a bitch, but I didn't even flinch.

'You've put on two hundred and fifty grams!' she screamed.

Whoop-de-fucking-do. Two hundred and fifty grams. I was in no mood for her bullshit.

'Maybe I need to confiscate your passport to teach you a lesson.'

I shrugged. 'Do what you like, I don't care anymore.'

The look on her face told me she was surprised by my outburst. I'd never backchatted her before.

'What did you say?'

Squaring my shoulders, I stood tall. 'I can't do this anymore. I hate my life. I hate you.' My confession surprised me. It's something I never thought I'd say out loud.

She was in my face in an instant. The murderous look in her eyes should've frightened me, but it didn't. Her hand came up, latching tightly around my throat.

'You ungrateful little bitch. You'd be nothing if it wasn't for me. You'd still be the piece of scum you were the day you came to live here.'

That's where she was wrong. I'd be everything I'd wanted to be if it wasn't for her. I may have been poor and unfortunate, but I was never scum—I was a victim of circumstances, nothing more.

Her grip on my throat tightened as she pushed my head roughly back into the wall. I tried desperately to take some air into my lungs. It was no use—my airway was completely restricted. 'The only way you'll ever get away from this profession, from me, is in a fucking body bag. Understand?'

The moment she uttered those words, some of the horrible things I'd witnessed her do over the years flashed through my mind. My gut told me she meant every word.

For a split second, I'd actually contemplated that death would be better than spending the next two years living under her iron fist, but that thought didn't last long. Brock had given me a small taste of how wonderful like could be. In my heart,

I knew that one day I'd get to experience that again. Maybe not with him, but anything would be an improvement on the life I was currently leading. There was so much more outside of this. *So much more.*

I refuse to die being the person nobody has ever loved. More importantly, I refuse to die a damn hooker.

*

I'd arrived at M's house around the same time as the other girls who are working tonight. Like everything else, M is big on punctuality. As usual we all have to go through a rigorous once-over before we head to our clients.

After M inspects what we're wearing, we're instructed to strip down to our lingerie. I hate this part the most. I can't tell you how many times I've been tempted to wear a huge pair of granny undies just to see the look on her face. Even thinking about it makes me smile.

'Very nice, Jade,' M says as she takes in my new lingerie. It's a set I bought from José while I was in New York. I knew she'd approve. I hear Rachel mumble some smart remark from beside me. Bitch. I get the impression the other escorts dislike me. I've heard the whispers and snickers when M leaves the room. They think I get special treatment from her, but I don't—she's just as horrible to me as she is to them.

We all pass M's inspection, and are allowed to get dressed and leave without suffering one of her rants, thankfully—it would spoil my mood. I'm actually looking forward to my weekend, which doesn't happen often. Theo James, my favourite client, is having a pool party at his mansion today. I'm his date. I love my time with him. Not just because he's gay: he's always kind to me, and fun to be around. He's like a big teddy bear.

*

BROCK

Sliding into my gold Lamborghini Murcielago, I punch Theo's address into my GPS. He texted me the information a few days ago, also telling me to bring a date. But I'm flying solo. I've just lost interest. Damn Snickers. She's ruined me.

To be honest, I'm not even in the mood to go to this party, but I said I'd be there, and I'm a man of my word.

When I reverse out of the garage, I dial Josh's number and put him on speaker. I have no idea what I'm getting into today, so I want to touch base.

'Hey pussy,' he says when he answers.

'Hey cocksucker,' I retort. I hear him gasp on the other end of the line, and it takes a few seconds for what I said to register. When it does, I burst out laughing.

'Very funny, arsehole,' he snaps. I clear my throat. Even though I have no problems with my little brother being gay, I definitely don't want images of him sucking some guy's cock in my head.

'Please tell me you're going to be at Theo's party today.'

'Sorry, bro. It's a business get-together. It's only for his straight friends.'

'What?'

'He's still in the closet. He keeps his business and personal life separate.'

'Oh,' I reply. 'Well, at least I don't have to worry about punching some fucker out for groping my arse, I guess.' This time Josh laughs. I'm glad he finds it funny. I don't think he'll ever let me live that night down.

'Your arse is safe today, big brother,' he says with amusement in his tone.

'Good to hear.'

'So, I've been meaning to call you, but time got away from me. Mum called me this morning.'

'She did?' That surprises me. I wonder if it had something to do with what I'd said to her?

'She did. She just wanted to see how I was going. It was weird. She hasn't spoken to me in years and then calls like nothing's happened.'

'How do you feel about that?' I know how much our parents have hurt Josh, but I also know this would've meant a lot to him.

'Honestly, it was nice. Weird but nice. She's not dying is she?'

'What? Fuck, no.'

'Okay. That's good,' he says. 'Her call had me worried. She wants to meet for lunch next week, Brock. She actually said she misses me.' I hear his voice crack and it tugs at my heart. I hate the way he's been treated. She better not hurt him again. For his sake, I hope my father doesn't get wind of this, because he'll put a stop to it, I'm sure. I'm proud of my mother for finally taking a stand and doing the right thing.

I end the call just as I arrive at Theo's mansion. There's an array of expensive cars parked in a neat row along the eastern wall of the property. Navigating the long driveway, I come to a stop outside the entrance to the house, where a valet is waiting.

One of the staff members at the front door takes my name before escorting me through the house and out onto the back patio. I find the other guests milling around the large in-ground pool. There must be close to a hundred people here. My gaze takes in all the bikini-clad babes. I'm suddenly feeling a little overdressed in my jeans and shirt. Only a few short weeks ago, this would've been my type of party. Losing myself in some random pussy tonight might be exactly what I need to help me forget Jade. A sinking feeling in my gut tells me it's going to take a lot more than that.

Scanning the partygoers, I search for Theo in the crowd. I can't see him anywhere.

'Would you like a drink, sir?' A waiter stops in front of me with a silver tray crowded with champagne flutes and bottles of imported beer.

'Thank you,' I say as I reach for one of the bottles. Wrapping my lips around the top, I take a pull. That's when I notice a leggy blonde eyeing me from beside the pool. I give her a wink as I set off in search of Theo. The blonde can wait. Business first.

The arse of a woman who's standing on the far side of the pool draws my attention. She's wearing a skimpy red bikini. Fuck me, what an arse. Of course I can't see her face, but from behind she's sexy as hell. Her legs go on for days. This one seems to have an instant effect on me. There's hope for me yet.

My gaze travels up her lean back to her long brown hair and thoughts of Jade flicker through my mind. Christ. Thanks but no thanks. I'll be steering clear of that one. I've had my fill of brunettes to last me a life time.

I only make it a few metres more before someone's hand lands on my shoulder. 'Brock,' Theo says. 'You made it.'

He's dressed in a pair of fluorescent pink swimming shorts and no shirt. He has matching pink zinc cream on his nose and aviator glasses place strategically on top of his head. I have to try to contain my amusement. It's wise to be sun smart, but he looks ridiculous. If he's trying to act straight, he's failing miserably. Pink zinc is for little girls.

'Hey,' I say, extending my hand to him. 'You forgot to mention it was a pool party.'

'I can see that. Sorry, mate. I can lend you something if you like.'

'All good,' I say, holding my beer up. 'Fluoro's not my thing.' My gaze moves back down to his coloured shorts. 'You know how it is, that colour clashes with my eyes.'

He slaps me on the back and laughs. 'I like you. Your brother said you were a cool guy.'

Theo leads me to a group of board members and introduces me. A few mention their concerns about the recent thefts, and that's my cue to explain what my company has planned to combat them. They're a tough crowd, and I can see why Theo thought it important for me to come here today. These men don't realise who they're dealing with, though. I'm Brock Weston. I'm a natural charmer. My mum always said I had the gift of the gab when I was a child, and she was right. It doesn't take me long to have them eating out of the palm of my hand.

I occasionally make eye contact with Theo as I give his men my spiel. I can tell by the smile on his face he's impressed. Then my words seem to fail me as I watch in disbelief. I swear I sensed her before I even saw her. Am I hallucinating, or is the world just fucking with me?

Like a goddamn apparition, the woman who's been haunting my dreams and taunting my every waking hour appears out of nowhere, Snickers. The kicker is, she doesn't even notice me standing here. Her eyes are firmly trained on

Theo as her hands wrap around his waist and she looks up at him with admiration.

What the ever-loving fuck?

'Hey baby,' Theo says draping his arm over her shoulder and leaning down to plant a loving kiss on her forehead.

'Get your hands and lips off my girl,' is what I feel like screaming, but of course I don't. She's not my girl.

This can't be happening. Seeing them together is like a sucker punch to the chest. Now I know why she fled New York. She has a fucking boyfriend, and going on what I've heard from Josh, Theo more than likely has a boyfriend as well. Could this get anymore fucked up?

CHAPTER TWELVE

JADE

'I'm sure you gentlemen remember my girlfriend, Jade. She's pretty unforgettable,' Theo says, winking at me. I smile up at him. He's such a sweetheart. Even if it's just an act, I can hear the sincerity in his voice. He has terrible luck with boyfriends, but he'll find Mr Right one day, I'm sure.

I look at the men in front of me and I greet them one by one, until I meet a pair of familiar steely brown eyes. My heart instantly drops, and I swear to God I feel all the colour drain from my face. What is Brock Weston doing here?

'I don't believe I've had the pleasure,' he says, never once taking his gaze off me. I don't think the others would've picked up on it, but I can clearly hear the sarcasm in his voice. The hurt and confusion I see in his beautiful eyes tug at my heart. It brings back all those horrible feelings from the day I ran from him.

'How rude of me,' Theo cuts in. I don't move because I'm frozen. 'Brock, Jade. Jade, Brock. Brock's going to be heading up the security at my development sites.'

Theo's words don't really register. I'm thrilled to see Brock again, but petrified too. He can't find out what I'm doing here. He just can't.

My gaze finally leaves his and lands on his outstretched hand. I pull myself together enough to wrap my fingers around his palm. I get that same electrified feeling I got when he touched me in New York. I need to keep my cool here. I can't afford to blow this. For Theo's sake, and for mine.

On the outside, Brock appears to be dealing with this situation a lot better than I am, but when his hand spitefully squeezes mine, I know, like me, it's all an act for our audience. He's angry. I guess he has every right to be.

'It's nice to meet you,' he says before dropping my hand. 'If you gentlemen will excuse me, I need a drink.' My eyes follow him as he walks away. Everything in me wants to chase after him and explain, but I can't do that. What am I supposed to say? It's not like I can tell him the truth.

Trying hard to pull myself together, I turn my attention back to Theo, forcing out a smile.

'Are you okay?' he asks, grabbing hold of my arm. 'You look like you've seen a ghost.' He's got that one right. Mr Delicious. A handsome, oh-so-fine ghost that I've been trying ever so hard to forget.

'I'm fine. I think I've just had a little too much sun. I might go and sit under the cabana, if that's okay with you?'

'Of course. Do you want to go inside and lie down?' I love that he appears to be genuinely concerned, and I feel awful for lying to him.

'Thank you,' I say, kissing his cheek. 'The shade will be enough.'

I don't even make it to the cabana before Brock grabs hold of my wrist, pulling me around the side of the house and out of sight of the others.

94

'So we meet again,' he says, pushing me up against the wall and caging me in with his arms. Unlike the first time he said that to me in the bar at our hotel, there's venom in his voice. My eyes lock with his, but words fail me. Having him so close brings all those feelings from New York back. He cocks an eyebrow when I don't reply. 'You have nothing to say, Miss Davis? Would you prefer to write it down on a piece of paper before running away? That seems to be more your style.'

His words sting. He's right. I'm a coward. He deserved so much more than what he got from me. He gave me the best moments of my life, and look how I repaid him. I bow my head in shame.

'I'm sorry,' I whisper.

'Sorry for what? For running? For lying to me? For having a fucking boyfriend?'

I flinch at the harshness in his voice. 'For everything.' I still can't bring myself to look at him.

He falls silent briefly before exhaling a deflated breath. 'I've missed you, Jade,' he says as his voice softens. He gently places his finger under my chin, bringing my gaze up to meet his.

'I've missed you too.' The words are out of my mouth before I even realise what I'm saying. Of course I've missed him. He's consumed my thoughts ever since I walked away from him, but I never meant to tell him that. This thing between us, whatever it is, can never happen again.

Without a second thought, he pulls me into his arms and crushes me against his chest. I feel every nerve in my body awaken. I love the feelings he ignites within me. How can something that feels so right be so wrong?

'You do know he's gay right?' he whispers.

I feel my lips slightly curve up at his words. Of course I know. I think everyone knows Theo's gay. Why he thinks he can fool people by parading around with me on his arm all the time, I don't know.

'Yes.'

'Enlighten me then. Why are you here with him? Is it the money? I have plenty of that, you know.'

His comment not only offends me, it pisses me off. I'm not a gold digger. I'd never be with a man just for his money. Well, I sleep with men for money, but that's not by choice. I'd give back every cent if I could be free of this miserable life.

'It has nothing to do with money,' I retort, backing away from him and folding my arms over my chest in annoyance. 'He …'

'He fucking what?'

I can tell by the tone of his voice that my vagueness is making him angry. It's none of his damn business why I'm here. I turn abruptly and walk away. I can't have this conversation with him. What can I say? *I'm Theo's escort. He hires me to pretend I'm his girlfriend.* Brock is the last person I'd want to know about my circumstances.

'Don't walk away from me,' he commands, reaching for my arm. 'Please, Jade … please. I haven't been able to stop thinking about you. About that night.'

His confession not only shocks me, it pleases me. 'That makes two of us,' I want to say, but I don't.

I turn to face him. The pleading look in his beautiful brown eyes makes my heart hurt. I can't tell him the truth, but I can't lie to him either. I need to do what's best for both of us.

'I'm sorry Brock. I need to get back to the party … to Theo.'

Tears sting my eyes as I walk away. I hate that I'm doing this for a second time. I honestly thought I'd never see him again. I tried to convince myself that I was over that night—over him, but I know now I'm not. Not by a long shot. Why couldn't I have run into him after my contract had expired? Why? This is so unfair.

I plaster on a fake smile when I join Theo again.

'Are you all right?' he asks, leaning down to kiss the top of my head. 'You're still awfully pale.'

'I'm fine. Honestly. I just have a bit of headache.'

'Go inside and lie down,' he urges as his kind eyes meet mine. Reaching up, he tucks a piece of hair behind my ear. 'You don't need to stay by my side if you're unwell, Jade.' I smile at his words. This is why I care for him so much. Underneath all those muscles and good looks, he has a heart of gold.

'Do you want to join me in the pool?'

I screw up my nose and shake my head.

'Come sit under the cabana then, out of the sun. I'll get one of the servants to bring you something for the headache.'

Hooking my arm through his, I get up on my tiptoes to kiss his cheek. 'Thank you.'

'No need to thank me,' he replies as he guides me to the line of sunchairs that are sitting under the shaded part. 'Just looking after my favourite girl.'

I can't help but smile as I watch Theo clowning around in the pool. I hate that he has to hide behind this charade. He has a beautiful soul. He'd give you the shirt off his back without hesitation. This world is full of narrow-minded people. It saddens me that he can't be the man he was born to be because he's afraid of ridicule from his peers. It shouldn't matter what his sexual preferences are. What's important is the person he is on the inside.

My gaze moves to the people milling around the pool. I haven't seen Brock since I rejoined the party. I'm not even sure if he's still here. It's probably best if he's left, even though that thought upsets me. I'm still reeling from seeing him again. I only wish things could be different.

My heart aches as the realisation we can never be sinks in.

*

BROCK

When Jade walks away from me for a second time, I'm consumed with hurt and anger. I'm not used to being told no. I hate that I'm hung up on someone who clearly isn't interested in me. Maybe she's my karma for all the hearts I've broken over the years. I sigh, tilt my head towards the sky and send the karma gods a huge 'Fuck you.' I walk down the side of the house and out the side gate. I can't go back to that party. I'll just text Theo later and tell him an emergency came up and I had to leave suddenly.

Once I'm in my Lamborghini, I rest my head on the steering wheel, trying to rein my emotions in. There's a part of me that doesn't want to leave because Jade's still here. Fuck, I'm pathetic.

When I feel calm enough to drive, I start the ignition. Something doesn't add up here. If she knows Theo is gay, why is she with him? Maybe he's bisexual. Pulling my phone out of my pocket, I dial Josh's number.

I'm driving through the gates and turning onto the street by the time he picks up.

'Bro,' he says when he answers.

'What's the go with the Theo?' I ask.

'What? Why?'

'I thought he was gay?'

'He is.'

'Then explain to me why I just met his girlfriend?'

Josh chuckles. 'She's his fake girlfriend. I told you he was still in the closet.'

'What do you mean "fake girlfriend"?'

'He hires her. She's an escort.'

I screech to a stop. *Not Jade.* It can't be true, even if it explains her reluctance to talk to me—and everything else, come to think of it.

'Brock? Are you still there?'

'I've gotta go. I'll call you later.'

Jesus. It can't be fucking true. I need to get to the bottom of this once and for all. Maybe then at the very least, I can move on. Turning the car around, I head back to the party to look for her.

Finally I see her sitting under the cabana, smiling as she watches the people in the pool. It kills me that she looks so happy when I feel so fucking miserable. Damn her and this whole situation to hell.

I greedily drink in her luscious body. I hate that she's so skimpily dressed in front of all these men, and I hate that I have to control my urge to take off my shirt and cover her up. Of course that babe in the red bikini earlier reminded me of her— it *was* her. Knowing I was drawn to her before I even knew who she was really messes with my head. What is it with this woman?

If what Josh says is true, she probably gets around in far less far more often. That thought fills me with rage. I move towards her and stop only when I'm standing beside her chair. She's so engrossed in watching the others she doesn't even notice me. I take a few more seconds to drink in her beauty before I clear my throat. Her head immediately snaps in my direction.

'I need to talk to you. You can come willingly, or I can make a scene. Your choice.' No more Mr Nice Guy. That ship sailed the minute I got off the phone with my brother.

'About what?' she asks hesitantly.

I don't reply. Instead I turn and walk back to the house. For her sake, she better be following me. I meant what I said. I'll make a damn scene if I have to. I need to know the truth.

When I enter the house, I spot a small corridor leading away from the main thoroughfare, so I head in that direction. Rubbing my face with my hands, I come to a stop at the end of the hall and turn around. I'm relieved when I find her approaching me. Smart girl. She stops when she's about a metre away, looking unsure of herself as her arms snake around her torso. How could this sweet woman be a whore? I just can't see it. Josh must be mistaken.

I try to think of the right words to say. I need to be careful how I put this, just in case I've got it all wrong. Unfortunately my brain and my mouth don't seem to be connected today, because what actually comes out shocks even me.

'You're a hooker?' I step closer and grab hold of her arm as I back her into the wall. Her pretty eyes widen. When her face drops and her mouth gapes open in shock, there's no need for a reply. I already know the answer. Disappointment floods me.

I'm gutted. The woman of my dreams is a fucking prostitute.

Letting go of her arm, my hands rake through my hair as I look at the ceiling. Devastation consumes me. I knew there was something about her, something she was hiding from me, but never in my wildest dreams did I entertain the idea it would be this. If anything was stopping her from being with me, I would've guessed it was a strict family. Her family—do they even know their daughter sleeps with strangers for a living?

'I can't believe I'm hung up on a fucking hooker,' I mumble to myself.

'I'm sorry,' I hear her whisper. *Sorry.* She's fucking sorry.

I feel my temper spike. 'I guess I was one of the lucky ones?'

'What?'

'I got a freebie. Or is my invoice for services rendered in the mail?' The second those words are out of my mouth I regret them. I feel like a prick for what I've just said. In my defence, I'm upset. I think I have every right to be, but I'll admit those words were spoken purely in anger.

Am I hurt by this revelation? You better believe I am.

Does is it lessen the feelings I have for her? Surprisingly not in the slightest.

I'm so focused on the tears that are now pooling in her beautiful jade green eyes that I don't even see her raise her hand until it connects hard with the side of my face.

A small sob escapes her as she sidesteps me and runs down the hall. My shoulders slump as my hand comes up to rub my stinging cheek. I need to go after her. At the very least, I need to apologise for my outburst.

'Jade!' I call out, as I follow her.

She runs up the main staircase and I'm hot on her heels. I need to make this right. I don't understand why she'd choose a profession like this, and I don't think I ever will. She has so much going for her: she's beautiful; she's smart.

And who am I to judge? I sleep around too, a lot. The only difference is I do it for free. Morally, I suppose that's no better.

'Please, Jade,' I call out again.

She glances over her shoulder before speeding up.

I don't think so, sweetheart. You ran away from me once. This time you're not getting away. I take the stairs two at a time, quickly closing the gap. I follow her down the long hall. She stops at one of the doors before opening it and darting inside. My hand reaches out just as she closes it in my face.

'Leave me alone,' she cries, trying to push the door closed the rest of the way.

'Let me in!'

'Why, so you can insult me again?' Her force on the door strengthens as she puts her whole body weight behind it. She's strong, but not strong enough. I managed to force my way inside, just in time to see her cover her face and slide down the wall in defeat. Sobs rack her body as she breaks down. My chest aches to see her like this. Even more so knowing I'm the cause of it.

'Come here,' I say as my hands reach for her, pulling her to her feet. The second she's standing, I pull her into my arms, crushing her to my chest. 'I'm sorry for what I said.'

She doesn't speak, so I continue to hold her. It's the only thing I can do. I can't take those awful words back.

The minutes tick by and eventually she settles. 'I knew you wouldn't understand,' she whispers into my chest. 'That's why I couldn't tell you. Don't think for a second I'm proud of what I do Brock, because I'm not.'

'Then why do you do it?' I ask as I pull back, cupping her face in my hands. Her eyes are red and puffy, but she's still as breathtaking as ever. 'Tell me, Jade.'

'I can't.'

'Are you in some kind of trouble? Let me help you.'

She shakes her head. 'There's nothing you can do.'

'Do you need money?'

'No. I have plenty of that. It's not about the money.'

'Then what?' I plead. 'Help me understand.'

'I have my reasons,' she mumbles as she looks down at the floor. I know in that moment I'm not going to get the answers I so desperately seek. I'll let it go. For now.

'Hey. Look at me,' I say softly. I don't speak again until her eyes meet mine. 'Is that why you ran?'

She nods. 'I never would've left you if I didn't have to, please know that.'

Her hand comes up to gently stroke the side of my face but I need to feel her lips on mine again. I suddenly don't care what her reasons are. All I care about is that I found her again. I won't be letting her go this time without a fight.

My heart starts to race the moment our lips connect. I can feel her body shaking as it melts into mine. My arms slide around her waist to pull her closer and her hands move up to my hair as she moans into my mouth. All the emptiness and uncertainty I've been feeling since New York vanishes and, for the first times in weeks, I feel alive again.

Reaching behind her, I click the lock on the door before I back her against the wood. I swear I can feel her heart beating against mine. This woman awakens something inside me whenever we're together. My hands run lightly over her skin before they cup her arse, and I lift her off the ground. I groan when she wraps her long legs around my waist.

I need her more than I've ever needed anything in my life.

'I've missed you so much,' I whisper against her skin as my mouth makes its way across her jaw and down her neck. 'I thought I'd lost you forever when you left me.' I've never been the type of man who expresses his feelings, but in this moment, I feel compelled to tell her how I feel. She's the first woman to ever make me *feel*.

'I've missed you too. Walking away from you that day was the hardest thing I've ever had to do. Those few days we spent together were the happiest moments of my life.' Her words touch a place deep inside as my lips curve into a smile against her skin.

I untie one of the bows that holds her bikini bottoms together. Her hands move from my hair and go to work on the buttons of my shirt. Within seconds she has it undone and pushes it off my shoulders. I tilt my head back and groan when her lips make contact with my chest.

Looking over my shoulder, I see a large bed behind me. 'Whose room is this?'

'Mine,' she replies.

'Yours and Theo's?' I need to know before this goes any further.

'Just mine,' she says, as her eyes meet mine. 'Theo is my friend. I've never been with him like that.'

That's all I need to hear. Smiling, I turn and lay her on the bed. I let my shirt fall down my arms and onto the floor. Sliding out of my shoes, I undo my jeans and pull them down my legs, taking my boxers with them. Kneeling on the mattress, I place my lips on her toned stomach as my fingers untie the other side of her bikini bottoms. I toss them aside as I go to work on the top. The second that's off, my lips are connecting with hers again as I position my body over her.

When she opens her legs for me, I eagerly settle between them. I want to take my time with her, but at the same time I'm desperate. Not only for her, but for this. I pull her hands above her head and lace our fingers together. Our eyes are locked as I slowly slide inside her heaven. Her eyes slightly roll back in her head the moment I push all the way in. She feels even more amazing than I remember. I know she feels this connection between us too. Surely I'm not imagining it? It's so strong.

I find myself wanting to freeze time. To freeze this moment. I want to stay buried inside her like this forever. I'm not sure where this is going, or what's going to become of us, if anything, after today. All I know is that I want to enjoy every second of my time with her. I took our time in New York for granted because I thought there'd be more of us. Now I know better.

I don't want to let her go.

CHAPTER THIRTEEN

JADE

I shed a few silent tears when I got in the shower this morning, because again I knew this was the end of us. I can't believe how emotional I've become lately. I still have one year, ten months and fifteen days until my contract expires. And yes, I am counting. I could never ask Brock to wait that long for me. It's incredibly selfish of me to even consider it. It's going to be even harder to walk away from him this time, I know it. He's still asleep in my bed, but Rupert will be here shortly to collect me so I need to get myself organised. It will be both our heads on the chopping block if I arrive back at M's late.

Brock and I had the most amazing night together. It even topped New York, if that's possible. It was wrong of me to let this go further, but I couldn't have stopped it, even if I'd wanted to. My heart and body needed him so much. I've fallen hard.

After dressing in a tight, red, sleeveless pencil dress, I dry my hair and apply my makeup. I need to look perfect when I reach M's. It's ridiculous, because I'll only be stripping off when I get home before heading to the gym, but this is my life, always pandering to M's ridiculous demands.

Once all my things are packed neatly in my small Louis Vuitton suitcase, I set it by the door. My heart is heavy as I go back to the bed where Brock is sleeping. I take a few minutes to watch him, before I kneel on the bed and place a kiss on his bare chest, just over his heart. My lipstick leaves a red imprint, bringing a small smile to my face. I wish I could leave my mark on him permanently.

My gaze moves up to his handsome face as my fingers skim lightly over his hair. He's so beautiful. He looks so relaxed and peaceful when he sleeps. I close my eyes and try to capture the image in my mind, so I can remember it forever.

I don't want to wake him, but I need to. I have to say goodbye. I never got to do that last time and it was one of my biggest regrets. Leaning forward, I gently place my lips on his. He groans as his arms encircle my waist, pulling me down on top of him. It makes me laugh.

'Good morning,' I say.

'Good morning, beautiful,' he replies with a smile. 'You're dressed?'

'Yes.'

'You look gorgeous.' The sincerity in his voice as he tenderly strokes the side of my face chokes me up inside. 'Where are you going?'

'Rupert will be here soon, I have to get going.'

'What?' he replies, shifting me to the side so he can sit up. 'Already?'

I sigh when I see his face drop. I'd give anything to be able to spend the whole day with him. 'Yes.'

'Why didn't you wake me earlier? I could've spent more time with you before you left.'

'You looked so peaceful,' I reply, forcing out a smile. I hate that I'm disappointing him once more.

'When am I going to see you again?'

I rest my forehead against his. 'I don't know.' Saying that to him makes my heart hurt.

'Can I get your phone number or something, so I can call you?' The hopefulness in his voice tears me up inside.

'I can't give you my number,' I whisper, as my eyes clench shut. I can't bear to see the hurt on his face.

'Why?'

'She checks my phone, Brock.'

'Who?'

'My madam.' This conversation is so humiliating.

'Aren't you free to do whatever you like in your spare time?'

'No,' I confess, turning my face away from him. 'She controls everything ... even my spare time.' My cheeks heat up as I speak. I'm so ashamed of my life and my circumstances.

'I want to see you again, Jade. No—I have to see you again,' he says, crushing me to him. He holds me so tight, like he's afraid to let me go.

'I want to see you again too. More than anything. But I can't see how. You have no idea how my life is—what she's like.'

I stand when he finally releases me, straightening my dress when I do. Pulling back the covers, he rises too. He's still naked and he's utter perfection. I could stare at him all day and never tire of it.

'I'll find a way. I promise. I won't let you get away again,' he says before picking his jeans up off the floor. I watch as he removes his wallet, pulling out a business card. 'Keep this. If you ever need me, just call. I mean it, Jade. For anything.'

'Thank you,' I say as my arms circle his waist.

'We're going to see each other again. We are.' He draws me closer. I'm not sure if he's trying to convince me or himself. We just stand there holding each other for the longest time. I hope he's right. I don't want this to be the last time I feel him in my arms.

When my phone rings he releases me, and I walk to my bag. I already know it's Rupert alerting me he's downstairs.

'Fuck,' I hear Brock groan from behind me.

'What?' I ask, turning around.

'You look fine in that dress, and you're wearing those damn shoes again.'

'What?' I feel my face screw up.

'Those red heels,' he says, pointing to my feet. 'You were wearing them at the airport. The day I met you.'

I can't believe he remembers what I was wearing on my feet that day. 'I was?'

'Yes, you were. I want to see you wearing nothing but those shoes one day.'

I chuckle as I retrieve the phone from the front pocket of my suitcase. Brock comes up behind me, grabbing hold of my waist and thrusting his pelvis into me.

'Fuck, your arse looks sexy in that dress.'

'Shh,' I say as I place my finger against my lips. 'Hi Rupert. I'll be down in a minute.'

When I end the call, Brock turns me in his arms. 'I miss you already.'

'I miss you already too,' I say, placing my lips on his.

'Take care of yourself, Jade.'

'I will. You too.'

'Please call me if you need anything, or even if you just want to say hello.'

'I will.' I'm trying hard to fight back the tears. I'm not usually an emotional person. I've cried more times since I've met Brock than I have in my entire life. And believe me when I say there were plenty of times that warranted tears when I was a child. Maybe opening my heart to him has finally made me feel.

'Until we meet again, beautiful.' He gives me a sad smile as he tucks a strand of hair behind my ear.

'Until we meet again, handsome.'

He picks up my suitcase and passes it to me. 'Bye,' I say as I place my lips on his for the final time. I open the door, taking a backwards step as my eyes drink him in one last time. 'You better put some clothes on before you go downstairs. I don't want Theo checking out my man.'

His face breaks out into a huge smile. 'Bye.'

I blow him a final kiss before turning and walking away. I have a huge lump in my throat. I only make it a short distance before Brock calls my name. Halting, I glance at him over my shoulder.

'For the record, I like being your man.'

*

BROCK

After washing my face and getting dressed, I head downstairs. I'll shower and change when I get home since I don't have any clean clothes with me. I'm hoping Theo is up so I can apologise for being MIA for most of yesterday. I also want to speak with him to see what he knows about Jade's situation. I have to figure out a way to see her again.

When I reach the landing I hear the sounds of a vacuum, so I head in that direction.

'Good morning, sir,' the elderly lady says when she sees me standing in the doorway. 'Is there something I can help you with?'

'I'm actually looking for Theo.'

'Last time I saw Mr James,' she replies, 'he was sitting out by the pool, having breakfast.'

'Thank you.'

'Here's the man of the hour,' Theo calls out as I walk onto the patio. 'Come join me for breakfast.'

'What do you mean?' I ask as I take a seat opposite him and reach for a piece of melon from the large serving dish sitting in the middle of the table.

'I walked Jade out to her driver when she left. She gave me a quick lowdown on you two. Should I be pissed off with you for getting it on with my girl?'

'She's not your fucking girl,' I grumble defensively, and he laughs. *She's mine.*

'I'm just messing with you. She's great. She needs a good guy like you in her life. You are a good guy, aren't you?' There's a touch of humour laced with scepticism in his voice.

I seriously contemplate my reply. Overall I'd say I'm a good guy. Yes, I've used women for sex in the past, but the majority of them were using me as well. For one thing or another, anyway. Jade is different. I care for her and would never do anything intentionally to hurt her, so I guess my answer to his question would be yes.

'I'm not using her and I'd never hurt her, if that's what you mean. I like her.' I pause. 'Really like her.' Why do I feel so unmanly for admitting that to another guy? I'm not good with this type of shit. I don't usually do feelings.

'I'm glad, because she really likes you too. She's had a pretty shitty life, so I need to make sure your intentions are honourable. She means a lot to me. I don't want to see her hurt.'

I nod as I try to take in everything he just said. 'What's the go with her, anyway?'

'What do you mean? Going on last night, it sounds like you know her better than I do.' He chuckles but I'm not amused. I give him a warning look. I've never been the type of guy to kiss and tell, but even more so with Jade.

'How long have you known her? Do you know much about her life?' I ask.

'Jade and I have been friends for about four years now.'

'And?'

'And what?' he says with a shrug. He seems like a nice guy, but his evasiveness is getting on my nerves. 'The things she's told me are in confidence. I'd never betray her trust like that, just like I know she would never betray mine.'

'Fair enough.' As much as I'd like more information on her, I totally respect him for that. 'I need to figure out a way to see her again. She told me her madam pretty much controls her.'

'Good luck with that one. M's a bitch. Poor Jade can't do anything without her permission. The way I see it, the only way you could swing that would be to hire her.'

I was afraid that might be the case.

'I want more than that,' I admit, and I'm not even surprised that I do. The last few weeks have proven how miserable I am without her. I like the way Jade makes me feel when we're together. She's like a breath of fresh air. 'Why does she allow herself to be controlled like that?'

'Because she's loyal and she has a contract.'

'A contract to control her life?'

'Basically.'

'That's totally fucked up,' I say, as my brow furrows. Who'd sign over their life to someone else?

'Tell me about it. M has brainwashed Jade into thinking she owes her, or some bullshit like that.'

'What do you mean?' His words only make my concern for Jade escalate.

'Look, I've said way too much. If Jade wants you to know more, she'll tell you herself.'

*

For the next few days my thoughts are solely about Jade. I'm desperate to see her again. I left Theo's house on Sunday with her madam's business card, and I've spent the majority of my time finding out everything I can about Madam Melody Sinclair, which isn't much. It appears this woman goes to great lengths to cover her tracks. So why does her name sound familiar?

By Wednesday, I'm struggling to focus on my mounting workload. I can't tell you how many times I've checked my phone, just hoping to see a text from Jade. By late afternoon it becomes apparent I'm probably not going to. If she's not going to make the move, then I need too.

Pulling out the card Theo gave me, I dial Madam Melody's number. Guilt consumes me as I wait for someone to answer. I feel like I'm breaking all the promises I made to myself growing up. I swore I'd never be anything like my father and resort to paying for sex. This isn't really about that, though. While sex with Jade is mind blowing, I'd forgo it if it meant

113

I'd see her again. I'm doing this for one reason only: to be with my girl. There's no level I wouldn't stoop to for Jade. If this is the only way I can spend time with her, then so be it.

I'm pretty sure I'd sell my damn soul for this woman.

*

Theo was right, Melody Sinclair's a bitch. She makes Clarissa look like a damn saint. It takes everything in me to keep my composure as I sit opposite her. I'm surprised she can even sit down with that stick that's been strategically placed up her arse. I'm finding it hard to mask my dislike for her, but I need to try harder. I can't afford to do or say anything that's going to jeopardise me seeing Jade.

'As I was telling you on the phone, Mr Weston, Jade is exclusive. I have a long list of girls who are available, and I'm sure any one of them could satisfy your needs.'

If this woman thinks she can intimidate me, she's mistaken. I've dealt with a lot worse than her, my father being one of them. I sit forward in my seat before speaking as calmly as I can. 'And as I told you on the phone, Ms Sinclair, I'm not interested in any of your other girls.'

'May I enquire why you have such an interest in Jade?' She picks up the three-page questionnaire I was made to fill out before she'd see me. Who knew seeing a prostitute would require divulging so much personal information? Granted, she runs a high-class establishment, but still.

'She came highly recommended to me.'

I see her lips slightly turn up at the corners. I think this woman's stern face would crack if she were to break into a full smile. 'By whom?'

'Theo James.'

'Hah,' she scoffs. I take a few deep breaths to calm myself as she continues to read over my paperwork. 'Interesting,' she says, leaning back in her chair and looking at me over the rim of her reading glasses. 'You're Maxwell Weston's son?'

Bingo. I should've known this woman would be familiar with my father. A sick feeling settles in the pit of my stomach at the possibility he may have been with Jade. 'You know my father?' I ask, barely managing to keep the disdain from my voice.

'We go way back.'

Of course they do. I'm struggling to contain the rage that boils inside me. Not that I'm surprised that my father is associating with madams. Clearing my throat, I sit up straight in my chair.

'You're in luck, Mr Weston. I'm prepared to make allowances now that I know you're Maxwell's son.'

'You are?'

'I am. Sometimes it's not what you know, Mr Weston, but rather whom.'

Although I remain calm on the outside, my heart thumps furiously against my rib cage as pure elation courses through me. I'm going to see Jade again. I think this is the first time in my life that I've ever been grateful that prick of a man is my father.

She picks up the phone. 'Bring me Jade's schedule for the next week,' she barks. This woman has absolutely no manners. A few seconds later, the plain-looking but meticulously dressed young woman who had me fill in the questionnaire enters the room. After she places a manila folder on the desk, I see Jade's name printed on the front. The woman immediately turns and leaves. I suppose she doesn't wait for a response because she probably has enough sense to know she won't get one.

My eyes scan the list of names when Melody opens the folder. I hate that I have to share her with other men. *She's mine.*

'When was the last time you were tested, Mr Weston?'

'Excuse me?' I look at her.

'Tested?' she snaps. 'For STDs.'

Oh. 'A few months ago.'

'That's not good enough. I'll require something more recent before this can go ahead. If you can get your test results to me by Friday, you can have Jade on Sunday evening.'

'I can arrange that,' I say as I stand.

'Sit. Mr Weston, we need to discuss a price.'

'I'll pay whatever the going rate is.'

'Fine,' she says, nodding her head. 'Jade is my number one girl, so if you insist on seeing her on her day off, know that she doesn't come cheap. She also comes with restrictions.'

'Which are?'

'We can discuss that once I have your test results.'

'I'll be in contact,' I say as I leave. I'm already on the phone to my doctor's receptionist, scheduling an appointment as I walk down the front stairs towards my car.

Sunday night, Jade will be mine again.

CHAPTER FOURTEEN

JADE

Sunday morning, I get a call from M requesting that I attend the house. She quite often does this, so I'm not particularly worried. But this woman is full of surprises, so I never know what to expect. I'd only just left the gym, so I rush home to shower and change. I knew she'd be pissed off at me for taking longer than expected, but she would've been even angrier if I turned up in my gym clothes looking like a hot mess.

'I shouldn't be long,' I tell Rupert after he pulls up outside her home.

'Good luck,' he replies, making me laugh. Hopefully I won't need it.

'You took your sweet time,' M snaps when I enter the house. 'I called you over an hour ago.'

'I was at the gym. I had to go home to shower and change.'

She walks towards her office, and I follow. 'Sit,' she demands. Once she's seated, she picks up a white envelope, handing it to me.

'What's this?' I ask.

'Your job for tonight.'

What? 'But it's my day off.'

Her eyes narrow as they meet mine. '*Was*,' she scoffs.

I deflate. I was looking forward to some *me* time. I've bought all the ingredients to try a new recipe I'd seen on the cooking channel. I've tweaked it a little and was excited to see how it would turn out.

'Okay,' I reply with a sigh. There's no point in arguing, I'd never win. 'With who?'

'A new client.'

'Not a regular?' My stomach churns at the thought. It's been a few years since I've had anyone new. I'm used to the men I have. I always know what to expect going in. What if he's like that horrible man I got on my first night? Or even worse? 'Who is he?'

'You'll find out tonight,' she says, picking up a pen and writing something down in her diary. 'Be back here at five for inspection.'

I sit there dumbfounded. I don't want to do this, but at the same time I know I don't have a choice.

'You can go.'

I have to bite my tongue when she flicks her hand at me. I hate her so much. The rude bitch doesn't even bother to look up at me when she speaks. Ever since my outburst when I returned from New York she's been a lot colder towards me than normal.

*

The nervousness I'm feeling when Rupert stops at the end of the long driveway of my new client's house must be showing, because he turns in his seat and locks his eyes with mine. 'You have my number, Jade. If you need me, don't hesitate to call. I'll be back here in a flash.'

I rest my hand on his shoulder. 'Thank you, Rupert. I don't know what I'd do without you.' He doesn't reply, but his hand is now covering mine and the gracious smile on his face is enough.

A sense of foreboding fills me as Rupert heads back to the street along the circled driveway. I admire a beautiful fountain before climbing the front stairs. When I reach the top, I freeze. All the fears I had as a foster child fill me—I don't know what awaits me behind that door, and I don't know if I want to find out.

Tilting my head back, I take in the opulent mansion that stands before me. It's breathtaking. The light grey render of the walls make the black finishes around the windows stand out. There's a beautiful wrought-iron balcony above me. I bet the view of the city would be spectacular from up there. Whoever lives here is extremely wealthy. That thought doesn't ease my worries at all. Some of the rich people I've associated with over the years think their social status comes with certain entitlements.

I have the sudden feeling my lucky streak is about to end. A new client usually always means sex. The fact that he's requested that I attend his house and stay the night virtually guarantees it. That thought makes me feel physically sick. Images of Brock flash through my mind and I have to fight back the tears.

The door before me flies open and I jump.

'Are you going to stand out here all night, beautiful, or are you coming inside?'

Oh. My. God. I blink a couple of times to make sure I'm not seeing things that aren't really there. 'Brock!' I squeal as I launch myself into his awaiting arms. 'What? How?' But before I get a chance to say another word, his mouth hungrily collides into mine. 'Mmm,' I moan as he draws me closer, my body melting into his. His kisses are intoxicating.

When we finally come up for air, he rests his forehead against mine. 'I've been dying to do that all week.' Happy tears well in my eyes, making his brow furrow. Tenderly, he cups my face in his hands. 'Hey. Don't cry.'

'I'm just … I'm just so happy to see you,' I say as I wipe my finger under my eye to catch the stray tear that has escaped.

'You have no idea how happy I am to see you, too. You've been on my mind night and day.' This time when his lips cover mine the kiss isn't so desperate, it's sweet and passionate. It not only melts my heart, it makes my toes curl.

'I love that your paperwork said that kissing was a hard limit for you, but you have no problems kissing me.'

'There are no hard limits where you're concerned,' I admit, because there aren't. I'm not a prostitute when I'm with him, I'm just plain old Jade. Even now that he knows the truth about me, I can tell he doesn't see me that way either.

'I'm pleased to hear that.' He reaches for the small suitcase I'm holding and grabs hold of my hand, lacing our fingers together. It sends my heart into a flutter. 'Let me get you inside.'

'Your place is beautiful,' I say. I've always wondered what his home would look like. It suits him perfectly. He's carried the black and grey theme inside and he has exquisite taste—well, his designer does. The rich wooden floors and staircase are stained in a dark charcoal grey. The wrought-iron bannisters are black. There are bright paintings framed in black on every wall, adding colour to the space.

'I still can't believe I'm actually here with you.'

Brock's hand tightens around mine as he places a soft kiss on the side of my head. 'You have no idea how happy I am that you're here, sweetheart.' The sincerity behind his words warms my heart. 'Come. We'll put your bag in my room and I'll give you a tour before we eat.'

'Do you live here all by yourself?' I ask as we walk up the stairs.

'I do. I had my brother living here for a few years, but he has his own place now.'

'How old is your brother?'

'Twenty-three, five years younger than me. We weren't close growing up because of the age gap, but we are now.'

'That's nice. Don't you get lonely living in this big house all on your own?'

'I like my privacy, but sometimes, I guess,' he says with a shrug.

When we reach his room, he sets my bag down just inside the door. 'I'm not sure if I trust myself having you in here right now,' he says with a chuckle. 'How about I give you a tour of my room later, otherwise we'll never eat.'

'Who needs food when I have you,' I say seductively as my arms slide around his waist. I'm used to acting like this around my clients, but with Brock, it isn't an act. With Brock, everything I say and do comes naturally. Nothing is forced. I hear a growl in the back of his throat as he draws my body in closer.

'Don't tempt me,' he moans, resting his forehead on mine. 'I'm already hanging by a thread here.' He places a chaste kiss on my lips before untangling my arms from his body. 'I didn't bring you here for sex, Jade. I wanted to see you, spend time with you.' Nobody has ever said that to me before. 'Mark my words, though,' he adds, 'I *will* have you in my bed before the night's out.'

'I look forward to it.' My finger trails a path down his chest. As much as I want him right now, I'm touched that he wants me for more than my body. That's another thing I'm not used to.

*

BROCK

After the tour, we head into the lounge room. I'm struggling to keep my hands off her, but tonight isn't about that. I want Jade to know she means more to me than a good time. That in itself proves how special she is to me. Until her, it was only ever about the sex.

I had contemplated taking her out to dinner tonight, but I'm selfish. I find myself wanting to give her everything she deserves, but I also wanted her all to myself. She's the first woman I've ever had in my home, apart from my mother. Before Jade came along, the last thing I wanted was one of my casual lays tainting my sanctuary.

'Sit,' I command, gesturing to the white leather couch. 'I hope you're hungry.'

'Are you cooking?'

Her comment makes me laugh. 'Hardly. My housekeeper usually cooks for me, but I've given her the night off. I had something else in mind.'

The moment she takes a seat, I have to quickly divert my eyes. Her sexy-as-hell white dress rides up, revealing more of her beautiful legs. Everything in me feels compelled to reach out and touch her. *It's not about the sex, Weston*, I try to remind myself. I'm pretty sure in her profession, she's used to being treated more like a sexual object than an actual person, but I don't want her to feel like that when she's with me. Ever.

'You have me intrigued,' she says, smiling, tapping the space beside her with her hand.

Against my better judgement, I sit. If I can't touch her right now, at least I can be near her. A few seconds later the doorbell rings.

'You ordered pizza,' she laughs when I walk back into the main room carrying the box and two bottles of beer.

I shrug. 'I did. I hope you don't mind. It's what we ate the first time we were together.' I'm suddenly feeling stupid. This kind of behaviour isn't me. I was trying to be sweet, but in all honesty, I'm far from it. This woman has turned my whole fucking life upside down and it scares the hell out of me.

After placing the box on the coffee table, I hand her one of the beers and sit. The moment my arse hits the couch, she grabs my shirt, pulling me towards her.

'It's a perfect choice,' she whispers against my mouth. 'Perfect, just like you.'

And there you have it, a few encouraging words from her and she's now made me glad I did it. *I'm fucking bewitched.*

'Shit, plates,' I say.

'Let's just eat straight from the box. We don't need plates.'

'Are you sure? You don't seem like a straight-from-the-box type of girl.'

When she throws back her head and laughs, it's like music to my ears. 'The real me—the Jade on the inside—is a simple girl at heart.' Taking a slice, she brings it to her mouth, taking a bite.

'That's what I love about you. You're a breath of fresh air.'

She looks away as a blush spreads on her cheeks. I get the feeling this woman isn't used to being complimented. And that astounds me. She's not only breathtakingly beautiful, she's smart, funny and so adorable. I have an urge to pull her into my arms and hug her tightly, but I don't. I ache to protect her and keep her safe. I want to shelter her from all the ugliness in this world. And surprisingly, more than anything I want to make her *mine*.

Once the pizza and beers are consumed, we both seem more relaxed. We've been talking about insignificant things, but I need more. I want to know everything there is about her, but I still get the impression she's not ready to open up. I don't want to force her into doing anything she's not ready for, but I'm hoping in time that will change.

'I almost forgot, I got you dessert.' I rise from the couch. 'I'll go grab it.'

'You bought me a Snickers bar,' she says when I walk back into the room and hand it to her. She hugs it to her chest, just like she did the day on the plane. She must really love chocolate.

'I did.' I sit down beside her.

'I still have the one you gave me on the plane.'

'You do?'

'I couldn't bring myself to eat it,' she admits. 'It was the sweetest thing anyone has ever done for me.'

I love that my small gesture meant so much to her, but it also saddens me to think nobody does nice things for her. Surely her family does?

'I want you to eat this one.'

'You're not having one?'

'I have something else in mind for me.' When I wink, a pretty pink blush spreads across her cheeks. How can this woman do what she does for a living, and yet still exude such innocence?

My eyes are glued to her mouth as I watch her eat. Lucky fucking chocolate. She offers me a bite, but I shake my head; I'm having too much fun watching her. Who knew watching her eat could be such a turn on?

'I'm so glad you're here,' I say, briefly placing my hand on her leg.

'Me too.' Her exquisite eyes gaze into mine as the world around us stands still. Our faces inch towards each other. The moment our lips touch, every part of me comes to life—it's like she flicks a switch inside me. Her lips are so soft and sweet. The only contact we have is with our mouths, but it's hot. Scorching.

I tilt her head back slightly and deepen the kiss. She moans and her hands grab my shirt again. Leaning back into the couch, she pulls me with her until my body is resting on top of hers. I groan when she hooks one of her legs over my hip. All my resolve vanishes. I need her like I've never needed anyone before in my life.

But tonight I'm going to take my sweet time with her. I'm going to savour every second. Who knows when I'll be permitted to see her again? I fucking hate that we're not free to see each other whenever we please, but I don't want to think about that now. I want to stay in the moment. I can worry about that tomorrow.

'Christ, you drive me wild,' I say as my lips trail a path across her jaw. 'I don't think I'll ever get my fill of you.'

Her fingers curve around the hem of my shirt as she slides it up my back. 'I need to feel your skin, Brock.'

Her wish is my command. Moving off her to kneel on the floor beside the couch, I pull my shirt over my head. My gaze moves down to her waist as she shimmies her dress over her hips, revealing a tiny pair of pink lace panties. Fuck me. Does she realise how sexy she is? She crosses her arms over her torso, pulling her dress up and over her head in one swift motion. Her barely there pink bra cups her breasts perfectly, and I realise I'm in love with her tits.

'You're so beautiful,' I whisper as I kiss a path up her leg. 'Perfection.'

'Brock,' she says breathlessly as her hands stroke over my hair.

'Lie back,' I command. My lips curve up against her skin when she does exactly as I ask. 'As pretty as these are, sweetheart, they've gotta go.' Sliding my fingers into the flimsy lace, I tear them effortlessly from her body, exposing her sweet pussy. My eyes hungrily drink her in. *Breathtaking.* I bunch up the lace in my hand before shoving it into my pocket. I'll add these to the pair I swiped from her in New York. If I get my way, I'll soon have a drawer full.

Hooking my hands under her legs, I place them over my shoulders. 'It's time for my dessert,' I whisper, blowing hot air against her sensitive flesh.

'Brock,' she pants, pulling my face forward. My greedy girl. The moment my tongue is on her, she moans. 'God, yes.' I smile as I watch her head tilt back and her lips slightly part as the pleasure takes over. I can't describe the feeling I get knowing it's me who's making her feel like this.

'You taste so sweet,' I murmur as my hand moves up her body to pinch her nipple through the thin lace of her bra. She whimpers, and I love how responsive she is. I slide the fingers of my other hand through her wetness, coating them, before moving down to her arse.

My mind drifts back to the paperwork M gave me on Jade. Her hard limits both thrilled and infuriated me. I can't even put into words the jealousy I felt towards the other men she sees. It ate away at my insides. I couldn't bear to think of what she's been through, or what she's done with them, for that matter. It only made my need to possess her—to make her solely mine—even stronger.

Immediately I feel the resistance when I slide the tip of my finger into her arse. I pause, giving her time to adjust. 'Can I?' I ask because I don't want to force myself on her. I know anal is one of her hard limits, but I won't be satisfied until she gives herself over to me completely. But in saying that, I don't want to take anything she's not ready to give me. For some reason, I need this with her. I don't want any restrictions when it comes to us. My need to claim every inch of her is overpowering.

She pushes her hips towards my face as I continue to work her over. 'Yes,' she moans loudly, so I push my finger in a little further and plunge my thumb into her pussy at the same time. When her grip tightens on my hair and her legs start to tremble as they squeeze my head like a vice, I know she's close.

Slowly I withdraw my finger and use her juices to lubricate it again before gently pushing it all the way back into her tight little arse. I can tell by the way her body pushes into my hand that she likes it. The second I suck her clit into my mouth, she falls over the edge.

'Oh God!' she screams as her whole body shudders.

Hearing her scream like that is almost my undoing, but I don't relent until I've drained every ounce of pleasure from her. When I'm done, her legs slide off my shoulders and she slumps back into the couch, exhausted. My girl is spent. Kissing my way back up her gorgeous body, her eyes flutter open when my face is hovering inches away from hers. The contented smile on her face hits me right in the chest.

'That was ... that was ... *amazing*,' she gasps, pulling my lips briefly down to hers.

'Get used to it, sweetheart,' I say, brushing her hair from her forehead. 'There's plenty more where that came from. I want to experience everything with you, Jade. Only you.'

She cups my face and smiles, but it doesn't quite reach her eyes. I can see a hint of sadness and possibly torment, reflecting back at me. It tears at my heart. Like her, I don't know what the future holds for us, but I pray it holds something. There is something truly special blossoming between us, and I know I'm powerless to stop it, even if I wanted to.

Standing, I scoop her into my arms before turning and heading for the staircase. I want to take her to my bed and show her just how much she means to me.

CHAPTER FIFTEEN

JADE

I woke to Brock's handsome face between my legs, which was a pleasant surprise. We barely slept. I've had the most amazing time here with him. I wish it never had to end.

'Morning beautiful,' he breathed against my sensitive flesh. 'I hope you don't mind, but I was hungry.'

I let out a small laugh as I ran my fingers through his hair. 'You'll get no complaints from me,' I said breathlessly. 'None whatsoever.' I'd love to wake up like that every morning.

Saying I'm feeling a little tender between the legs would be an understatement. I love that I'll be feeling the effects of being with him long after I've left here. After Brock had me for breakfast, he took me up against the tiles in the shower, but it was wonderful.

Now we both have sombre looks on our faces as he carries my bag downstairs. After placing the suitcase by his feet, he pulls me into his arms. 'I wish I didn't have to let you go.'

Tears sting my eyes, but I don't reply. I'm scared if I do, I'll cry.

'I'm going to swing by M's on my way to work this morning. I need to see you again, Jade. Is that okay with you?'

He cups my face in his hands as he awaits my reply. I still can't bring myself to speak, so I smile and nod instead. His kiss is so sweet that I have to clench my eyes shut to stop the tears from falling.

'Look at me,' he demands when he pulls back from me. My watery eyes open to meet his. 'This isn't goodbye, sweetheart. We will be together again. I promise.'

My arms tighten around his waist as I hold him. I hope he's right. I'm not sure how I'd cope if I never saw him again.

He reaches into his pocket and pulls out a small box. 'I bought this for you. It's a phone. Do you have somewhere to keep it where M won't find it?'

'You bought me a phone?'

'I did. I've programmed all my numbers into it. Home, work, mobile. I'm going to go out of my fucking mind if I can't communicate with you.'

'But M—'

'Don't worry about her. Everything is registered under my name, so there's no way it can be traced back to you. The last thing I want is to get you in trouble.'

'You're sweet.'

'Can you call or text me sometimes to let me know you're okay?'

'I can definitely do that,' I reply as my mouth meets his. 'Thank you.' I'm so overcome by his gesture. I miss him so much when we're apart. I can't say how many times I thought of calling him after he gave me his card at Theo's, but it was just too risky. M checks all of our phone records, and I saw what she did to poor Anna the day she found out some guy from the university she attends had called her phone. It turned out to be something innocent, but M still flipped her lid.

M slapped Anna's face and threatened her in front of all of us. It was awful.

'You're welcome,' he says tucking a strand of hair behind my ear. The look he gives me melts my heart. Apart from Rupert, nobody has ever watched out for me before. 'I'll wait impatiently to hear from you.' I let out a small laugh when he says that. 'I don't want to risk calling you in case she's around. I don't want to do anything that's going to jeopardise this arrangement and keep us apart.'

*

The second I climb into the back of the limousine after my inspection with M, I tear open the white envelope that contains my schedule for the next few days. I smile when I see I'm attending a function with Theo this evening and my smile widens because I have tomorrow night off. My gaze moves down to Wednesday and my heart sinks. Frank Agostino. Great. He's one of my clients that always expects sex. Bye-bye lucky streak.

A few weeks ago that wouldn't have bothered me. It would've been just another job that I'd suffer through as best I could, but things are different now. Now that I've reconnected with Brock, I'm going to feel like I'm being unfaithful to him. I know that's stupid because we're not what you'd call an item, but he's more than just a client. I've never felt this deeply for a man in my life—for anyone, for that matter. And it fills me with hope.

I pull out the phone I'd hidden under the seat of the limo before we arrived at M's. Removing it from the box, I turn it on. The first thing I see is Brock's beautiful face: he's put an image of himself as the screensaver. I gently run my finger over the glass.

Opening the messenger app, I type him a short message.

Jade: *I miss you already. xx*

He replies almost instantly.

Brock: *I miss you too, beautiful. I'll be arriving at M's shortly. Hopefully I can arrange to see you again this week. x*

I hope so too.

Jade: *I'm free on Tuesday. Tonight I have a function to attend with Theo.*

I'm not going to mention anything about my Wednesday night appointment. If by some miracle he can convince M to agree to tomorrow night, I'll discuss it with him then. I hate to think how my situation must make him feel. I know if the roles were reversed I'd be devastated. I don't want to share him with anyone. I want him all for myself. Maybe I need to open up more, so he understands the predicament I'm in. It's not like I have a choice.

Brock: *Brilliant. I'll work on tomorrow night then. Can I call you?*

I'm not sure that's a good idea while I'm still in one of M's cars. Being the controlling bitch she is, it wouldn't surprise me if she has her vehicles bugged.

Jade: *I'll call you once I arrive back at my apartment. I'm still in the limo.*

Brock: *I look forward to it. <3*

I'm smiling as I clutch the phone to my chest when I see the heart at the end of his message. Is this what it feels like to be in love? If it is, it's the most *wonderful* feeling in the world.

*

'You look beautiful,' Theo says, when Rupert drops me at his house. The function we're attending tonight is formal, so I'm wearing a gorgeous silver gown. It's strapless with a bead-encrusted bodice above a skirt that falls softly to the floor in a wave of tiny pleats. The only jewellery I'm wearing is a pair of diamond stud earrings. My personal hairdresser has styled my hair into a loose low bun that sits at the nape of my neck. I feel like a princess. Getting to dress up on a regular basis is the only perk that comes with this job.

'Thank you. You look rather dashing yourself,' I say, when he kisses my cheek. There's something about a man in a tuxedo, especially someone as handsome as Theo. I can just imagine how dreamy Brock would look in one.

'Is there anything special I need to know about tonight?' I ask him once we're seated in the back of his limousine.

'Nope. Just smile and look beautiful as always, leave the rest to me.'

'So be your arm candy, in other words?' I hope he can hear the humour in my voice.

He laughs. 'Something like that.'

'How are things going with Adam?' Theo's been dating Adam for a few months now.

'We split up.'

'What? Oh no, Theo.' I rub my hand gently down his arm. 'What happened?'

'He didn't like the double life I was leading. He hates that I pretend that I'm straight when I'm not. We had a heated argument, and he gave me an ultimatum. I don't like ultimatums, so we broke up.'

'I'm so sorry to hear that. Doesn't he realise why you do it?'

'Yes, but he doesn't understand my reasons.'

'Oh, Theo. One day the right man will come along, you'll see. He's going to love you so completely, the only thing he's going to care about is being with you. Nothing else will matter.'

'Like you and Brock.'

'I wish,' I say with a sigh, hooking my arm through his and resting my head on his shoulder. I don't think this thing between Brock and me will ever be more than it is, but a girl can dream. Dreams are free. I'm sure he'll eventually tire of having to pay to see me. 'I like him so much, Theo. So much that sometimes my heart hurts. I've never felt like this before. Never.'

'I get the impression he's smitten with you too, pretty girl. You're an easy person to love. If I didn't bat for the other team, I would've snapped you up years ago.'

His comment makes me laugh. 'You really think he's smitten?'

'I know he is.' He rests his hand on mine.

I walk into the grand ballroom of the luxurious hotel with Theo, smiling and greeting everyone he stops to talk to. These events can get pretty boring, but I'd much rather be here with him, than with the majority of my other clients. And after his revelation in the limo, there's no way I'm going to be able to stop smiling.

My mind drifts to Brock while Theo listens to some short, chubby man babble on about how successful he is. I really don't understand people who feel the need to constantly big note themselves. I guess Theo feels the same, because within minutes I hear him say, 'If you'll excuse me, I think I'll take my gorgeous date for a spin around the dance floor.'

'You hate dancing,' I say, laughing as he guides me across the room.

'I know, but I'd rather suffer on the dance floor than spend another second listening to that tool blow his own trumpet. Just one song, I promise.'

'Fair enough,' I reply, as he spins me around and pulls me into his arms. 'You really should take lessons in preparation for situations like this, though. I'm not sure if my poor toes can handle a whole song with you.'

He throws back his head and laughs. 'I'll try my best not to step on your feet this time.'

We only get a third of the way into the song before we're interrupted.

'Do you mind if I cut in?'

My heart flutters when I turn my head and see Brock standing beside us. He's dressed in a tuxedo, and like I imagined, he looks absolutely breathtaking.

'Be my guest,' Theo says, stepping aside.

Brock gives me a pantie melting smile as his arms slide around my waist, drawing my body flush with his. 'You look beautiful in that dress, sweetheart. Absolutely exquisite.'

'What are you doing here?' As thrilled as I am, he's the last person I expected to see tonight.

'When you said you were going to a function with Theo, I called him. I couldn't wait until tomorrow night to see you again.'

'You came here tonight just to see me?'

'Yes. Does that surprise you?' He glides me effortlessly around the dance floor. *Wow, can he dance.*

'A little,' I admit.

'You obviously have no idea how much you mean to me then. I'd travel to the ends of the earth if it meant I'd get to see you, Jade. And I couldn't wait until tomorrow night. You mean too much to me.'

'M agreed?'

He nods.

'Why didn't you tell me?' I want to hit him for keeping this secret from me.

'I needed to see your face when I told you.'

Swoon.

*

Theo made sure Brock had a seat at our table, and although I was there as his date, my eyes spent most of the night fastened on my man. We even played footsie under the table a few times, and at one stage he held my hand. It's like we crave some kind of physical contact when we're in each other's presence. That's how I feel—I crave him. I've never felt so drawn to someone as I am to him. It's both scary and wonderful.

Theo was kind enough to let me travel back to his house in Brock's car. I even got to kiss him goodnight before Rupert arrived to collect me. I floated all the way home.

All day Tuesday I'm on a high, anticipating our impending date. By the time I arrive at M's for inspection, you couldn't have wiped the smile off my face if you'd tried. Which in hindsight, was a huge mistake on my part. I'm so caught up in my own little world that I'd forgotten to hide my new found happiness from M.

'What are you looking so pleased about?' she asks suspiciously the minute I enter her parlour.

Shit. 'Nothing,' I reply, trying to keep my cool but failing miserably.

'Don't lie to me, Jade,' she says as she comes to a stop in front of me. She latches onto my hair, yanking it hard as she pulls me to her. 'Do you think I'm a fool? Does this sudden mood change have anything to do with Mr Weston? He was very persistent about seeing you tonight.'

Double shit. If she even suspects that there's something going on between us, I know she'll forbid us from seeing each other again.

'No … no,' I stammer. 'I'm just feeling happy today. It has nothing to do with Mr Weston. Why would you ask that? He's just another client.' I know I'm babbling, but I can't seem to control it.

Her evil eyes narrow, but I get the impression she may just believe me. She releases my hair from her death grip, and my scalp stings. 'I'll be keeping a close eye on you two,' she warns. 'If I suspect for a second there's more to this, I'll put a stop to it immediately. Do you hear me?'

'There's nothing going on between us,' I say, determination setting in. I'm not going to say anything that could blow my chances of seeing Brock. 'As I said, he's a client, nothing more.'

'Make sure it stays that way.' The look she gives me has my stomach in knots. I know she means every word, and now that her suspicions are raised, we'll have to be extra careful.

*

'Are you okay?' Brock asks as we travel back to his house after dinner. He took me to a lovely restaurant overlooking the harbour. I enjoy every second of my time with him, but M's words were still playing on my mind. Maybe the wise thing to do would be to keep our distance for a while until things cool down, but the thought of not seeing him makes me sick to the stomach.

'I'm fine,' I say, forcing out a smile.

'Are you sure? You don't seem yourself. Has something happened?'

I shrug my shoulders as my gaze moves down to my lap.

He doesn't pry any further, but reaches across the centre console to grasp my hand in his before giving it a comforting squeeze, there's worry etched on his handsome face. I love that he cares. I'm pretty sure this won't be the end of this conversation.

It's a warm night, so when we arrive back at his house, he suggests that we sit on the back patio. After retrieving glasses and a bottle of white wine, he comes to sit beside me. It's so beautiful out here. The patio overlooks a magnificent in-ground pool that has lights around the perimeter, illuminating it in the night. I can see the steam rising off the water from here, so I'm guessing it's heated. The surrounding gardens, with their perfectly manicured hedges, are immaculate. I presume Brock has a gardener by the amount of work that's gone into the landscaping. Running such a large corporation wouldn't leave him much time to do it himself. The lounges and dining chairs have plush white cushioning, softening the space. There are a number of large black ceramic pots placed strategically around us. The beautiful greenery of the palms stand out against the dark furniture and tiles.

'Here,' he says passing me a glass of wine.

'Thank you.' Lifting the glass to my lips, I take a sip. 'It's lovely out here.'

'Thank you.' I feel his eyes on me as he sits back further into the chair. 'Jade,' he says suddenly, as he exhales deeply. 'I don't want to put any pressure on you—I get the feeling you have enough of that going on in your life already—but I wish you'd open up to me. I'm worried about you.'

'I'm okay, honestly,' I tell him, placing my hand on his leg. I'm touched by his concern. Maybe if I tell him what's on my mind, he'll relax. It's probably wise that he knows she suspects something. 'M is a little suspicious of us, that's all. She warned me before coming here. If she finds out that there's something going on between us, Brock, she won't let me see you anymore.' My gaze moves down to my glass. 'I'd hate that,' I whisper, because I would. Since I've met him, my life is so much richer.

He takes the glass out of my hand and places it on the table in front of us. 'I'd never let that happen,' he says, pulling me into his arms.

'You don't know her like I do,' I whisper into his chest.

'She doesn't scare me, Jade. I've been around people like her all my life.' There's such conviction in his voice, but he doesn't know M like I do. If only he knew the things she's already done.

'She scares me.'

He cups my face in his hands. 'I'd never let her hurt you.' His thumbs tenderly stroke my cheeks. 'Never.' The sincerity in his voice makes my smile. 'How did you ever get mixed up with someone like her anyway?'

'She adopted me when I was eleven.' The words are out of my mouth before I even realise what I said. His hands instantly drop away from my face.

'She what?' There's shock in his voice. He holds his palm up in front of me for a moment as he processes what I just said. 'That woman is your mother?'

I shrug my shoulders. 'I guess ... well, kind of? My adoptive mother. My real mother died giving birth to me.'

'Jesus.' He abruptly stands and starts pacing. 'Fucking hell.'

My stomach churns as I wait for him to calm down. Have I just ruined things between us by telling him the truth? Does he think I'm disgusting? Weak?

A few minutes pass before he stops. I'm sure my apprehension is showing as I gaze up at him. In one swift motion, he pulls me off the lounge and into his arms.

'I'm so sorry, sweetheart.' When he holds me close I can feel his body trembling against mine. I have no idea why he's sorry. He's done nothing wrong.

He clings to me for the longest time. Neither of us speak. I know I've already said too much, but I suppose my confession may help him better understand my situation, if nothing else.

'How long?'

'How long what?' I ask, pulling back from him so I can see his face.

'How long have you been subjected to this?'

'I signed a contract with her when I was eighteen. I've been working for her for five years now.'

'How long did you sign for?' Even though there's anger in his voice, the softness in his features tells me it's not directed at me.

'Seven years. One year for every year she cared for me.'

'Christ,' he murmurs, letting go of me so his hands can fist in his hair. The anger is just rolling off him. 'How could she do this to you?'

'She told me I owe her for everything she did for me when I came to live with her.'

'Bullshit, Jade. You owe her nothing. Not a damn thing. She was supposed to *care* for you. It was *her fucking job* to care for you.'

I flinch at the harshness of his words. 'She saved me, Brock. I had the most horrific childhood before coming to live with her.' I don't know why I'm defending M, because everything he says is true. But I'd hate to think where I would've ended up if it wasn't for her. As much as I dislike her, and the situation she's forced me into, I think there will always be a tiny part of me that will be grateful she rescued me from the horrors I faced in foster care.

She saved and ruined me, I guess.

CHAPTER SIXTEEN

BROCK

I'm trying hard not to lose my cool here. The last thing I want to do is frighten Jade. This situation is so much grimmer than I originally thought. By the sounds of it, she's already been through way too much in her short life. My heart is bleeding for her right now. Everything in me wants to march straight over to that bitch's house and wring her neck for what she's put Jade through. Never in my life have I had the slightest inclination to hurt a woman, but if M was in front of me now, I'm afraid that's exactly what I'd do. This shit ends today.

'I'm going to help you,' I say.

A brief smile forms on her lips. 'Thank you, but I can't let you do that, Brock. She's dangerous and I'd never ask, or expect you to put yourself in harm's way to protect me.'

I kiss her. For now, this conversation is over. Doesn't she realise the lengths I'd go to for her? I'm not afraid of M. I'm prepared for anything that monster throws at me. I grew up with a ruthless bastard, so I've learnt from the best. I'm Maxwell Weston's son. What type of man would I be, if I stood by and watched this injustice continue?

I won't give Jade up without a fight. I won't give Jade up, period. There's nothing I wouldn't do for the people I care about, and fuck me if I don't care about her.

'Please don't do anything that will jeopardise what we already have,' she begs.

I have no intention of doing that. What I have planned will guarantee that we can be together, and whenever we please. That sick and twisted bitch will not dictate our relationship any further.

The pleading look on Jade's face tugs at my heart. It's time for a distraction. I don't want her worrying about this. From this day forward, her worries will be firmly placed on my shoulders. She is mine, and I'll protect her with everything I have.

My right hand moves from her waist to under her arm as my fingers slowly slide down the zipper of the black dress she's wearing. I use both hands to push the straps off her shoulders until the garment pools at her feet. Then I take a step back to admire what was hidden beneath. A primal growl permeates from deep in my chest. 'You take my breath away, sweetheart,' I whisper.

She's standing before me in black stockings that stop mid-thigh. They're connected to a black lace suspender belt, with tiny black satin panties and bra completing the ensemble. Every drop of blood racing through my veins flows straight to my cock. Her body is pure sin, yet she has the face and demure of an angel. This woman is no angel, she's sex on legs. *A walking fucking wet dream.*

My heart is thumping furiously against my ribcage as I lean forward and place my lips on the swell of her breast. I inhale the intoxicating scent of the perfume on her skin. She smells just as good as she looks. My dick strains painfully against my pants.

'There's so much I want to do to you,' I breathe.

'Then take me, I'm yours,' she says, reaching behind herself to unclasp her bra. The moment it drops to the floor, my fingers glide over her toned stomach until I'm palming her spectacular tits. 'Brock,' she moans, letting her head fall back when my lips close around a hardened nipple. I'll never tire of hearing her say my name like that.

I fall to my knees and she rests her hand on my shoulder as I help her step out of the dress. Her black heels are almost as sexy as her red ones. My fingers slowly move up the inside of her leg until they're rubbing over her satin panties. I can already feel her arousal through the fabric. *I need to taste her.* These may be a little harder to tear because they're not lace, but nothing gets in the way of a man on a mission.

'I'm going to run out of panties,' she giggles when I tear them from her body.

'I'll buy you more,' I say as I shove them in my pocket before my fingers glide through her folds. I love how wet she gets for me.

'*Yes,*' she whimpers as she spreads her legs wider, allowing me better access.

'I think I'm in love with your pussy,' I moan against her flesh the moment I taste her. I've never said that to anyone before, but it's true. I am.

'I know I'm in love with your mouth,' she replies, making me chuckle.

I slide a finger inside her as my tongue goes to work on her clit. When her legs start to quiver, I snake my arm around her waist to hold her up. Eating her pussy is my new favourite thing.

I could do it all day. Before her, it was more about me. I always made sure I pleased the women I was with, but there were other ways to do that. Everything seems different with Jade.

It only takes a few minutes before she's calling out my name. 'I love how you make my body feel,' she says finally, looking down at me with a sated look on her pretty face.

'I'm only just getting started,' I tell her, placing a kiss on her pelvic bone next to the lace of her suspender belt. 'How do you get these undone?'

I watch her unclasp the front, so my hands move around the back to do the same. My lips trace a path down her legs as I roll the stockings off, one by one. I'd leave these on because they're as sexy as fuck, but I want to take her in the pool. If I get my way, in time I'll christen every inch of this place with her.

Jade goes to work on the buttons of my shirt as I slide out of my shoes and undo the zipper and button on my trousers. I remove my boxers at the same time, pushing them down my legs. I help her undo the last few buttons before shrugging out of my shirt and scooping her into my arms.

'Are you up for a swim?' I ask, walking towards the pool.

'I'm up for anything with you, Mr Weston.'

'That's my girl,' I say as I walk down the steps and into the water. Thank fuck the water's heated. I can't have my dick shrivelling up in front of her. I have a reputation to keep.

The moment we're chest deep, I let her go. Her arms snake around my neck and her luscious long legs wrap tightly around my waist. Her tits are now firmly pressed into my chest, and as much as I'm enjoying the feel of her soft skin against mine, my need to be inside her is overpowering. She's my addiction.

My lips find hers as my hands move down her back before coming to a rest on her arse. Shifting her body slightly, I draw back before entering her in one swift movement, impaling her with my cock. We moan in unison as I bury myself balls deep inside her.

I wrap her long hair around my wrist and tug on it gently making her head fall backwards. My tongue licks a trail up her neck.

'Jesus, Jade,' I groan as her hips grind against me in a circular motion.

I could easily lose myself in this woman forever.

*

I set my plan in motion while Jade's in the bathroom drying her hair, getting ready to leave. I barely slept after our marathon sex session last night. I kept going over everything in my mind. She has no idea what's about to happen. I thought it best to keep my ideas to myself for now, otherwise she'd worry unnecessarily, or worse, try to talk me out of it. But my mind is made up, there's no going back.

Thankfully, in my line of work I need to have a lot of cash on hand. You never know when a crisis will pop up in the middle of the night. This may not be work related, but it's a crisis nevertheless—a huge motherfucking injustice to someone I care very deeply for.

After gathering what I need from the safe, I write a quick note to enclose with the money. Fuck, I hope this goes the way I've planned. Otherwise, the only way Jade will be going back to work for that monster is over my dead body. For Jade's sake, I hope it doesn't come to that. She's going to need me now, more than she realises.

I'm standing in the foyer admiring her as she prances down the stairs carrying her suitcase. I take a moment to appreciate everything she is, to appreciate *her*. I'm not sure she's even aware how extraordinary she is. Now that I've had time to absorb her revelation from last night, I'm filled with nothing but admiration for her and the predicament she's been living with. She's not only incredibly smart, but courageous, breathtakingly beautiful, and so damn sweet. Her most admirable quality, though, is her strength. The world is her oyster, or it could be. And if I get my way, it will be. It only makes me hate M even more for putting Jade in this situation.

Jade has so much to offer, and if I'm lucky enough to be given the chance, I'm going to make it my mission in life to see she gets everything she deserves. A huge statement coming from someone like me, but that's exactly how I feel. I want to fulfil all her desires, and I'm not just referring to the bedroom either.

I take the suitcase out of her hand and place it on the floor beside us.

'Rupert's outside,' she says. I already knew that. I heard him pull up before she came downstairs. She's trying to play it down, but I can clearly see that she feels apprehensive about leaving here.

'Do you trust me?' I ask, cupping her beautiful face.

Her brow furrows. 'Yes, why?'

'Good. I need you to wait here for me. I'm going outside to talk to Rupert for a minute. Okay?'

'Sure. Okay.' There's uncertainty and confusion on her face as she tries to make sense of what I'm saying.

'Just give me a few minutes with him, and then I'll explain everything.' Her brow furrows again, but she doesn't reply.

It hits me right in the chest. I have no idea what lies ahead for us, but I know that I'll protect and care for this woman with everything I have. Pulling her into my arms, I hold her face protectively against my chest. 'Everything is going to be okay, sweetheart,' I say, trying to reassure her. 'Promise me you'll stay here.'

'All right.'

Fuck, I hope I'm doing the right thing.

Rupert leaves the car when I walk down the front steps. 'Mr Weston,' he says as I stop in front of him.

'Rupert,' I reply, extending my hand to him.

'Is there a problem with Jade?' he asks, looking down at his watch. 'I need to get her back to M's.'

'She's not going back.'

'Excuse me?' he says, frowning.

'She's staying here with me. I refuse to send her back there.' I wait for him to react, but he doesn't. Instead I see his features relax and the corners of his mouth turn up slightly.

'Is that what she wants?' he asks.

'She doesn't know yet, but I'm almost certain she'll be fine with it.'

'Are you sure you know what you're doing? She's not going to give Jade up without a fight. She has an unhealthy obsession with her.'

'I'm not afraid of her,' I scoff, because I'm not. 'If she wants to fuck with me—or someone I care about—then she better bring her best show, because I'll fight her with everything I have.'

'I'm glad to hear that,' he says, placing his hand on my shoulder. 'Jade needs someone like you in her life. But, I must warn you, be prepared for anything and everything. This woman is the lowest of low. She'll stop at nothing to get her way. I've never met anyone like her before—she's one of a kind.'

'You obviously haven't met my father then.' I chuckle, but there's no humour in it.

'No, I haven't.'

'If you have such a dislike for her, why do you continue working for her?'

He looks away, running his fingers through his hair. 'I have my reasons.'

I get the impression there's a story there, but I don't have time for that right now.

'Can you give this to M for me? There's a note enclosed that explains everything.' I pass him the grey backpack that contains one million dollars in cash. The note explains if she tears up Jade's contract and gives me something in writing to that effect, I'll give her a further two million dollars. That should more than pay for the remainder of time Jade has left with her. Money talks, and this woman is greedy. Whether she accepts my terms or not, Jade will not be returning. 'I'm sorry to put you in this position, but I couldn't see any other way.'

'Don't worry about me,' Rupert replies. 'I can handle myself. To be honest, I'm grateful for what you're doing. Jade deserves to be free of the life she's been leading. It's no place for a sweet girl like her. If I wasn't in the position I'm in, I would've taken her away from it a long time ago.'

'You still have my card, right?'

'I do,' he answers.

'If you need anything, just call. There'll always be a job waiting for you here if you decide not to continue working for that bitch. I mean that.'

'I need to stay where I am for now, but thank you. If the opportunity arises where I can leave, I'll definitely take you up on that offer.' He reaches into his pocket and pulls out a card. 'Here's my number as well, just in case you ever need anything.'

'Great. Thank you.' I shake his hand once more.

'Look after Jade for me. I'm going to miss her, she was the highlight of my job.' There's definitely a hint of sadness in his voice. I'm sure they've grown close over the years.

'I will. I'm pretty sure she'll miss you too. You're welcome to come visit any time you like. I appreciate everything you've done for her over the years, mate. I know she's very fond of you.'

I'm quite concerned for his wellbeing as he gets back into the car to leave. The shit is going to hit the fan when he gets back to M's. I feel like a prick for putting him in this position, he seems like a decent guy. I hope he doesn't suffer any fallout from the decisions I've made.

I wait until he reaches the end of the driveway before I turn and walk up the front stairs. Now to face the music with Jade. I hope she doesn't hate me for what I've just done.

*

JADE

Butterflies churn in my stomach as I wait for Brock to re-enter the house. I have no idea why he needed to see Rupert alone, but it concerns me. Maybe he's going to ask him to keep a closer eye on me. There's no need for that. Rupert takes great care of me. I'd be lost without him in my life. I know he's under M's iron rule just as much as I am, but he helps me out whenever possible.

Minutes pass and Brock still doesn't return. Pulling my phone out of my bag, I check the time. What's taking them so long? M is going to be pissed off if we don't leave soon.

My head snaps up the moment the front door opens. The solemn look on Brock's face does nothing to ease my mind. My heart starts to beat out of my chest as he approaches me.

'What's going on?' I ask.

'You're staying here.'

'What?' Has he requested me for another night?

'Jade,' he says, pulling me into his arms. I can hear his heart beating rapidly as my face rests against his chest. 'I can't send you back there in good conscience. Not now that I know the truth.'

I put my hands on his abdomen and push away before taking a further step back. 'What do you mean I'm not going back there? I have to go back,' I blurt in a panic. Of course I don't want too, but I know I don't have a choice. God, what has he done? Brock's delusional if he thinks he can refuse to take me back without consequences. My hands are trembling as I cover my face with them. Images of what she did to one of the girls who tried to leave the profession flash through my mind.

This will not end well.

'I'm not sending you back there, Jade. That's final.'

I can tell by the forceful tone of his voice that he means what he's saying. Has he lost his fucking mind? No one makes demands like this to M. *Nobody* tells her what to do. She'll rip him apart, and me for that matter.

'Look at me, sweetheart,' he says, pulling my hands away from my face and crouching down slightly so we're at eye level. When my eyes meet his, he gives me an unsure smile. 'I won't let anything happen to you, I promise. You're safe with me.'

'You don't know her like I do, Brock—she's ruthless.'

'I'm not afraid of her,' he states matter-of-factly.

'You should be.' M's middle name might as well be crazy-arse-she-devil-bitch.

'Well, I'm not. I'll protect you. Please tell me you're not angry at me for doing this. I can't bear the thought of you going back there. I want you here with me.'

Tears rise to my eyes. I'm so overwhelmed. Am I actually free of her—and my shitty life?

'Are you happy to stay here with me? At least for the interim, anyway. Until we sort this mess out.'

'Yes ... no ... I, um, I don't know.' Is this really happening? 'I want to be wherever you are,' I wanted to say. Even though it's the truth, I had no intention of telling him. I don't want him to think I'm clingy or needy, because I'm not. I've been alone all my life. I'm used to rejection. Nobody has every truly wanted me.

Raising my head, I make eye contact with him again. 'I *don't* want to go back there, but she's not going to just roll over and accept this.'

'She doesn't have a choice. My mind is made up.'

His words surprise me, but annoy me as well. 'Do I even get a say in this?' I snap as I put my hands on my hips. I'm hurt by the statement he just made. Don't get me wrong, I love that he feels so protective towards me, but I refuse to be dictated to. I've had to deal with shit all my life—I refuse to let him do it to me as well.

'Of course you have a say, as long as it doesn't involve you going back to work for her.'

I narrow my eyes at him.

'Don't look at me like that, Jade. I'm not trying to control you, I'm trying to protect you.'

'By doing whatever it is you've just done, you've put me in danger. You've put both of us in danger. You didn't even discuss it with me first.'

'She won't get anywhere near you.' He places his hands on my shoulders as he stares into my eyes. 'I couldn't risk having you talk me out of this. That's the only reason I didn't discuss it with you first. I care about you, Jade. I've never cared for a woman like I do you.'

I fight hard to suppress my smile when he says that. I care about him too. Nobody has ever made me feel like this before, but all that is irrelevant at the moment. We have a bigger problem to face—M.

'You can't protect me twenty-four-seven, Brock. And what if she does something to you? How am I supposed to live with that?' Once again, I'm feeling completely overwhelmed. My legs are threatening to give way. 'I think I need to sit down,' I say.

'Come,' he replies, sliding his arm around my waist and leading me into the main room. The moment he's seated, he pulls me onto his lap, wrapping his arms around me. 'I'm sorry to just spring this on you, but it was a spur-of-the-moment decision. I haven't thought much beyond right now, I'll get a more structured plan in place today. I'm confident M will accept my offer.'

'What offer?' I ask.

'I'm not naive enough to think she'd let you out of your contract without payment.'

'You paid her?' Jesus. What is it with rich people? They think because they have money, they can use it to buy whatever they like. I'm sorry, but I'm a human being. I'm not for sale. I work for M because she made me feel like I owed her. I don't owe Brock shit. I go to stand, but he tightens his grip on my waist.

'Don't run from me, Jade. I did the only thing I could. Money talks, especially to someone like her.'

'So you bought me?'

'No. I bought your freedom, sweetheart.'

I sigh at his words. Although they melt my heart a little, I don't like this situation. I don't like it one bit. M thought she owned me. Is that how Brock's going to see things now?

'I'm sorry, it's just, I don't want to feel indebted to you. That's what got me into this whole mess in the first place.'

'You're not indebted to me. That's not why I did this. I'm doing it for you, I don't want you to live like that anymore.'

'How much did you give her? I want to pay you back.' I wasn't in a position to pay M back when she first told me I'd be working for her. I was eighteen and penniless—I'm not anymore.

'It's irrelevant.'

'Please, Brock. This is important to me. I have money in the bank. I've been saving everything I've earned since I started working for her. It was money for my future. It was what I was going to use to buy my restaurant when my contract had expired. I'd happily give that dream away if it meant I had my freedom.'

'I'm sorry, but I'm not taking your money, Jade, and that's final.'

'Yes, you are,' I snap. 'I'm not comfortable with this. I don't want to feel like I owe you.'

'Listen,' he says sternly. 'You don't owe me jackshit, Jade. You're free to come and go as you please. Well, after I know you're safe, that is.' He rubs his hands over his face before continuing. When his eyes meet mine again, I can see the uncertainty etched in his features as his voice softens. 'I'd really like you to stay.'

Everything in me wants to believe him. I want to believe that what Brock and I share is special, and that I really do mean something to him. But when you've been let down and screwed over your whole life, it's hard to trust.

'I want to be with you,' he says.

My heartbeat quickens. 'Why?' I'm used goods; he couldn't possibly want me for more than that.

'Why not?'

'It won't work. We're from two different worlds.'

'Yes it will,' he says with confidence.

'But what if we fall?' I don't know if I could take a blow like that. Not where he's concerned.

'But what if we fly?'

I love his optimism.

But it's too much, too soon. I'm not sure I can wrap my head around any of this. All I know is I have that sick feeling in my stomach again. It's the same one I used to get when I was a little girl. There's definitely trouble looming, I'll put money on it.

For the next few minutes, Brock soothingly rubs my back as we sit in silence. I'm happy, but also scared. I'm unsure of what lies ahead, but I'm grateful he's trying to help me escape M. Even though I'm pretty sure it's impossible.

Nobody has ever done anything like this for me before. It's something I've always wished for since I was a child: someone to care enough to not only want what's best for me, but to care enough to remove me from my living hell.

'Are you okay?' he asks, using his fingers to turn my face to his.

I shrug. 'I don't know.' That's the most honest answer I can give him right now.

He places a soft kiss on my lips as my arms snake around his neck. I need to seek comfort in him. He's the only one who has the power to do that.

'Everything is going to work out. I promise.'

I'm glad he's so confident.

CHAPTER SEVENTEEN

JADE

Forty minutes is all it takes for all hell to break loose. Forty minutes from the time Rupert left, to the time M is banging on Brock's front door like a psychotic crazy woman on a mission to take me back to my living hell. I knew it.

'Go upstairs and lock yourself in my bedroom,' Brock demands.

Even though I'm trembling again, there's no way I'm leaving him to face this on his own. 'I'm staying right here.'

'Listen to me, Jade,' he says, forcefully gripping my arm. 'Go upstairs and lock yourself in my fucking room *now*.'

'No.' I'm trying my best to act calm and not let my true feelings show, but truth is, I'm petrified of this woman. Still, I refuse to leave him.

'I know you're in there, open this door immediately!' we hear M scream, in that don't-fuck-with-me voice I've come to know well over the years.

'Jesus fucking Christ,' Brock snaps. 'I can't protect you if you don't listen to me.'

'I'm staying, so you may as well open the damn door.'

Brock exhales a large breath, pinching the bridge of his nose in frustration. 'Fuck,' he mumbles. 'So help me ... if she lays one finger on you, I'll kill her.' He gathers me protectively behind him as he approaches the door. 'Do not leave my side.'

'I've come to collect Jade,' M says calmly the minute Brock opens the door. I'm surprised by how this woman has so quickly regained her cool.

'As I told you in my letter, she won't be returning to work for you.'

'Listen here, you arrogant fuck,' M spits. I'm still strategically placed behind Brock, so she hasn't noticed I'm here yet. 'I'm not having some cocky little prick dictate to me. She is under contract to me and I suggest you return her immediately.'

'Or what?' Brock says. 'You don't scare me. You know as well as I do that contact will not stand up in court.'

'I'll ask you one more time, Mr Weston. Return Jade to me this instant or I won't be held responsible for what happens.'

'Do you have my million dollars?' he asks, and for a split second my heart drops. He's not actually planning to give me back to her is he?

'What million dollars? I have no idea what you're talking about.'

'Bullshit,' he snaps.

When M laughs, I know she's lying. I don't even need to look at her face to know she received that money. She's a snake. She'd rip off her own mother if given the chance. I can't believe he gave her a million dollars for my freedom.

'Jade,' she screams. 'Get your traitorous arse out here now.'

'Hey. Show some respect. Who the fuck do you think you are? I refuse to stand by and let you talk to her like that.' Brock takes a step in her direction. I follow suit because I'm still shielded behind him. I feel like a coward, hiding from her like this. If I wasn't so afraid of the repercussions, I'd step forwards and face her. I've waited five long years to tell her what I really think. 'I won't tolerate it,' he growls. I feel inclined to wrap my arms around his waist and thank him for sticking up for me like he is.

'Respect. Ha,' she scoffs. 'She's a common whore, Mr Weston, or have you forgotten that?'

I cringe at her words, but she's right, I am.

'No thanks to you. You're the scum of the earth for what you've put her through. You should be ashamed of yourself for taking advantage of someone as sweet as Jade.'

'I have no problems sleeping at night.' *Smug bitch.* She wouldn't because she has a black heart. I don't know why her words hurt me, but they do. 'I see I trained her well. One taste and she's turned you into putty. *Pathetic.* I'm sure your father would be very proud,' she says with disgust in her voice.

God, I hate her. I refuse to stand by for one more second while she continues to insult him.

'Jade. You've got one minute to show your face or I'm coming in to get you.'

I know she means what she says, but surprisingly her words don't scare me like they usually do. I feel safe with Brock by my side. It's time for me to stand up to her.

'I'm not coming back,' I say, squaring my shoulders and stepping out from behind Brock.

He growls at me, before manoeuvring me behind him again. I try to fight him, but I'm overpowered by his strength.

'You coward,' M sneers. 'I brought you up better than this. Stop hiding and face me, you ungrateful little bitch.'

'Don't you dare speak to her like that,' Brock yells. 'You brought her up to be a damn hooker, so don't put on the high-and-mighty act with me. I know exactly what type of person you are.'

'She was trash when she came to live with me. I alone shaped her into the woman she is today.'

'I've heard enough. The real Jade is nothing like the person you've tried to mould her into. The only trash here is you. You've mistreated her for the last time. We have nothing more to say to you. Leave my property before I call the police.' Brock extends his arm, ready to close the door.

'I don't think so,' a male voice says. M's henchman, Rocco. Shit. He must've been standing out of sight, waiting for her to give him the word to pounce. My heart drops into the pit of my stomach. This man is crazy, completely unstable. He's always frightened me. My gut feeling was right. This isn't going to end well.

I step out from behind Brock again, and to my horror I find Rocco standing there with a gun aimed at Brock's head.

'Come here, you conniving bitch,' M snarls, tugging me towards her by my hair.

'Get your fucking hands off her,' Brock yells, grabbing my arm and trying to manoeuvre me behind him again. I already know it's useless. He has a gun only inches away from his face. We've lost. The thought of her taking me away from here—from him—fills me with dread. She can dish out any physical punishment she likes, but taking me away from Brock is the only thing that will truly hurt. My legs threaten to give way for the second time today.

'Move and I'll put a bullet in you,' Rocco says to Brock.

'Do whatever he says, Brock,' I beg. I don't want any harm to come to him. I know how these people work.

*

BROCK

I should be concerned that there's a gun pointed at my head, but I'm not. My only concern in this moment is Jade. The stupid prick doesn't even know how to hold a gun properly. His finger is resting alongside the barrel instead of hovering over the trigger. I'm grateful for that. It assures me that, whenever I make my move, the gun won't go off. I just have to bide my time, then this fucker's going down. I'm highly trained for situations like this.

My eyes are locked on him, but in my peripheral vision I can see Jade being pulled through the doorway by her hair. Rage consumes me. Fuck. I should've locked her in my damn room myself. I promised I'd protect her, so I need to act fast.

'Let me go,' I hear her whimper as my gaze leaves the gunman's for a split second. Seeing her being manhandled like this sets off something inside me. My eyes move back to the cocksucker standing before me. He gives me a smug look and I use that as my cue. He may be built like a damn brick wall, but I already know he doesn't have the brains to go with his brawn. The faster I unhinge this situation, the sooner I can get Jade to safety again.

He's so busy silently gloating about having the upper hand that he doesn't even see me make my move until it's too late. My hand flies up at lightning speed and my fingers tightly grip his wrist. Using all my strength, I bend his arm back until

I hear a sickening pop. I know I've successfully snapped his wrist when he cries out in pain and the gun goes crashing to the floor with a thud.

'My arm ... my arm,' I hear the pussy cry as he clutches it to his chest. He's not so tough now. Without hesitation I retrieve the gun from the floor. He takes a few steps backwards when I point it at his head.

'You've got three seconds to get back in that car before I put a bullet in you,' I say calmly. I won't hesitate to shoot this fucker if I have too. 'One.' The gutless prick turns on his heel, hastily making his way down the stairs. *Smart man.* That's when I turn the gun on M. I could shoot this bitch right now for what she's done and not have any remorse for my actions. *None whatsoever.* She is the lowest of low. 'Let her go, or I won't hesitate to blow your fucking brains out.'

She lets go of Jade's hair with a shove and I hear my girl cry out softly as she lands with a thud.

'Are you okay?' I ask without taking my eyes off M. I don't trust this woman as far as I can kick her. I blindly reach out with my free hand, helping Jade to her feet.

'Yes.'

'Go into the main room,' I command. This time she does as I ask. I'll check her over as soon as I get rid of these two. 'Leave,' I say to M. The murderous look she gives me doesn't bother me in the slightest. I have the upper hand now. 'If you set one foot on my property again, I'll have you charged.'

'I don't take well to idle threats, Mr Weston, and I always get my way in the end. You haven't heard the last of me,' she spits, before turning and storming down the stairs. What she fails to realise is I always get my way as well. This is one battle she won't win.

I glance at her friend, who's now standing beside the car. My lips curve into a smile when I see him still clutching his broken hand to his chest. He looks like he's going to cry. Fucking pussy. I can't help the laugh that bubbles from my mouth when I see M give him a clip across the head with an open palm before she gets into the car in a huff. I may have just started World War III, but I'm prepared for anything she dishes out. I won't be giving Jade up.

Period.

CHAPTER EIGHTEEN

BROCK

My hand gently skims down the side of her beautiful face as I watch her sleep. I'm in awe of this woman. How she can sleep so peacefully after everything that's happened today astounds me. It also breaks my heart. The poor thing has obviously been through so much in her life that she's used to this kind of behaviour. And I hate it.

She's held herself together like a real trouper today. I, on the other hand, not so much. Maybe on the outside, but not internally. I'm not worried for myself, but I'm concerned for Jade. What if I can't protect her like I promised? The way M grabbed hold of her hair made me sick to the stomach. I can't bear to think of what Jade's endured over the years at the hands of that woman. She'll never have to face anything like that again if I get my way.

This whole caring for another person thing is so new to me. I hope I can pull it off. Rest assured, I'm going to try my damn hardest. By the sounds of it, Jade's been to hell and back, so the last thing I want to do is let her down. I'd like to be the person she can count on, if she'd let me.

It's ironic how one person can enter your life and turn

everything upside down in a blink of an eye. I've never been the commitment type. Settling down was never on my agenda, but a part of me thinks there's definitely a possibility with Jade. That scares the fuck out of me. I can't believe I'm even entertaining the idea. What if I can't give her what she wants— or worse, what if she doesn't want what I'm prepared to give?

I take a deep breath as I try to calm down. I need to get some sleep. I have a big day ahead of me tomorrow. I've already put some plans in place to keep Jade safe, but I'm going to need a hell of a lot more if I'm going to succeed. M's crazy and I know she'll stoop to anything to get her way.

A crushing pain settles in my chest at the thought of it. I'd hate to see what would become of Jade if M got her filthy hands on her again.

*

I'm up before Jade wakes. I feel like shit, but I want to make her some breakfast. She hardly ate yesterday. I can't cook to save my life, but I'm sure I can manage to cut up some fruit. I have some of that muesli crap too. Looks like damn bird seed if you ask me, but I know she likes it. I asked my housekeeper, Erika, to buy some.

I've given Erika the next few days off. I don't want her hovering around with all this shit going on. She usually comes when I'm at work, but I won't be going into the office until I can sort out what I'm going to do with Jade.

After turning on the coffee machine, I wash some strawberries and grapes under the tap. Placing a few scoops of muesli into a bowl, I grab a tub of yoghurt out of the fridge. I've seen her use that instead of milk. I place it all on a tray so I can carry it back to the bedroom. As I go to lift it off the bench, I feel her arms wrap around my waist.

'Good morning,' I hear her say in a sleepy voice as she places a kiss on my bare back. I think I could really get used to having her around. Turning in her arms, I cup her face in my hands. Her face is free of makeup, but she's still as beautiful as ever.

'Good morning,' I say when she smiles up at me. 'How are you feeling today?'

'Okay,' she replies with a shrug. 'I'm here with you, so that's a plus.'

I kiss her and I can taste mint, so I know she's just brushed her teeth.

'Mmm,' she moans into my mouth.

'Is that my shirt you're wearing?' My hands slide down her back, coming to rest on her arse.

'Yes. I've run out of clothes. I hope you don't mind.'

'I don't mind at all. I like seeing you in my clothes,' I say, because, surprisingly, I do. I feel bad that she has nothing here. She was only supposed to stay overnight and it's too risky to go back to her apartment right now. 'How about we go on a little shopping spree today?'

'Really?' she asks, her face lighting up.

'Really.' As much as I'd be happy to see her walking around the house naked, I know that's not practical. Plus women like shopping, don't they? I want to do whatever makes her happy. I'll get a few of my boys to tag along in the background, just in case.

'Oh, my purse ... I don't have it with me.'

'You don't need money, Jade,' I say, tightening my embrace. 'I'll figure out a way to get your things from the apartment.'

'I'm not letting you pay my way, Brock. I have my own money.'

'We'll work all that out later.' I kiss her again softly on the forehead. I don't want to say anything that will upset her, but if she thinks I'm taking money from her, she's mistaken.

'How did I get so lucky?'

Funny, I feel like the lucky one here.

I end up taking Jade on the kitchen counter before I feed her some breakfast. I couldn't resist after seeing her dressed in nothing but my white button up shirt. She's so fucking sexy. Sitting there watching her eat, I'm ready for round two. Throwing her over my shoulder, I carry her upstairs before taking her again in the shower.

This woman is going to be the death of me.

Once showered, she dresses in my white shirt again. She needs to wash one of her outfits before we leave. As great as she looks, even I know my shirt isn't appropriate attire to wear outside the house. After showing her where my laundry is, she sets about washing what little she has. Thank fuck she knows how to use the machine, because I have no idea. Erika sorts out that stuff for me.

While she's busy, I head into my home office to make arrangements to leave the house later today. I genuinely feel bad that Jade won't be able to go home for a while. I plan on making up for it on our shopping spree—I'm going to buy her whatever she wants. Lord knows how long she'll be here.

A few hours later, we're in my car heading to the shops. I have my guys in two cars, one travelling in front, the other trailing behind. Jade is completely unaware. I thought it best not to say anything that may frighten her.

She won't even notice them when we're out, but they'll be close by if needed. She seems relaxed enough under the circumstances, but I did notice her scanning the grounds when we were leaving the house. She's wearing the light blue dress she had on yesterday, with matching blue heels. How many shoes does this woman own? I'll admit I love every pair I've seen so far, but those red ones will forever remain my favourite.

Her hair is down and completely straight. She's only put a bit of gloss on her lips. And she looks beautiful. As gorgeous as she is all dolled up, her natural beauty is something else. She takes my fucking breath away. How she looks now reminds me of the time we spent together in New York. She was a different person over there. I get the feeling it's the person she's been yearning to become. I'm sure if I can keep her away from M, she'll continue to flourish.

'Are you okay?' I ask, placing my hand on her knee. She's awfully quiet, and it's unnerving.

'I'm great,' she says, placing her hand on top of mine and looking at me with a sweet grin on her face. 'I'm happy to be here with you.'

'I'm glad you're here as well.' She has a lot of adjustments ahead of her, but she'll get there. I know it. Her life is only going to improve from here. I'll make sure of it. My hand moves slightly up her leg and under the hem of her dress. I growl when she parts them slightly, allowing me access. My eyes move back to the road as my hand automatically travels a little further.

'Where are your panties?' I ask, briefly looking in her direction.

'You tore them.'

That's right, I did.

'Mmm,' she moans as my fingers glide through her wetness.

My eyes dart in her direction again just as her eyelids flutter shut and her sweet mouth slightly parts. This woman drives me wild. Flicking the indicator, I manoeuvre the car to the side of the road.

'What are you doing?' she asks.

Quickly putting the car in park, I remove my seatbelt at lightning speed. 'Come here,' I command, leaning my body across the centre console and crashing my lips to hers. Sliding one of my hands into her hair, I tug on it lightly, tilting her head further back and deepening the kiss. My other hand moves back under her dress, towards her little piece of heaven.

'Will this unhealthy craving I have for you ever be sated?' I say against her mouth. She doesn't need to answer because I'm already pretty certain it won't. She's under my skin and slowly worming her way into my heart. The scary thing is, I'm powerless to stop it.

*

JADE

The moment his fingers slide inside me and his thumb circles my clit, I push my head back into the seat, moaning into his mouth. I'm quickly becoming addicted to his kisses and his touch. For someone who hated sex, it's surprising how quickly I've changed. He's like a drug.

'Yes ... that's it ... fuck my fingers, beautiful,' he murmurs against my lips as my hips push forwards. His dirty talk only turns me on even more. I can't believe we're on the side of the road in broad daylight, and he's bringing me to orgasm. I'm not bothered, though, I'm too consumed by him and these incredible feelings.

It doesn't take long at all for him to take me over the edge. 'B-B-Brock,' I stammer breathlessly, as my whole body starts to quiver. I grip his hair, pulling his face even closer to mine. I devour his lips as he drains every ounce of pleasure out of me.

When he removes his fingers, he draws back to make eye contact. I watch as he raises his hand and places two fingers inside his mouth. His eyes briefly close like he's savouring the taste of me. God I love it when he does that. It's so hot.

My hand reaches across the centre console and skims over the coarse fabric of his denim jeans, until I'm cupping his crotch. I can feel his erection straining against his pants and that only seems to turn me on more. I love that I can do that to him.

'Not now,' he says as his hand covers mine.

'Let me please you.'

'You already have.'

'I think it was you who pleased me,' I say.

'I love pleasing you,' he replies as he starts the ignition again. 'I have something more important to do.'

'Like what?' I ask.

'I need to get you some damn panties. My boner won't go away as long as I know you're not wearing any under that dress.'

No more words are spoken as we head to the lingerie store. I'm sure he even broke the speed limit a few times. After parking the car, he hastily heads around to my side to open the door. I notice him untucking his shirt as he goes.

I presume he's still hard and trying to hide it, but I did offer to relieve that earlier.

Tugging on my hand, he pulls me out of the car and towards the street front store. The sheer desperation in his movements is amusing. From the moment we enter, though, his urgency shifts dramatically and his eyes dart everywhere as he comes to an abrupt stop. I fight to suppress a laugh. I must admit, Brock looks extremely uncomfortable surrounded by so much silk and lace. He hangs back as I grab a selection of things off the racks. I adore lingerie. That and shoes are my weakness.

I see the sales assistant approach. She's tall, blonde, and extremely attractive. The moment she goes to speak, her eyes land on Brock. Sidestepping me, she makes a beeline for him. Initially it annoys me, but when I see his face turn red as he nervously tugs at the collar of his shirt, I smile. Poor thing.

'I'm with her,' I hear him say in a panic, as I let out a small laugh. I shouldn't find this situation humorous, but I do. He only has himself to blame. If he hadn't ripped all my underwear, we wouldn't be in this position to begin with.

'You okay?' I ask when he comes to stand beside me.

'Uh huh. You seem to be finding this situation very amusing.'

'I don't know what you're talking about.'

'I bet you don't.'

Turning my head, I cover my mouth to muffle my laugh. When my gaze finally moves back to him, he shoves his hands in the pockets of his jeans, cocking an eyebrow.

'Liar.' Leaning forwards, he places his face within an inch of my ear. 'I may have to punish you later, for telling fibs.' I'm not sure if it's his words or his warm breath dancing over my skin, but a shiver courses down my spine. 'Then again, you'd probably enjoy that.'

'If you were dishing out the punishment, I'd definitely enjoy it.'

He gives me a knowing look that holds so much promise.

'What do you think of this?' I ask, holding up a pretty pink silk corset. It has two strips of black lace running down the front, either side of the eyelets, which are laced with black silk ribbon. 'It goes with these,' I add, showing him a tiny pink and black G-string.

Instead of replying he growls, adjusting his crotch at the same time.

'I think I might try these on.'

He growls again when I give him a flirtatious smile.

I know I'm treading on thin ice, but I'm enjoying making him squirm. It's playful and fun. My life's always been so structured and serious, it's nice to act carefree for a change.

I guess my life is far from carefree at the moment. It's like the calm before the storm—the M storm. I don't want to think about that right now. I want to enjoy my new found freedom for as long as it lasts.

'Is it okay if I try this on?' I ask the sales assistant as I pass on my way to the dressing rooms.

'Sure,' she replies, without making eye contact. Her gaze is fixed firmly on Brock as he trails behind me. There's a smile playing on her lips as she looks him up and down. Ugh. She's lucky I'm not the jealous type. He is perfection, so I can't really blame her, but it's obvious we're here together. I find her behaviour trashy.

'Where are you going?' I ask Brock, when he tries to follow me into the cubicle.

'To help.'

'I'm capable of doing it on my own,' I inform him as I push him back out.

'I want to see what it looks like once it's on.'

'I'll consider it,' I say, closing the door in his face. The look he gives me is priceless. I'm smiling to myself as I set the lingerie down on the red velvet chair in the corner.

'I mean it, Jade,' he warns, making me laugh. I love this dominant side of him.

As I set about getting undressed, I hear the sales assistant speak. 'Is everything all right in here?'

'Yes, thank you,' Brock replies.

I stop what I'm doing, listening intently to their conversation. Of course she was waiting until I wasn't around for a chance to talk to Brock alone. Some women have no shame. It's not half obvious that she's attracted to him. Who wouldn't be?

'Great. Let me know if your friend requires any assistance, handsome.'

'She's my girlfriend,' he replies flatly. *He called me his girlfriend*. My lips turn up in a huge grin as I do an inner fist pump. Even if he's just saying that for her benefit, I'm still thrilled. I've never had a boyfriend before.

'Oh.' She doesn't say another word after that. Thankfully, she got the message loud and clear.

After tightening the ribbon, I admire my ensemble in the mirror. It looks gorgeous.

'Jade,' I hear Brock call softly, after knocking on the cubicle door.

'Yes.'

'Can I see now?'

The hopefulness in his voice brings a smile to my face again. Without replying, I unlock and open the door slightly. He pops his head in and the look on his face does something to me. I'm so lost in it, I don't even realise when he pushes the door open further, worming his way inside and turning the latch to relock it.

'What are you doing?' I whisper.

'Sweet Jesus,' is all he says as his arms wrap around my waist, drawing my body towards his. 'You look incredible. We're definitely buying this.'

'You like?' I ask as he gropes at my arse.

'I fucking love. Turn around.'

I do as he asks.

'Christ,' he groans as his fingers skim up the outside of my legs until they're resting on my hips. In the reflection, I see his eyes planted firmly on my behind. He takes a step forward, rubbing his body against mine. When his gaze meets mine in the mirror there's pure desire in his eyes. Nobody has ever looked at me the way he does. *Nobody.*

His hands encircle my waist as he draws me closer, pressing into my back. 'What are you doing to me?' he murmurs as his lips graze over my shoulder. I have no idea, but I'm pretty sure it's the same thing he's doing to me.

I moan softly, resting my head against his chest while his mouth trails a path up my neck. One of his hands palm my breast through the corset, and the other moves down between my legs. I'm so lost in his touch that I totally forget we're still in the dressing room at the lingerie store.

I'm pulled back into reality when I hear the tearing of

fabric. 'Brock,' I say, when my eyes fly open to see him shoving the now ruined panties I was just wearing into his pocket. 'I haven't even paid for them yet.'

'Shh,' he whispers in my ear as the hand on my breast moves up to cover my mouth. 'I'm going to fuck you now. I can't wait another second.' My eyes widen at his comment. Has he lost his mind? We can't have sex in here. I see his other hand in the reflection of the mirror disappear behind me and the distinct sound of a zipper rings out in the silence that has now fallen over us.

My stance widens automatically. My head knows what we're about to do is wrong, but apparently my vagina didn't get that memo.

'Do you even realise how sexy you are?' he whispers as his hand finds its way between my legs again.

'Mmm,' I moan into the palm of his hand, my body trembling with anticipation.

'I'll remove my hand if you promise to be quiet. Okay?'

I nod. I still can't believe we're going to do this.

'Place your hands on the mirror,' he demands. I do exactly as he asks. It's ironic how I've hated being controlled my entire life, yet I have no qualms about following his orders. The way Brock takes control is sexy.

He rubs his cock between my legs as I push my hips towards him. I'm no longer concerned about what we're doing. I want to feel him inside me.

I bite down on my lip when he slides inside me, trying hard not to make a noise.

'Christ you feel amazing,' he breathes as he pulls out slightly before pushing all the way back in.

'Oh god.' One of his hands grasps my hip, holding me in place, while the other tugs on my hair, tilting my head back so his mouth can cover mine.

'I said no noise.'

My eyes roll back in my head as he deepens the kiss before picking up the pace. He slams into me in short, hard strokes. It feels incredible. The risk of the sales assistant discovering us only seems to heighten the experience.

It doesn't take long for him to have me on the edge. 'I'm ... I'm,' is all I get to say before we're interrupted.

'Is everything all right in there?' I hear the skanky sales assistant ask. Shit. There's no holding back. I'm coming whether I like it or not.

'Ahh,' I moan into Brock's mouth as my body starts to quiver and my orgasm hits me full force. His hand quickly moves from my hip, snaking around my waist, using his strength to hold me up. When he pulls out of the kiss, I see a smile tug at his lips as his eyes lock with mine in the mirror.

'We're fine,' he says in a breathless tone that has him sounding like he's just run a damn marathon.

I see his eyes clench shut as his movements become more desperate. I can feel my vagina still pulsing around him and I know he's about to come as well. Shit, could his timing be any worse?

'I was just helping her come undone.'

He did not just say that. There's humour in his voice as my face flushes red. I softly elbow him in the ribs, causing him to laugh. Then the dreaded inevitable happens.

'Christ,' he says in a loud, drawn-out moan, as his body starts to shudder.

'Oh … okay,' is all the sale assistant says before I hear her high heels clinking on the tiles as she walks away in a hurry. God, she knows what we're up to. Someone kill me now.

'Why did you say that?' I whisper, when his body stills.

'I wasn't lying, I am helping you come undone.' He chuckles as he unties the silk ribbon on the corset, sliding his hand inside to pinch my nipple between his finger and thumb. Closing my eyes, I bite my lip again trying to suppress my moan.

How am I going to face that woman when I walk out of here?

*

BROCK

When I'm done, I put my cock away before turning Jade around and pulling her into my arms. Although she's clearly embarrassed, I know she enjoyed it. The minute I saw her dressed in that lingerie, I had to have her. I've never wanted anyone like I want her. It's crazy. Losing ourselves in each other helps escape the cloud that's looming over us, even if it's just for a short time. No drama or pressures. No outside world. Just us becoming one.

Christ, I sound like a damn pussy.

We've heard nothing from M since she left my place in a huff yesterday morning. I'd be foolish to think that was the end of it, because in my heart I know it isn't. Like me, she's not prepared to let Jade go. I only hope that we can stay one step ahead of her. I don't want that psycho bitch anywhere near my girl.

'Do you need some help getting dressed?' I ask, placing a kiss on the top of her head.

'I think I can manage. You've already helped enough.'

I don't miss the sarcasm in her voice. It makes me chuckle.

'I'm glad you find it amusing. We still have to face that woman out there,' she angrily whispers. It doesn't faze me in the slightest. I've been caught in compromising positions more times than I care to admit.

Cupping her pretty face in my hands, I place a chaste kiss on her lips. 'I'll be outside if you need me,' I tell her, trying hard not to smile. She may be embarrassed, but she'd do it all again in a heartbeat. I know her body like the back of my hand. There's no denying this strange pull we have towards each other. I don't think either of us can control it.

While she's getting dressed, I walk back out onto the shop floor. The sales assistant eyes me suspiciously, but it doesn't bother me in the slightest. The uneasiness I felt when I first walked in to this store is now gone.

I head towards the rack that contains more of the kind of panties I just destroyed. Pulling them out of my pocket, I check the size. I then proceed to grab every pair available. We're gonna fucking need them.

Moving to another rack, I grab a few more items that take my fancy. Making sure to grab extra panties, of course. By the time Jade exits the dressing room, my arms are overloaded.

'What are you doing?' she asks, coming to stand beside me.

'Stocking up, sweetheart.'

'How many pairs of panties do you have?' I see her eyes widen as she riffles through what I'm holding.

'Not enough,' is my reply. She lets out the sweetest laugh. I fucking love that sound.

'You do realise this is a high-end boutique? These garments don't come cheap.'

I shrug at her comment. Money's no object to me. She obviously has no idea how wealthy I am. 'As long as I get to rip them off your luscious body, they're worth every fucking cent.' When her smile widens, I lean forward and brush my lips with hers.

Yep, I'm a goner.

*

Jade hesitantly asks the sales assistant if she could use the bathroom while the purchases are being rung up.

'That comes to two thousand, seven hundred and fifty-five dollars,' the sales assistant says a few minutes later. Jade was right, this stuff doesn't come cheap.

Jade comes back and stands beside me. She still has a slight pink tinge on her cheeks, which I love. I drape my arm over her shoulder, pulling her into my side. I can't seem to keep my hands off her.

'Oh and these,' I add, pulling the damaged pair of panties out of my pocket and placing them on the counter. The sales assistant's eyes move from Jade to me, and then down to the torn undergarment. I see a blush creep over her face before she shakes her head. Turning to Jade, I find her head bowed.

Fucking woman.

'I don't know my own strength,' I say with a shrug before clearing my throat. I feel Jade stomp down on my foot. I thought my explanation would help, but obviously not. I open my mouth to speak again, but she gives me a look that has me closing it straightaway. I can't explain why I find this whole situation amusing, but fuck me, I do.

Back in the car, my fingers grip the steering wheel when Jade pulls a pair of panties out of the bag and shimmies into them. I have to get this need for her under control.

We drive to the mall and spend the next few hours buying her new clothes. I've never enjoyed shopping, but today I do. I love spending time with her. I'm pleasantly surprised by her selections. Rather than the classy outfits she usually wears, she opted for more casual attire, jeans and shorts mainly. It pleased me no end for some reason. Jade oozes class and sophistication, but on the other hand she seems to crave normality. I'm yet to find one thing I don't like about this woman. Understandably I hate her occupation, but I no longer have to worry about that. Well, I hope I don't.

Around lunchtime, we head towards a café to get something to eat.

'Would you mind if I had a burger and fries?' she asks, looking at me over the top of her menu.

'Of course not. Have whatever you like.' I'm taken aback that she'd even ask me that.

'Thank you,' she replies, smiling. 'I've never eaten a burger before.' I hate that she thinks she needed my permission.

'Jade,' I say, reaching for her hand across the table and grasping it in mine, 'I'm not M. You can eat, wear, say and do whatever you like. I'd never try to control you ... I mean, I won't give up control in the bedroom, but everything else, you're free to do what you please.'

'I know,' she says with a sigh. 'It's just going to take some getting used too. I've been dictated to my entire life.'

Her words break my heart.

*

The next two days pass without incident. There's still no word from M, and it's disconcerting. She wouldn't give up that easy. I wish I knew what she had planned, so I could stay one step ahead. I have a feeling she'll pounce when we least expect it.

Jade, for the most part, seems okay. On occasions, when she thinks I'm not watching, I see the worry etched on her beautiful face. I haven't gone to work for that very reason. As long as we're together, she's safe. I've been doing what I can from home, but I'll have to go back in to the office eventually. I was hoping the situation with M would've been sorted by now.

The time I've spent with Jade this week has been amazing. She's smart, witty and completely fucking adorable. She's down to earth and just a pleasure to be around. I love how easy-going she is. Most of the women I've been with in the past are high maintenance.

Even if things don't last between us—and I find myself hoping they do—I know I'll cherish every second I've spent with her. I've realised a moment of something incredible is far better than a lifetime of nothing special, which is exactly what I've had until she came along.

Erika, my housekeeper, came in briefly this morning to do a bit of cleaning. Jade gave her a list of things to pick up from the supermarket—she's been cooking for me all week. Her culinary skills are extraordinary and would rival the best of the best. What blows my mind is she's had no formal training. I'd love to see her fulfil her dream of opening a restaurant one day. It's plain to see she's in her element when she's in the kitchen.

'Hi,' I hear her say from the door of my office.

'Hi.'

'I'm not disturbing you am I?'

'Not at all,' I say, rolling my chair out from under my desk and tapping my hand on my knee. Pushing off the door frame, she comes over to me. As soon as she's in reaching distance, I grasp her hips, pulling her down onto my lap. 'I'll always make time for you.' I place a soft kiss on the side of her head and draw her body closer.

'I've really enjoyed my time here,' she says before resting her head on my shoulder and sighing. She seems content, which I love. 'I just wanted to let you know that dinner will be ready soon.'

Who knew playing house could be so enjoyable? Not me. I honestly thought I was happy living here on my own, but now I know that's not the case. Jade has changed me in so many ways. I'm truly going to miss her when she goes. To my huge disappointment, she's voiced her desire to leave numerous times over the past few days. When it's safe to do so, she has plans of returning to her apartment, or finding somewhere else to live. Every time she mentions it, I get a stabbing pain in my chest. There's a huge part of me that doesn't want her to go. But I'll worry about that when I have to.

I can understand why she'd want her freedom after the life she's led, but I hope that her going home doesn't mean the end of us.

'Have I got enough time for a quick snack?' I ask as my lips kiss a path up her neck.

'Always,' she replies, smiling and turning her head to capture my lips.

I groan into her mouth. Lifting her off my lap, I place her on the desk in front of me. My fingers go to work undoing the button and zip on her shorts. When my eyes meet hers again, she's doing that damn lip-biting thing again. Fuck, she's beautiful, in every sense of the word.

She lifts her arse slightly off the desk so I can remove her shorts and panties. Placing my hands on the back of her calves, I lift her legs and position her feet on my shoulders before my mouth bears down on her.

'Brock,' she moans. We've slowly been making our way through this massive house over the past few days. When I'm finished with her, it will be time to tick *Christening my office desk* off the list. I won't be satisfied until I can't enter any room in this house without thinking of her.

CHAPTER NINETEEN

JADE

Saturday morning, I get a nice surprise. 'What's going on?' I ask when Brock leads me into the lounge room.

'I have a work function to attend tonight, and I was hoping you'd be my date.'

'Really?' I ask.

'Really. Will you come with me?'

'Yes,' I say without hesitation, even though butterflies swarm in my stomach at the thought of going. I'm not even sure why, I've attended these kinds of events a thousand times in the past. I guess this is the first time I'll be going as someone's date instead of their client—as Jade the person, not Jade the escort.

'Great,' he replies, pulling me into his arms. After placing a kiss on my forehead, he turns towards our guest. 'Jade Davis, this is Brendan. He's a stylist and friend of my brother's.'

'It's lovely to meet you,' he says, taking my hand and placing a kiss on my knuckles. 'You're simply stunning.' He shifts my arm out to the side as his eyes travel the length of my body. 'It's going to be an absolute pleasure working with you, Miss Davis.'

'Thank you,' I reply, forcing a gracious smile. I've received compliments on my looks my entire life, but I don't think I'll ever be entirely comfortable hearing them. And although the look Brendan gives me isn't sleazy or creepy, Brock picks up on my uneasiness.

'Can you give us a second alone?' he says to Brendan, before leading me back into the main foyer. 'Are you okay?' he asks, cupping my face in his hands.

'I'm fine.' Because I am, but I don't elaborate.

'He's gay,' he says. 'You have nothing to worry about.'

I let out a small laugh. He's obviously misread my uneasiness. 'He can try all he wants,' I reply, sliding my arms around Brock's waist. 'I only have eyes for one man.'

'Really. And who would that be?'

'I'm not sure if you know him,' I say. When he growls, I laugh. I place a soft kiss on his mouth. 'You,' I whisper.

It's hard for me to put myself out there like this. When you've been rejected your entire life, you come to expect that from everyone you meet. So letting your true feelings be known is only setting yourself up for heartache.

Brock gives me the most beautiful smile, revealing his perfectly straight teeth. 'I'm glad to hear that because I only have eyes for you too, sweetheart.'

I finally manage to convince him that I'm comfortable being alone with Brendan, so Brock heads into his home office to do some work. I hate that I've been keeping him away from his business for the majority of the week.

While Brendan takes my measurements, his assistants wheel in two racks full of beautiful gowns. I'm used to this kind of treatment, but I'm touched that Brock has gone to so much trouble to please me.

I jump when I hear the front door slam shut, it makes my heart rate accelerates. I hate being on edge like this. What if it's M?

'Anyone home?' I hear a male voice call.

An attractive young man comes barrelling into the room a few seconds later. 'Well. I'll be damned,' he says, approaching me. 'You must be the woman who's captivated my brother's heart.'

'Shut up, Joshua,' Brock snaps from behind him as he enters the room as well. While Brock appears to be unimpressed by his brother's outburst, Joshua seems quite amused. I even hear Brendan snicker beside me.

'I'm Joshua,' the new arrival says, extending his hand to me. 'I'm the good-looking one in the family.'

I laugh. He's very handsome. His features are similar to Brock's, but in my eyes, he has nothing on his brother. Brock is perfection in every sense of the word.

'I'm Jade.'

'Wow. I can see why my brother is so taken with you.'

'Ignore him,' Brock says, coming to stand beside me and draping his arm possessively over my shoulder. 'What brings you here, anyway?'

Joshua winks at me before turning his attention to his brother. 'I just needed to see her with my own eyes.'

'I don't understand what the big deal is.' Brock's words only seem to amuse Joshua more. When my gaze moves to Brock, I find his eyes narrowed.

'Calm down, bro, you did well,' Joshua says, placing a hand on his brother's shoulder.

Brock clears his throat while shoving his free hand into his pocket. He's clearly uncomfortable with this situation.

They've totally lost me. I have no idea what they're talking about.

'Well, you've seen, now you can leave.'

'Nope,' Joshua says, taking a seat on the couch and placing his feet on the coffee table. 'I think I might hang around for a while.'

'How did you get in here anyway?'

'I still have my key.' Joshua removes it from his pocket and dangles it from his finger. I can tell he's enjoying getting under his brother's skin, but despite that, I like him. My gut instincts are usually pretty spot on. Their playful banter tells me they have a good relationship. I've heard the way Brock talks about Joshua, so I know they're close.

'If you're going to continue to drop in unannounced, you can return it.'

Joshua chuckles before shoving the keys back into his pocket. I find myself envying their relationship. I pined for a sibling growing up. I still do. A real family of my very own—someone who would love me unconditionally and make me feel like I wasn't so alone in this world.

The pair of them sit on the couch while my fitting continues. However, I only get to try on three of the dresses that Brendan brought to the house. The moment I enter the room wearing the strapless emerald green gown, the guys unanimously choose it. They all say the colour of the dress makes my green eyes pop. It feels weird parading around in front of them, even though it's something I've been forced into doing my whole adult life. Being on show is something I'm not fond of. Remembering two of the men are gay and the other is Brock makes it a little easier.

Once the decision's made, Brock stalks across the room towards me. 'You look breathtaking. I'm going to enjoy stripping you out of this dress and fucking you tonight when we get home,' he whispers so only I can hear. His finger lightly skims a path down my neck and comes to a stop at my cleavage just above the bodice of the dress, making a shiver ran through my body. I have to clench my thighs together at the desire that washes through me. The effect he has on me is so strong.

Bring it on, Mr Weston ... bring it on.

Brendan and his assistants leave a short time later. He measured my feet before leaving, saying he'd have some shoes delivered to the house later that day. When they arrive, I instantly fall in love with the gold strappy heels. He also sends a small gold clutch to accompany them. He has exquisite taste.

I guess Brock can see how comfortable I am with his brother, because after we ate lunch he left me with him while he ran a few errands. I was fine with that. Brock has been cooped up in this house with me all week and I'm sure I've been holding him back from doing a lot of things.

Besides, it gives me the perfect opportunity to pick Joshua's brain and get a little inside info on Brock.

*

When I exit the ensuite, I find Brock standing on the other side of the bedroom, in front of the mirror. He's already dressed in his tux and tying his bowtie. I take a minute to drink him in. His strong back and broad shoulders are accentuated in his tailor-made jacket. My eyes move towards the reflection in the mirror and I'm again left breathless by him.

The moment he notices me watching him, he swings around. His lips curve into a smile as his eyes move down the length of my body. Being dressed up is nothing new for me, but I find myself hoping he likes what stands before him. Appearance has never been high on my agenda. On M's yes, but never on mine. In this moment though, it means everything. I want to look beautiful for him. I want Brock to be proud to have me by his side tonight.

Something has shifted between us recently. I think we've both let our guard down—I know I have. It's hard for me to let people in when I'm so used to being rejected. For some reason, Brock is different. The things he makes me feel both frighten and thrill me. For once in my life I'm willing to remove the barrier I erected around my heart years ago. Only for him. He's the first person in my life who's ever made me want to take that leap of faith. I only hope I don't come to regret it.

Dropping his hands from his tie, he stalks across the room and pulls me into his arms. 'You look stunning,' he says, placing his lips against my neck. My hair is slicked back into a tight bun at the nape of my neck. Since I didn't have my hairstylist for tonight, it was the best I could do. My makeup is done to perfection, smoky eyes and my signature red lips. 'God, you smell amazing. How am I going to be able to keep my hands off you tonight?'

'You'll manage,' I reply. 'Let me do this for you.' I tie the bow quickly and flawlessly. It's one of the many things I learnt during my training to become an escort.

I love looking after him. I can't even put into words how wonderful it's been. Even with the uncertainty of M hanging over our heads, these past few days have been the happiest times of my life. If I've learnt anything over the years, it's nothing good ever lasts, so you should enjoy every second while you can.

'I bought you something when I went out earlier,' he says, reaching into his coat pocket and pulling out a blue velvet box. 'I hope you like them.'

My hands are trembling slightly when he passes the box to me. Tears sting my eyes the moment I lift the lid. Inside is a mass of teardrop-shaped emeralds, strung together to make the most exquisite pair of earrings I've ever seen. 'They're beautiful,' I whisper. I don't know what else to say. Nobody has ever bought me anything this extravagant before.

'When I saw you in the dress this afternoon, I felt compelled to get you something to wear with it.'

'They're perfect,' I say, brushing my lips against his.

'I knew nothing I bought would ever be able to outshine your beauty.' He lets out a small sigh. Our eyes lock, but neither of us speak. Time seems to stand still as we gaze at each other. Butterflies settle in my stomach as I'm suddenly overwhelmed by the feelings I have for this man.

'You've already done so much for me. I'm not sure I'll ever be able to repay you.'

His fingers tenderly glide across my cheek. 'I'm pretty certain there's nothing I wouldn't do for you.'

Tears burn my eyes. 'Thank you,' I whisper as I pull him tightly against me.

I know I'm thanking him for more than the earrings.

*

BROCK

We're both quiet on the drive to the function. I crossed a line before we left. It's a line I was certain I'd never cross. But that was until Jade came into my life. As I stood gazing into her eyes after giving her the earrings, something happened that I can't put into words. It was like a sucker punch to the chest. A kind of epiphany, you could say. The feeling hit me like a tonne of fucking bricks, and I'm not sure what to think about it. I'm in way over my head here.

'You ready?' I ask, lacing my fingers through hers as we walk towards the function centre. Tonight is huge for me. Jade is the only girlfriend I've ever had, so bringing her here to meet my family and work colleagues is a big fucking deal. I'm apprehensive, but also excited to show her off to everyone. I'm pretty sure she'll love my mum. My dad is a whole other story.

'Ready as I'll ever be,' she says, tightening her grip on my hand. She seems nervous.

'I think it's only fair to warn you that you'll be meeting my parents tonight.'

'Really? Your parents? You've never mentioned them before.'

I shrug. They're not my favourite subject. 'My mum's okay most of the time, but our relationship is a little strained of late. Let's just say they weren't very accepting when Joshua came out.'

'Oh,' she says as her pretty green eyes widen. 'That's a shame.' Yes, it is. Josh told me today that Mum has been calling him daily since they've reconnected. I only hope it lasts. He's been hurt enough.'

'How is your relationship with your father?'

I was afraid she'd ask me that. 'My dad's a prick.' It's best to prepare her because you never know what to expect from that man. I don't bother elaborating, she'll find out for herself soon enough.

'Oh.'

I feel all eyes on us when we enter. Jade squares her shoulders and I have to repress my smile. I love her strength. I hope tonight is a pleasant experience for her. As we cross the room, I stop to greet a few of my colleagues. The shock on their faces is evident when I introduce Jade as my girlfriend. I guess I should've expected that with my reputation, but it annoys me nevertheless. Is it so hard to believe Brock Weston has a girlfriend?

Who am I kidding? Even I can't believe it.

As we make our way to the table where my parents are seated, my gaze lands on Clarissa. Fucking great. She has nothing to do with our company, so I don't see why my father insists that she always attends. Her face lights up when she sees me, but the moment she spies my date, her smile turns into a frown. She better keep her fucking distance. I won't tolerate her upsetting Jade tonight.

'Brock,' my mother says, beaming, when we reach the table. I do love her, but I don't approve of her behaviour sometimes. I know my father intimidates her, he tries to intimidate everyone, but I wish she'd grow a backbone. Her husband is a damn snake and she deserves so much better.

'Mother.' I lean down and place a kiss on her cheek.

'Who's this lovely lady you have with you tonight?' She's always been polite to my dates, even if she doesn't agree with my philandering ways.

'This is my girlfriend, Jade. Jade this is my mother, Elaine.' A smile spreads across her face when my words register.

'Your girlfriend!' Mum repeats in shock.

Yes, I have a fucking girlfriend. Maybe I should've put an announcement in the company newsletter in preparation for tonight.

Standing, my mother embraces Jade with a warm hug. 'It's so lovely to meet you.'

'It's lovely to meet you too, Mrs Weston.'

'Please, call me Elaine.' When she finally lets go, Mum wraps her arms around me as well. This is the loving and caring mother I have missed. 'I'm so happy for you both,' she says. I see tears glistening in her eyes. Fuck me. By the way she's carrying on, you'd think I'd just told her we were getting married or something.

I look at my father and immediately know he's not impressed. *Fuming* would be a better word. Fucker. He better not start any shit tonight.

'Father, this is Jade Davis. Jade, my father, Maxwell Weston.'

'It's nice to meet you, Mr Weston,' Jade says sweetly, extending her hand to him.

Nodding his head curtly, he briefly takes her hand giving it a half-hearted shake. The rude prick doesn't even stand. When I see Jade's face drop, I have to control the urge to lunge at him. I hate that I have this arsehole's blood running through my veins.

'Ignore him,' I whisper in her ear when Jade straightens. 'I told you he was a prick.' She smiles up at me when I drape my arm over her shoulder and place a soft kiss on the side of her head. I notice her smile doesn't quite reach her eyes, and again I want to throttle my father.

After seating Jade next to my mother—and away from that prick—I head to the bar to grab us both a drink.

I almost crash into my father when I return to the table. Lifting the drinks in the air, I come to an abrupt stop.

'You brought that fucking whore here?' he seethes. His words both surprise and worry me. Does he know who

Jade is, or is it just a general comment? Maybe he's just been associating with Clarissa for too long. She always refers to my women as whores.

'Watch it, old man, you're already skating on thin ice.'

'I'm just speaking the truth. I raised you better than that.' His comment makes me laugh.

'Like father like son,' I retort, side-stepping him. I need to put some distance between us, and fast. 'And if you refer to her as that again,' I add, looking over my shoulder, 'I won't be held responsible for what I do. And that's not a threat, it's a promise.' Because, by Christ, it is. Jade has no control over her past. I won't stand by and let anyone disrespect her.

'You better turn up to the office on Monday, or so help me ...'

I was thinking of returning to work Monday, but not now. I'll go back Tuesday just to spite him.

*

JADE

Thankfully, Brock stayed by my side for most of the night. His mum seems really lovely and kept making conversation with me, but unfortunately I can't say the same about his father. I tried my best not to look at him after the unfriendly greeting he gave me. The one time I did, I found him glaring at me. I gather he doesn't approve of me dating his son.

Meeting Elaine and Maxwell Weston made me think of my own parents. I hate that I have no family to introduce Brock to. I've wondered about them a lot over the years, but I try not to do it often. It hurts too much. My mother died, but my father obviously didn't want me, because he gave me up.

That speaks volumes. He mustn't have loved me, otherwise he never would've done it.

Why am I so unlovable?

After dinner, Brock heads back to the bar and I'm left sitting with his parents again. My heart drops when his mother says, 'I'm just going to duck to the ladies' room.' Everything in me wants to go with her so I'm not left here alone with Maxwell, but that's childish. If I can live with M for years, I'm sure I can sit at the table with this man for a few minutes.

Elaine is only a few step away from the table when Maxwell strikes. 'You know my son is only having fun with you, right?'

'Excuse me?'

'My son is of good breeding, but in saying that he's also a stereotypical male. We have certain needs, you could say. Men of our standards don't marry trash like you, so don't get too comfortable. He'll throw you aside when he's had his fill, mark my words.'

I gasp at the harshness of his words, before turning away from him. Hopefully that will be enough to make him leave me alone. Briefly clenching my eyes shut, I fight back tears. I won't give this man the satisfaction of seeing me cry.

His words swim around in my head. He's right, Brock does deserve better than me. But I already knew that. It doesn't seem to lessen the sting though. I'd be foolish to think I was anything more than a good time to Brock. A fool is exactly what I've been. I truly believed he cared.

My eyes seek out Brock, and that's when I see him standing at the bar talking to a tall, beautiful blonde. She's a woman of *good breeding*. A lump rises to my throat when I see her affectionately rub her hand down Brock's arm as she smiles at something he's said. She turns her head slightly to look in my direction. When our eyes meet, her lips curve up. It's not a pleasant smile; *smug* would be the best way to describe it. I'd like to march over there and tell her to get her hands off my man, but I can't do that, because truth is, he's not mine. He'll never be mine.

Coming here tonight was a huge mistake.

I don't belong with these people. All the money M spent making me so refined over the years was a waste. My training is just a mask to hide the real me. The scum, as she so rightly put it. The girl nobody has ever wanted, or loved.

Rising from my seat, I move hastily across the room. Tears rise to my eyes, but I manage to contain them. Breaking down in front of these people is the last thing I want to do. I'm already humiliated enough.

When I see Elaine exit the ladies' room, I head in that direction.

'Jade. Are you all right?' she asks as I hurry past her.

'I'm fine, Mrs Weston,' I reply, glancing at her over my shoulder and forcing out a smile. 'Nature calls.'

The large sitting area is empty when I enter. I cross the room, heading for the cubicles. The moment I'm locked inside, I take a few deep breaths to try to calm myself. My body is trembling. I'm not going to cry ... I'm *not* going to cry. I've been treated a lot worse than that in my life, but Brock was right, his dad's a prick. He'd get on famously with M.

I wait a few minutes until I've pulled myself together before heading back out to the sitting room to check my appearance in the mirror. I'm washing my hands when the door flies open and the blonde who was talking to Brock waltzes in like she owns the place.

Her eyes meet mine in the mirror and she gives me another one of those smug smiles. I'd like to slap it right off her perfect face. I'm in no mood for her.

'I don't believe we've met,' she says coming to stand beside me. 'Although I'm not usually interested in meeting any of Brock's whores.'

'Excuse me?' I gasp, turning to face her. Does he hire prostitutes on a regular basis? Does she know who I am?

'I'm Clarissa, Brock's fiancée.' She extends her hand to me, but I ignore it.

She's what? I take a few seconds to try to process what she's just said. She's fucking what? My erratically beating heart drops into the pit of my stomach.

'Don't look so shocked. You honestly didn't think you had a chance with him, did you?'

I suddenly feel like I'm in a world of M's. First Brock's father, now this bitch. Her words swim around in my head as I try to make sense of it all. It can't possibly be true. 'I don't think Brock would have me staying with him at his house, or would've introduced me to his parents as his girlfriend tonight, if he was engaged to you.'

She falters briefly as her eyes narrow at me in the mirror. 'That's where you're wrong. Brock and I have an arrangement. His sexual appetite, as I'm sure you know,' she says with an eye roll, before beginning to reapply her lipstick, 'is insatiable. I decided to let him fulfil his needs elsewhere until we're married, then it's going to stop. I won't share him after that.' She speaks calmly, like it's no big deal. It's a big deal. A huge fucking deal.

I think I'm going to be sick.

'Excuse me,' I say, pushing past her and accidentally knocking her arm in the process. The lipstick she was applying leaves a hot pink smudge up the side of her face. If I wasn't on the verge of a total meltdown, I would've found that amusing. Crazy bitch. Who in their right mind would let their fiancé sleep with other women?

I leave the toilets and hurry towards the door that leads to the hotel foyer. The second I step out onto the street an ugly sob escapes me as a crushing feeling settles in my chest. I'm suddenly finding it hard to breathe. I wrap my arms around my body to try to comfort myself. I have nobody else to do it. Again, I'm all alone. My heart feels like it's shattered. I've endured a shitload of betrayals in my life, but nothing has hurt as much as this does. I feel like a fool for letting my guard down and trusting Brock. He's a snake just like the rest of them.

Those damn barriers were there for a reason.

CHAPTER TWENTY

BROCK

'Where's Jade?,' I ask my mother when I arrive back at the table. After getting stuck listening to Clarissa whinge for five excruciating minutes, I was stopped by one of my clients. Normally it wouldn't bother me, but I didn't want to leave Jade at the table with my father for too long.

'She went to the ladies' room about ten minutes ago, but hasn't returned,' my mother tells me. For some reason, that gives me a sick feeling in my stomach. Slamming the drinks down onto the table sends the liquid flying everywhere, but that's the least of my worries at the moment. What if something's happened to her? Christ, M. I break into a run as I head across the room. My heart is beating so hard I can hear it thumping in my ears.

'Jade,' I call out, bashing on the door of the ladies' room. I'm sure I look like a dick, but I don't care. 'Jade!'

Relief floods through me when the door swings open, but it doesn't last long when I see Clarissa glaring back at me.

'Is Jade in there?'

'Who?' she replies, screwing up her face.

'Jade. My date. The one I came here with tonight.'

'Oh, your whore. Nope. I haven't seen her.'

Fucking bitch. She's just jealous she'll never have me. I hear her laughing as she walks away. I need to put a stop to her attending these events.

'Jade!' There's still no response. I'm going in. Pushing open the door to the ladies' room, I call out her name again. All the stalls appear to be empty. Where could she be? Turning on my heel, I head back out. I can see from here she hasn't returned to the table. I search the room. When I can't see her, I head towards the exit.

'Is everything okay, Mr Weston?' the doorman asks as I approach the front of the hotel.

'Did you see the woman I came here with leave? She was wearing a green dress.'

'I remember her, yes. She left a few minutes ago. She looked distressed. I hope everything is okay.'

The only words that register are 'she looked distressed'. Fucking hell. I need to find her.

'Was she alone?'

'Yes, I believe she was. She asked where she could get a taxi. I had reception order one for her. You may find her waiting out front.' I don't even wait to hear if he has anything else to say—I'm out the door in a flash and running towards the street. It's not safe for her to be out here alone.

'Jade! Jade!' I call. I get a few strange looks from people milling outside the hotel, but I don't give a shit. All I care about is finding Jade and making sure she's okay. My head swings from left to right as I frantically search the surrounding area. 'Jade!' *Christ.* Where the fuck did she go?

My hands are trembling as I reach inside the breast pocket of my tux to retrieve my phone. I need to call her and find out what the fuck's going on. Maybe she's tried to contact me. My heart drops when I realise I don't have her number. I only have the number of the phone I gave her, but she didn't bring that one to my house. Shit!

Searching through my contacts, I find Rupert's number. It's too late to call, so I text him on the off chance he's still awake.

Hi Rupert, it's Brock. Do you have Jade's phone number?

I head towards the valet to collect my car—I can't stay here when she's out there all alone, anything could happen—but I only make it a few step before I see her. She's leaning against the wall of the hotel. Her arms are wrapped protectively around her body, but her eyes are on me. She doesn't look impressed. She looks downright pissed.

'Jade,' I breathe in relief as I approach her.

I'm taken aback when she pushes off the wall and starts walking in the other direction.

'Jade, wait up.' I'll admit I'm perplexed by the way she's acting. She's never acted this cold towards me. She seemed fine when I left her sitting at the table earlier. This is exactly why I don't get involved with women. They're so fucking unpredictable.

I break into a jog and catch up to her in no time. Reaching out, I attempt to halt her. She abruptly swings around. Anger is rolling off her, but it's the sadness I see in her beautiful green eyes that tugs at my heart.

'Don't touch me,' she spits, ripping her arm from my grip.

'What's your fucking problem?' I ask.

'Just leave me alone.'

I don't think so, sweetheart. Reaching for her arm again, I gently but forcefully guide her around the side of the building.

This time she doesn't put up a fight. The second I back her into the wall, I use my arms to cage her in. I'm not letting her go until she tells me what's wrong. She better not say 'nothing', or I'll lose my shit.

She bows her head when I move my face within inches of hers.

'Look at me,' I demand.

'No.' She crosses her arms over her chest. It only manages to push her perky tits up further. I can't let that distract me, I need to know what the hell is going on. Why am I finding her attitude a complete turn on? Is there something wrong with me? To my dismay, it only proves yet again that this woman owns my balls. If anyone else acted this way towards me, I wouldn't care. I'd walk away without a backwards glance, wishing them a nice life in the process. Fuck me, why can't I do that now? She has me tied up in fucking knots. 'Goddamn it, Jade,' I say, trying to calm my voice. Using my finger I tilt her face up to meet mine. 'Talk to me.'

Her determined gaze locks with mine. *She's so stubborn.* I've never seen this side of her before. I'm usually a good judge of character but maybe I've been wrong about her. Then, in an instant, her beautiful green eyes well with tears and I know I haven't been mistaken—she is the sweet person I believe her to be. She's just hurt or angry and I have no idea why. I can't fix it if I don't know what the hell is wrong.

Drawing her towards me, I wrap her in my arms. 'Talk to me, sweetheart,' I plead. She doesn't answer for the longest time and it does nothing to calm my racing heart. Saying I'm confused would be an understatement.

'I just met your fiancée,' she finally whispers into my chest.

I almost want to laugh because the notion of me having a fiancée is quite comical. *Why would she even think that?*

Drawing back, my eyes search her face and I can tell she honestly believes I'm engaged.

'You're joking right? I don't have a fiancée.' My response doesn't sound very convincing, but it's true.

Her brow furrows before she places her hands on my chest, pushing away from me. 'Deny it all you want, Brock, but she told me you were engaged.'

'Who told you?' I ask, pinching the bridge of my nose. This conversation is giving me a fucking headache.

'Your fiancée,' she says, ducking under my arm to head back to the street.

Here we go again. I should just let her go, but I can't. I don't want to lose her over a stupid misunderstanding. I don't want to lose her period.

Who would say such a thing? My mind is swimming in a haze. Then realisation hits. Fucking Clarissa. She must've confronted Jade in the ladies' room.

'Fuck, Jade, stop walking away from me,' I snap as I go after her again. 'Do I even get a chance to explain?'

'I think I've heard enough for one night,' she replies glancing at me over her shoulder and narrowing her eyes. She's so fucking sexy when she's angry. I see her raise her hand to flag down the taxi as it pulls up to the kerb. If she thinks I'm letting her go, she's delusional.

The moment she opens the door, I reach over her shoulder and push it closed. We have a silent standoff, before the driver interrupts us. 'Do you wanna ride, or not?' he asks impatiently, winding down his window. We answer in unison.

'Yes.'

'No.' Of course my reply was the 'no'.

Ignoring me, she tries to open the back door of the cab—again I close it.

'For fuck's sake, Brock,' she snaps, and I smile. I think that's the first time I've heard her use a profanity. I shouldn't be turned on by her attitude, but I am.

'I don't have all night, lady, are you in or out?'

Reaching into my pocket, I remove a fifty dollar bill and pass it to the driver. The satisfying look on Jade's face tells me she's relieved I'm letting her leave.

'She's out,' I say, before bending my knees slightly and wrapping my arms around her legs.

'Let me go, you pig!' she screams as I haul her over my shoulder.

I laugh. 'Can't do that, sweetheart,' I reply smugly, walking towards the valet.

'I'd like to collect my car myself,' I tell him as Jade thrashes around on my shoulder. The valet gives me a quizzical look, but doesn't argue. My company uses this luxury hotel often for functions, so they know me. 'She's had too much to drink,' I say, trying hard to suppress my smile when she slaps my back.

'Sure, sir. Let me get you the key to your vehicle.'

'Let me down, Brock,' Jade pleads when the valet walks away.

'Nope.'

The valet approaches again, handing me the keys to my Lamborghini. 'Take that door over there,' he says, pointing. 'Your vehicle is on the first floor, in the second row.'

'Thank you.'

'You can't take me against my will,' Jade cries as I climb the flight of stairs. 'This is kidnapping.' When I chuckle, she pinches my arse.

'You didn't exactly give me a choice,' I say. 'You forced me into taking drastic measure when you refused to hear me out.'

'I've heard enough lies from you, I don't need to hear anymore.'

Her comment gets under my skin. I pride myself on my honesty. And I've never lied to her.

When I reach the car, I slide her down my body, pinning her against the side of the vehicle. 'Listen here, I've never lied to you.'

'Really? You just forget to mention that, while I've been living at your house and sleeping in your bed, you're engaged to someone else? You snake.'

I chuckle when she calls me a snake, I can't help it. I've been called a lot worse in my time, but I find what she said, and the way she said it, amusing. Especially coming from her sweet mouth.

'You think playing with someone's emotions is funny?' she says, pushing on my chest. 'I thought you were different.'

When I see tears well in her eyes again, I feel like a prick for making light of this situation. I hate that this has hurt her. I could fucking strangle Clarissa.

'Jade,' I say, cupping her face.

'Get your two-timing hands off me.'

This time I manage to repress my amusement. I can't lose her over this. 'I'm not engaged. I never have been, and I never will be.'

'Tell that to your fiancée,' she snaps.

'Clarissa is not my fucking fiancée, goddamn it.'

'Oh, but you know who I'm referring to without me even mentioning her name.' She tries to push out from underneath me, but I hold her firmly in place.

'Because she's a psycho bitch, that's why. Our fathers are friends. They've wanted us to get married for years. I can tell you right now, it's never going to happen. I can't stand that woman. Do you really think if I was engaged to her, I'd be here tonight with you?'

'She told me you had an arrangement.'

'There's no fucking arrangement.'

Her green eyes lock with mine as she tries to absorb what I've just told her. Fuck—I hope she believes me, because it's the truth. 'Please believe me,' I plead as my hands settle on her shoulders. I've never had to beg anyone like this before. I never wanted to, but she isn't just anyone—she's Jade.

'I've told my father—and Clarissa—numerous times that I have no inclination to marry her. I'm not the marrying kind.'

'You're not?' she asks, and I see a flash of hurt cross her face. My thumbs tenderly caress her cheeks. Marriage has never been on my agenda. My parents haven't set a great example in that department.

'No, I'm not, but if there was one person on this earth who could change that, it would be you.' And that's the truth. Having her staying at my home has opened my eyes to the possibility. Well, it's planted a small seed, anyway. I still don't think I have it in me.

'Me. Really?' she breathes as a small smile plays at her lips.

'Yes, you.' Closing my eyes, I exhale a large breath. It's not until my forehead is resting against hers, that I open them. I can't believe I'm about to admit this out loud.

'I think I'm falling in love with you, Jade.'

*

JADE

I gasp at his words. Taking a moment, I give myself time to let them sink in. The way he struggled when saying it makes me believe he meant what he said. I'm not sure if it's hearing those words or if it's just a combination of everything I've been through this week, but when the tears come I'm powerless to stop them.

I cover my face with my hands and I start to cry. Like, really cry. Cry as I never have before.

'Jesus, Jade,' he said, pulling me into his arms again. 'That's not the reaction I was hoping for.'

He holds me for the longest time until the tears finally stop. I feel foolish for crying in front of him. I hate showing anyone my vulnerable side. I've become a master at disguising my weaknesses over the years; I learnt at a young age that only the strong survive.

Placing his finger under my chin, he lifts my face to meet his. The look in his eyes tugs at my heart. The confident Brock I'm used to seeing is gone.

'Do you really think you're falling in love with me?' I ask. My heart rate accelerates as I wait for his answer. I don't usually allow myself to hope, but that's exactly what I'm doing now. Hoping it's true—hoping he really means what he said.

Using the pads of his thumbs, he wipes the tears from my cheeks. 'I've never felt like this before,' he admits. 'I'm consumed by you, Jade. I've never been in love, so I can't say with all honesty that I know what it feels like, but if wanting to be with someone every minute of every day, feeling like a part of you is missing when they're not around, not being able to imagine your life without that person in it, or finding it hard to function properly because all you can think about is them, then yes, I'm in love with you. Because you make me feel all of that and so much more.'

Tears rise to my eyes again. 'Nobody has ever told me they love me.'

'Oh sweetheart,' he whispers as he holds me tight. 'You're such an easy person to love.'

I've always imagined what it would feel like to hear somebody say those words to me, but I can't even put into words how wonderful it is to finally be loved.

CHAPTER TWENTY-ONE

JADE

Thankfully, Brock didn't want to go back to the event. He did offer to go and confront Clarissa with me though, which helped me believe he was telling the truth about not being engaged. The more I thought about it on the way home, the more I realised how unrealistic her claims were: Brock's been with me the whole time; there were no visits, no phone calls; and the fact he introduced me to his parents as his girlfriend. Maybe that's why his father was such an arse to me—he'd been pressuring Brock to marry that skank.

Brock held my hand the entire journey home, only letting go to change gears. After parking the car in his garage and entering the house, he scoops me into his arms, carrying me up the stairs towards his bedroom.

The moment we enter, he puts me down and turns me. 'I've been dying to remove this dress all night,' he whispers as his lips find my neck. Moaning, I tilt my head to the side to allow him better access. 'Your skin is so perfect ... everything about you is *perfect*.'

My skin pebbles with goose bumps as he slowly unzips my dress. 'I think you're perfect too,' I admit. I'm grateful that he didn't let me walk away tonight. I should've allowed him the chance to explain, but I was heartbroken to think he'd deceived me. I honestly thought he was going to feed me a bunch of lies and excuses. My heart wouldn't have been able to take another blow.

The moment my dress pools around my feet, Brock turns me in his arms before his lips capture mine. The way he kisses me shows that things have changed between us. As though his confession has removed the last of his resolve. I think he's finally ready to give me his all. Like I am to him, but I can't profess my love for him just yet. I've never uttered those words before, so it's a huge step for me—definitely one I'm not ready to take. I'm sure if we continue to blossom, one day I'll be ready, but not tonight.

My hands move to untie his bowtie before going to work on his buttons. While I'm doing that, he shrugs out of his jacket. His hands are all over me the moment it's removed. Pushing his shirt off his shoulders and down his arms, I pull out of the kiss to trail my lips over his chest before I fall to my knees. I look up at him through my lashes as my fingers undo the buckle on his belt.

The moment I get the button on his trousers undone I slide down the zipper. He growls when I reach into his boxer briefs and wrap my hand around his hard, impressive length. Hooking his thumbs into the side of his pants, he pushes them down around his thighs before cupping my face and drawing it towards him.

I work him over with my tongue before sliding my lips around his erection. I don't stop until it hits the back of my throat. He releases a primal sound, tilting his head back in the process. I have no gag reflex so I can take most of him in my mouth.

'Fuck, you suck a mean cock,' he groans as he gently pumps into my mouth. I wrap my fingers tightly around the base of his shaft and use my other hand to gently massage his balls. I love that I can please him like this, it turns me on just as much as it does him. With my clients I tried my best so it would be over quickly. With Brock I do it because I want to give him as much pleasure as I can. He goes out of his way to please me.

'Jesus, Jade,' he grates out a few minutes later as his body starts to shudder. I know he's close, so I pick up the pace, sliding my lips down his shaft, swirling my tongue at the same time. It only takes a few seconds before he starts groaning loudly. After a few short thrusts his body stills, but I continue to suck until I've milked him of every last drop.

He places his hands under my arms, pulling me to my feet and devouring my lips. His hands are everywhere again and a moment later I hear that familiar tear as my panties are ripped from my body. He's ruined five pairs since our trip to the lingerie store. If he keeps this up, we'll need to make another visit.

Reaching behind me, he unclasps my strapless bra with one hand, tossing it across the room. Without breaking the kiss he walks me backwards to the bed. When the back of my knees come into contact with the mattress, he gently lays me down.

Standing to his full height, he gazes down at me, a smile gracing his face. 'Do you have any idea how breathtakingly beautiful you are?' Unlike the other men, his compliments don't make me feel uncomfortable—they make me feel beautiful, desired.

Kneeling beside the bed, he places a kiss on my stomach as his hand skims over my skin until it reaches my breasts. His other arm moves behind my knee, lifting my leg so his lips can trail a path down my inner thigh, stopping before he reaches the good part. I'm desperate to have his mouth on me.

He hooks my leg over his shoulder and lifts the other one to repeat his kisses. He appears to be taking his sweet time tonight, like he's savouring every moment. It only makes my need for him intensify. Every word, every touch, every kiss, every look—I'm intoxicated by him.

'I need you, Brock,' I whimper as my hands grip his hair. I need him so much I'm aching.

'All in good time, beautiful.' After running his tongue along my pelvic bone, he blows hot air over my sensitive flesh. If he's trying to kill me, he's succeeding.

Using all my strength, I push his face forward until it connects with my vagina. *Enough of the teasing.* He chuckles against my skin, causing a vibration.

'Please,' I beg.

'I like it when you beg me,' he says as his tongue licks a path up my centre, making me moan. 'I love those sounds you make too. It drives me crazy.'

'You drive me crazy,' I whisper. He lets out a small laugh before slipping a finger inside me. That's exactly what I need. I push my hips forwards as he withdraws from me before adding a second finger, burying them both deep inside me. 'Oh God.' I tug on his hair, pushing his face even closer. I can't get enough of him. He has spectacular oral skills.

He withdraws his fingers again, sliding them down between my arse cheeks. I want him to touch me there again. When he did it the first time, the orgasm was so intense I

212

thought I was going to pass out. I swore it was something I'd never do—that's why I made it a hard limit. But I want to give Brock a piece of me that nobody else has ever had.

I hope he takes the hint when I push my arse into his hand. He groans against my clit before running his fingers around the hole and inserting a tip. He stills, giving my body time to adjust to the invasion before pushing in a little further. The combination of that and his tongue lapping at my clit brings me to the brink within seconds.

'Brock,' I moan tugging on his hair again. 'I'm going to … I'm—'

'Christ,' Brock growls and I let out a scream as my orgasm takes hold. Again I'm seeing stars as the sensation reaches every nerve ending, making my toes curl. While his finger is still inserted in my arse, he pushes his tongue deep inside me as my muscles continue to pulse.

When he's finished he raises his head and licks his lips before giving me the most majestic smile. I snake back on the bed as he crawls towards me.

'I'm going to take that sweet arse of yours one day,' he says as his mouth meets mine. I smile against his lips. Did he just read my mind? *Bring it on, Mr Weston*. In the short time we've been together he's turned my thoughts about sex completely around. He's taken my personal idea of hell and transformed it into something magical. What I feel when I'm with him is like nothing I've ever experienced. He's wiped away all the shame that once consumed me and replaced it with something beautiful. I no longer feel used and dirty—I feel desired and wanted.

Once he's settled between my legs, he gazes down at me and smiles. Running the back of his hand tenderly down the side of my face, he slowly eases inside me. My eyes flutter shut and my head presses back into the pillow as he pushes all the way in, filling me completely. I feel so connected to him when we're together like this. It's like we become one.

'Open your eyes,' he commands, and I do. My eyes lock with his as he draws back before pushing all the way back in. 'I love you, Jade.'

I pull his mouth down to mine. My kiss is full of passion, conveying everything I can't say. His words were spoken with not only sincerity, but confidence. Most importantly, he didn't say he *thinks* he loves me this time, he said he *did*. I clench my eyes shut to stop the tears of joy from escaping. For the first time in my life, my empty heart is so full, I think it's going to burst.

I'm almost afraid to admit this to myself, but I'm hopelessly in love with him too.

CHAPTER TWENTY-TWO

BROCK

We spend the majority of Sunday in bed, only getting up to eat and shower. Even though our relationship is moving along fast, it feels right—I'm not going to fight it. I'm actually looking forward to the journey ahead. I'm surprisingly comfortable with how things between us are progressing. I don't want to leave this little bubble that Jade and I have created over the past week. It's been absolute bliss. With every day that passes I see her blossoming into the person she's always wanted to be … the person she was meant to be. It's such a beautiful thing to witness.

But I have to head back into the office. As much as I hate the idea, I don't have a choice, because I'm falling behind. Amy having to courier over some contracts for me to sign forced my hand. I can't continue working from here. Before this week, I hadn't taken a day off since I started running the company.

There's still no word from M, which concerns me. No news is good news they say, but that rule doesn't apply where she's concerned. Because there are no rules where M's concerned. Pulling my phone out of my pocket, I decide to call Rupert. Maybe he can give me some insight. He replied to my text yesterday morning, giving me Jade's number and asking if everything was okay. I told him it was, but didn't elaborate further.

'Rupert,' I say when he picks up. 'It's Brock, can you talk?'

'Of course. How's Jade? After your text, she's been on my mind.'

'She's doing great.' I feel myself smiling as I talk about her. 'She's happy, Rupert. We both are.'

'I'm pleased to hear that. She deserves happiness. She's been through a lot.'

'I know. I'll do my best to make sure she gets it,' I tell him, and I will. 'Her happiness means everything to me.' The line goes quiet. I hope he doesn't think I'm not blowing smoke up his arse, because I'm not. I mean every word.

'Have you heard any more from M?' he asks, changing the subject.

'No. That's why I'm calling. I was wondering if anything had been mentioned at your end.'

'All's quiet here. She's made me her personal gopher since Rocco can't drive with his broken wrist.' He chuckles. 'You really did a number on him.'

'He had a gun pointed at my head. That fucker deserved it and a lot more.'

'No arguments here,' he says. 'I can't stand that guy. I'm glad someone was able to bring him down a peg or two.'

'If either of them set foot on my property again, I won't be so kind. I won't take any chances when it comes to Jade's safety.'

'Just be prepared for anything. She won't let this one go, I know it.'

'I'll protect Jade with everything I have. She's not going back there. Ever.'

'I'm glad to hear that.'

'Let me know if you hear anything, will you?' At least I know I have him working on the inside. It's something I guess.

'Of course. I'll keep my eyes and ears open. Tell Jade I said hello.'

'I will, mate. She misses you. Once things settle down, will you come to the house and visit her?'

'I'd like that,' he says.

*

I begin to miss Jade the moment I walk into the office. I offered to bring her with me, but she declined. It was probably for the best. I know I wouldn't have gotten much work done with her here. I left one of my best men at the house, he's highly trained to handle any situation and under strict instructions not to let Jade out of his sight. She didn't seem impressed about him being there, but there was no way I was leaving her alone.

'Amy,' I say into the intercom on the desk. 'Can you get Natalie to come up to my office when she's free?'

'Yes, Mr Weston,' she replies, clearing her throat. I chuckle to myself when I realise why. I'm a changed man and in time she'll see that. Leaning back in my chair, I run my hands through my hair. Fuck me. I really am. Realisation of how much my life has changed in such a short time hits home. The love of a good woman can do wonders for a man's philandering ways, I suppose.

I fucking hope she loves me. If not, then I pray she will in time. She feels something for me, I know that much. It was a huge step for me to even admit that to her, but I needed her to know I'm all in, because, by Christ, I am.

'You wanted to see me?' Natalie says when she enters my office. I can see that familiar glint in her eyes as she approaches the desk. When she licks her lips, I have to adjust the tie around my neck. I'm surprised I'm not the slightest bit tempted to go there again.

'I didn't call you up here for that,' I say, clearing my throat. 'I have a girlfriend.'

'Then it's true,' she says in a disappointed tone.

'What's true?'

'The talk around the office. They're saying you've finally settled down.'

'I haven't exactly settled down,' I say with a chuckle, 'but yes, I'm in a committed relationship.'

'Lucky girl,' I hear her mumble under her breath as she takes the seat opposite me. But I'm the lucky one.

'I need a favour,' I ask, trying to change the subject. Things are getting awkward. 'I want you to go over the accounts for the last ten years and see if you can find anything on a Melody Sinclair.'

'Sure, I can do that.' I watch as she jots the name down on a notepad. 'When do you need the information by?'

'As soon as you can get it.' Before I even knew who she was the name sounded familiar. The fact that she's associated with my father, I wouldn't be surprised if she shows up on the books somewhere. My father's a snake and I can practically guarantee he's used the company's funds to pay for his whores.

'Is there anything else I can do for you before I leave?' she asks with a dash of hopefulness in her voice. The old Brock Weston would've had her on her knees and under the desk in a heartbeat, but all that's changed. I've changed. Wonders will never cease. I'm committed to one woman, and couldn't be happier.

My phone chimes and I pull it out of my pocket as Natalie leaves. I smile when I see a message from Jade.

Jade: *This man is following me everywhere! EVERYWHERE!!!*

I chuckle. That's exactly what I asked him to do.

Brock: *He's just doing his job sweetheart.*

Jade: *Well, it's driving me crazy. The only place I can be alone is in the bathroom. I'm surprised he didn't follow me in here as well. I bet you anything he's waiting outside the door. I've been hiding in here for an hour. I'm playing Candy Crush on my phone. FYI, I hate Candy Crush. I suck at it. Stupid candy.*

I laugh out loud at her reply. She's so adorable.

Brock: *I'd give anything to be locked in there with you right now. The things I'd do to you ...*

Jesus, just thinking about it is giving me a hard-on.

Jade: *I wish you were in here with me too. Tease!!!*

Brock: *I'll make it up to you when I get home. I promise. I'll bend you over the bathtub and have my way with you. I've been thinking about your heavenly pussy all day.*

I groan to myself. Now my dick is so hard it's straining against my pants.

Jade: *Oh God. Now I'm thinking of you doing exactly that. Can you come home for a quickie? Having you here would be so much better than playing this damn game. It's giving me high blood pressure.*

I laugh out loud again, adjusting my aching cock at the same time. This woman is going to be the death of me. As I go to type my response, the phone chimes again.

Jade: *OMG! He just knocked on the door to check I was still in here. Where did you find this guy ... the Gestapo???*

Brock: *I wish I could come home, but I have a meeting in twenty minutes. Be patient with him. He's only doing what I asked him to do, and that's keep you safe. I need to know you're going to be okay when I'm not there to look after you.*

Jade: *I know, and I appreciate that. I just miss you. x*

Brock: *I miss you too, sweetheart. x*

It's official, I'm pathetic. I do fucking miss her though.

*

As busy as I am, the day seems to drag on forever. I'm desperate to get back to my girl. Going home to that big house was never something I looked forward to in the past. Having her waiting for me has changed that.

Jade texts me constantly throughout the day. She has me in fits of laughter at one stage; I can tell she's bored out of her mind. I hate that she's cooped up in the house all day. I'm going to have to find something stimulating for her to do until this mess with M blows over.

As much as she says she hates it, I think she's becoming addicted to Candy Crush. She rings me, at one stage, squealing because she's gotten past a hard level she'd be stuck on for over an hour. 'Woo hoo! I kick level forty-seven's sweet little candy arse,' are her exact words.

Amy buzzes me as I'm getting ready to leave, to say Natalie wants to speak with me. When she's seated in my office, she leans forwards, passing me a thick manila folder.

'I'm guessing you found something,' I say, opening it.

'I did. I went back over the accounts for the past ten years, but when her name kept popping up so frequently, I dug a little further. She's been on the company payroll for the last eighteen years. Until today, I'd never heard of her. Who is this woman?'

'A friend of my father's.' I'm not getting into the technicalities of the situation with my staff.

'A very wealthy friend,' she retorts. 'In the past eighteen years, she's been paid close to ten million dollars.'

'She fucking what?' I seethe as I flick through the paperwork in front of me. There was an initial payment of one million dollars, then they ranged anywhere from five to ten thousand dollars a week. It doesn't take a genius to figure out exactly what those payments were for, especially given my father's history. My blood boils at the thought of him paying so much for his whores, and with company funds, no less. My poor mother. Maybe it's time I let her know just how despicably low her husband is.

After thanking Natalie for the information, I ask her to keep this between us. I know I can trust her. I'm a lot more easy-going than my father and I have a good rapport with my staff. Maxwell has a reputation of being a tyrant around here.

My good mood has vanished. I travel down in the lift to the underground carpark where my driver is waiting. I can't believe my father's spent so much money on sex over the years. I need to plan my attack carefully, but I won't be letting this go.

This shit has to stop.

*

I've calmed down somewhat by the time I arrive home. Well, not really, I'm fucking furious with my father. Everything in me wants to call my mother and tell her, but at the same time

I don't want to hurt her. I'm not even sure if she's aware this has been going on. Maybe that's why I've never told her about the things I witnessed when I was growing up.

My father used me as a ruse for years. He'd take me everywhere with him so my mother wouldn't get suspicious of him leaving the house so often. We'd always end up at the same hotel. He'd sit me in front of the television, surrounded by junk food, before disappearing into one of the bedrooms with one of his whores. If I asked questions, he'd always say it was a top-secret meeting, or secret spy stuff, which, as a kid, I thought was super cool. As I got older though, I soon realised it was all a lie.

Growing up, my dad was my hero. I wanted to be exactly like him. That's until I found out he was a lying, cheating snake, and then I wanted to be nothing like him. Over the years my hate for him grew. I hated him for his dishonesty, but more than anything I hated him for having such disregard for my mother, their marriage and our family as a whole.

I sit in the back of the limo and take a few deep breaths before I exit. I don't want to be in a bad mood around Jade. I've been dying to come home to her all day, and I hate that my father has put a dampener on that. One day karma will come back to bite him on the arse for all of his past indiscretions. I only hope I'm around to see him get his comeuppance.

After placing my briefcase in my office, I head to the gym. I can hear loud music pumping through the walls so I know that's where she is. I find Brad leaning against the door frame watching her when I round the corner. It makes my already high blood pressure spike. I'm not paying him to perve on my girl, fucker.

When I'm standing behind him, I clear my throat. He immediately spins around to face me.

'Are you right there?' I ask, raising my eyebrow in annoyance. The venom in my voice is obvious.

'Sorry, boss,' he mumbles, bowing his head. He's lucky I don't knock him the fuck out.

'You can go now.'

'Do you want me back here in the morning?'

'I'll let you know. I may have a change of plans.' If he wasn't the best man for the job, I'd say hell fucking no, but the fact is, I know he could look after her in any situation that may arise. That's my main priority right now.

I growl when he takes one more look at Jade over his shoulder. I can't believe how protective I feel towards her.

'Damn,' he says shaking his head. 'You're one lucky bastard.'

'You know where the door is.' I trust this man with my life. He's been working for my company for years. I know he'd never do anything inappropriate where Jade's concerned, but I'm not comfortable with him admiring her either. She's for my eyes only.

The moment he's out of sight, I turn to her. She's so engrossed in working out, she's oblivious to what just went on. She looks so fine in those tiny gym shorts. No wonder Brad couldn't keep his eyes off her. I stand there for a moment, drinking her in. She's doing squats and holding her arms out, weights clutched in both hands. I hate to interrupt her workout, but I have something else in mind for her.

I'm a few metres away before she even notices me approach and her face lights up as soon as she sees me. The sight hits me straight in the chest. Placing the weights on the floor, she launches herself into my arms.

'I missed you today,' she says as her lips meet mine. God, I missed her too. As much as I hated being away from her, I could get used to coming home to a greeting like this every day.

I pull her legs up until they're wrapped around my waist and walk towards the door.

'Where are you taking me? I haven't finished my workout.'

'I have a better workout in mind. I believe we have a date in the bathroom. You bent over the bath and me buried balls deep inside you.'

'Oh that sounds amazing,' she says, nipping at my neck.

CHAPTER TWENTY-THREE

JADE

I'm sprawled out on top of Brock in satisfied bliss. After he bent me over the bathtub as promised, he filled the tub with warm water and bubbles and we both climbed in.

'I can't believe in the six years I've lived in this house, I've never taken a bath,' he says.

'I love soaking in a warm bath. This is the first time I've ever shared one though.'

'We should do this more often, it's nice.'

'We should.' I raise my head off his chest and smile at him. He threads his fingers in my hair before pulling my face to his.

'How would you feel about going to Josh's place for the day tomorrow?' he says when the kiss ends.

'Really?' I ask. 'You're getting rid of the Gestapo?'

He chuckles before he replies. 'No, the Gestapo stays. But if you're with Josh, I can get the Gestapo—I mean Brad—to hang back.'

'Really?' I grin. I like Joshua. I'd love to spend the day with him and get to know him better.

'Really,' Brock replies. 'I hate the thought of you being cooped up in this house.'

'You're the best,' I say, wrapping my arms around his neck.

'I know.' His modesty makes me laugh.

His lips meet mine again and when he deepens the kiss, I shift my legs so I'm straddling him. I'm trying so hard not to get attached to him, but I'm failing miserably. Every second we're together just makes me crave him more. I'll never tire of these feelings. It's like nothing I've ever known. How am I going to cope if this thing between us doesn't last?

Brock's hands move down to my waist. He lifts my body slightly before sliding the head of his penis inside me. We moan in unison when he pushes all the way in, filling me completely. I rock my hips gently against him, never once taking my lips off his.

This is different to the other times. It's not primal or desperate, it's beautiful. Two souls coming together as one. This is not sex … this is making love.

*

'So, do you have a boyfriend?' I ask Joshua when we sit down for lunch.

I've had the best morning and we've become friends fast. His looks are similar but different to Brock's, if that makes sense, though their personalities are miles apart. Joshua has a soft and vulnerable side to him. A big teddy bear. He reminds me a lot of Theo. Whereas Brock is cocky and exudes confidence.

'No, I don't have time for that.'

'Well, you should make time. You're a great catch. Being alone sucks. Trust me, I know. Until your brother came along, I was very familiar with that feeling.'

'I'm a great catch?' he replies, shaking his head. 'Says the girl who's only met me twice.'

I laugh. I knew within minutes of meeting him he was a sweetheart. Don't ask me how, I just did.

'I'm a pretty good judge of character. Hey, what about Theo? I think you two would be perfect for each other.'

'Oh, we're playing matchmaker now?'

I shrug. Of course I'm playing matchmaker.

'I just think everyone should have someone special in their life. Your brother is the best thing that's ever happened to me.'

'I've never seen him like this before,' he admits. 'I'm so glad you've found each other. I honestly thought he'd never settle down. I couldn't have chosen a better sister-in-law if I tried.'

'You're getting a bit ahead of yourself there,' I say with a nervous laugh.

'He's not going to let you go, you know that right? He's crazy about you, Jade.'

'I'm crazy about him too,' I say as my eyes lower and a blush creeps onto my cheeks. Why is it so hard for me to talk about things like this? Perhaps it's because I've never felt this way about anyone before. 'I'm lucky to have him in my life.'

'He's lucky to have you too.' When Joshua reaches across the table and places his hand on mine, I give him an appreciative smile. *Is Brock lucky to have me?* Sometimes I wonder about that. He has so much to offer, me not so much.

We are both silent for a few moments. I'm not sure either of us know what to say.

'So, about Theo,' I finally blurt, trying to divert the conversation away from me.

'What about him?'

227

'He's hot, he's single, and he's sweet, just like you.' When I wiggle my eyebrows at him, he laughs.

'I don't know,' he says with a shrug.

'Not your type?'

'He's so my type, but am I his?'

'Are you kidding me? I know you have a mirror in this place, because I just cleaned it.' I'm a little OCD like that. 'You're gorgeous. If I wasn't with your brother, and you—you know—didn't prefer men, I'd so do you.'

He throws back his head and laughs. 'You're fucking adorable, you know that right?'

*

'Are you drunk?' Brock asks when he draws back from the kiss. I'm not what you'd call drunk, but I am definitely tipsy.

'Just a little,' I reply, holding my thumb and forefinger up and squeezing them together.

'What the fuck, Josh. You got her drunk,' he calls out across the bar.

'Hey. Don't speak to him like that, he's been teaching me how to make cocktails.' I giggle when I say that word, playfully poking him in the chest. 'Mmm ... *cock*tails.' I grab Brock by the crotch.

'Jesus, Jade,' he gasps, removing my hand.

'You're no fun,' I say, pouting.

'I'll give you plenty of fun when we get home.' His eyes slightly narrow when he speaks. He's obviously not impressed that I'm kind of intoxicated. It wasn't my intention, but some of the cocktails we made were so yummy, I had to drink them. 'Bringing you here was a mistake,' he says, shaking his head.

'Bringing me here was a brilliant idea. Can I come back tomorrow? Pretty please?' I fold my hands together as though praying. I see him fighting to suppress his smile as he looks down at my clutched hands before moving his gaze back to my face.

'Maybe.'

'Josh,' I say, looking at him for backup.

When he comes out from behind the counter to stand beside me, he drapes his arm around my shoulder. 'I'm not sure if I want to give her back,' he says. 'I think I wanna keep her.' You can tell he's trying to get his brother to bite.

'What the fuck?' Brock snaps, pulling me to him and placing me possessively by his side. 'Like fuck you're keeping her, she's *mine*.' Mission accomplished.

When he takes the bait, Joshua and I both burst out laughing. Brock growls when he realises what just happened.

'Seriously, though,' Joshua says when he finally stops laughing, 'you've got a keeper there, bro. She cleaned my apartment and cooked for me.'

'You put her to work?' Brock frowns.

'I offered. He tried to stop me,' I say in Joshua's defence, because he did. Unlike his brother, Joshua doesn't have a maid to pick up after him. His apartment is quite spacious. It's about the same size as mine. It only took me a few hours to get it spick and span. He's very tidy, but the place was in need of a good vacuum and dusting. I'm not sure if that's the mothering side of me coming out, or the fact that I was forced into cleaning at some of the foster homes I lived in, not to mention severely punished if it wasn't done to their satisfaction. I've had a phobia about mess ever since.

'I had a really nice time here today, Brock.'

'I'm glad,' he says, before wrapping me in his arms and kissing the top of my head. 'You can come back here tomorrow,' he whispers, so only I can hear.

My man is the best.

CHAPTER TWENTY-FOUR

BROCK

Jade and I fall into a comfortable routine. It's ironic how normal it feels to have her in my life. During the days she's with Josh at the club. They've become very close, which I love. They're the two most important people in my life, so I need them to get along. It's like we've been together for years, not a few weeks. She feels like a part of me now, in every sense of the word. Not having her around just wouldn't feel right. I love going to bed with her every night and waking up with her every morning.

After collecting her on the way home on Friday, we head back to my place. I've been taking the Lamborghini to work since Jade has been spending the weekdays with my brother, it's just easier. There's still no word from M. You'd think the longer she stayed away, the more relaxed I'd feel. Sadly, that's not the case. The silence only seems to put me more on edge with every passing day.

'I'm looking forward to having you all to myself over the weekend,' Jade says as we pull into the driveway.

'Me too, sweetheart.' I reach for her hand. I've been rushing through my work all week just to get home to her sooner.

The moment I press the button to open the automatic garage door, my phone rings. My mood sours when I see my father's number on the screen. I still haven't confronted him about paying for his whores with company funds. Or the fact that he's been screwing around behind my mother's back for the past eighteen years. I'll pounce when the time's right and he won't know what hit him.

'Father,' I say with disdain in my voice.

'Don't use that tone with me, boy,' he spits.

'What do you want? I'm busy.' I look over at Jade and smile. I need to get her in the house so I can bury myself in her heavenly pussy. Even though I had her before leaving this morning, she's still been consuming my thoughts all day. She's addictive.

'I need a favour.' Of course he does. He'd never ring to see how I was, or just to say hi. Prick.

'What?'

'I need you to head over to Phelan & Sons to sign the contract. I'm stuck in a meeting.'

'Can't you reschedule?'

'It's a five-million-dollar account. We can't afford to screw this up.' As if that would worry him. It's only half the amount of the money he's squandered away on his whores.

'You should've thought of that when you made the appointment,' I snap. No wonder this business wasn't growing until I took over. Incompetent fucker. 'You only have a handful of clients to look after.'

'Are you going to do it or not?'

I exhale a frustrated breath before I answer. Do I even have a choice? Unlike him, I pride myself on professionalism. 'What time is the meeting?'

'Six.'

'That's in thirty fucking minutes. I'll be lucky to make it to the other side of town in this traffic. You couldn't have given me more notice?'

'I'll get my secretary to call them and let them know you're on your way.'

'Next time don't make appointments you can't keep,' I hiss before disconnecting the call.

'I've gotta head back out,' I say pinching the bridge of my nose. 'It won't take long.'

'That's fine. I can get a start on dinner. Is everything okay?'

'I'm not leaving you here on your own, Jade.' I can't take her with me either. If I drive her back to Josh's, I'll never make the meeting. Shit. 'And yes everything is okay,' I add, trying not let her see the inner battle I'm having with myself.

*

JADE

Brock was apprehensive about leaving me, but I'm fine being alone. It's not like M would even know I was here by myself. Nevertheless, he made me promise to keep my phone on me at all times, and left strict instructions to call him if there was a problem. He said he'd keep his phone on during the meeting just in case. He's worrying for nothing.

Once I get all the food prepped for dinner, I decide to head upstairs to soak in the bath. Brock won't be home for at least another hour, so it's too early to start cooking. It's nice to be able to cook for someone other than myself.

I shove my phone into my pocket before heading to the main staircase. I've only climbed the first few steps when someone knocks on the front door. My heart drops into the pit of my stomach. It couldn't be Brock, and even if it was, he wouldn't be knocking.

'Jade, it's Maxwell Weston. Are you in there?'

Brock's father. What is he doing here? After the way he treated me the other night, he's the last person I want to see. My heart is hammering against my chest as I climb a few more stairs.

'Jade!' he calls out again, as his knocking intensifies. Even though there's urgency in his voice I have no intention of answering the door. 'Please, if you're home, answer the door, Brock's been in an accident.'

One hand goes to my mouth and the other reaches for the bannister as my legs threaten to give way. What does he mean? When I'm able to put one foot in front of the other, I hastily make my way to the door.

'Is Brock okay?' I ask in a panic as I fling the front door open. My body is trembling and my legs feel like jelly.

Brock's father eyes me sceptically. 'You need to come with me,' he replies, reaching for my elbow.

'I'm not going anywhere with you.' I pull my arm out of his grasp.

He pinches the bridge of his nose as his eyes meet mine. That's a trait Brock has picked up from his father. 'It's no secret I don't agree with this situation between you and my son, but he's asking for you, so I'm prepared to take you to him.'

'Where is he? What happened—is he okay?' I can hear the desperation in my voice. I need to know if he's going to be okay.

'I'll fill you in on the way. We don't have much time.'

My gut is telling me not to go anywhere with this man, but my heart is screaming to be with Brock. I hesitate only briefly. Closing the door behind me, I follow Maxwell down the front stairs. When he opens the back door of the waiting limousine, I climb in. I scoot over as far as I can so I'm not sitting anywhere near him. He may be Brock's father, but that doesn't mean I have to like him.

'Please tell me what you know about Brock,' I beg as soon as he's seated and the limo starts to pull away. 'Is he hurt seriously? Is he going to be all right?' A small sob escapes me. Please let him be okay. I can't lose him, he's all I have.

'You're shaking,' Brock's father says as his gaze moves down to my hands, which are clutched in my lap.

'I just need to know he's going to be okay,' I cry, wiping the tears from my eyes.

'Here, drink this. It will help calm you.' I watch as he pours a small amount of amber liquid from the crystal decanter into two glasses.

Taking the glass he offers, I drink the liquid down in one gulp. I feel the burn as it slides down the back of my throat, but I welcome it. When I hand him back the glass, I notice his is untouched.

'Please tell me what happened,' I plead as my watery eyes meet his. I'm confused when I see a smile play at his lips. There's nothing funny about this situation. Doesn't he care about his son?

Panic rises within me as a woozy feeling spreads throughout my body. A tightness stretches across my chest and my breathing becomes laboured. I try to move but my arms and legs are heavy and weighted. I open my mouth to ask what's happening to me, but the words come out slurred.

Everything feels fuzzy. I've been slightly drunk before, but it's never felt like this and certainly not from just one drink.

I hear Brock's father laugh beside me. 'You stupid, naive bitch.'

I attempt to turn my head in his direction, but I can't seem to make it move. This man is worse than I thought. My eyes begin to droop as I struggle to keep them open. I feel like I'm slipping into unconsciousness. I try to call out to Brock, but I can't. Nothing comes out except a strangled sound.

Just as my eyes are closing, the partition in the limousine lowers.

'Hello, my dear,' M says. 'I knew when the timing was right, I'd get you back. You're going to regret the day you tried to run from me.'

CHAPTER TWENTY-FIVE

BROCK

The meeting goes longer than anticipated. I'm on edge the whole time, constantly looking down at my watch. The thought of Jade being home alone makes me uneasy. I should've brought her with me. I've had no word from her so I presume all is okay. Nevertheless, I'm busting to get home.

The second I'm out of that office I'm dialling her number. I'm concerned when she doesn't answer, but not alarmed. I'm sure there's a logical explanation. When I try another three times and she doesn't pick up, I start to panic.

I continuously call on my drive home, but nothing. I find myself driving a little more recklessly than usual, weaving in and out of traffic. The uneasy feeling in my gut has me desperate to get to her. I'm hoping it's just my overactive imagination, but something is telling me it's not. The longer I'm delayed in city traffic, the more agitated I become. Why isn't she fucking picking up? I told her to keep her phone on her at all times. I bang my hand against the steering wheel in frustration when again there's no answer.

I finally pull into my driveway, screeching to a stop at the front of the house. Taking the stairs two at time, I bash on the front door, calling out her name, while frantically fishing my keys out of my pocket.

'Jade!' I scream loudly when I enter the house. My place is so huge, she could be fucking anywhere. When there's no reply I head to the kitchen, since it seems to be her favourite place. The food for dinner sitting covered on the countertop somewhat calms me. She has to be in the house somewhere. I have a good mind to throw her over my knee and spank that sweet arse of hers for not following my orders.

I check the gym while I'm downstairs, but again, there's no sign of her. My adrenaline rises as I take the main stairs two at a time. 'Jade,' I call, praying she's soaking in a bath or in the shower and unable to hear me.

When I find the bedroom and bathroom empty, I start to panic again. I call out her name a few more times as I rush back down the stairs and head towards the back deck. She isn't in the pool either.

Where the fuck is she? Pulling my phone out of my pocket, my trembling hands dial her number. When there is still no answer, I feel like I'm going to throw up. Something is wrong. *Something is terribly wrong.*

*

I spend the next thirty minutes searching every inch of my house and surrounding grounds. She's nowhere to be seen. I'm fucking beside myself by this point. I spoke with Josh twenty minutes ago and he hasn't heard from her. He's on his way over. I'm grateful because I'm going out of my mind. Surely she wouldn't just up and leave without telling me? What if M has her? Jesus.

After trying her phone for the umpteenth time, I decide to give Rupert a call.

'Rupert,' I blurt as soon as he picks up. 'Jade's gone, have you heard from her?'

'What? No. Where did she go?'

'If I knew I'd fucking be there.'

'Calm down. Did you two have a disagreement?'

'Fuck, no. Everything between us is fine. I had to go out for a short time, and when I returned, she wasn't here. She's not answering her phone. What if they have her, Rupert?'

'Shit. I haven't heard anything. I'll head over to the house and see what I can find out.'

'I'll meet you there.'

'No,' Rupert snaps. 'If they do have her, we need to be smart about this. Going off all half-cocked isn't going to get us anywhere. It's only going to put Jade in more danger.'

'Fuck.' He's right, but sitting around and doing nothing when she could be in danger isn't an option.

'I'll call you back once I've scoped out M's. Call me in the meantime if you hear from her.'

Ending the call, I place the phone in my pocket. I close my eyes and chant a silent prayer: *Please let her be okay.*

Thank fuck Josh soon arrives to stop me from heading over there, because that's exactly what I want to do. I haven't stopped pacing. There's still no word from her. Rupert calls to tell me she wasn't at her apartment when he went there to check and that he was heading to M's house. I call Theo as soon as Rupert confirms Jade isn't at her apartment. He's the only other contact I have for her, and when I tell him she's vanished, he offers immediately to help.

Everything in me wants to go over to M's and tear that house apart until I find her, but what if she isn't there? I don't want to alert M to the fact that Jade may be somewhere alone and vulnerable, even though my gut tells me she is behind this. Jade wouldn't walk away from me, I know it.

When Theo arrives, Josh and I leap into the car with him to drive blindly around the city, hoping to catch a glimpse of her. My heart picks up whenever I see someone with long brown hair, but it drops the minute I realise it isn't her.

It's no fucking use—we won't find her this way—but I feel powerless doing nothing. If she's not at M's, where the fuck is she?

I feel like I'm going out of my mind.

*

It's some ungodly hour in the morning when Theo, Josh and I finally give up and head back to my house. I tell Josh and Theo to go home, but they refuse to leave me alone. I appreciate that. We brainstorm ideas for a few hours, but it's futile. We have no leads and nothing to go on.

Josh and Theo fall asleep on the sofa, but not me. As exhausted as I am, I can't sleep. I won't rest until I have her back. I clutch my head in my hands as images of her flood my mind. I don't know what I'll do if I don't find her soon.

What if I never find her?

I'm jolted from my thoughts by my phone. Looking down at the screen, I see it's Rupert calling. I hope he has some good news.

'Brock.'

'Rupert, do you have anything?'

'Yes.'

My adrenaline picks up and I bolt upright in my seat. 'You found her?' I ask hopefully.

'I think so.'

'What do you mean you fucking think so?' I snap. 'You either did or you didn't.'

'Calm down.'

'How the fuck can I calm down? Where is she? Is she okay?' I'm usually in control, but right now I'm a fucking mess.

'It only dawned on me a few hours ago to do a track on her phone. I had a program installed when I was looking after her. Just in case something ever went wrong.'

Jesus, why didn't I think of that? 'And?'

'M's address came up.' I fucking knew it.

'I'm coming over there,' I say standing.

'No.'

'You can't fucking stop me, Rupert. If she's there, I'll tear the place apart until I find her.'

'Listen,' he says, and I can hear he's trying to remain calm, 'her phone is there, but that doesn't necessarily mean she is. Use your common sense. You can't come over here like a charging bull. It won't do her any good.'

'So we're going to just sit around and do nothing?' Like hell. She's not safe with that woman and Rupert knows that as well as I do.

'This is exactly why I didn't call you earlier. You're too emotionally invested. I have a plan, but you need to trust me on this.'

I rub my hand over my face in frustration. He's right, I'm no good to her like this.

Get your shit together, Weston, your girl needs you.

I'll hear him out, but if I'm not happy with his idea I'm going to take charge. Situations like this are what I do for a living.

'What's your plan?'

'As I said, Jade's phone is there, but that doesn't necessarily mean she is.' He's right, M would be crazy to leave her in that house where we could easily find her. 'However, I do happen to know there's a passageway that leads to a secret room. I stumbled across the floorplans a few years ago. If Jade is in the house, my guess is that's where M's keeping her.'

'She's there, I know it.' Although I'm relieved we finally have something to go on, my concern for Jade only deepens. I saw firsthand how that bitch manhandled Jade that day she came to retrieve her, and that was in front of other people. God only knows what she'd do when they're alone.

'Don't get ahead of yourself,' he says. 'There's a good possibility, but I won't know until I look.'

'So go and fucking look.'

'You know as well as I do that I can't just barge in there. We have to be smart. I've been parked out in the street for the past few hours, waiting for everyone to leave and for M to retire for the night. I'm getting ready to go in now. That's why I'm calling. If I need backup, I'll let you know. If something happens and I don't come out, at least you know M is responsible for Jade's disappearance. I know you won't rest until you find her.' His voice cracks slightly as he speaks.

'Jesus, Rupert.'

'I'll call you as soon as I know.'

'Please do, and for God's sake, be careful.'

Despite what he says, there was no way I can just sit here and do nothing. I head straight for the car.

*

Twenty minutes after Rupert called me I'm parked not far from M's house. There's still no word from him. I'll give him ten more minutes, and then I'm going in.

A few minutes pass before my phone rings and I jump. I'm on edge.

'I found her,' Rupert says when I answer. I can't explain the emotions I feel when I hear those words. Thank Christ.

'How is she? Is she okay?' I ask, exiting the car and walking towards the front gates of the property. The house is bathed in darkness.

'She's not in a good way. I'm going to need you to call an ambulance. I'm getting ready to move her now.'

'What the fuck? What do you mean she's not in a good way? What did that bitch do to her?' Jesus. I'll fucking kill her.

'She'll be okay. Don't panic. I think she's been drugged, because she's barely conscious. I've gotta get her out of here before we're discovered. Can I rely on you to get the paramedics? She really needs to be seen to as soon as possible.'

'Of course. I'll do anything for her, you know that.'

My hands are trembling as I dial triple zero. I can't give them any more information other than what Rupert told me, but they assure me help was on its way. My heart beats furiously against my rib cage as I pace outside the wrought iron gates, waiting for Rupert to emerge with Jade.

Dread fills me when I see a light come on in the upper level of the house, followed by another. M must be awake. Instinctively, I set about climbing the eight-foot-high fence. As I'm sprinting down the long driveway towards the house, I hear the sirens in the distance. Help is on its way.

I hear the distinct sound of a gunshot coming from inside the house as I near the front door.

I freeze.

*

BROCK

I recover quickly and, after removing my gun from my shoulder holster, I reach for the doorhandle. By some grace of God, it's unlocked. *Thank you, Rupert.* My heart is beating out of my chest, but I try to remain focused. This is the kind of thing I'm trained for. Unlike in other situations, though, my whole existence seems to be riding on the outcome of this one.

Please let Jade be okay.

The foyer is bathed in darkness, but I can see light streaming from a room at the back of the house. I head quietly in that direction, stopping briefly when I reach the doorway. I take a deep breath and raise my gun.

With my back to the wall, I peer inside the room. My eyes immediately scan the area. Jade is lying on the floor, unmoving. Her wrists and feet are bound. A combination of fear and fury rises inside me at the sight. Rupert is lying beside her, blood seeping from his shoulder. Rupert's not moving either, but his moaning tells me he's still alive. For how long, I can't say. His injury looks bad and there's a pool of blood beside him. I'm unsure of the severity of Jade's injuries. I can't see any blood from here, but she doesn't appear to be conscious. Please let her be alive.

M's standing a few metres away with a gun trained on Rupert. I need to disarm that bitch.

'After everything I've done for you, this is the thanks I get,' M spits as she takes a step towards them, raising her gun. 'You've left me no choice. Now I'm going to have to get rid of you both.'

Like hell. M's back is to me, so she's still unaware of my presence. Moving quickly and quietly, I'm behind her in a flash.

'Drop the gun or I'll blow your fucking brains out.'

The colour drains from her face as she swings around and makes eye contact with the barrel of my gun.

'Drop it!'

When her gaze moves up to meet mine, her eyes narrow slightly. A bitch right to the end. I'm sure she can tell by the look on my face that I mean every word, because, by Christ, I do. I'll get immense pleasure from taking this woman out.

'Just try to fuck with me,' I warn.

We're in a silent standoff. This woman has balls, I'll give her that.

'Police! Open up!' we hear, followed by a loud bang on the door. I watch as M's shoulders slump in defeat before the gun finally slips from her hand, landing with a thud.

Twisting the sleeve of her dressing gown in my hand, I hastily march her towards the door. I need to get her out of here so I can go to Jade.

There's no doubt in my mind that M will be serving time for this little stunt. I'll do my best to make sure she faces the maximum penalty.

CHAPTER TWENTY-SIX

BROCK

My heart is heavy as I sit beside Jade's hospital bed, her tiny hand clutched in mine. Hours have passed and she's still out of it, sleeping now, rather than comatose. She's stirred on a few occasions, but remains incoherent due to the narcotics that are still in her system. The doctor assures me she'll be okay once they wear off, which is a huge relief.

I got word that Rupert survived the surgery to remove the bullet that was lodged in his shoulder. He remains in a critical but stable condition in ICU. He has some extensive physio ahead of him, but should make a full recovery. I'm yet to see him and thank him for all he has done, because I'm unable to leave Jade's side. When she finally comes round and I know for sure she's going to be all right, I'll go to him. He put his life on the line for my girl, and I'll be forever indebted to him for that.

Josh called earlier when he realised I was no longer at the house. As far as I know, he and Theo are still sitting in the waiting room, both eager to see Jade when she wakes.

I skim the back of my hand lightly down the side of her face. She's so pale and fragile looking and I can't help but feel responsible. I promised her I'd protect her, and I didn't. I shouldn't have left her alone.

'I'm sorry,' I whisper as a lump rises to my throat. I'm grateful to have her back, even though I'm not sure I deserve her anymore—I've caused her nothing but harm. I'll never let her out of my sight again. I only hope she can forgive me for letting her down.

'Brock,' she whimpers in her sleep. Concern fills me as her head thrashes from side to side. I hate to think of the trauma she's faced at the hands of that evil bitch.

'I'm here, sweetheart.'

When I feel her grip tighten on my hand, I know she heard me. Standing, I slip off my shoes to carefully climb into bed beside her and fold her protectively in my arms. 'You're safe now,' I whisper, kissing the top of her head. 'I've got you, and no harm is going to come to you again.'

I'm not sure how long I lay there holding her, but exhaustion finally takes hold and I'm awoken some time later by Jade's soft moans. My eyes spring open to find her gazing at me.

'My body aches all over,' she says and moans again as she pushes on my chest, trying to sit. 'I feel so weak. What's wrong with me?'

'You're going to be okay,' I reply, pulling her back down to me.

'Where am I? Am I in the hospital?' she asks as her eyes dart around the room. With all the drugs that have been pumped into her system, she may not have any recollection of what has happened.

'Do you remember anything?'

Her brow furrows and her eyes squeeze shut.

'It's okay if you don't remember,' I say as my hand gently strokes her hair. It's probably a good thing if she doesn't. I can only imagine how confused she must be feeling. 'For now you just need to rest, I can explain everything to you later.'

She doesn't open her eyes again, and I presume she's gone back to sleep. Seconds later her eyes fly open. Tears rise in them before her grip on me tightens. 'Oh, Brock. Thank God you're all right. I was so worried about you.'

She's obviously confused. I find it amusing that she was worried about me. Does she have any idea of the utter fear and hopelessness I've been feeling since her disappearance? My heart goes out to her. I can feel her body trembling as she clings to me like her life depends on it.

'There's no need for you to worry about me.'

'When your dad came to the house and said you'd been in an accident—'

I cup her face in my hand. 'There was no accident. You must've dreamt it.'

Her brow furrows again. I hate that she's disorientated. I hope that bitch gets put away for a long time for everything she's put Jade through.

'No, I didn't dream it, I remember your dad coming to the house. It wasn't long after you left for that meeting. I was heading upstairs to take a bath when he knocked on the door. I wasn't going to answer, but then he said you'd been in an accident.'

At first I don't take stock of anything she's saying—it has to be either a dream or a hallucination caused by the drugs. The more she speaks though, the more concerned I become. Surely my father had nothing to do with her disappearance?

'I was wary about going with him after the way he treated me the night I met him, but I needed to know you were okay.

'Once I was in the back of the limousine, he gave me something to drink, to calm me. Understandably, I was upset and worried about you.' She smiles at me briefly before concern again crosses her beautiful features. 'I thought you'd been hurt, Brock. Please don't be angry with me.'

'I'm not angry at you,' I say, pulling her back into my arms. My mind is spinning as I try to make sense of what she's saying. But it can't be true—my father would never betray me like that.

'It wasn't until I drank what he gave me that I realised he must've put something in it. Everything went fuzzy. That's when … that's when …' She takes in a few deep breaths. Her voice is shaky as she continues. 'That's when the partition in the limousine came down and I saw M sitting in the front seat.'

'Jesus, Jade.' I tighten my hold on her.

'I don't remember anything after I saw M's face,' she whispers.

I'm gonna fucking kill him.

*

I try to keep my shit together for the next few hours. Everything in me wants to hunt down my father and rip him apart, but my heart wins out. My need for Jade is stronger than the retribution I crave.

My father and I haven't been close for years, but deep down, I know I was foolish to believe he cared about me. I'm his son. I may not like or respect him, but I love him if for no other reason than he's the man that gave me life. And as much as I've grown to hate the person he has become, I never thought he'd stoop this low. How could he do something so despicable to his own flesh and blood? He knows how much Jade means to me. Does he have such little regard for my feelings? He may not like me being with her, but that's irrelevant. This is the ultimate betrayal. I'll never forgive him.

Pushing thoughts of my father out of my mind, I focus on comforting Jade and telling her everything she can't remember about the incident. She's understandably distressed when I tell her about Rupert being shot, even when I assure her he's going to be okay. I promise to take her to see him as soon as she's allowed out of bed.

The doctor comes to examine her, and my desire to pay my father a visit becomes almost unbearable. Standing back, I watch as the doctor checks her vitals, and it only makes my fury intensify. I'm grateful I got her back in one piece; things could've turned out so differently. The blame belongs squarely on my father's shoulders. Without his deviousness, M never would've got her filthy hands on my girl.

The doctor informs Jade that he'll be keeping her in for another twenty-four hours, purely for observation, which pleases me. As much as I want to take her home where I can care for her myself, she's in the best place for now. When Jade asks about visiting Rupert, he suggests she wait until tomorrow. She's still extremely weak, so for the interim he'd prefer she remained on complete bed rest. I know she's busting to see him, but I agree bed rest is what she needs.

The moment the doctor leaves, I pull the chair over beside the bed. My need to be close to her is overwhelming. My fingers stroke her hair once I'm seated. When she starts asking questions about M, Rupert, and how we came to find her, I'm hesitant to give her more detail, but in true Jade form, she takes it all in her stride and again I'm left awestruck by her strength. She's been through such a traumatic experience, but seems to be coping better than I am. I only wish I was half the person she is.

'You're amazing,' I say, gazing into her beautiful green eyes.

'How so?'

'I love your strength, and your ability to accept the shitty things life continues to hand you. Your strong will to go on no matter what's thrown your way.'

She shrugs. 'I've learnt over the years that there's no point dwelling on things you can't change. Accepting things for what they are and moving forward as best I can is something I've mastered. It's how I survive. I could easily let it get me down, but what good would that do me?'

'I'm so glad you ran into me that day at the airport,' I confess. 'Meeting you has enriched my life in so many ways.' And that's the truth. Before Jade, I was just existing—going through the motions of life, not feeling, not really living. I've had the world at my feet my entire life, and I took it all for granted. She's had to fight for everything she has, sometimes just to survive. She's opened my eyes and made me see my life in a totally different light.

'I'm glad I did too,' she says, reaching for my hand and lacing her fingers through mine. I'm again reminded of what she's been through when I see the bandages covering the rope burns around her wrists. It kills me inside. 'Although if I could redo that moment, I'd definitely lick the chocolate off my teeth before I smiled at you.' A sweet blush spreads across her cheeks. I wouldn't change a second of that moment, or the chocolate on her teeth. It was adorable. Knowing her has made me a better man—a better person.

We talk about everything and nothing. Eventually, I see her eyelids getting heavy and I know she's tired. 'Close your eyes and get some sleep, it will do you good,' I suggest, tucking a strand of hair behind her ear.

'I feel rude sleeping while you're sitting here, but I'm tired.'

'Don't. You need your rest. The quicker you get better, the sooner I can take you home.'

I hope she'll come back to my place when she leaves here. Now that M is no longer a threat, she's free to go back to her apartment, but I find myself hoping that's not the decision she makes. Still, I won't pressure her, even though I'd like too.

Rolling onto her side, she tucks her hands under her face and smiles at me. It astounds me how quickly she became my world, because that's exactly what she is.

She still won't close her eyes, so maybe it's best if I go. I don't want to leave her, but my need to see my father is just as strong as my desire to stay here. I'm struggling to comprehend that he'd actually be a part of this.

When my mind is made up, I say, 'I actually need to step out for a while. Would it be okay if Josh and Theo came and sat with you while I'm gone?'

I see a smile tug at her lips before she speaks. 'Are they out there together?'

'I guess,' I reply.

'Have they been out there the whole time?'

'Yes.' Her face lights up and I wonder what she's up to. I lean down and place a small kiss on her cheek. 'I won't be long, I promise.'

'Okay,' she replies, as her eyes finally close.

'I love you.'

She doesn't say it back. As much as I'd like to hear her say she loves me too, I'm okay with it. I close my eyes and briefly rest my forehead against hers. Why is the thought of leaving her again tearing me up inside? Perhaps it's because, only hours ago, I wasn't sure if I'd ever see her again.

I give Josh strict instructions not to leave Jade's side until I return. He gives me the keys to his car since I'd travelled here in the back of an ambulance. I intend to go and see my father, have it out with him and make sure he never goes anywhere near Jade again.

*

By the time I reach the office it's safe to say I'm consumed with anger. God help my father when I get my hands on him.

'Mr Weston, your father is in the middle of an important call. He asked not be disturbed,' his secretary, Renee, says as I approach.

I walk straight past her without replying.

Reaching for the handle, I ignore her comment, flinging the door open with so much force it crashes into the adjoining wall with a loud bang. My father's head immediately snaps up and his eyes meet mine. When the colour drains from his face, I know he understands why I'm here. I close the door to his office, locking it behind me. There will be no escaping this conversation.

'Look, I'll have to call you back,' he says in a shaky voice before ending his call. He has good reason to be worried.

Stalking around the desk, I grab the lapels of his suit jacket before reefing him out of his seat. 'You were behind Jade's disappearance?'

'She's a damn whore. I was only returning her to her rightful owner. She has no place being with you.'

'You had no right to interfere. She was forced into working for that monster. I saved her, and you threw her back without any regard for her safety or my feelings.'

'I did you a favour.'

I let go of his jacket and he falls back into his seat. I clench my hands by my sides to stop myself knocking his smug head off his shoulders. I shake with the effort. How can we be related? How can this man's blood be running through my veins? We're so different. *I have a heart.*

'Pack your shit and get the fuck out of my building. You're fired.'

'You can't fire me,' he says. 'This is my company. I founded Weston Global.'

'And then you gave it to me, remember? I'm CEO now. Either you go or I do.'

'Giving you this company was the biggest mistake of my life.'

Is he for real? I made this fucking company. It was going nowhere until I took over.

'Then tell me, Father, why did you sign it over to me?'

'Because you're my son!' he screams, smashing his hand down on the desk. 'I wanted this company to be my legacy. Was that too much to ask?'

It isn't, but since when did he give a fuck about his family?

'I can't believe you're going to throw everything away over a piece of pussy.'

'She's not just a piece of pussy. I'm in love with her.' I don't even know why I'm telling him this. He's proved countless times over the years that he has no compassion for anyone but himself.

He laughs. 'You're pathetic.'

It takes everything in me not to lunge at him. 'At least I'm capable of having feelings.'

'I thought you were different, but I was wrong. You're just like your brother. I wanted sons, but instead I got fucking pansies. I'm ashamed of you—both of you.'

'Listen here, old man,' I grate through clenched teeth. My hands latch onto the armrests on either side of his office chair so I can lean right into his face, and my fingers dig painfully into the leather. I've never experienced rage of this magnitude before. 'You've managed to push me pretty far in the past, but believe me when I say you've never seen me pushed to my limit. I'm warning you now, I'm teetering on the edge. So, I'd shut that fucking mouth of yours if I was you. Don't test me because, trust me, it will *not* end well.'

'You think I'm scared of your idle threats, boy?' He knows damn well this isn't an idle threat. He may be wearing a composed look of his face, but his dilated pupils tell me an entirely different story. I'm trained to read body language. I know all the tell-tale signs. It's time to show this fucker just how serious I am.

Letting go of the chair, my hands roughly grab his tie as I draw him even closer. Our noses are practically touching. If he wasn't twenty-eight years my senior, I'd knock him out.

'Put it this way, Father, you go anywhere near Jade again and I'll fucking kill you.' I give him a shove as I let go, making the chair tilt backwards when he lands with a thud. 'Consider yourself warned. I despise you. I'm ashamed to be your son,' I say. I don't even wait for a reply as I turn to leave. From this day forward he's dead to me.

Fuck him, and fuck this company. I don't need any of it. Storming past Renee and down the corridor, I head for my office. I need to calm the fuck down before I get behind the wheel again. As I pass my secretary, Amy, I hold my hand up to stop her before she speaks. The last thing I want to do is lose my cool with her. I'm fucking livid.

I slam my office door so hard the windows rattle. I wouldn't give a fuck if they broke. I swipe my hand angrily across my desk, sending everything flying across the room. I want to scream—no, I want to hit something or someone. Unlike my father, though, I know the meaning of respect.

A crushing feeling forms in my chest as I slump into the chair and rest my head in my hands. I'm angry, but more than anything, I'm hurt. How could my father have such blatant disregard for his own flesh and blood? I've disliked him for years, but I still loved him—he's my father and I'm his son. It's quite obvious to me now that the love only runs one way. A father is supposed to love his children.

All those feelings from the moment I learnt my father wasn't the great man I'd always believed him to be, come flooding to the surface. I actually feel like doing something I haven't done since I was a kid—cry. Fuck him, I won't give him the satisfaction.

A knock on my door pulls me from my inner turmoil.

'Go away!'

'Mr Weston,' Amy calls. I shouldn't take my foul mood out on her, but I'm in no state to talk to anyone at the moment. I'm on the verge of losing my shit and I don't want her to be in the firing line. 'Mr Weston, please, I need to speak to you urgently. It's about your father.'

'Fuck my father,' I retort.

'Please,' she begs. 'It's important.'

The desperation in her voice has me rising from my chair. I stalk across the room.

'Please just give me some time calm down,' I say when I open the door.

There's concern on Amy's face—she actually looks like she is on the verge of tears.

'It's your father, Mr Weston—he's … he's dead.'

CHAPTER TWENTY-SEVEN

JADE

When I wake, I find Theo asleep in the chair in the corner. There's no sign of Joshua, or more importantly, Brock. The moment Theo opens his eyes, I know something terrible has happened. I ask him where the boys are, and I'm in no way prepared for what he tells me.

My first instincts are to go to Brock, but Theo won't take me. Although Maxwell Weston was far from my favourite person, I can imagine how his death will be affecting his sons.

'Brock hasn't taken the news well,' Theo says. 'I've promised him I'll look after you. Don't worry, when he's ready, he'll come.'

His words both shock and confuse me. Maybe given the history between his father and me, they shouldn't, but they do. I'm afraid to ask Theo if Brock has specifically said he doesn't want to see me, because I have a feeling in my gut that he'd say yes. My instincts are usually pretty spot on.

I try to push that thought out of my mind. I still can't believe that Maxwell Weston is actually dead. Apparently he'd collapsed in his office. Joshua told Theo that Brock's efforts to revive him had been futile. That only made my need to go to Brock intensify.

Later that morning, the doctor finally discharges me. With Theo by my side, and Brock forefront in my mind, we head straight for Rupert's room. There was no way I was leaving this hospital without seeing him.

I pause momentarily at the doorway of his room. Boy, I've missed Rupert. This is the first time I'd seen him since I stopped working for M. For years he'd been a huge part of my daily life, so having no contact with him has been hard. This was not how I hoped our reunion would be though.

Hesitantly, I step into the room. The moment my eyes land on Rupert, I take a sharp breath. I'm usually pretty good at keeping my emotions in check, but seeing him lying in that bed, connected to so many machines, is too much. Knowing he'd risked his life and had taken a bullet for me fills me with a mixture of gratitude and guilt.

'I'm all right,' he says when I cross the room and hug him, weeping softly into his chest. I have so much to say to him, but for now all I can manage to get out is a measly, 'Thank you.' I'll be forever indebted to him for what he did.

'You don't have to thank me, I'm just glad to see you're okay.' His voice is raspy as he speaks.

When I eventually pull myself together, I draw back and wipe my eyes with the back of my hand.

'How are you?' he asks, concerned. I can't believe he's worried about me. I'm not the one with a gunshot wound.

'I'm fine,' I say, giving him a reassuring smile. 'How are you?'

'It'll take more than a bullet to bring me down.' He chuckles, before screwing up his face and placing his hand on his bandaged shoulder. It hurts to see him like this.

Theo brings a chair over, placing it beside the bed. When I'm seated, I reach for Rupert's hand, giving it a squeeze. After rewarding me with a smile, his gaze moves to Theo.

'Mr James,' he says. 'It's good to see you again.'

'You too,' Theo replies, 'but I wish it were under better circumstances.'

I watch as Rupert's eyes move towards the door and then back to me. 'Where's Brock?'

My shoulders slump. 'His father passed away.'

'Shit.'

I'm glad he doesn't ask any other questions because there's nothing more I can tell him.

We stay by Rupert's side for a few hours, but as time wears on, I can see he's tired and he needs to rest. It's hard for me to leave him, but I promise to come back tomorrow. I have no idea if he has any family, and I hate myself for not knowing. He's always seemed like a private person and has never talked about his life outside of work. I'm going to make it my mission to find out more about him. The real him. The man he was before coming to work for M. Our relationship has always been more than just a working one. I care about him, and the fact that he has risked his life for me tells me he cares about me as well.

Theo has his driver pick us up from the hospital. 'We'll grab what you need from your place before heading back to mine,' he says.

'I'll be fine staying at my apartment on my own, but thanks for the offer.' He's already gone out of his way for me,

I don't want to disrupt his life any more than I already have: he's spent the past two days at the hospital.

'Nice try, but I'm not letting you out of my sight. I promised Brock and Josh I'd look after you, and that's exactly what I plan to do.'

'I'm quite capable of looking after myself,' I say with a laugh. I've looked after myself for most of my life. 'M's not a threat to me anymore.'

'She may be behind bars for now, but for how long? You know as well as anyone that she has some pretty powerful friends.'

I sigh. He's right. I know for a fact that she has judges and politicians on her payroll. A few of them are my clients. I wouldn't put it past her to call in favours or threaten bribery to help beat the charges. She's as corrupt as they come and would stoop to any level to save her own skin.

'I'm not going to put you out, Theo.'

'You won't be. I adore your company, you know that.' He covers my hand with his. 'It's a done deal, babycakes, I'm not letting you out of my sight until Brock comes and collects you.'

I smile at his pet name for me. He hasn't called me that in a long time. But I'm not impressed about being bossed around yet again, even if I understand he's only doing it because he cares. I can't be angry at him for that.

There's still no reply from the boys when I check my phone. I can't get them out of my mind. I'm tempted to ask Theo if his driver can swing by Brock's house too, but I don't want to force myself on him. He's obviously grieving; I'm sure he knows I'm here when he's ready.

Theo asks his driver to wait for us out the front of my building. I'm both surprised and thrilled to find everything still intact when we enter my apartment—I was expecting to see the place trashed.

'Would you mind if I had a quick shower before we leave?' I ask Theo. There was no point in me having one at the hospital because I had no clean clothes.

'Of course not. Knock yourself out.' He plops down on my couch and reaches for the television remote that's sitting on my coffee table, making himself at home.

Even though I only live in an apartment, it's very spacious and occupies the entire tenth floor. My lounge area and dining room are open plan, with the living space on the right and dining on the left. Through the archway is a large kitchen, and there's a long hall that leads to the bedrooms and bathroom. I've converted one of my spare rooms into a large walk-in wardrobe, which I adore. The other remains empty—I've never had anyone stay. Before Brock came along, I was a loner, which was the way I liked it. My time was my own. When I was here, nobody could tell me what to do.

I let out a huge sigh of relief when I reach my bedroom. I'm grateful it's the way I left it. I love my room, it's my favourite part of the house—my sanctuary. The first thing I do when I enter is head towards the windows to open my blinds and let the light in. The room is all white. My bed, my furniture, the linen, even the walls—everything. I have a number of candles placed throughout as well. Taking a deep breath, calmness settles over me. That's what this space does for me. I look down at the view of Sydney Harbour below.

After returning from being with my clients I would crave the purity of this space, because pure was the opposite of how I felt. No matter how many times I scrubbed myself in the shower, it was impossible to get that dirty, disgusting feeling off my skin. Brock's the only person who has managed to remove the sins of my past.

My bedroom is the only real place I've ever felt comfortable and I truly love it here. But I know I can't stay. Once things settle down, I'll have to find somewhere safer to live. Somewhere where M won't find me. Disappointment about leaving my sanctuary weighs heavily on me.

I sit on the edge of my bed as my thoughts turn back to Brock. I hate to think of what he's going through right now. I know his relationship with Maxwell wasn't great. Nevertheless, he was still Brock's father.

I contemplate calling him as I unravel the bandages on my wrists. I just need to know he's okay. My heart is aching for not only him, but for Joshua and their mother. My hands slightly shake as I pick up the phone and dial Brock's number. I'm not sure why I'm nervous, but I am.

'You've reached Brock Weston. Please leave your details and I'll get back to you.' Hearing his sexy, confident voice in the recorded message sends my heart into a flutter, despite my disappointment. It's only been a day, but I miss him.

'Hi Brock, it's Jade. I just wanted to say again, I'm sorry about your father. I've been discharged from the hospital and I'm heading to Theo's house. I just thought you may want to know. I'm here if you need anything. Take care of yourself.' I clutch my phone to my chest and fight back the tears when I end the call.

Please let us be okay.

CHAPTER TWENTY-EIGHT

JADE

A week has passed and there's still no word from Brock. Nothing. With every day that goes by my concern not only for him, but for us, escalates. I've spoken with Joshua—he came to Theo's to touch base and make sure I was doing okay. When I asked him how Brock was, his reply was 'not good'. To my disappointment, he didn't elaborate. I had a thousand questions I wanted to ask, but for some reason words failed me.

When he was leaving, he wrapped me in his arms and kissed my forehead, just like Brock used to. Tears stung my eyes. 'Give him time,' he whispered, before letting me go. If those words were meant to soothe me, they didn't. They only served to worry me more.

I've been spending the majority of my days at the hospital with Rupert. He's improving every day, which brings some light into my darkness. We don't speak about Brock. Rupert knows me well, so I'm sure he can sense that there's trouble in paradise. The fact that I'm being dropped off and picked up by Theo every day would tell him everything.

When Theo's home, he does his best to keep me occupied. I'm grateful for that. For the most part it works, but Brock is always on my mind. It's been hard. I'm fighting to stay strong, and not let it bring me down. Some days are better than others, but there are times when I feel like I can't breathe without him, and I hate that. This is why I don't usually allow myself to get close to people.

It's the nights I'm struggling with most. I haven't been sleeping well. I feel like a part of me is missing without him. I've drafted countless messages, but haven't had the guts to send any of them. I don't want to appear needy or desperate, because I'm not. I'm used to rejection so this should be nothing new. This hurts more than all the other times combined. I honestly thought he meant it when he said he loved me. I understand he's going through a hard time, but his desire to have no contact with me during this difficult time is hard to digest.

I'm lost without him.

Tomorrow is Maxwell Weston's funeral. Theo is going, but I'm not sure if I can. I'd feel like a hypocrite attending the funeral of a man I hate. On the other hand, I'm desperate to see Brock, even if it's just from distance. I have to do something to ease my mind and see firsthand how he's really doing. Sometimes we need to put our own feelings aside to help the people we love. He's given me so much. If I can return the favour in any way, I will.

*

'You're coming?' Theo asks, when I enter the kitchen the next morning dressed in a black pencil skirt and tailored jacket. I sat up half the night debating whether I should go or not, but my heart won out in the end. I'm doing this for Brock—and no other reason.

265

'I guess,' I reply, shrugging. Taking the mug from his outstretched hand, I sit at the breakfast bar. 'I want to be there for Brock.' I look at the coffee in front of me. Theo probably thinks I'm pathetic.

'Hey,' he says, placing his fingers under my chin and tilting my face up. 'You're a better person than I am. You're a fucking saint, Jade. Brock's a damn fool if he doesn't see that.'

I know his words are meant to comfort me, but they seem to have the opposite effect. A sick feeling settles in the pit of my stomach, because it's the first time he's mentioned Brock in days. Does he think we're over too? My head has been telling me Brock and I are through, but my heart still refuses to believe it. I guess today will give me the answers I'm seeking.

I'm on the verge of throwing up when we arrive at the cemetery. The family have opted for a graveside service. It's fitting, I suppose. What little I know about Maxwell Weston tells me he wasn't a religious man. I'm pretty sure he's earnt himself a one-way ticket to hell, along with M. There'll be no pearly gates for either of them.

'You're shaking,' Theo says when he reaches for my hand across the centre console. Everything in me is screaming not to get out of this car, but I do. I've faced worse in my life, and my need to see Brock is too strong.

Theo comes to a stop in front of me as we walk around the front of the car. 'Are you sure you want to be here, babycakes?'

'It's ironic I'm here to pay my last respects to a man I have absolutely no respect for,' I reply with sarcasm in my voice. 'Despite everything, Theo, both Brock and Joshua have been wonderful to me, so I want to be here for them.'

'You're amazing. This is exactly why I love you.' He places a chaste kiss on my forehead. 'If at any time it feels too much, just say the word and we're gone.'

'Thanks, Theo. I'm grateful for everything you've done for me.'

'It's been no hardship, Jade, I love being around you. You're not only the best fake girlfriend a gay guy could ask for, you're the dearest friend I have.'

'I adore you too,' I say as my hands snake around his waist and my head rests on his chest. It doesn't escape me that he just told me he loved me, and again I couldn't say the words back. What is wrong with me? Why can't I tell the people I care about that I love them? Brock has expressed his true feelings towards me, yet I've never once told him I reciprocated them. Now I'm afraid I'll never get the chance to tell him how I really feel about him.

Theo's hand is firmly clasped around mine as we walk across the grassed area towards the people milling by the freshly dug grave. This is the first funeral I've ever attended and I'm grateful when he comes to a stop at the back of the crowd. I'm happy to stay here; it's not like either of us were close with this man. I'm not sure if Theo even met him when he was alive.

My chest tightens and my breath hitches the moment I see Brock. He looks awful. Well, not awful—this is Brock Weston we're talking about, it would be almost impossible for him to look awful. What I should've said is he looks tired, and kinda lost. I can see the black rings under his eyes from here. He looks like he hasn't shaven or slept in days. The sight of him tears at my heart.

He's staring at the coffin in front of him. His face is totally void of any emotion. I just want to run over there and wrap him in my arms. My gaze eventually moves to his mother, who is seated beside him. Her head is bowed as she wipes a tear from her eye. I notice Brock's hand is tightly gripped around hers. Joshua is sitting on the other side of her, his hand placed on her knee for comfort. I'm glad she has her boys looking after her.

When my eyes meet Joshua's, I'm surprised to see him looking straight at me. I give him a weak smile when he nods his head. I watch as he leans slightly across Elaine to whisper something to his brother.

Brock's head snaps up and his eyes scan the mourners until finally stopping on me. I have to fight back the tears when I see him sigh before the corner of his mouth turns up slightly. Unfortunately, it's gone as quickly as it appears, and the solemn look returns to his face. Is he happy I'm here? I hope so.

All the air seems to leave me when a woman places her hand on Brock's shoulder. *Clarissa*. There's a smug, satisfied look on her bitchy face that has me wanting to slap her. Why does this woman bring out the worst in me? Is this why I haven't seen or heard from Brock? Has he been seeking comfort from her?

I stare at the grass by my feet. Regardless of my misconceived notions, coming here today was a mistake. I feel Theo's arm slide around my waist as he pulls me protectively into his side. I guess he just witnessed the same thing I did.

Eventually, things get underway. Nothing the priest says registers. My mind is in a complete haze. On the few occasions I involuntarily look at Brock, I'm surprised to find his eyes firmly fixed on me. His expression is still empty, so I'm finding it hard to judge what he's thinking. Clarissa's perfectly manicured yet grubby little hand hasn't left his shoulder. I know I shouldn't let her get to me, but she does. A lot. I don't want her or her hands anywhere near Brock.

Once the coffin has been lowered, the priest invites the family to place dirt into the hole. Brock helps his mother to her feet. My eyes shamelessly rake over his tall, lean body in his tailor-made black suit.

Elaine goes first, followed by Joshua. I concentrate on Brock as he squats down, sprinkling the dirt onto the casket. Tears fill my eyes when I see him mouth the word 'sorry', as he looks into the hole. I have no idea why he'd feel the need to say that. Maybe he's having regrets about the tumultuous relationship he had with his father. It pains me to think he's suffering.

I'm rooted to the spot as the guests begin to offer their condolences to the family. I don't want to go over there. I'm scared. But this might be the last time I ever get to be near Brock, so my legs are moving in that direction before my brain even realises what's happening.

I reach Joshua first. His arms encircle my waist as he squeezes me tight. 'You're the last person I expected to see here today, but I'm so thankful you came.'

'I needed to see Brock,' I confess.

'He may not show it, but I know he's grateful you came.'

Giving Joshua a brief smile, I go to his mother. 'I'm sorry for your loss, Mrs Weston.'

'Thank you, Jade. It's lovely to see you again.'

'It's lovely to see you as well, I just wish it wasn't under these circumstances.'

'Thank you. Please consider coming back to the house for some refreshments. I'd love to catch up with you,' she says, giving me an affectionate hug. I get the impression she knows nothing about what went on between her husband and me. Nevertheless, I smile and thank her for her offer before stepping away.

Butterflies dance in my stomach as I approach Brock. The moment his eyes lock with mine, I see his face soften and a small smile play on his lips. Hope surges in my heart. Reaching for his hand, I give it a squeeze. The contact is brief, but it sends tingles up my arm. 'I'm sorry about your father,' I say quietly.

He stares at me for the longest time before replying. 'Thank you.' I hear his voice slightly crack as he speaks, and it tugs at my heart. I desperately want to pull him into my arms, but before I get a chance, he takes a step back. My shoulders slump and my heart shatters when he turns away from me, exhaling a large breath and fisting his hands in his hair. That small gesture tells me everything I need to know.

We're over.

Turning, I walk hastily towards Theo's car. I need to get out of here as soon as possible.

'Hey, wait up,' Theo calls out, jogging to catch up to me. 'What's the big rush?' Grabbing my elbow, he pulls me to a stop. 'Jade.' When my watery eyes meet his, I see his face drop before he pulls me into his arms. 'Jesus, what happened?'

'Please just get me out of here,' I beg. I'm grateful when he ushers me towards the car. 'Can you please take me to my apartment?'

'Why? What's happened?'

'Nothing,' I say, turning my face away. 'I just want to go back to my old life and forget everything.'

My life of loneliness and solitude.

CHAPTER TWENTY-NINE

BROCK

I feel like a prick, an absolute lowlife, for doing what I just did to Jade, but I panicked. I haven't shed a tear since my father's death. Not one fucking drop. The moment I saw the sympathetic look on her sweet face and felt the tender touch of her soft hand wrapped around mine, it was too much. I had to turn away because I was on the verge of breaking down. Every emotion I experienced this week came bubbling to the surface. This woman will forever be my undoing. I couldn't let her see me fall apart. I just couldn't.

Fuck, I've missed her.

Today was the first time I've felt anything other than numbness. My world has been shrouded in darkness ever since I spent ten futile minutes trying to revive my father on the floor of his office. My last words to him were, 'I despise you. I'm ashamed to be your son.' How do I live with that? I can never take those words back. I killed him, and I'll never be able to forgive myself.

Frankly, I'm amazed that Jade attended the funeral. My father tried to destroy her, luring her away from the safety of my home and handing her over to the devil herself. How could she even find it in her to come today? Even if it was just for my benefit. She has the heart of an angel. This is why I love that woman. I'll always love her, but I'm just not in a good place at the moment. I refuse to bring her down with me. She's been through enough.

Pushing my thoughts to the back of my mind, I turn my attention to my mother. 'How are you, Mum?' I ask, placing my hand on her leg as we travel back to her house in the limousine. This week has been rough for her too. I'm yet to confess that I'm the cause of my father's death. That's because I'm a fucking coward.

'Surprisingly, I feel okay. Is it wrong that I feel like a weight has been lifted from my shoulders? I loved your father, but I didn't exactly like him. I've been extremely unhappy for years.' Tears of guilt rise to her eyes.

She has every right to feel that way. My father was a monster for the way he treated her. One good thing has come out of his death: Mum, Josh and I are closer now. I haven't left her side since I drove to my parent's estate to break the news. I wanted it to come from me, nobody else. Since I was the cause of his untimely demise, the least I could do was be there for her as her world crumbled. It was the first time I'd been back since they kicked Josh out.

*

I'm consumed with disappointment when Jade doesn't arrive at the house. I'm certain I heard my mother invite her back here at the cemetery. But I can't blame her after I gave her the cold shoulder like I did. I'm eager to apologise. My heart sank at the funeral when I finally turned back around to find her gone.

Heading for the bar in my father's office, I pour myself a drink from one of his 25-year-old bottles of scotch. He's been collecting these for years. It's been my drink of choice this week. My father would roll over in his grave if he knew I was pissing away his beloved scotch, but it's no good to him now. You can't take it with you. He should've drunk the fucker while he had the chance.

His death has made me realise just how short life really is. One day you're here, the next you're not. We all should live each day like it's our last.

I get a pain in my chest as my mind flashes back to that day. I'll never be able to get the image of his lifeless body out of my head. He must've had a major heart attack because I couldn't even get a pulse as I worked on him. In truth he deserved everything he got—you reap what you sow, so they say. I just never expected to have a hand in his death.

Downing the scotch in one gulp, I pour another before heading back out onto the patio. It turns my stomach to hear people reminisce about my father, saying what a great man he was, as I pass. He wasn't a great man at all.

'There you are, Brock,' Clarissa whines, coming to a stop beside me as I stand by the pool. Her voice makes the hairs on my neck stand up. To my dismay, she's been dropping by the house almost every day. I'm sure it was only because she knew I was staying here. I got the impression she was even getting on my mother's nerves. Like me, I'm certain Mum can see straight through Clarissa's façade. My father was the only one she could fool.

'I'm not in the mood for your shit today, Clarissa, leave me alone.' Harsh, but it's the truth. Sometimes brutal is the only thing she understands. I still haven't forgiven her for the trouble she caused with Jade.

'Come on, babe,' she says, hooking her arm through mine. I hate when she calls me babe, I'm not her fucking babe. 'I'll excuse your rude behaviour because you buried your father today, but I think we should discuss our future. Maybe it's time we granted him his dying wish. You know how much he wanted to see us married.'

I can't help but chuckle bitterly at her brazenness. Is this woman for real? My father's dying wish, my arse. She'll stoop to any level to get what she wants.

Removing her arm from mine, I take a step back. 'When are you going to get it through your thick head? I have no intentions of ever marrying you. I have a girlfriend, remember?' Well, I hope I still do. I need to pull my head out of my arse and make things right with Jade before I lose her forever.

'The whore from the function.' Clarissa stamps her foot as she speaks, like the annoying brat she is. 'Wasn't she at the funeral today with another man? They looked awfully cosy.'

Her statement pisses me off. I'll admit I felt insanely jealous when Theo had his arm around Jade. I know their relationship is completely platonic, and I'm extremely grateful that he's been caring for her all week while I've been unable too, but I wanted to be the one holding her, instead of him.

'She's not a fucking whore,' I snap.

'If the shoe fits,' Clarissa retorts, raising one of her perfectly sculpted eyebrows.

Something inside me snaps. Reaching out, I place my hand on her scrawny chest, giving it a slight shove. It doesn't take much. She's so thin I'm surprised the wind doesn't carry her away. I have to suppress my laugh when I see the look of horror on her face as she tumbles backwards, falling straight into the pool. Everyone around us gasps when she lands in the water with a splash. That should cool her down a bit.

She's coughing and spluttering when she finally comes up for air, looking like a drowned rat. 'Brock!' she screams, banging her hands down on the surface in one of her temper tantrums.

Ignoring her outburst, I turn away and head towards my brother.

'Did you just push Clarissa in the pool?' he asks. The amusement in his voice doesn't go unnoticed.

'I may have accidentally-on-purpose knocked her in.' When he holds up his hand, I give him a high-five. She's not his favourite person either. She gave him such a hard time when he came out. She's just as narrow-minded as my father was. 'Listen, can you keep an eye on Mum? I have to duck out for a while.'

'You better be going where I think you're going, or I may have to kick your arse. I saw the way you treated her at the cemetery. She—'

'I know,' I say holding up my hand to stop him. 'I'll grovel at her feet if need be. I have to make things right between us.'

'Good. Theo called me earlier. He dropped Jade off at her apartment. He wasn't happy about leaving her alone, but she insisted. You better grovel. She's perfect for you,' he says, placing his hand on my shoulder. 'I want her as my sister-in-law.'

'You're getting a bit ahead of yourself there.' He gives me a look that almost makes me squirm. I'm not ready for anything like that. I'm still getting used to having a damn girlfriend.

When—or should I say if—I ever am, she'll definitely be the one. *It'll only ever be her.* That's if I can get her to forgive me for acting like a dickhead. I may have been suffering, but shutting her out was inexcusable.

But I'm a selfish prick. I always get what I want, and Jade is no exception.

*

I have an uneasy feeling in the pit of my stomach when I knock on Jade's apartment door. I'm not sure what type of reception I'll get. I hope she gives me a better one than I gave her. I'm desperate to see her—to touch her. I need her more now than I've ever needed anything in my life.

She's my air.

I knock a few times, but there's no answer. I refuse to leave until I've seen her. 'Jade, it's me, Brock,' I call out.

A few seconds later the door opens slightly. I'm pleased to see the safety chain is latched. When she doesn't speak, I do. I put this wedge between us, so now it's up to me to make things right.

'Can I come in?'

Stepping back, she closes the door and for a moment my heart sinks, but then I hear her removing the safety chain. She's letting me in. That's a start. A huge fucking start.

'Hi,' I say the minute she opens it.

'Hi.' From the tone of her voice, I'm unsure if she's happy to see me. Nevertheless, my eyes drink her in as she stands before me. I've never seen her so casually clad before. She looks sweet, wearing a T-shirt that's five sizes too big. It looks awfully familiar.

Her face is clear of makeup and her long dark hair is piled into a messy bun on top of her head. Obviously, she wasn't expecting company. I feel my dick twitch as my gaze moves down her long, bare legs to the hot pink polish painted on her perfect little toes.

She's my saviour. She's the only one who can make me feel. She's my ticket out of this dreary dark hole I've fallen into. Just being in her presence has me feeling lighter than I have in days. Why have I left it so long to see her?

'Is that one of my T-shirts?' I ask, trying not to smile when she wraps her arms around her torso, trying to shield her appearance.

'No ... yes ... maybe.' The defiant look she gives me has my lips curving up at the corners. I love her spunk.

'It either is or it isn't,' I say teasingly, taking a step towards her. I hear her breath hitch when I place my hands on her hips, my fingers digging into her flesh as I draw her body into mine. My recently unfeeling heart starts to race as I look into her exquisite green eyes and I raise a hand to cup her pretty face. 'I've missed you, sweetheart.'

I feel like an arse when she bites her bottom lip to hide a quiver. Steely determination crosses her face as she wills herself not to cry. I love her strength, but I hate that she feels the need to be strong around me.

'I'm sorry,' I confess as my thumb moves down to free her lip from the death grip of her teeth.

'Sorry for what? For ignoring me all week, or giving me the brush off today?'

I deserve that, and so much more. 'For everything ... I've been in a dark place.'

'And not being around me helped?' The venom in her voice doesn't go unnoticed. She has every right to be angry.

'No. Being away from you didn't help.' I release a long breath before continuing. 'I've been miserable without you.'

'I wish you hadn't shut me out like you did. It hurt me, Brock.'

'I didn't want to bring you down with me.'

'You wouldn't have.'

Oh, I would have. It's time to admit the truth—to tell her something I haven't had the guts to say out loud, until now.

'The last thing I said to my father before he died was that I despised him and I was ashamed to be his son.'

She gasps at my words, just like I knew she would. I bow my head because I can't bear to see the judgement in her eyes when I tell her the rest.

'I walked out of his office and a few minutes later he collapsed and died. I killed him Jade.'

'What? No!' She cups my face and raises it to meet hers. This time she doesn't hold back the tears that now fall from her eyes. 'You didn't kill him.' The conviction in her voice has me almost believing her, but sadly I know better. I'll forever feel responsible for his death.

Confessing what I've done makes me feel lighter somehow, like a weight has been lifted. I know it won't change anything, but I feel freer for finally voicing my guilt. It's ludicrous the amount of trust I have in her after such a short amount of time, but I trust her with my life.

She's my happy place.

Walking her backwards, I enter her apartment and kick the door closed with my heel. Spinning her around, I pin her to the back of the door before crashing my lips into hers.

'I need you, Jade … I need you so much, I ache.' I hear my voice crack as I speak. I can't hold my emotions in any longer.

It's time to lose myself in my girl and try to forget all my problems for a while.

*

JADE

Brock's hands and mouth are everywhere. I've been pining for him all week and I'm craving this just as much as he is. I honestly thought we were over ... I'm so glad that's not the case. I've missed him more than words can convey.

When I feel dampness on my cheek, I know he's shedding silent tears, and that breaks my heart. I hate that he shut me out, but more than anything, I hate that I wasn't there to comfort him during his suffering.

Sliding his hand behind my knee, he lifts my leg, placing it on his hip. His fingers dance over my skin until he's cupping my arse in his hands. I moan into his mouth when he pushes his erection against my centre.

I slide my hands underneath his jacket and push it off his shoulders. Shrugging out of it, he tosses it across the room. I undo the tie around his neck. Gripping the hem of my T-shirt—or should I say *his* T-shirt—he rips it over my head.

'I love that you're not wearing a bra,' he breathes as he palms my breasts. When his hands skim down to my hips and grasp the side of my underwear, I quickly place my hand over his.

'Please don't rip these, they're my favourites.'

Pulling out of the kiss, his hooded eyes meet mine before he takes a step back. I feel my face flush red when his eyes travel down my body, a smug smile tugging at his lips.

When I arrived home from the funeral today, I headed straight for my bathroom. I'll admit I shed a few tears when I was in the shower, but I sucked it up the minute I was out. My heart was hurting bad, but I knew losing Brock had the potential to destroy me if I let it. I flat-out refused to let this thing between us beat me. Like the rest of the shit I've been through in my life, I knew I'd bounce back eventually. I always do.

Although my future without him looked bleak, it didn't stop me from shamelessly dressing in my Brock attire. It was all I had left. I wanted to feel close to him anyway I could. I spent the rest of the day vegging in front of the television watching the cooking channel and binge eating an entire tub of Ben & Jerry's choc-chip cookie dough ice-cream.

'Is that my underwear?' I can tell he's trying not to laugh as he speaks.

'No … yes,' I finally admit. Somebody kill me now. This is the pair I brought back from New York.

'And here I thought you couldn't get any sexier. Goddamn, woman.' His words only seem to heighten my embarrassment. 'Looks like someone was missing me as much as I was missing them,' he says smugly, stepping forwards and pressing his hard body into mine.

Of course I was missing him, but I refuse to admit it. I've already embarrassed myself enough by getting caught wearing his clothes like a damn stalker. His mouth trails kisses across my jaw.

'I love that you're wearing my clothes,' he whispers in my ear. 'Fucking love it,' he adds, sucking my earlobe between his lips, 'but, they need to go.'

Reefing the boxer briefs down my legs, I step out of them and kick them to the side. As I reach for his belt buckle, he captures my hands, lifting and pinning them above my head. Sliding his loosened tie from around his neck, he wraps it around my wrists.

'Don't move your arms from this position,' he commands. There's something so hot about him ordering me around. Pushing his knee between my legs, he parts them. His mouth captures mine again as one of his hands slide between my thighs. 'Christ, you're so wet,' he groans into my mouth, as his fingers circle my clit.

'Oh, Brock,' I moan as my legs begin to tremble. I've missed his touch. His other hand moves behind me, sliding over my arse cheeks and between my legs from behind. I already feel like I'm going to come when he plunges two of his delicious fingers deep inside me. Pushing my hips forwards, I widen my stance. God, this feels incredible.

Within seconds he brings me undone. Tilting my head back I whimper as wave after wave of pleasure seeps through my body.

'I owe you a whole week's worth of orgasms, so I'm not going to stop until you come for me again, beautiful,' he whispers seductively in my ear as his fingers continue their assault.

'I'm not sure if my legs will withstand it, but bring it on, Mr Weston,' I reply with a pant.

He's true to his word. He doesn't stop until he milks another mind-blowing orgasm from me. This time my legs buckle, but he uses his strength to hold me up. He frees my wrists before dropping the tie on the ground.

'I need to be inside you,' he growls. 'I can't wait another second. I'm going to fuck you hard and fast then take you to your room and make love to you nice and slow.' His words make my body tremble with need. I hear him undo his zipper before he lifts me off the ground. 'Wrap your legs around me.'

The second I do, he pushes inside me, filling me completely. He didn't even bother to remove his pants.

We moan in unison as he withdraws before pushing all the way back in. It feels wonderful. Picking up the pace, he pounds into me as his lips find mine again. He's never taken me so roughly before, but I love it. I love *him*.

Within minutes, he throws his head back and groans as his body shudders before stilling.

'I've fucking missed you,' he says as his eyes lock with mine.

'I've missed you too.' I cup his face with my hand as my lips softly connect to his.

'Which way to your bedroom?'

'The last room at the end of the hall.' He'll be the first person other than me to ever enter my sanctuary ... he's the only person I want to share it with.

He turns down the hall with me in his arms, his cock still inside me, and I find myself wishing we could stay connected like this forever. Pausing at the door, his eyes dart around my space.

'I always wondered what your room would look like,' he says. It pleases me that he's thought about me in that way. 'It's very ... white.'

I laugh. 'It's calming.' What else can I say? I don't want to delve into the demons of my past. That's all behind me now. This room was the light in my darkness, but I don't need it now, I have him. He's changed everything—he's changed me. Maybe it's time I added some colour in here. Something to signify what he's added to my life.

Withdrawing himself, he gently places me on the middle of my bed before standing to full height. I'm overcome with the loss of our connection. 'I've barely survived this week without you,' he says, sighing. 'I don't want to ever experience that again.'

I don't want to be without him either.

I admire his exquisite body as he hastily undresses before settling over the top of me. 'I love you so much, Jade.' My heart swells as his eyes lock with mine and he tenderly brushes the hair from my face. I'll never tire of hearing him say that. Never!

My mind drifts back to this morning, when I was having regrets about never telling him how much I cared for him. It's time I rectified that. I don't want any more regrets where he's concerned.

The words fall from my mouth before I chicken out. 'I love you too, Brock.' Finally. It wasn't as hard as I thought it would be. His face lights up and his mouth curves into a smile. It's the first real smile I've seen since he arrived here.

'You really love me?' he asks, like he's unsure if I'm telling the truth. Doesn't he realise how much I've struggled to voice my feelings?

'I do,' I reply, stroking his face. 'It's the first time I've ever said those words, but I wanted you to know how I feel. I truly love you, Brock ... with all my heart.'

I see tears well in his eyes and it tugs at my heart. His kiss is soft and sweet—full of love. Nothing like the hungry and desperate kisses he gave me a few minutes ago. He slides inside me again, connecting us in the most beautiful way, and I feel whole again.

We're going to be okay.

CHAPTER THIRTY

JADE

It's midmorning when we both finally wake. We spent countless hours reconnecting before falling asleep wrapped in each other's arms. It's the best I've slept since we've been apart.

'Morning, beautiful,' he says, rolling onto his side and caressing the side of my face. He looks refreshed, which pleases me. His gorgeous brown eyes don't look as troubled as they did yesterday, and the dark circles under them are barely visible.

'Morning, handsome,' I reply, snuggling into him. 'How did you sleep last night?'

'Great. Better than I have in days. I can thank you for that.' He places a soft kiss on my forehead.

'Because I wore you out?' There's humour in my voice as I speak. I think we wore each other out.

'No. Because just being near you again has helped ... more than you know.'

'Having you here has helped me too,' I admit. 'I've struggled without you, Brock.' Being honest like this something I rarely do, but something changed between us last night. I don't want to hold back when it comes to him. I finally gave my heart completely, and it's a wonderful feeling. I only hope he takes care of it.

'Move in with me permanently, Jade. If being separated from you this week has taught me anything, it's that I'm nothing without you by my side.'

'I can't.'

His brow furrows as my words sink in. 'Why not? Are you having second thoughts about us already?'

'Of course I'm not having second thoughts about us. I meant everything I said last night. I love you.'

'Then why?'

'It's too soon. If this week has taught *me* anything, it's that we rushed into everything before. I want us both to be sure that this is what we really want before making such a huge commitment. I can't have a repeat of what I went through this week. It almost broke me.'

'I'm sorry,' he says, resting his head against mine. 'Hurting you was the last thing I wanted. I'm sure about us. I've never been more certain about anything in my life. You're it for me, Jade.'

'You're all I want too, but I still think it's wise if we take things a little slower this time.'

Sighing, he pulls my face into his chest. I can hear the erratic beating of his heart as his grip on me tightens. 'If that's what you really want. I don't want to force you into doing anything you're not ready for. I guess I'll be spending a lot of time here then, because I refuse to spend another night without you.'

'I can live with that,' I say, smiling.

'You don't really have a choice. That part of the deal is not up for negotiation.' I laugh when he flips me over onto my back and settles between my legs. 'I need you with me, Jade.'

Threading my fingers into his hair, I pull his mouth down to mine.

I need him with me too.

*

After we make love again, we shower and dress. I have no food in my apartment, so Brock offers to take me out for breakfast. We swing past his place on the way so he can change. He even packs some extra clothes into a bag to leave at my apartment. It's going to be nice having him stay over.

It's the first time going back to Brock's since the incident, and I'll admit I feel sick as we pull into his driveway. I'm grateful that apart from being in the car with his father, I don't remember anything. The drugs in my system and the rope burns were the only injuries I sustained. I had a bruise on my shoulder and hip, but those have faded now. Rupert said they would've been from when he was shot and collapsed, with me in his arms.

After breakfast we head to the hospital to see Rupert. His face lights up the moment he notices Brock standing beside me. Even though our hands are linked, I'm sure the smile I give him in return tells him Brock and I are okay. He hasn't mentioned Brock much when I've visited, but from what little he did say, I knew Rupert was concerned about us.

'It's good to see you again, mate,' he says, reaching out to shake Brock's hand. 'I was sorry to hear about your father.'

Brock's body stiffens when Rupert mentions Maxwell's passing. He's been acting more or less like his old self since waking this morning, but occasionally I see him drift off. It worries me. I hate that he's feeling responsible for his father's death. This afternoon, Brock and Josh are meeting with the coroner. I hope once the autopsy results are known, it will give Brock some peace. Logically, there's no way he could've killed his father. Even if he suffered a heart attack like Brock believes, there must've been some underlying heart condition.

'It's good to see you as well,' Brock says. 'You're looking much better than last time I saw you.'

'I owe my speedy recovery to Jade. She's been coming to visit me daily, and cutting up my food because I can't move this damn arm. She's done a good job of keeping me sane. Being cooped up in this place is hell. Hopefully I'll be able to leave soon.' Rupert looks at me. An appreciative smile graces his face.

I've enjoyed looking after him—he's been looking after me for years. I'd like him to come and stay with me when he's discharged, just until he gets on his feet again. I haven't asked him yet, but I hope he says yes. Apart from Brock, he's the closest thing I have to family.

'And I've enjoyed every minute of it,' I admit, kissing his cheek. We've always been close, but this week we've bonded on a totally different level.

'She's one in a million,' Brock says, draping his arm around my shoulder.

'She is.' The huge smile on his face tells me Rupert's pleased to see us together again.

Makes two of us.

Brock leaves me with Rupert while he goes to his appointment with the coroner. I can't help but feel apprehensive—he promises to pick me up when he's done, but that's what he said the day his father died. I didn't see him again for a week.

'So, what are your plans once you're discharged?' I ask Rupert.

'I'll go back to my apartment. The doc says I have a few months of physio ahead of me.'

'Do you live alone?' Again I feel bad that I've never asked him before. He's been my minder for over five years.

'I do.'

'How are you going to cope on your own? I heard the doctor say you'll have limited movement in your arm for a while. Do you have family to care for you?'

'Nope. It's just me,' he replies, sighing. The turmoil in his eyes tells me there's a story there, but I'm not one to pry.

I place my hand on top of his. 'Would you consider coming to stay with me? You know, until you regain some movement.'

'I couldn't do that.'

'Yes, you could. I have plenty of room. Please. It would make me so happy.' I give him the look I've often given him over the years. I know he can't say no to that look. It's low of me to even pull that move, but I want him to come stay with me. It's the least I can do—I'm the one who got him into this mess.

'I wouldn't want to be a burden. You've only just regained your freedom.' His words are telling me no, but the hopeful look I see on his face tells me he wants to accept my offer.

'You could never be a burden. You're like family to me.'

'You're like family to me as well.' I'm surprised to see tears glistening in his eyes.

'So come stay with me. It will be just like old times. I've missed being around you. It's not like you can go back and work for M. We're both out of a job now.' Although there's nothing funny about the way M's treated us, there's a touch of humour in my voice.

'Are you sure you want me there?' There's vulnerability in his voice and it tears at my heart. I've never seen this side of him before. He's always seemed so sure of himself, so put together.

'Absolutely.'

'Okay,' he says, grinning. 'That'll be nice. Thank you.'

'You don't need to thank me. You've looked after me for years.' We sit in comfortable silence for a while.

'Can you pass me my wallet?' Rupert says eventually. 'It's in the top drawer.'

Doing as he asks, I pass it to him. He opens it and hands it straight back.

'I had a family once.'

He's showing me a photo of two very attractive women. One looks to be around forty, the other is a teenager. They're both blonde, and look like mother and daughter. There's something familiar about the younger girl, but I can't quite put my finger on it.

'Is this your family?'

'Yes. My wife and daughter.'

I hate that I don't know this. 'They're beautiful.'

'Thank you,' he says. 'Not a day goes by that I don't miss them.'

'Where are they now?' I have a feeling I'm not going to like his answer, but he brought it up for a reason.

'I lost my wife fifteen years ago, to breast cancer.'

'I'm sorry, Rupert,' I say, clutching his wallet to my chest.

'She was the love of my life,' he says. The sadness in his voice tugs at my heart. 'Her name was Beth. We were high school sweethearts.'

Covering his hand with mine, I give it a comforting squeeze. 'It must be hard for you. What about your daughter?'

'I lost her too. Twelve years ago.'

'What?' I gasp. 'How?'

'She went missing.'

'And you've had no contact with her since?' His shoulders slump as he lets out a sigh.

'She would've contacted me if she was still alive. Her bank account hasn't been touched since she went missing.'

'You think she's dead?' I whisper, squeezing his hand. 'Have you tried to find her?' Pulling his wallet away from my chest, I look down at the picture again. I know I've seen that face before.

'Yes. I've spent the last twelve years searching. That's how I came to work for M. After my wife died, I fell into a deep depression. I started drinking heavily. I wasn't there for my daughter when she needed me most. I was so wrapped up in my own grief that I didn't even stop to think that she was going through the same thing.'

'Oh Rupert.' I don't know what else to say.

'She ended up getting involved with the wrong crowd, and started taking drugs. It was her coping mechanism. I'll never forgive myself for not being there. If I was, maybe she'd still be alive. She was only sixteen when her mother passed.'

I see him wipe a tear from his eye and a lump rises to my throat.

'She was such a good girl. A straight-A student, until our family fell apart. She never gave us any trouble. The day before she went missing, she came to me. She told me about the drug addiction and how M had cleaned her up and given her a job. Can you believe, in that moment I felt gratitude towards that woman for helping my daughter. I was so misguided.' He shakes his head as he speaks.

'Your daughter worked for M?' I ask in disbelief. That's why she looks so familiar. I must've seen her at the house.

'Yes. The night she came to see me, she told me she wanted out. She'd met a young man and they were in love.'

Knowing M as well as I do, I know that wouldn't have gone down well. 'Do you think M had something to do with her disappearance?'

'I know she did. That's why I started working for her. I thought being on the inside, I'd be able to find out more. That's how I came to know about the hidden room. The one I found you in. I'd gotten hold of the plans of her house, hoping it would give me a clue. Anything.'

'Jesus. Did you find anything?'

'Nothing. Not a damn thing.'

'What was her name?'

'Sasha ... Sasha Taylor.'

Oh. My. God. The moment he says her name, memories of that night, and M's voice, flash through my mind. It's a name that has haunted me for years. *Nobody walks away from me, Sasha. Nobody!* M had screamed into the girl's face. *Do you understand me?* I've tried to block out memories of that night for the past twelve years, but no matter how hard I try, the dreams and flashback still come. I look at the picture again. She's a lot younger in this photo, but there's no doubt in my mind that it's her.

Dread fills me. 'Sasha was your daughter?' I ask.

'You remember her?' His face lights up and he groans, clasping at his shoulder, as he tries to sit up.

'Oh Rupert.' Tears are freely falling down my face. I'll never forget what happened. 'I remember the night she came to the house. I'd only been living with M for a few weeks.

I was woken by the sounds of screaming. It frightened me. It was coming from downstairs. Sneaking out of my bedroom, I went to the staircase. Sasha and M were arguing in the foyer. I wanted to run back to the safety of my room, but I didn't. I squatted down and watched through the bannister.'

'Do you remember what happened? What they were saying?'

'Yes,' I whisper. 'You're not going to like it.'

'I need to know … please.'

I look at my lap—I don't want to see his reaction to my news. 'Sasha was crying, and M was screaming at her.' Sighing, I close my eyes I transport myself back to that night. 'She said she'd met a man and they were in love and were planning to get married. M was furious and told her she couldn't leave, and then—then …' My hands cover my face, just like they did that night. 'M grabbed her around the throat. She was choking her, Rupert.'

When I hear a sob escape him, I look up. He's crying, and I feel awful.

'I'm so sorry.'

'Don't be,' he replies, wiping his eyes with the back of his hand. 'I've been searching for answers for the last twelve years. It's ironic that we've been working together for all this time, and you've had them all along. It's the not knowing that's been the hardest thing to live with. I accepted her death years ago—I didn't have a choice. In my heart I knew she was never coming back.'

'Oh, Rupert.'

'I need to find my baby and give her the proper burial she deserves. That's all I've ever wanted. I won't be able to find peace until I do. I want to bring her home and lay her to rest beside her mother.'

I lean over the bed and wrap him in my arms as we both cry. My heart is truly breaking for him. I hate that he's suffered for so long.

We stay like this for the longest time, comforting each other, until I pull away. To my knowledge, M has no idea I witnessed what happened. That night changed me—in my heart I knew I was no longer safe living under her roof, and that's what unknowingly gave her the power to control my future. Fear.

A brief conversation M had on the phone immediately after the murder replays in my mind: '*Bring something heavy to weigh down the body.*'

Dear God.

'I think I know where her body is, Rupert.'

CHAPTER THIRTY-ONE

BROCK

'He was a selfish prick right to end,' Josh says shaking his head in disgust.

'How so?' I ask, fastening my seatbelt and turning the key in the ignition of my Lamborghini so we can head back to our mother's house.

'You heard the coroner. He was diagnosed with a brain aneurysm three fucking years ago. Why is this the first time we're hearing about it? I bet you anything Mum doesn't even know.'

I look at Josh, sighing heavily as my eyes meet his. 'Just before he died I told him I despised him,' I confess. 'I said I was ashamed to be his son. I thought I was the reason for his death, now I know better.'

'You know as well as I do that it would take more than words to kill that man. He was a ticking time bomb. It was just bad timing on your part.'

'I know, but I still regret what I said, even if I meant every word.' I just didn't think it would be the last thing I ever said to him.

'I'm sorry,' Josh says, placing his hand briefly on my knee. 'Is that why you took his death so hard?'

'Yes. I felt responsible.'

'You should have talked to me.'

'I know.'

'He's said a lot worse to us over the years. Well, to me he has. Karma finally caught up with him.'

'I guess.' Even so, that day will still haunt me.

Josh was right, my mother knew nothing of the aneurysm. She's just as shocked as we were when we tell her. I shouldn't be surprised, keeping secrets from her was my father's speciality. I leave Josh with Mum, so I can head back to the hospital to collect Jade. I'm itching to see her. Being with her last night wasn't enough—we have a whole week of missed time to catch up on. Although I was absent, I made sure the boys were looking after her. I was in no place to care for her myself, but at the same time I wouldn't have been able to cope not knowing if she was okay.

My heart rate accelerates as I travel in the lift to Rupert's ward. These feelings Jade ignites in me still freak me out, but at the same time I love them. She's my drug.

I find myself smiling as I approach Rupert's room. I feel lighter than I have in days. I know it's because of her. Sure, I still have misgivings about what happened in the moments before my father's death, but I'm relieved to know I wasn't the cause of it. Like the coroner said, he was a ticking time bomb. He was surprised my father lived as long as he did, given the size of the aneurysm.

My excitement turns to confusion when I step into the room and find Jade and Rupert crying. What the fuck? 'Jesus, Jade,' I say, crossing the room.

'Oh Brock,' she cries, wrapping her arms around my waist. 'I'm so glad you're here.'

'What's happened?' I frown as I look at Rupert. He looks just as devastated as Jade, if not more.

'You'd better sit down,' she says, wiping her eyes.

Fuck. I'm not sure if I can take any more bad news. Things were just starting to get normal for me again. Once I've taken a seat next to the bed, I pull Jade onto my lap. I hate seeing her upset.

'Is someone going to tell me what the hell is going on?' I ask, when nobody speaks.

She looks at Rupert. 'We think M killed Rupert's daughter.'

'What? Hold on—what?' I didn't even know Rupert had a daughter.

'Rupert's been working for M because he was trying to find his missing daughter. Her name is Sasha. I remember her, Brock. I remember what happened. It was not long after I came to live with M.'

*

It's two in the morning by the time we arrive back at Jade's apartment. It was after midnight when detectives finally left the hospital. Jade insisted that we stayed with Rupert until he was settled. My heart went out to them both. Especially Rupert. Poor guy. I had no idea he'd been through so much. It also explained a lot about Jade and M's relationship. No wonder she was so frightened of her.

Jade said she'd covered her eyes when M started choking Sasha. A few minutes later she heard a loud thud, so she peered through her fingers. That's when she saw Sasha lying on the floor by M's feet. She explained how she'd stayed on the landing, too frightened to move. That would've been a tough thing for a kid to see. My heart bled for the little girl she once was. I don't even think Jade realises now just how amazingly strong and resilient she is.

She never faltered once while giving her statement, and remained composed the whole time. Despite her horrendous childhood, she never gave up. I can't even begin to comprehend how it would feel to be all alone in this world, with not a soul to turn to. Nobody you could trust. Her strength and will to survive despite all the odds blows me away.

I knew M was a cold hearted bitch, but what shocked me more than anything was the phone call Jade told us she made to Rocco: *'Rocco, it's M ... I need you to come over ... I don't care that it's the middle of the night ... Shut up and listen to me, you fool ... I need you to take a trip to the quarry ... Yes ... Sasha ... Bring something heavy to weigh down the body.'*

It surprised us all that Jade could remember so much detail after all this time. I suppose those poignant moments in our lives seem to stick with us. Just like I know my father's last minutes on this earth will stay with me forever.

I didn't doubt anything Jade had said. Both hers and Rupert's stories gelled together perfectly. There's no way they were making it up. Still, the detectives said since the incident happened twelve years ago, and Jade was a minor at the time, they'd need to do some investigating before they could take the case any further. They said they were going to question M and Rocco though.

Now Jade is exhausted. All she wants is to go to bed, but I'm able to talk her into having a bath first. She needs time to wind down, otherwise she's never going to get a restful sleep.

When I leave the bathroom after filling the bath, I find her sitting at the foot of her bed, her head buried in her hands. Seeing her like that hurts my heart. All I want is for life to give her a damn break.

'Hey sweetheart,' I say softly, kneeling in front of her.

Raising her head, her watery eyes meet mine. 'My heart is breaking for Rupert.'

'Come here.' I pull her into my arms. I love how caring she is towards others. With the way she's been treated over the years, I find it very admirable. When I let her go, I stand, holding my hand out to her. 'Your bath is ready.'

'Will you join me?'

'Of course.' She didn't need to ask me—I need her comfort just as much as she needs mine.

I help her into the bath before climbing in behind her. 'I hope they find Sasha,' she says as she relaxes back onto my chest. 'Rupert deserves to know what happened to his daughter.'

'I'll make it happen.' I don't know how, but I will. I'll place a few calls in the morning and see if I can pull some strings.

'For years I wondered who that girl was. I presumed, like me, she had no family—that's why nobody ever came looking for her. Now I know differently, and that breaks my heart. Poor Rupert.'

I tighten my grip around her waist when she swipes a hand across her face. 'I hope M rots in hell for what she's done.'

'That so easily could've been me,' Jade says.

'I'd never let that happen.' Guilt floods me. I almost let it happen. I'll never forgive myself for leaving her alone that day.

'When I got back from New York I told her I wanted to quit, and the first thing she did was grab me around the throat.'

Jesus Christ. I didn't think it was possible to hate that woman any more than I already do. Rage surges through me. I place a kiss on top of Jade's head. Words elude me. I can't even begin to imagine the horrors she's faced over the years. She'll never have to worry again. She's safe with me, and I'll make sure nobody ever hurts her.

'At least now she won't be able to harm anyone else,' Jade whispers.

*

Two days later I'm standing beside a large dam at the bottom of a quarry. It took numerous calls and a lot of pulled strings to make this happen so quickly. Now we wait while the police divers scour the murky waters below. Both Jade and Rupert wanted to be here today, but I managed to talk them out of coming by offering to be present on their behalf. I can understand them wanting to come, but this is no place for either of them. A father watching as his daughter's remains are removed from her watery grave is just unfathomable. As for Jade, she's already been through way too much. There was no way I was letting her come here. She's my responsibility now and I aim to protect her from here on in. I left her at the hospital with Rupert, promising to let them know as soon as I had any word.

Thirty minutes later the divers find the first human remains. A mix of relief and sadness floods through me when I think they've found Sasha. Within the hour though, more remains are discovered, and that's when we realise this is a lot more sinister than we first thought. The authorities eventually decide to call in the divers and have the dam drained. It looks like Sasha isn't the only victim to fall prey to M.

*

One week later and a total of nine bodies have been recovered. It appears we have a mass murderer on our hands. Of course at this stage, there's no certainty that M is the culprit, but in my heart I know better. All the bodies had been tied and weighed down using identical materials. It doesn't take a genius to figure out it was all the work of the same person.

The discovery makes me realise just how lucky we were. As Jade says, she could've easily been M's tenth victim. That thought makes me sick to the stomach.

The police say it's going to take a number of weeks before any of the identities will be known, and some of the remains may never be identified, but at least they have Rupert's DNA. If Sasha is among them, we'll find out soon enough. For his sake, I hope he gets the answers he's been craving. He's waited twelve painful years.

The police are organising a search to be carried out at M's and Rocco's houses. As well as looking for evidence, they're going to try to match the list of missing persons against M's past employees. Rocco has been taken into custody on suspicion of murder, and M is still on remand for kidnapping Jade. The detective assured me that until they had proof otherwise, neither of them would be walking free. For the interim at least, we can breathe easy.

CHAPTER THIRTY-TWO

JADE

Rupert was finally discharged from the hospital and is settling into my apartment. He seems content to have me doting over him. I'm enjoying looking after him. Brock has finally gone back to work, so having Rupert here means I have company during the day while he's gone.

Brock spends his nights here. The only time he ventures back to his place is to collect more clothes. Not only am I keeping him from his home, we aren't getting much alone time. Even once we go to bed we have to be careful not to make too much noise. *Easier said than done.* Maybe once Rupert's well enough to look after himself again, Brock and I can start spending more time at his house. For now, Rupert needs me.

'Here you go,' I say, passing Rupert a cup of tea and placing a plate of biscuits on the small table beside his seat.

'Thanks. You don't have to wait on me like this. My arm may be out of action for a while, but I'm not an invalid.'

'I know, but I want to. You may not admit it, but I can tell you're enjoying having someone looking after you. I know you better than you think.' I give him a wink and he blushes as he tries to suppress his smile.

'It's been a long time since a woman, or anyone for that matter, has looked after me like this. I may be slightly enjoying it.'

I laugh at his reply. Slightly, my arse—he's loving every minute of it.

'Well, get used to it. I like looking after you. You looked after me for years.'

'Thank you.'

Taking the seat beside him, I place my hand on his arm. 'How are you holding up?' I worry about him. He's been quiet and withdrawn for the past few days. Waiting for news about Sasha is hard for him.

'I need confirmation.' He scrubs his hand over his face. 'It's taking too long. I'm so close, but not knowing is eating away at me. In my heart, I know one of those bodies pulled from the dam is my baby girl.' When he chokes up, tears rise to my eyes. 'I just want to bring her home and give her the burial she deserves.'

'Oh Rupert,' I say, wiping a stray tear from my eye before reaching for his aging hand. 'We should hear something any day now.'

*

Three more agonising days was how long poor Rupert had to wait before the answers finally came. He seemed to sink deeper into himself with every day that passed. Brock and I were concerned for him so when the call finally came through, we accompanied him to the coroner's office. He needed all the support he could get.

'Take a seat,' the coroner offers the moment we step into his office. As soon as we're seated, I reach for Rupert's hand.

It trembles in mine. He's barely spoken a word since the call came through.

'Mr Taylor,' the coroner begins, 'I'm sorry it has taken so long for us to get back to you. I'm sure this hasn't been an easy time for you. Let me assure you, my team has been working tirelessly over the past few weeks. So far we've managed to identify four of the nine bodies recovered. All four of the females identified to date worked for Melody Sinclair at some point in time.' The coroner pauses. 'I'm sorry to inform you, sir, that one set of remains has been positively identified as your daughter, through the DNA you supplied.'

I knew the coroner was going to say Sasha was among the victims, but knowing doesn't stop a gasp from escaping me. Rupert rips his hand from mine and stands. The coroner, Brock and I watch as he starts to pace back and forth. Even though we were prepared for this outcome, Rupert's reaction tears my heart in two. He pauses briefly before clutching his head in his hands and stays like that for a few seconds before covering his face. Then his shoulders slump, and his entire body starts to shake. Tears rise to my eyes when a heart-shattering cry of pain tears from deep inside him, before he collapses to his knees and sobs his heart out. I'm off the chair and wrapping him in my arms before I even register what I'm doing. I just hold him for the longest time while he grieves for his only daughter. What else can I do? There are no words strong enough to comfort a parent who has lost their child.

My heart breaks for Rupert, but even more so for Sasha. She was still young and had her whole life ahead of her before it was so cruelly and viciously taken away. Her death seems so pointless. It was just another example of how calculating, selfish and uncaring M really is.

When we get home, Rupert locks himself in his bedroom for two whole days. I desperately want to go to him, but Brock insists that I leave him be. I leave trays of food outside the door, but none of it is touched.

By day three, I can't stand it any longer; I'm ready to break down the door. But he emerges showered and dressed, without me even having to go to him. It's a relief.

The first thing he does is wrap me in his arms. 'Thank you for finding me the answers I needed,' he says as he squeezes me tight. I can't respond. That day will haunt me forever. Even though the night Sasha was killed has come full circle, it doesn't seem to lessen the guilt I feel about that night. I was just a young girl, but I wish I'd done more. Logically I know that was an impossibility. It probably only would've served to get me killed as well.

I help Rupert with all the funeral arrangements. It's hard for him, I can tell, but he keeps himself together. Understandably, he wants to make it special for his daughter. He chooses a white casket and a beautiful arrangement of pink tulips to adorn the coffin. Apparently they were Sasha's favourite flowers. A few of her favourite songs growing up are chosen to be played at the service, including one he used to sing to her when she was a little girl. He also places an advertisement in the local paper where they once lived, in the hope that some of her friends will attend.

On the way home from the funeral parlour, Rupert and I stop by his apartment to collect a black suit, and he emerges from his bedroom with a large framed picture of Sasha to place in the church on the day of the service. I know he'll never get over the loss of his daughter, but I'm hoping once the funeral is over, he finds some peace.

When the day of the funeral rolls around, we're all on edge. I'm dreading it. I'm worried for Rupert, and Brock— it was only a few weeks ago he laid his father to rest. I'm even concerned for myself. Sasha's death has been playing on my mind for years, but finding her remains has brought the trauma and pain to the surface. I even had a nightmare about her. It was awful. I'd woken with a start, my body trembling and covered in perspiration. I was able to slip out of bed and pull myself together before Brock noticed I was missing. He doesn't need to add my nightmares to his worries.

None of us eat breakfast before we leave, but Brock had managed to force a cup of coffee into Rupert and me. Brock's been wonderful throughout this whole ordeal. Not only to me, but to Rupert as well. I'm sure staying in my apartment and having Rupert with us hasn't been easy for him, but he hasn't complained once. I'll make it up to him once all this is over.

We follow the funeral car all the way to the church. The three of us are sitting in the back of the limousine; I'm in the middle. Brock's fingers are tightly laced through mine, and my free hand is resting on Rupert's leg. He hasn't voiced it, but I know he's grateful to have us both by his side. There's an appreciative look on his face whenever we make eye contact.

'Are you okay?' I ask as we near the church.

'As good as I can be,' he replies, placing his hand over mine. I don't think any of us were expecting a big turn out today, but when we pull up, there's a large group waiting: easily fifty people, maybe more. Rupert immediately sits up straight, gazing out the window.

'All these people have come to say goodbye to my baby,' I hear him whisper, and a huge lump rises to my throat.

Once we're out of the car, Brock and I stand back while Rupert heads towards the group standing near the entrance.

'How are you holding up?' Brock asks me as his arms slide around my waist, drawing me into him.

'I'm okay,' I lie. Truth is, my stomach is in knots. I'm dreading every aspect of today. Learning about Sasha from Rupert over the past week hasn't helped. She seems so real to me; no longer just a face and a name.

When Brock tightens his embrace and places a soft kiss on the top of my head, I get the impression he doesn't believe me. Having him here helps. He's my rock. Spending my days with Rupert has been emotionally draining, but losing myself in Brock at night has been my salvation—my escape from the harsh realities of life. He's the best thing that's ever happened to me.

He's so much more than simply the love of my life.

CHAPTER THIRTY-THREE

Three months later ...

BROCK

The past few months have done wonders for all of us. My mum has blossomed now she's no longer living under my father's thumb and our relationship has come along in leaps and bounds. For the first time in years, Josh, mum and I feel like a real family again. I'm still haunted by my father's death, but I've come to terms with it. I know it wasn't my fault. It was just unfortunate that his aneurysm chose to rupture moments after our heated altercation.

Rupert seems like a new man as well. *Lighter.* His daughter's funeral was hard on him. The following day, he decided he needed some time away. Jade tried her best to talk him out of leaving, but in the end it was to no avail. We never asked where he went, but when he arrived back a few weeks later, he was a different person. Wherever he went had done him the world of good.

Rupert has become family to us, especially Jade. So when I finally talked her into selling her apartment and moving in with me, he came along too; my house is plenty big enough for the three of us. We set him up in one of the bedrooms on the ground level, so Jade and I still have our own space and privacy. I gave him a job in my company: he's my chief liaison officer. Although he's old enough to retire, he was keen to get back to work and I was thrilled to have him join my company. With his integrity, he'll be an asset.

The coroner and his team have now identified eight of the nine bodies. Along with Sasha, the seven other women went missing while working for M. One of them was only seventeen. The ninth body is male, and they're yet to figure out who he is. He wasn't an employee, so they think he may have been either an ex-lover, a client, or just someone who pissed M off.

M has yet to go to trial, but there's no doubt in my mind she'll get life. The detectives have a mountain of evidence against her and assure us they have an ironclad case. Her assets were seized by the police department, as profits of crime. So, even if she was to ever walk free, which she won't, she'll be homeless and broke. Jade's apartment was safe because it was in her name and paid for out of her earnings. Rocco's charges were downgraded to an accessory to murder when he sang like a bird and became a crown witness. He'll still be facing a hefty sentence, but might get to see the light of day in years to come.

Today, I'm excited and a bit anxious on my drive home from work. I have a surprise planned for Jade and I'm not sure what she's going to think of it. She told me a few weeks ago that her time with me has been the best of her life. I feel exactly the same. I'm totally besotted by her. The love I feel for her only seems to grow stronger with each passing day. I never believed life could be this good. I couldn't imagine life without her in it. She's my happy place—my best friend, my lover and the reason I look forward to waking up every morning.

As I pull into the driveway, something she said to me last week when we were lying in bed, plays over in my mind. *I'm looking forward to making a lifetime of beautiful memories with you.* It's ironic that her words didn't freak me out in the slightest. The bachelor life I once led is long forgotten. Thanks to Jade, I'm a new man. A lifetime with her by my side is exactly what I want. Hence my surprise. If my girl wants beautiful memories, then that's exactly what she's going to get.

I told Rupert of my plans for tonight, so he organised to go out for a few drinks with some of the guys from work. I have her all to myself for the next few hours.

When I enter the house, I head straight to the kitchen; I have no doubt that's where she'll be. She's still keen to open her own restaurant, and has been taking part-time classes at the local TAFE. She's already an exceptional cook, so in my opinion the classes aren't needed. In saying that though, when I see her face light up as she talks about the things she's learnt that day, I'm glad she's doing something she loves. Seeing her happy is all I want.

'Hey, sweetheart,' I say, snaking my arms around her waist and burying my face in the crook of her neck. 'Something smells delicious.' And I'm not just referring to the food. Her scent is my drug.

'Hey,' she replies turning in my arms and sliding her hands around my neck. My heartbeat accelerates when she looks into my eyes. I'll never tire of her beautiful face. 'How was work?'

'It was good, but I missed you,' I say, brushing my lips against hers. I always miss her when she's not around.

'I missed you too.' She laces her hands through my hair before pulling my lips down to hers.

Groaning into her mouth, I deepen the kiss as I lift her onto the counter. It's only on rare occasions I get to take her anywhere I want now. I don't mind Rupert living here—he's a great guy—but I do miss the spontaneity our sex life once had.

My hands travel up her sides, taking her shirt as I go.

'What about Rupert?' she enquires when I draw back from the kiss, pulling her shirt over her head.

'He's having drinks with some of the guys from work. He won't be home until later.'

'I love how well he's fitted into your company,' she says, reaching behind herself to hastily remove her bra.

'And I love you,' I reply as my hands cover her magnificent tits.

'Oh Brock,' she moans the moment I replace one hand with my mouth. I'll never get my fill of her.

'Wrap your legs around me,' I command. When she does, I lift her, carrying her over to the island in the middle of the kitchen. Laying her down, I step back and pull her yoga pants down her incredible legs. I wanted to give her the gift first, but that will have to wait now. She always manages to distract me.

Dropping her pants to the floor, my fingers trail a path over the silk fabric of her panties. A growl forms in the back of my throat when she arches her back and pushes her hips towards my hand. I crave her so much sometimes it scares me. Entwining my finger and thumb in the side of her underwear, I tear them easily from her body before shoving them into my pocket. Even though Jade lives with me now, my obsession with ripping off her panties hasn't diminished in the slightest. I've set up an account for her at the lingerie store. It's an expensive habit, but it's worth every fucking cent.

I delve my fingers into her sweetness and she whimpers at the contact, throwing her head back. The noises she makes are like music to my ears. My cock is so hard it strains painfully against my pants. Since we're alone, I wanted to take my time with her, but my good intentions have flown out the window. I need to be inside her more than I need my next breath.

I pull down my zip and free myself before drawing her to the edge of the bench. I slide inside her heaven as she wraps her legs tightly around my waist. Moving my hands behind her body I draw her torso to mine. Pulling my hips back slightly, I push all the way inside her again. I can feel her tits pressed firmly against my chest through my shirt as my mouth crashes into hers. I need skin against skin, but I don't have time to remove my clothes. I'm too lost in these incredible feelings she gives me.

'I love you so much,' she whispers against my lips, making mine curve into a smile.

She doesn't tell me often, but when she does, it's amazing. I can't even find the words for how it makes me feel.

*

After we shower, we head back downstairs for dinner. I still use Erika for the housekeeping and shopping, but Jade cooks all the meals. I wouldn't have it any other way—I love her cooking. Her talents are endless.

'I made the most amazing caramel and apple tarts in class today,' she says, when I take a seat at the breakfast bar so I can watch her as she prepares our food. 'We're going to have them for dessert.'

Shit, that reminds me—the surprise.

'You know I'm going to get fat eating all these sweets you keep bringing home.'

'Never. I'm more than happy to help you work off the extra calories.' She gives me a knowing look, and my cock stirs again. If she keeps this up, we'll never eat.

'You enjoy those classes, don't you?' I ask, trying to change the subject. If I don't, this conversation will only end one way—more sex. Rising from the bar stool, I pick up my suit jacket.

'I do,' she replies smiling as she glances over her shoulder. I love seeing her happy. She's a different person to the woman I met all those months ago. She's more carefree.

After stashing the envelope in the back pocket of my jeans, I clutch the small pouch in my hand as I approach her. Standing behind her, I dangle it in front of her eyes.

'What's that?' she asks, turning to face me.

'It's a gift. I bought it for you today.'

Her gaze moves between the pouch in my hand and my face as she smiles.

'Open it,' I say, laying it in her palm.

'Wow ... it's beautiful.' She gazes down at the round glass locket in her hand.

'It's a memory locket. You said you wanted to make beautiful memories with me, so I thought this would be a great way to keep a record of them. I've already added a few charms to get you started.'

'Brock,' she whispers as her eyes meet mine. 'I—I don't know what to say.'

She doesn't need to say anything, she's given me so much already. More than she'll ever know.

'The love charm speaks for itself, but the other two charms are to go with this.' I remove the envelope from my pocket. After she places the locket on the counter beside us, I hand it to her. Her hands slightly tremble as she opens it. She carefully unties the ribbon and unfolds the invitation. I hear her gasp. I'm not sure if that's a good sign or not, but I'm hoping it is. It took a lot of work to set this up for her.

'Pierre Hermé,' she says, as her wide eyes meet mine.

'I've heard you mention him a few times, so I've arranged for us to fly to Paris so you can spend a day with him. You're attending one of his creative workshops.'

'But—'

'What? You don't want to do this?'

'Are you kidding me? Of course I do, I'm just shocked. You do realise he's one of the most famous pastry chefs in the world? How …?'

'I know who he is, and I have my ways.' I smirk. Money talks, and there's nothing I wouldn't do for her.

She pauses briefly before looking down at the invitation in her hand again. As she rereads it, her smile grows. She then picks up the locket and studies the charms inside.

As well as the word *love*, there's a plane and a tiny cake. They represent our journey to Paris and her day with Pierre Hermé. I intend to fill the locket with lasting memories before we return to Australia. If anyone deserves them, it's her.

When her eyes finally meet mine again, I'm surprised to see them welling with tears. By the width of her smile I'm guessing they're happy ones. 'Thank you,' she squeals with excitement as she throws her arms around my neck. 'I love you so much.'

Hearing her say that is all I'll ever need.

CHAPTER THIRTY-FOUR

BROCK

Jade is showered, dressed and ready for her big day with Pierre before I even wake. I can tell she is filled with a mix of excitement and nerves.

We'd arrived in Paris at some ungodly hour in the morning the previous day. It was a long flight with a five-hour layover in Dubai, and we had no plans for the rest of the day, so we spent it in bed.

After I shower, I return to the bedroom wrapped in a towel. Dropping my towel, I smile to myself as I watch her eyes rake over my body from the edge of the bed where she's sitting. After sliding into a pair of jeans, I stalk towards her, pulling her off the bed and into my arms.

'I can't believe I'm in Paris with you,' Jade whispers as she snuggles into my chest.

'There's no other person I'd rather be in the City of Love with,' I reply, kissing the top of her head. 'I plan on travelling the entire world with you. This is just the beginning, we have our whole lives ahead of us.'

We're going to stay on in Paris for a few days after Jade's class before flying home. I would've liked to stay longer, but it's a busy time for my company at the moment. Things are going ahead full steam. I no longer have my father breathing down my neck, so I can make decisions without fear of retribution or backlash from him. He was old school and wasn't comfortable taking risks. On the other hand, I thrive on shit like that. My vision is finally being realised. Within the next few years, I plan to make Weston Global the number one security firm in the world.

'You're awfully quiet,' I say. 'Is everything okay?'

'I'm just nervous,' she replies. 'What if I stuff things up and look like a fool?'

She has nothing to be nervous about; she has a natural talent for cooking, so I'm sure she'll impress. Placing my finger under her chin, I raise her face to meet mine. 'Impossible. You've got this in the bag, sweetheart. You may even show him a thing or two.'

'That's very sweet of you to say, but I highly doubt it,' she says, laughing.

'Don't underestimate your talents. I've eaten at some of the finest Michelin-starred restaurants in the world. Your cooking rivals the best, and I'm not just saying that to get in your pants.'

'You have a permanent invitation to my pants, Mr Weston,' she says, placing a soft kiss over my heart.

'I'm glad to hear that.' I move my hands down to squeeze her incredible arse. 'Now let me get dressed before I do something that's going to make you late.'

Smiling, she releases me and takes a step back. 'I left a mark on you. Let me get a tissue to wipe it off.'

Looking down, I see the red imprint left by her lipstick. It's sitting right over my heart. 'No, leave it. I like being marked by you. Last time you did that, I didn't want to wash it off.' I wish I could leave it there permanently.

*

JADE

Brock's confidence in my ability gave me the pick-me-up I needed. Though I'll admit I'm a little starstruck when we meet Pierre, I'm completely taken aback when Brock drapes his arm around me and introduces me as his girlfriend instead of Jade, and then proceeds to give me a scorching hot, toe-curling kiss right in front of Pierre. I get the impression he's uneasy about me spending the day with another man, so I quickly forgive him for his little performance. I never would've picked him for the insecure type. Pierre is short, plump and middle-aged, so I find Brock's actions ridiculous, but adorably sweet at the same time. He has no need to worry. Even if Pierre were young and gorgeous, nobody could ever come close to Brock. He's everything I'll ever want.

My day flies, and I am genuinely sad when it is over. It's the most amazing experience—so much more than I could've imagined. In the six hours I'm with Pierre, I learn so much. Being a fourth-generation pastry chef, you could say it's in his blood. He shares a lot of industry secrets as well as the one behind his world famous macarons. It's nice to spend time with someone as passionate about food as I am.

His English is good, but I speak fluent French. I'd learnt to speak a few foreign languages at the private schools M had me attend growing up, including Italian and German. Pierre tells me he's impressed with my culinary skills, and compliments me a number of times throughout the day. He even goes so far to say he wouldn't hesitate to hire me to work in one of his restaurants. It's a huge compliment and I'm pretty sure I smiled like a fool when he said that, but my home is in Australia with Brock. I'm keen to start my own business when I return. Nothing flashy, just something small that I can call my own. Something worlds away from my previous profession.

When I tell him of my plans, Pierre promises to look me up if he ever comes to Australia. It's kind of him to say, but it will probably never happen. I'd probably keel over and die if he ever walked into my restaurant.

I find Brock waiting across the street when I exit Pierre's building. His long, lean, sexy-as-hell body is resting up against the convertible sports car we hired at the airport. His legs are crossed at the ankles and his arms are folded over his strong chest. A beautiful smile spreads across his face when he notices me walking towards him. The sight of him sends my heart into a flutter.

'How was it?' he asks when I approach.

'One word: *amazing*.' I pass him the white box that's filled with all the delicious treats I made, and watch as he leans over and places it on the back seat of the car before pulling me into his arms.

'I'm glad,' he says, pressing his lips to mine. My body melts into his. Nothing else seems to exist when we're together like this. He has the power to stop my world from spinning. Like we're the only two people on this planet. 'I missed you today,' he whispers against my mouth.

'Me too,' I reply, before drawing back. 'How was your day?'

'Interesting.' His smirk tells me he's been up to something, but he doesn't elaborate, so of course I have to ask.

'What did you do?'

'Stuff.' He chuckles, letting go of me and opening the passenger side door.

'What kind of stuff?' I ask, my brow furrowing as I seat myself in the car.

'You'll find out soon enough,' is all he says, leaning down to kiss the top of my head before closing the door. Ugh! Why is he being so vague?

'So, are you going to tell me what you did today?' I ask once we're seated in the restaurant where we're having dinner. I'm dying to know what he's been up to.

'Of course,' he says, trying to suppress his smile.

When he doesn't continue, I raise my eyebrow. 'Well?'

'I promise all will be revealed before the night's out.' When he picks up his menu and holds it in front of his face, I swear I want to reach over the table and smack him.

Sighing, I pick up my menu as well. I hate secrets, and surprises scare me. I'm not a fan of the unknown. That's what I've faced my whole life. I've learnt firsthand how horrible the unknown can be. Past experience tells me good things never last, but that's my insecurity rearing its ugly head again. I want us to last more than anything I've ever wished for in my life, and believe me when I say the younger Jade wished for so much. *So, so much.*

We're quiet during dinner, apart from the few questions Brock asks me about my time with Pierre. I grow agitated. I know he wouldn't do anything bad to me, but I'm concerned as to why he won't tell me about his day. He's quiet and a little withdrawn.

'Are you wearing your locket?' he asks suddenly, as we wait for the waiter to bring our bill.

'Yes, of course,' I reply, pulling it from underneath my top to show him. He smiles before reaching into his pocket.

'I have a few more charms for you to add.'

My hands tremble slightly as I unwrap the small piece of tissue paper he places in front of me. My smile grows when I find a tiny Eiffel Tower charm inside.

'You're taking me to the Eiffel Tower?' I've been to Paris many times and I've seen the tower from ground level, but I've never been up to the top. When I came with M, touristy things weren't allowed. When I was older and came alone, it's something I never wanted to do on my own.

'Yes.'

'Can we travel to the top?' I can hear the excitement in my voice as I speak.

'You better believe it,' he says.

I give his hand a squeeze across the table. Removing the necklace from around my neck, I carefully open the glass locket and store the little tower inside with my cake, plane and love charms. Excitement ignites inside me, and all my insecurities seem to vanish.

'Thank you,' I say as my eyes meet his.

'Before you close it, I have one more charm.' This time he reaches into a different pocket.

I laugh when I see a tiny red high heel inside the tissue paper. 'It's so cute.'

'Well, that's not really a memory for you. It's more for me,' he says with a chuckle. 'You were wearing those sexy red shoes the day we met. I fucking love those shoes.'

*

When we arrive at the base of the tower after dinner, we join the end of the long queue to ride the lift to the top. It looks like we're in for a bit of a wait, but I'm okay with that. It will be worth it.

Ten minutes pass and the line hardly moves. I'm personally not bothered by this, but the way Brock keeps looking at his watch tells me he is.

A short time later, he says, 'I'll be back in a second.' He doesn't even give me the chance to ask him where he's going.

When he returns, he reaches for my hand. 'Come,' he says, tugging gently on my arm.

'Where are we going?'

'Up to the top.'

'But, the line—'

'It's all sorted.'

'I'm not pushing in, Brock. These people have been waiting too.' I pull on his hand, trying to stop him, but to no avail. He's on a mission. Not only do we move to the front of the line, but it appears we're riding up on our own.

'They're on their way up,' I hear the staff member say into his handheld radio in French.

'I feel awful for pushing in,' I say when the doors close. 'Did you pay them, or something?'

'Or something,' Brock replies.

I give him a sceptical look. Something fishy is going on here. Shoving his hands in his pockets, he finally looks at me. He doesn't say a word, but his face says everything. He looks extremely anxious and that makes my stomach churn for some reason.

'What's going on, Brock?' My arms reach for him as I take a step in his direction.

320

'Just give me a second okay?' he says. When he holds up his hand and retreats a step, I let my arms drop to my side.

'Are you afraid of heights?' That's the only rational explanation for his sudden mood change.

'No,' he replies with a nervous chuckle. 'I just didn't think this would be so hard.'

'Didn't think what would be so hard?' My brow furrows.

Before he gets a chance to reply, we're interrupted by an announcement asking us to exit on the second floor before taking another lift to the top. The doors open and I give him a puzzled look as he places his hand on the small of my back.

'Monsieur et madame, de cette manière s'il vous plaît,' a man says, smiling pleasantly.

'Why does he want us to follow him?' I ask as my hand latches around Brock's elbow.

'He's taking us to the lift that will take us up to the top of the tower.'

For a minute I thought—I don't know what I thought, but whatever it was, it wasn't good. I guess Brock weirding out on the way up has put me on edge. But I hope bungee jumping off the Eiffel Tower is illegal, that's all I'm saying.

The moment we step into the other lift, Brock goes all weird again, pacing back and forth like a caged animal. It makes my stomach churn. He's never acted this way with me before.

'We don't have to do this if you don't want to,' I whisper. I'm grasping at straws, trying to find out what's going on inside his head, all the while hoping to God it has something to do with heights or confined spaces, and nothing to do with us or our relationship.

'Do what?' he asks as he stops pacing and turns to face me.

'Go to the top.'

'But I want to go to the top. Why would you think I didn't?'

'Because you're acting distant and weird.' There's no point in lying.

'Am I?' he asks. His eyes lock with mine as he exhales a large breath. Quickly closing the distance between us, he wraps me in his arms. 'I'm sorry. I didn't realise it was so obvious.' Like that statement is going to ease my mind. Not. It doesn't explain a damn thing.

Brock reaches for my hand and laces our fingers together when the lift arrives at the top of the tower. Maybe I'm just being paranoid.

Even though the lift we travelled in was glass, I didn't get a chance to admire the view on the journey up since I was preoccupied by Brock's mood swing. So, the moment we step onto the landing, I gasp. It's breathtaking. 'Wow.'

Heading straight for the edge, I let go of Brock's hand and my fingers curve around the wire cage. I take a few minutes to absorb the view before turning my attention back to him. He's standing beside me, hands in his pockets, but instead of looking at what's before us, he's staring at me.

'I love you,' he says as he smiles.

'I love you too,' I reply, slipping my arms around his waist. 'Are you sure you're okay?'

Raising his hand, he tenderly strokes my face. 'I'm with you, so I'm perfect.'

His sweet words fill me with joy. Yay! My Brock is back.

He briefly places his lips against mine, before taking a step backwards. Digging his fingers into his pocket, he pulls out another small fold of tissue paper. 'Another memory for your locket,' he says, placing it in my palm. 'I hope you like it.'

He already gave me the Eiffel Tower charm at dinner, so I can't imagine what this one will be. Maybe it's something to symbolise our next journey. Carefully unwrapping the paper, my eyes widen and my mouth gapes when I see what's inside. It's a ring. A teeny-tiny ring charm with a stone set into the top. Is it? Could it be? I'm scared to ask in case I'm wrong.

The moment Brock gets down on one knee before me I know I'm right. *Oh. My. God.* My heart starts to beat out of my chest as tears fill my eyes.

'Jade,' he says, reaching for my hand and clearing his throat. I can feel his fingers slightly trembling as they wrap around mine. Now I know why he's been acting so weird.

There's people all around us, but I don't care. I want to hear him say it. I want to hear the words that I never thought I'd hear.

'From the moment you crashed into me at the airport and gave me a big chocolatey grin, you've captivated my heart.' I feel my face flush at the mention of the chocolate on my teeth. 'The more I got to know you, the more I realised that you were *it*—the part that's been missing from my life. You complete me, sweetheart, and I can't imagine my life without you in it. You make me happier than I thought I could ever be. I don't want to ever lose that feeling, and what we share. Will you do me the honour of becoming my wife, so I can make you mine forever?'

I don't even need to think about this. There's no one else I'd rather spend my life with. 'Yes,' I blurt out, pulling him to his feet and leaping into his arms. 'Yes … yes … yes,' I repeat as I rain tiny kisses all over his face. Tears of joy cascade down my cheeks.

'Thank fuck you said yes,' he says into the crook of my neck as his arms tighten around me. 'I was worried you were going to turn me down.'

Is he kidding? Why wouldn't I want to marry him? He's the man of my dreams, and has so much to offer. I on the other hand, am just me. Plain old Jade Davis, the orphan—the kid nobody wanted—the hooker. The person who, until he came along, was sure she was unlovable. He could have anyone he wanted, but thankfully he wants me.

*

I feel like I'm floating when we arrive back at the hotel. I want to pinch myself to make sure I'm not dreaming. After Brock produced the engagement ring from his pocket and slid it on my finger and we received a round of applause from the onlookers, we headed back down to watch the incredible light show. The Eiffel Tower on its own is a magnificent structure, but when it's lit up—no words can describe how beautiful it looks. There's something magical about this place, but I never felt it until I came here with Brock.

When we enter our room, there's another surprise awaiting me. Brock organised for the hotel staff to line our bedroom with candles. There's a bottle of champagne sitting on ice beside the bed, and red rose petals sprinkled all over the white bedsheets.

'Brock,' I whisper as my eyes take it all in.

'I wanted to give my future wife something special to come home too.'

I love the sound of that. *His future wife*. Mrs Jade Weston.

'What if I'd said no?' I joke as he pulls me into his arms.

'I wouldn't have taken no for an answer. I need you in my life, Jade. I have no intentions of letting you go.'

'There's no place I'd rather be,' I say as my lips brush against his. 'Thank you for wanting me when no one else did.'

'Oh, sweetheart. I'll always want you. You're my life now. You mean everything to me.'

'When we're married, you'll officially be my family. I never thought I'd have that.'

'Always,' he says, kissing the top of my head. 'Have you ever tried to find your father?'

'No. I'm scared he still won't want me.' As far as I know, he's never tried to find me. That in itself says a lot.

'If it's something you ever decided to do, I can help you. I have the best investigators in the field working for me.'

'I'll think about it.' Who am I kidding? It's practically all I think about. Finding the man who abandoned me has consumed me for years. There's a part of me that wants to know, and a part that doesn't. I'd love to meet my father and find out why he gave me up. But then there's that old saying: what you don't know can't hurt you. That's what's holding me back: *I'm tired of hurting.*

'We can talk about this another time,' he says, cupping my face. 'Tonight we celebrate.'

'Okay. Do you mind if I have a quick shower first?'

'Of course not. I'll pour us a glass of champagne while I wait.'

After pulling me in for a scorching hot kiss, he releases me and walks toward the bed. I quickly grab what I need before ducking into the bathroom.

Emerging a short time later, I find Brock sitting at the foot of the bed. His arms are positioned behind him, taking his body weight. His long legs are extended out in front of him and are crossed at the ankle. He's unbuttoned his shirt, and I can see a hint of his toned and tanned chest. There's a sexy smile on his lips and a glint of what's yet to come in his eyes. It makes my pulse quicken.

His gaze leaves mine and slowly travels down my body. He was wrong about the red shoes being his memory, because they're about to become our memory. He told me once that he'd like to see me wearing nothing but these shoes.

Wish granted.

A smile explodes onto his face when he gets to my feet. 'Fuck me,' he gasps. 'My favourite shoes.'

He goes to stand. I immediately hold my hand out to stop him. I'm nervous, but I want to do something I used to do for some of my clients. I know how much they loved it, and I'm hoping he does too. I want to share every part of me with him.

His eyes widen as one of my hands glide over my torso and settles between my legs. My other hand moves up to caress my breasts. I close my eyes and tilt my head back and moan as my fingers slowly circle my clit and I pinch my nipple with my other hand.

'Sweet Jesus,' he whispers, as my eyes open and lock with his. My gaze moves down to his waist when I hear the sound of a zipper. I moan again when I see him free his impressive, hard length and slowly stroke it. Now I know why my clients like it so much. Seeing him pleasure himself is hot.

It only takes a few minutes for me to come undone. Having him watch me turns me on. I never felt anything other than disgust when I did this for the others. I try to keep my eyes on him as my body starts to tremble and the ecstasy courses through me, but I can't. My head tilts back as a long, drawn-out sound escapes me.

Before I get a chance to open my eyes, Brock's in front of me, lifting me off the ground. My back is roughly pushed into the wall, as his lips crash into mine.

'That was the most beautiful thing I have ever seen. How did I get so lucky?' he groans into my mouth, as he hoists my legs around his waist, impaling me in one swift motion.

*

Our vacation comes to an end way too fast, but I've enjoyed every second. I came here with my lover and I'm leaving with my fiancé. I still can't believe I'm going to be married to the man of my dreams. Could my life get any better?

Looking down at the beautiful heart shaped diamond ring on my finger, I can't help but smile. My other hand clutches the locket around my neck that contains all my memories of Paris. This morning, Brock gave me a red lip charm. I'll never forget the magical time we spent here.

After my little show last night, and him taking me up against the wall, he revealed a red lip tattoo he had gotten while I was with Pierre. It sits right over his heart, right where I kissed him that morning. 'Now I have your mark on me permanently,' he'd said.

Sadness washes over me when the announcement comes saying we can board the plane. I know we have a lifetime of beautiful memories ahead of us, but I'm not ready to go home yet. There's no pressure here. No worries. None of life's troubles. Just us, and sheer bliss.

Before we board the plane, Brock hands me another tiny piece of tissue paper, and I'm immediately smiling.

'This is the last charm I'll be giving you on this trip,' he says. 'To me it's the most important one of all.'

I can't imagine anything more important than the tiny ring charm he gave me just before he proposed. Every charm is special, but that will forever be my favourite. The night he asked me to marry him is a night I'll never forget.

Eagerly, I unwrap the paper to find a tiny red jewel inside. It's been carved into the shape of a heart.

His expression suddenly turns serious as he shoves his hands nervously into his pockets. His vulnerable side is emerging and it puzzles me. The moment he speaks I understand why.

'You're the first person I've ever given my heart to, Jade, please look after it.'

'Oh Brock,' I whisper. He has no need to worry about that. I'll treasure his heart for as long as it belongs to me. Clutching the charm to my chest, my watery eyes lock with his. 'I promise.'

CHAPTER THIRTY-FIVE

BROCK

I find Jade in the kitchen when I arrive home a week after our return from Paris. She gives me a beautiful smile as I place an envelope on the table and go to her. It hurts my heart to know I'm about to wipe that smile off her pretty face. I'm having serious misgivings about pushing her into this now. But I've found information on Jade's family, and everything she needs to know is now sitting in that large white envelope. Her father's lawyer was very helpful, but the news is going to gut her.

At least she won't be left wondering for the rest of her life.

I plant a soft kiss on her lips. 'Hi, beautiful.'

'Hi, handsome.'

Stepping back, I pull her with me until I'm seated at the table and she's on my lap.

'Is everything okay?' she asks. 'You look grim.'

'I have some good news, and some bad news.' I watch as her eyes move to the envelope sitting in front of us. 'It's about your father.'

'You found him,' she whispers as her hands cover her mouth. Her eyes fill with tears.

'I found out what happened to him.'

'Oh. Is it bad?'

'Yes,' I answer immediately.

She rises from my lap and walks back over to where she was preparing the food.

'Jade.'

She ignores me.

Leaping off my chair, I head towards her. I slide my hands around her waist and turn her in my arms. The tears are running down her face now. It makes a lump rise in my throat. It kills me to see her upset.

'Is my father alive?' she whispers, and the pleading look in her eyes tears me apart.

'No.' I sigh when she covers her face with her hands and sobs. 'I'm so sorry, sweetheart.'

'How?'

'Suicide.' No point sugar coating it.

'I'll never get the answers now.'

That's where she's wrong. I have all the answers, including a letter from her father. I just don't know if I have it in me to give it to her.

'Come sit back down,' I say, when her crying stops.

'How long ago did he die?' She wipes her eyes with the back of her hand.

'Come sit with me,' I say again, gently pulling her towards the table. I'm relieved when she doesn't try to fight me. 'When you're ready I have all the answers to your questions.'

I pull her onto my lap and her head comes to rest on my chest. 'I'm ready,' she says.

'We don't have to do this tonight.'

'I've waited twenty-three years for answers, I'm ready.'

When I reach for the envelope, she sits up straight and squares her shoulders, bracing herself for what I have to say.

'Before I show you what's in the envelope, let me tell you what I know. Your parents' names are Colin and Patricia Davis.'

'Colin and Patricia,' I hear her whisper as a small smile crosses her face.

'Your mother died during childbirth.'

'I already know that,' she says. 'What about my father?'

I pause. 'He died when you were six months old.'

'Oh,' she says, her shoulders slumping. 'That would've been around the time I went into foster care.'

'Yes.'

'I hope it wasn't because of me.'

I can't answer that. There's a letter addressed to her, and though I haven't read it, I can't imagine that being the case.

Reaching into the envelope, I pull out four photos. They were left with her father's lawyer, along with the letter. 'These are pictures of your parents,' I say, placing two on the table in front of her. She picks them up one by one and studies them.

'You can see a bit of you in both your parents, but mainly your mother.'

'I know. I can't believe I'm finally seeing what they looked like.' She gently runs her fingers over the images. 'It's something I've always wondered.'

Placing the next two photos down, I wait for her reaction. One is of her parents with a small boy, and one of her and the boy together. 'Who's this?'

'It's your brother, with your parents,' I say, pointing to the first photograph. 'And this one is of the two of you together.'

'Oh. My. God,' she squeals, turning on my lap to face me again. I can see tears pooling in her eyes again. 'I have a brother?'

'Yes. His name is Tate. He's three years older than you.'

Her gaze moves back to the photos, as she studies them both.

'I can't believe I have a brother,' she whispers. 'Please tell me he's still alive?'

'I haven't been able to track him down yet, but yes, as far as I know, he's alive.'

'I have a brother,' she whispers again.

'I'll promise I'll find him for you.' It's a huge promise to make, but I won't give up until I do.

*

A week later, and our postponed announcement dinner is back on. I'm eager to share our news. I know my mum and Josh will be over the moon to hear about our engagement. Jade wants Rupert and Theo there because they're the closest thing she has to family. It's taken her a while to recover from the shock of finding out her father is dead and her brother is probably alive. Not that I've managed to uncover any more information about Tate. Christ, I hope I can track him down. She deserves some good news.

Mum, Josh and Theo all arrive together. Apparently Theo had his driver pick them up on the way over. Jade has set the table on the back deck, since it's such a lovely night. Once we're all seated with drinks in hand, Jade gives my leg a squeeze under the table, signalling it's time to share our news. I stand and help her to her feet. Once I have everyone's undivided attention, I speak.

'We invited you all here tonight for a reason. You are our family, and we wanted you to be the first to know our news—'

'Brock's asked me to marry him, and I said yes,' Jade squeals, holding out her hand to show off her ring. I can't help but laugh at her outburst.

We receive a few cheers, and Mum starts to cry. I guess they're as happy with our news as we are. Jade hugs me, looking just as happy as I feel. Rupert is first to stand and congratulate us. After shaking my hand, he wraps Jade in his arms. 'I needed some good news. If anyone deserves a happily ever after, it's you.'

'I'm so happy, Rupert' she says as she looks at me over his shoulder. The smile she gives me hits me right in the chest. Seeing her happy is all I've ever wanted. I know we're going to have a wonderful life together.

'I love you,' I mouth.

Her smile widens before she draws back to make eye contact with Rupert. 'Will you give me away at the wedding?'

I love how close they've become since he's been living here. He's the closest thing to a father she has. Hopefully one day I'll be able to track down Jade's brother. She'll always have us, but I'd love to be able to find him for her.

'I'd be honoured to give you away,' Rupert chokes out. They both wipe the tears from their eyes when they part.

'My turn,' Theo says as he pulls Jade into his arms, squeezing her tight. 'You deserve happiness, babycakes.'

'Thanks, Theo,' she whispers. 'You'll get yours one day too.'

'I guess I'll have to start telling people we've officially broken up.' We both laugh at Theo's comment. Going to his house all those months ago was the best decision I've ever made … It was the day Jade and I reunited and the day I realised I didn't want to live my life without her in it.

'I'm glad you didn't let this one get away, bro,' Josh says extending his hand as he comes to stand beside me. 'A guy couldn't ask for a better sister-in-law.'

My mother is still crying when she pulls Jade and I into a group hug. 'Don't make me wait too long for grandbabies.'

'Jesus, Mum. Give us a break, we're not even married yet.'

We've come so far since our run-in at the airport, and the brief yet wonderful time we spent together in New York. She not only changed my life, she changed me. I'm blessed to have met her, but more importantly, to be loved by her.

CHAPTER THIRTY-SIX

Six months later ...

JADE

I haven't stopped smiling since the moment I got out of bed this morning. Even though Brock already feels like family to me, today it becomes official. In under an hour I'll be Mrs Jade Weston and I can't put into words how happy that makes me. I feel like I've waited my whole life for this moment. *I'll finally belong to someone.*

'You look beautiful,' Rupert says as he straightens my veil. 'I'm honoured to be giving you away today.'

'There's no one else I'd rather,' I reply. And that's the truth. 'You're the closest thing I have to a father.'

'I'm so proud of you, Jade.' I have to fight back the tears when I hear his voice crack. 'From the moment I met you, I hoped that one day you'd find happiness. I'm so glad I get to witness it.'

'I love you, Rupert,' I say as I wrap my arms around him. I've never told him that before, but I do.

'Jade,' he replies, choking up. 'I love you too. Although I lost a daughter, I've gained another in you. I'm extremely grateful to have you in my life. You were the one who kept me sane for all those years.'

I wipe the tears from my eyes and see Rupert do the same. 'I don't know what I would've done without you either. You made my life bearable.'

Our moment is broken when Brock's mother enters the bedroom. Brock and I decided to get married at his—our—house, and I'm getting ready in our bedroom. Brock is using one of the bedrooms on the ground floor.

'Oh my gosh,' Elaine says, holding her arms out wide. 'Look at you. You're breathtaking. I can't wait to see my son's face when he sees you.'

I feel like a princess in this dress. It's simple but elegant. The mermaid-style dress is white, which is quite ironic, of course. It's tight fitting until mid-thigh, before flowing loosely to the floor. It has a sweetheart neckline and dips low down my back. The dress is covered in a sheer lace that extends over my breast bone and down my arms. My hair is pulled back in loose curls that are pinned into a bun at the base of my neck.

'Thank you. I hope Brock likes it.'

'He's going to love it,' Elaine says, closing the distance between us and folding me into her arms. 'Thank you for making my son so happy.'

'He makes me happy too.' Happier than I ever thought I'd be.

'I know. Oh, that reminds me, he sent me in here to find Josh, and to give you this.'

I have no idea where Joshua is and, come to think of it, Theo is missing as well. I asked him to be my brides-man today. It's unconventional, I know, but he's my best friend, so I wanted him by my side. Brock asked Joshua to be his best man.

I find a note from Brock inside the envelope Elaine gives me.

Today we become one.
I'm looking forward to making a lifetime of beautiful memories with you.
I love you, sweetheart.
Forever yours,
Brock.

Tears rise to my eyes when I unwrap the tiny piece of tissue paper enclosed with the note to find a bride and groom charm to add to my memory locket.

*

The wedding should have started five minutes ago, so when there's still no sign of Joshua and Theo, Rupert and I split up to find them. We know they're here somewhere. There are only so many places they can be.

'What the hell?' I screech, coming to an abrupt stop when I open the door to one of the spare bedrooms. 'Did you forget we have a wedding here today?' I say, trying not to laugh as I cover my eyes with my hands.

'Fuck. I'm sorry, babycakes,' Theo says, clearing his throat.

'I'm sorry to,' Joshua chimes in. 'We lost track of time.' I can hear them both shuffling around the room, but my hands are still over my eyes so I can't see what they're doing.

'There'll be plenty of time to make out after the wedding. Brock's waiting for me.'

'We'll be down in a minute,' Joshua says.

Stepping back into the corridor and closing the door, I do a little fist pump. It looks like my matchmaking has finally paid off. Theo and Joshua are perfect for each other.

I'm smiling as I head back downstairs to find Rupert. It's time for me to marry the man of my dreams.

*

BROCK

As I stand under the gazebo by the pool area with the wedding celebrant, I rub my sweaty palms down the front of my trousers. I've been looking forward to this day, so I'm surprise by how nervous I am. It was my idea to rush through the wedding plans. I was eager to make Jade my wife.

We opted for a small wedding. Jade invited a few people she's met through her cooking classes, and I have some work colleagues and a couple of friends I've kept in contact with over the years. Since there's only thirty people in attendance, we set up the back patio with a long table overlooking the pool for the reception later. I've hired chefs to cater the event, as well as waiters and bar staff. I would've liked to have been able to give her something a little more elaborate, but this is what she wanted.

I smile at my mother when she comes to stand beside me. 'She'll be out soon,' she says. 'She looks beautiful, Brock.' I didn't doubt that for a second. I can't wait to see her.

'I bet she does.'

'How are you holding up, you look nervous?'

'I am, Mum. I honestly thought marriage wasn't on the cards for me, but when I met Jade all that changed.'

'The love you have for each other is rare. Hold on to that.' I have no doubt in my mind that we will. She means everything to me and I intend to cherish her for the rest of my life. *She completes me.* 'You're going to give me the most beautiful grandchildren.'

I chuckle at her comment. She's brought the subject up a number of times since we announced our engagement. My mother has flourished since my father's death, but there are times where she seems lost. Grandchildren would help fill that void I gather. She's very active in mine and Josh's lives now which is great. I love having her around.

'Hopefully one day we'll be able to give you grandchildren.' It's not like Josh will be able too. Leaning forward I place a soft kiss on her cheek. I would love nothing more than to start a family with Jade one day, but for now I just want to enjoy her.

'I'm going to go and take my seat. Good luck, honey,' she says, rubbing her hand affectionately down my arm.

I roll my shoulders and take a deep breath trying to calm myself. Where the fuck is Josh? I look down at my watch. They're late. A few minutes pass before my brother comes rushing down the red carpet that was laid on the lawn earlier. He's breathless as he comes to a stop beside me.

'Where the fuck have you been?' I ask in an angry whisper.

'Long story,' he replies. By the look on his face I know he's been up to something and that makes me feel uneasy. Before I get a chance to pry further, the music starts playing, signalling Jade's arrival. She chose the song Endless Love sung by Stan Walker and Dami Im, to walk down the aisle too.

'Shit,' I mumble nervously to myself as I turn and face the house.

'You've got this,' Josh encourages, placing his hand briefly on my back. 'You guys were made for each other.'

The moment she appears on the patio I take in a sharp breath. She looks even more beautiful than I imagined. Theo walks down the aisle first, but I barely notice him because I can't take my eyes off Jade. Her arm is linked through Rupert's as they slowly make their way towards us. My heart is thumping rapidly against my ribcage. When she is within metres of me, she gives me a breathtaking smile. The tears that glisten in her eyes bring a lump to my throat.

I reach for her hand and lace our fingers together when she comes to a stop beside me. 'You look beautiful, sweetheart,' I whisper. Her grip tightens around my hand as we both face the marriage celebrant. I'm eager to start my new life with her by my side.

She's my best friend.
My dream girl.
My soulmate.

EPILOGUE

Five months later ...

JADE

I leave the kitchen carrying a batch of freshly baked Snickers cookies. It's my own recipe and one of my bestsellers. Buying that chocolate at the airport turned out to be the best decision I've ever made. That insignificant moment changed my life. Brock still says that, to this day, he can't walk past a Snickers bar without thinking of me.

The bell above the door chimes just as I place the hot tray on the counter. Taking off my oven gloves, I turn to greet my first customer for the day. It's been almost three months since I opened my patisserie. It's everything I dreamed it would be, and more. I decided to name it 'Life's Sweet', because that's exactly what life has become—sweet. I've come a long way from where I once was. Thanks to my husband and new found family, the horrors of my past seem like a distant memory.

As hard as it was for him, Brock didn't interfere, and let me pay for everything with the money I'd earnt from working for M. He likes to spoil me, but he knew how much it meant for me to do this on my own. He's very understanding and supportive. I worked hard for that money, sacrificed my soul for it, so I got immense satisfaction from seeing it put to good use. It helped make everything I went through worth it. In the end, those hard times not only helped me fulfil my dreams, they led me to Brock. That can't be a bad thing.

'Morning,' I say as the man approaches the counter. He's around my age, and quite handsome with his dark hair and rugged features.

'Morning,' he replies with a genuine smile as he comes to a stop in front of the display cases. The moment our eyes meet, my heart starts to race. His eyes are identical to my jade green ones.

'Jade?' he says hesitantly.

'Tate?' My eyes instantly cloud with tears. When he nods his head, I clutch my hands to my chest. My brother.

I've found my brother.

Before I even realise what I'm doing, I'm on the other side of the counter, launching myself into his arms. I don't mean to cry, but I find myself sobbing into his chest as we hold each other tight. I finally have a real blood relative, something I've wished for my entire life.

'Your husband wanted me to come to the house for dinner tonight, to surprise you,' he tells me, tightening his embrace. 'I feel bad for ruining this for him, he seems like a great guy, but I couldn't wait another second to see you. I've been waiting my whole life for this moment. The minute my plane touched down, I headed straight here.'

'I'm so glad you came,' I manage to say. 'So glad.'

Tate spends the rest of the day with me at the shop. We don't stop talking the whole time. I call Brock and he comes over in his lunch break to meet him. He isn't upset that his surprise was ruined, he's just happy to see us together again. I have the most amazing husband.

Tate was adopted a few months after we became wards of the state. The family that took him already had three daughters and desperately wanted a son. Maybe that's why they didn't want me as well. He was only three years old when we were separated, so in time, he forgot about my existence. He tells me that when Brock contacted him four days ago, he called his adoptive parents and asked about me. They told him he cried for weeks when he first came to live with them, and kept asking for his bubba.

Hearing that breaks my heart.

He confesses to dreaming about me the night after finding out he was adopted. He says he was standing beside my crib and reached in to take hold of my hand. He distinctly remembers saying the words, 'I love you, bubba,' which makes my cry. We were both robbed of so much.

Tate tells me he always felt like a part of him was missing, growing up. Even though he had a good life, and his adoptive parents loved him, he confesses to never truly feeling like he belonged. He tells me how his sisters resented him for being the son their parents always wanted, and gave him a hard time for it; how he left home as soon as he was old enough. He's been working abroad for the past five years. That's why Brock had trouble tracking him down.

We sit up into the early hours of the morning catching up. We laugh and cry. It's an amazing feeling to be reunited with him. I hate that we've missed out on so much, but we have the rest of our lives to make up for lost time.

*

I don't have the nerve to bring out the letter that my father had written before he died until a few days after Tate arrives.

'What's that?' he asks when I place it on his lap.

'It's all the information I have on our family. There's some photos inside, and a letter from our father.'

'Really? What's it say?'

'I haven't read it yet. I was waiting to find you so we could read it together.'

Tate holds the letter from our father in his hands. 'Are you ready to see what it says?'

'Yes.' It's the last piece of our puzzle. Hopefully it will tell us why he took his life. It's the only thing we don't know. My brother's hands slightly shake as he removes the letter and unfolds it.

To my dear children Tate and Jade,

I couldn't leave this earth without explaining my reasons for doing what I've done. Please don't think for a minute that I don't love you both, because I do, but my heart belongs wherever your mother is. I can't physically go on without her by my side. It may be incredibly selfish of me to think that way, but it is what it is. She owns my heart and soul. She has since the moment I met her. The day I lost her, I lost my will to go on.

I hate the thought of leaving you both in this big ugly world all alone, but I know you have each other and I have to find some comfort in that.

Tate, look after your little sister. Even though you're still young, I already see the love you have for her. You're a good boy, and I know you'll watch out for her and keep her safe when you're older.

Jade, my precious baby girl. You're so much like your mother. Not only in looks, but personality. You're sweetness right to the bone. She would've loved you so much if she'd got the chance to meet you. She always wanted a daughter and it breaks my heart knowing she gave her own life just to get you.

I hope one day you can find it in your heart to forgive me for leaving you, but your mother is all alone, so I need to go to her. I'm no good to you like this, and I know you'll always have each other.

My wish is that you both have a wonderful, rich full life. I can no longer give you that, but always know your mother and I love you and will be watching out for you from above. Until we meet again.

Always,

Your father, Colin.

We're both quiet for the longest time once we've read our father's parting words. I have a kaleidoscope of emotions running through me. I'm sad that he was so broken by her death, but at the same time, it was nice to hear how much he loved her. At least I'm the product of love.

I feel guilty my mother died giving birth to me. My birth ruined all our lives and ripped our family apart. I'm also angry that my father's decision tore me away from Tate and led me into a life of abuse at the hands of my carers, before being adopted by a woman who forced me into prostitution. That's a hard pill to swallow.

I wish he hadn't taken his own life, leaving us to fend for ourselves. Tate's life wasn't that bad, but my childhood was horrific. My life would've been so different if he'd stuck around.

'I'm sorry I wasn't around to look after you,' Tate says.

'It was out of your hands. You were just a kid. I had a good life,' I lie. There's no point dredging up the past. Telling him the truth will do no good. Squeezing his hand, I force out a smile as pieces of my childhood flash through my mind.

'I'm happy to hear that.' He pauses. 'Would you come to the cemetery with me tomorrow?' he asks.

'Of course.' I don't need to think about it. It will be good for us both.

It's a two-hour drive to the small town where Tate and I were born, and where our parents are buried. Brock is with us, but opts to stay in the car when we reach the cemetery. He thinks it's something we should both do together, but assures me he's here if I need him. I'd be lost without that man.

We stop off in town and buy some beautiful white roses to place on their grave. As we approach the gravesites, I clutch the flowers to my chest as Tate bends down to clear the leaves that have gathered over their headstones. A lump rises to my throat when I read what they say.

When Tate straightens, he drapes his arm over my shoulder. 'Mum, Dad, it's us, Tate and Jade. It's taken twenty-four years for us to find each other again, but we wanted you to know that we're finally together.' He turns his head and smiles at me. 'And I'm so glad we are.'

'Me too,' I say, putting my arm around his waist and resting my head on his shoulder.

I pass one of the bunches of flowers to him and he bends down and lays them on our father's grave. 'I promise I'll look after her,' I hear him whisper.

Crouching down, I lay my bunch of flowers by my mother's headstone. 'I'm sorry.' I was just a baby, but I can't help but feel responsible for her death. Suddenly, it all becomes too much and I cover my face with my hands and sob. I feel relieved I finally got to say that to her, it's played on my mind my entire life. I wish more than anything that things could've been different.

'Come here,' Tate says, pulling me to my feet and into his arms. He hugs me tightly as we both cry for our parents, for our family, and for the life we missed out on. It's cathartic. It's closure. I know coming here today is the first step in truly healing. It will help us both. You may not be able to change the past, but you can shape your future.

*

M's trial finally rolled around. Both Rupert and I were subpoenaed as witnesses. I'd be lying if I said I wasn't nervous, but on the other hand, I was eager to see this through to the end—to finally be able to put M, my past, and everything I went through behind me. I have a wonderful life now and a family who loves me, so there's no point dwelling on something I can't change. I know Rupert is keen to see justice served, and the monsters responsible for his daughter's death finally held accountable.

To my dismay, I'm the first to be called to the stand. I've been dreading this day. Under the circumstances, the court offered to let me give my evidence by video link, but that would be the coward's way out. I refuse to let her take one more piece of my dignity. I'd forever be disappointed in myself if I didn't face her. I firmly believed standing up to M is exactly what I need to finally be free. It's something I've yearned for. She bullied and intimidated me for far too long. With Sasha's death always in my mind while I lived with M, it gave her the power to control me in the worst possibly way.

Butterflies churn in my stomach the moment I enter the courtroom, but like every other tough situation I've faced in my life, I plan to tackle it head on. Squaring my shoulders, I put on my you-can't-fuck-with-me-face as I walk to the witness box. My eyes briefly meet Brock's as I pass. He nods, giving me a reassuring smile. His presence is all I'll ever need. He's my rock. Tate, Joshua and Theo are here with him to give Rupert and I moral support.

'This way, Mrs Weston,' the bailiff says as I approach him.

I see M's head swing around from where she's sitting with her lawyer. I'm momentarily taken aback by her appearance. She's no longer the immaculately dressed woman I once knew. Her hair isn't meticulously styled like it used to be, and her face is bare. What really shocks me is the horrid prison green overalls she's dressed in. They're very unflattering. Karma's a bitch.

Her eyes narrow as soon as they meet mine. I swear if looks could kill I'd drop dead on the spot. Nice try. Her days of instilling fear in me are over. She can no longer hurt me, where she's going.

'Bitch,' she mumbles as I pass.

Looking her square in the eyes, I plaster a pleasant smile on my face and reply. 'It takes one to know one.' I refuse to let her intimidate me.

Her mouth gapes at my brazenness and I see her lawyer place his hand on her arm, stopping her before she reacts further.

I walk across the room with all the confidence I can muster. I feel liberated already. Once I've taken the stand, the bailiff makes me hold the bible up in front of me. 'Do you swear to tell the truth, the whole truth, and nothing but the truth so help you god?' he asks.

'I do.'

After I give my evidence, I'm not allowed to enter the courtroom again and the trial drags on for five tedious days. I sit in a small room just off the corridor and wait. Thankfully, Brock fills me in on all the comings and goings each day.

The biggest shock of all comes on the last day of the trial, when Rocco takes the stand. Not only does he give his account of all the murders, he identifies the male remains and the reason behind his death.

Brock tells me everything Rocco said. Apparently M wasn't responsible for the man's death, but was present on the day it happened. The victim's name was Robert Sanderson. He was one of M's many lovers, and the first body to go into the dam. The kicker was he was shot by Maxwell Weston. 'He's still fucking with me from the grave,' Brock murmurs. 'I never thought he was capable of murder. I guess he was more ruthless than I thought.'

Going on what Rocco said, around twenty years ago, M and Maxwell were apparently having an affair. One day, Maxwell walked in on M and Robert in a compromising position, and shot him in a fit of jealousy.

'You double-crossing dog,' was apparently what M had screamed across the courtroom when Rocco said this. She never once tried to deny his claims. I can tell by his body language that it was heart-wrenching for Brock to hear this about his father, but it also explained a lot. Brock went on to tell that Maxwell had given M one million dollars only days after the murder had taken place and had gone on to spend millions more on M's escorts. This may also explain

Maxwell's involvement in my kidnapping: Brock and I think he was bribed into taking part. M was no stranger to bribery; she thrived on it and always used it to get what she wanted.

M's lawyers successfully appealed to have the ninth murder charge downgraded to an accessory to murder, but fat lot of good that did her. She was found guilty of the other eight deaths as well as a string of other offences, and sentenced to life imprisonment without the possibility of parole.

It's gratifying to see her finally get her just deserts, but it will never bring back the lives she's taken, or undo all the damage she caused over the years.

Nevertheless, Rupert and I agree the past is now the past, and that's exactly where it is going to stay. M can no longer harm another soul, and we take solace in that, making a pact to never mention her again.

She's dead to us.

*

It's a few minutes before midnight on Christmas Eve, and I'm so excited I can't sleep. We have the whole family staying at the house with us. Elaine, Joshua and Theo, my brother, Tate, and of course Rupert, who's still living with us. Brock's huge home was once empty, and it's now bursting with life.

This will be the first Christmas I'm surrounded by people I love, and who love me back. We have a beautifully decorated tree that's bursting with presents. I'm really looking forward to tomorrow. I have a huge feast planned.

'Brock, are you awake?' I say, nudging him.

'I am now,' he groans, rolling onto his side to face me. 'Is everything all right?'

'I can't sleep. Can I give you one of your presents now? I don't want to give it to you in front of the others.'

Opening one eye, he studies me for a few seconds. 'I sincerely hope you wouldn't give me one of your magnificent blowjobs in front of our family.'

I can't help but laugh as I playfully slap his arm. 'It's not a blowjob.' Rolling over, I turn on the bedside lamp before reaching into the drawer to retrieve the long thin box. 'Open it,' I say, passing it to him.

Sighing, he squints as he sits up. Unwrapping the ribbon, he removes the lid. I'm pretty sure he's going to like what's inside, but the butterflies churn in my stomach nevertheless.

'What the—' His wide eyes meet mine.

'It's a—'

'I know what it is,' he says. 'One of those stick things—a pregnancy test.' Of course he knows. We've been trying to fall pregnant for months now. He's sat with me on the side of the bed numerous times waiting and hoping. This time I did it without him. I hated to see the look of disappointment on his face every time we got a negative result.

'Have a look at the lines.'

I see a smile form on his lips. 'You're pregnant.'

'Yes. We're going to be parents.'

'Are you sure?'

'Yes. I got confirmation this afternoon from the doctor.'

Tossing the stick aside, he pulls me into his arms. 'I'm going to be a father,' he whispers.

'Merry Christmas, Brock.'

'Merry Christmas, sweetheart.'

'I love you so much,' he says as he lays me back into the mattress and covers my body with his. I see tears glisten his eyes.

'I love you more.'

'Not possible, sweetheart,' he says before his lips meet mine.

*

It's funny how one person can change everything. Change you. How one fleeting moment in time has the ability to redirect your path in life. To give your future meaning and hope. How something as simple as love can heal even the most damaged heart.

That's exactly what one man has done for me. My saviour. My knight in shining armour—Brock Weston. He may not have ridden in on his beautiful white stallion like I hoped, but that's insignificant. He came, he conquered, and he did everything I dreamt he would.

He saved me.

He gave me a taste of how good life could be when we first met in New York, but even that doesn't compare to how rich my life is now. As hard as things were for me growing up, I'd do it all again in a heartbeat if I knew I'd end up exactly where I am today. I take back everything I said at the beginning of my story. I'm not cursed at all. I'm lucky, I'm blessed, I'm wanted, and I'm *loved*.

Love is like water,
you can fill up on it,
you can drown in it,
but most importantly,
you cannot live without it.

JAX

Author of the #1 Bestseller BASTARD

J.L. PERRY

My name is Jaxson Albright. To my friends I'm known as Jax. I'm the disgraced son of well-known politician Malcom Albright. You could say I was born with a silver spoon in my mouth. I was supposed to follow in my father's footsteps and move into politics. My whole childhood was spent being groomed for this role, but that wasn't what I wanted. I had other plans.

To my family's disgust, I'm inked, I'm pierced and I own and run a tattoo parlour in Newtown, in Sydney. I fit in here. I can be the man I was destined to be, the man my family are ashamed of. The son they regret having.

I wouldn't be where I am today if it wasn't for my saviour, Candice. My pink-haired angel. We grew up in the same circle, but like me, she's an outcast. She refused to conform to society's ways. She's the only one who stuck by me and not only encouraged, but supported my dream.

I love her. No, correction—I'm in love with her. I have been for as long as I can remember. She has no idea how I feel. It's a battle I struggle with daily. I've kept my secret all these years because I couldn't risk losing her. That's a chance I'm not prepared to take, because she's my best friend; my only real family.

I've spent the last few years pounding random hot chicks, trying to mask these feeling I have. But it doesn't help—I can't get her out of my head. She still owns my heart.

How do you get over the girl you know you can never have? And how do you live without the one person on this earth who was made for you?

She's my soulmate.

KEEP READING FOR A SNEAK PEAK OF

PROLOGUE

The Past ...

JAX

'Where do you think you're going?' my father snaps as I walk down the main staircase, heading for the front door.

'Out.' I'm nineteen and a legal adult. I don't have to tell him jackshit.

'Not dressed like that you aren't.'

Here we go a-fuckin-gain. Is this man ever going to let up? I've lived my entire life doing what he's asked. I'm tired. I can't be the person he wants me to be anymore, I just can't. I'm not cut out to be a politician. That shit may be running through his veins, but it sure as hell ain't running though mine.

I scoop up my skateboard from beside the front door, tucking it under my arm. Out of the corner of my eye I see him storming towards me. I know exactly what he's going to do, he's done it a million times in the past. And that shit is getting old.

'Get that fucking thing off your head!' he screams, reaching for my baseball cap.

I manoeuvre my head to the right and then back to the left, avoiding his attempts to snatch it.

There's a murderous glare in his eyes as he tries one last time. 'You're an Albright, not some common thug. I won't have my son walking the streets dressed like that.'

'It's just a hat. Get the fuck over it.' I've never spoken to him like that before, I've always managed to bite my tongue. When I reach for the door handle, he roughly latches onto my arm, tugging me backwards.

I think the fact my father's long awaited plan is finally coming to a head is the reason for my bad attitude. In two days, I'll be heading to university. Of course he's making me study politics, which is the last thing I want to do. I feel trapped in a world I hate, far removed from the person I want to be. The only plus is I'll be getting out of this godforsaken town and away from him—away from my whole family. My mother and brother aren't much better. Sometimes I swear I'm adopted. How can we have the same blood in our veins, yet be nothing alike?

'You're an adult now, when are you going to start acting like one?' he sneers, tightening his grip on my arm.

'One day … maybe,' I retort, pulling my arm away.

'I'm not finished with you, boy.'

Ignoring him, I make a hasty retreat out the door and down the front steps. I drop my skateboard onto the concrete before placing my foot on it. He may not be finished with me, but I'm sure as hell finished with him.

'I don't know why I wasted my money on that damn car,' he yells at my back as I skate away.

I don't drive it because it's the same type of car he and my brother have. The type made specifically for preppy, pole-stuck-up-their-arse show ponies. It just screams, *Look at me I'm a pretentious dickhead*. That's not who I am. Give me my skateboard any day.

When I graduated high school last year, my father asked me what type of car I'd like. I told him I wanted a classic, something cool like a 1967 Mustang. Instead I got a brand new Alfa-fucking-Romeo. I don't mean to sound like an ungrateful prick, but honestly, I would've preferred a beaten-up Toyota or something. Why can't he see I'm nothing like him, and no matter how hard he tries, I'll never be?

I hate my life.

Without even thinking I head to the one place I don't have to try to be someone I'm not. Candice's house. She's not only my candylicious, blonde, blue-eyed bombshell, she's my best friend. The only person on this earth who gets me. We're kindred spirits. Like me, she's a social outcast. Neither of us belong in the fake high-class society we were unfortunate enough to be born into.

I've had a secret crush on her since the first day we met. Keeping my hands to myself has been a constant struggle, but I'm not the commitment type. And we'd never last. I'd rather have a life-long friend then a fleeting good time. I'd never want to lose what we have. She's the only one who keeps me sane in the fucked up world I exist in.

I honestly don't know how I'm going to survive the next few years at uni without her.

'Jesus Christ, Sophia, give it a rest. It's only hair. It's not the end of the world!' I hear Candice screech, moments before she opens the front door. Sounds like she's having a similar day to me.

Who invented parents anyway?

'Whoa!' I blurt out in shock the second she appears in the doorway.

'Great. Not you too,' she snaps as her shoulders slump.

'Hey. I like it,' I say as my eyes move down the length of her very pink hair.

'You do.'

'It's very candylicious. Very ... you.' I smile when I see her face light up. I love seeing that look. It never gets old.

'Come in, you dork,' she says with a light-hearted laugh, reaching for my arm and dragging me into the foyer, 'and stop calling me that.'

'What, candylicious?' I chuckle when she playfully elbows me in the ribs, narrowing her eyes. I'm the only one who's ever gotten away with calling her that name. I watched in amusement one day when one of the preppy guys at school groped her arse and called her candylicious. She swung around and grabbed hold of his crotch, hard. I almost pissed myself laughing when his eyes rolled back into his head as he fell to his knees in agony. She's a top chick, just don't mess with her.

'Jax. Thank god you're here.' Sophia sighs with relief as she rushes into the foyer from one of the side rooms. 'Look what she's gone and done.' I see tears glistening in her eyes as she points to Candice's hair.

Candice's mum is an ex-supermodel, so appearance is extremely high on her agenda. She's constantly having work done to maintain her beauty as she ages. So much so, she could easily pass as Candice's sister, instead of her mother.

'I like it,' I state, winking at Candice before looking back to Sophia.

'Great. Of course you would,' she cries, throwing her arms in the air in defeat. 'I should've known you'd stick up for her. You always do.'

And that will never change. I'll always have her back, just like I know she'll always have mine.

'It's just hair.'

'Bright fucking pink hair!' Sophia screams before covering her face and sobbing. She's a little on the dramatic side, but she has a good heart.

'I honestly don't see what the big deal is,' I confess.

Candice shakes her head, giving me a look that has me closing my mouth and not speaking another word. When her mother lets out a dramatic howl, I'm glad I stopped.

'Come,' Candice says, reaching for my hand and dragging me towards the staircase. 'I'll show you what the big deal is.'

'I'm making a hair appointment for you tomorrow, missy,' Sophia calls out as Candice pulls me up the stairs.

'Fine. Make an appointment,' Candice replies sarcastically, 'good luck getting me to go.'

Candice not only inherited her mother's beauty, she also inherited her pigheadedness. They have a fantastic mother– daughter relationship on a whole, but when they have a disagreement—let's just say it's explosive.

'Where are you taking me?' Usually we hang out in the games room, or by the pool.

An image of Candice's sinful body in one of those tiny bikinis she wears enters my mind. Do you know how hard it is to be best friends with someone you carry a permanent fucking boner for? Torture is the first word that springs to mind.

'To my room,' she replies.

'Hell no,' I say, tugging my hand out of hers. That's dangerous territory right there. Me in Candice's bedroom? Not happening.

'Get over yourself. I just want to show you something. You're delusional if you think I'm going to attack you or anything.'

When she puts her finger in her mouth and fakes a gag, I lunge for her, throwing her over my shoulder.

'Jax, put me down,' she squeals.

'Not until you take that back.'

'Take what back?' She laughs as I run up the stairs with her.

'That fucking gag you just did.'

'Never,' she says through her laughter.

'Take it back,' I demand, bringing my hand down on her arse. It only seems to make her laugh harder. When I get to the top of the landing, I slide her down my body before pinning her to the wall. 'Take it back.'

'Nope. Make me.' She has that stubborn look in her eyes, and I already know I've lost.

Growling, I bring my face close to hers. Big mistake. We always muck around with each other, but never this close up and personal. I can feel her sweet breath on my skin, and my heart starts to race. We're both breathless. The moment my eyes lock with hers, something shifts between us. Things go from playful to serious in a millisecond.

My face involuntarily moves towards hers. I hear her breath hitch just before our lips connect. Christ, they're just as soft and sweet as I imagined that'd be.

What in the hell am I doing? Reality hits like a bolt of lightning. Pushing off the wall, I take a step back. I can't lose her.

'Fuck. I'm sorry,' I whisper. 'I don't know what came over me.'

I swear I see hurt flash through her eyes, but it's gone as quickly as it comes. 'Don't be,' she says with a shrug, as she casually walks away, heading towards her bedroom. 'Are you coming or what?'

I pause momentarily. This is a bad idea, but I don't want things to be weird between us. That's the closest we've ever come to crossing the line. *We can't cross that line.* It's too risky. If I walk away now, that's exactly what it will be—weird. Sighing, I follow her. I don't have a choice.

'What the?' I say the second she opens her door. Her bedroom is very pink, just like her hair. But that's not what surprises me, it's the huge display cabinets running the entire length of the wall. Rows and rows of trophies line the shelves. 'Did you do a ram-raid on a trophy factory?'

'Very funny, arsehole,' she says, nudging my shoulder. 'No, I won them.'

'What? How?' I walk towards the cabinet closest to me and read the inscription on one of the trophies. Fuck me. 'You're a beauty queen?' I ask in amazement, swinging around to face her. How did I not know this? That's when I spot all the sashes that are proudly displayed along the wall above her bed.

'Yes,' she replies, her shoulders slumping. 'I'm supposed to be in the running for Miss Australia, hence the pink hair. But I'm not cut out for this kind of thing, Jax. I hate it.'

'Then why do you do it?'

'Sophia,' is all she says, letting out a deflated breath. I still find it weird that she calls her mother by her first name. Apparently, being called 'Mum' makes Sophia feel old.

'Oh.' I get that. My dad has been controlling my life for as long as I can remember.

'This is why she freaked out about my hair,' she says gesturing around the room with her hand. 'The Miss Australia pageant is only two weeks away. This crap means everything to her.'

'But not to you?' I'm still shocked by her revelation. My candylicious is a beauty queen. Sure, she's got the looks for it, she's a fucking babe, but the Candice I know is far from that type of girl.

'Exactly. You know me better than anyone, Jax. This is not who I am.' She's always so bubbly, so it hurts to see her so deflated. I want to pull her into my arms, but I can't— dangerous territory.

'Did you tell Sophia that?'

'Yes. I've been telling her for years. I don't know,' she says, raising her arms in frustration. 'I guess she misses her old life, so she's trying to live vicariously through me.'

'That's fucked up.'

'I know, right? Welcome to my life.'

'You know, mine's not much better. I wish our parents would just let us live our lives the way we want.'

'I'll drink to that.'

She prances across the room and my eyes follow. Her sweet apple scent lingers in the air as she breezes past me. I'm fucking addicted to the way she smells. On any other occasion, I'd probably be checking out her arse, but our little encounter in the corridor has me spooked. When she bends over to retrieve something out of the bottom drawer, I quickly divert my gaze to the ceiling.

'So how long have you been doing this beauty thing?' I ask trying to pull my thoughts out of the gutter.

'Since I was four,' she replies with a roll of her eyes.

'I can't believe you never mentioned it.'

'It's not something I'm proud of.' The sadness in her voice tears at my heart. 'Here.'

When she passes me a shot glass, I raise it to my nose, inhaling. The strong scent of aniseed invades my senses. Sambuca. Nice.

'Bottoms up,' she says, holding her glass in the air. 'Or should I say, penises up.'

My face screws up at her comment, then I look at the glass in my hand. Why did I not see that before? It has a tiny penis handle, and the words 'I Love Peckers' written in bold letters across the front.

'No fucking way,' I snap, shoving the shot glass into her hands before frantically wiping my fingers down the front of my jeans to remove the pecker germs. 'What the hell is wrong with you? I'm not drinking out of a cock cup.'

Candice throws her head back and laughs at my outburst. I'm glad she finds this amusing. 'It's just a glass, Jax, get over it.'

'A glass with a cock on it. Would you drink out of a pussy cup?' I ask, smugly.

'Um, yeah. It's just a damn cup. The shape or design hold no significance.'

How did we go from talking about beauty queens to genitals? I rub my free hand over my face. Christ, I really need to get out of her room before I do something I'm going to regret for the rest of my life.

'It does if you're male and it's shaped like a cock,' I retort.

'Fine. More for me.' She downs her shot, quickly followed by mine. Clenching her eyes shut, she shakes her head slightly as she swallows the liquid. I grin as I watch her. She's like no other girl I know. I think that's the thing I love about her most. When her eyes spring open, she looks at me sceptically.

'When did you become a homophobe?'

'I'm not a damn homophobe. I have no problem with a guy drinking out of a cock cup, as long as it's not me.'

When she laughs again, I swear I hear her mumble pussy under her breath, but I'm not entirely sure, so I let it go.

Stalking across the room, I grab the open bottle of Sambuca off her dresser and bring it to my lips.

I'll give her pussy.

*

Two hours and an empty bottle of Sambuca later, it's safe to say we're both a little drunk. We're sprawled on her bed, lying side by side and staring at the ceiling. Being on her bed with her is a bad idea, but the alcohol seems to have robbed me of my common sense.

'I'm going to miss you while you're away,' Candice whispers, reaching for my hand. I'm gonna fucking miss her too. My chest aches just thinking about it. 'Oh, that reminds me, I got you a little present.' Sitting up, she leaps off the bed.

'It's not cock paraphernalia is it?'

'No, you dick.' She laughs, coming to sit back down on the side of the bed. 'Here.'

I look at the parcel in her hand. 'You shouldn't have,' I say rolling onto my side and propping myself onto one elbow.

'I wanted to. I hope you like it.'

I'll like it just because it's from her. When she extends her hand, I take the present before pushing myself into a sitting position.

'Candice,' I whisper when I see what's inside.

'I know you're not studying art at uni, but one day you'll get to fulfil your dream. In the meantime, you can keep all your sketches in there.'

A lump rises in my throat as I gaze down at the black, leatherbound sketchpad. It has *Jax's Dream* stamped in silver across the front, and underneath the words *Wicked Ink* curve around an image of a skull-and-crossbones. This gift signifies so much. She's the only one who's ever supported me. I love her for that alone.

'Thank you,' I say as my eyes meet hers.

'You will open your own tattoo parlour one day, Jaxson Albright, I know it.' I love the conviction in her voice.

A sudden sadness washes over me. 'How am I going to survive the next few years without you?'

She sighs and looks away from me to watch her fingers swirl a figure-eight pattern in the comforter.

'Hey,' I say, placing my finger under her chin and dipping my head to make eye contact with her. When I see tears pooling in her baby blues, it's like a sucker-punch to the chest. I pull her into my arms. 'Hey, don't cry.'

'You're the bestest friend a girl could ever ask for,' she sniffles.

'And you're the bestest friend a guy could ever ask for.' Shit. Did I just utter those words? That would have to be, hands down, the unmanliness thing I've ever said. It's that fucking cock cup, it's messing with my head. I hear her chuckle through her tears, and I know she's thinking exactly what I am—I'm a pussy.

'When am I going to see you again?'

'There's a spare room at my apartment in Sydney. Once I'm settled, you can come down and stay some weekends.'

'I'd like that,' she whispers.

My thumb sweeps across her cheek, wiping away her tears. It kills me to see her so upset. I wish I didn't have to leave.

Her eyes lock with mine, and just like in the corridor, something shifts. It's like the universe has suddenly stopped spinning. I'm frozen. When her gaze flicks down to my mouth, and her tongue darts out to moisten her lips, my need to kiss her again is almost my undoing. I've gotta get the fuck out of here. I'm trying to be the good guy, but failing.

Before I get the chance to do anything, her face moves towards mine as her eyes drift shut. The moment our lips connect, all my resolve vanishes. My fingers thread through her hair as I draw her closer, deepening the kiss. I'm so lost in this moment, I'm powerless to stop it.

'Jax,' she whispers against my mouth as her body leans forwards, pushing me back down on the mattress. The second she straddles my lap and her sweet lips meet mine again, I know I'm a goner.

'Candice,' I breathe as my fingers trail up the length of her legs, coming to rest on her arse. This is my wildest dream and my worst fucking nightmare all rolled into one. I've dreamt and dreaded this moment since I first laid eyes on her.

She's my fucking kryptonite.

I groan into her mouth when she rotates her hips over my rock hard dick. I need to put a stop to this, but I can't. I crave her too much.

When she abruptly pulls out of the kiss, I'm filled with mixed emotions. I'm thankful that, unlike me, she has the strength to stop this, but I'm gutted too.

She manoeuvres her body down mine, sliding her hands underneath my T-shirt as she goes.

Maybe I misunderstood.

When she leans forwards, running her tongue across my abdomen before raising her face and giving me a mischievous smile, I know I've misunderstood. Sweet Jesus, have I misunderstood.

I swear my heart skips a beat when her fingers move to the waistband of my jeans. Is this really happening? I can't tell you how many times I've jacked off to the image of her lips wrapped around my cock.

She makes easy work of undoing the buttons, which is unnerving. I'm not naive enough to think this is her first time. Actually, I know it's not.

Candice was dating one of my brother's loser mates when we first met. I'll never forget it. They were all hanging around by the pool, so I decided to go for a swim. It was only to piss my brother off. He and his preppy mates have always thought they were too good for me, and I get pleasure out of riling them up. They were playing some pansy-arse game of water polo or something, so I ran out onto the back deck, doing a mother of bomb right in the middle of their game. I hadn't even noticed her sitting on the edge until I heard her sweet laugh when I broke the surface.

My head snapped in her direction, while my brother and his mates screamed profanities at me. She was fully dressed and soaked from the splash, but surprisingly, she was smiling. It was a beautiful fucking smile too. I've never been a believer in love at first sight, but fuck me if I didn't fall a little in love with her in that moment. If it had been any of the other stuck-up bitches my brother hangs around, all hell would've broken loose.

Two days later, I ended up beating the crap out of her boyfriend in our kitchen after I heard him bragging about her exceptional oral skills to my brother and his dickhead mates.

Thankfully, she saw the light and broke up with him a week later. We've been hanging out together ever since.

I'm pulled back into reality when her hand slides inside my boxer briefs, causing me to inhale a sharp breath. I'm torn. I want this more than I want my next breath, but it's what comes after that petrifies the hell out of me. I can't lose her.

'Holy crap,' she whispers once she's freed my cock. 'I had no idea you were packing this monster in your pants.' Her comment makes me laugh. 'This thing should come with a warning label.'

'You're not the first person to say that,' I reply with amusement. When her eyes slightly narrow and her grip on my cock tightens, I get the impression she doesn't want to hear about the other girls I've been with. I don't blame her.

I'm positive that's part of the reason I beat up her ex. One, because he was telling his mates how well she sucks cock, and two, the thought of them together like that really fucked with my head.

I take a deep breath and hold it as her face inches towards my dick. Part of me is screaming, 'Stop this before it goes any further!' But I can't. Maybe the alcohol coursing through my veins is affecting my rational thinking, or maybe it's because all the blood in my head is now rushing to my cock.

The second her sweet mouth wraps around the head, every ounce of fight leaves me. 'Candice,' I moan as my hands thread through her hair. '*Fuck.*' My eyes roll back in my head as my hips involuntarily thrust towards her mouth. She takes me deep into her throat, palming my balls in her hand at the same time. I bet you a thousand bucks one of those trophies in her cabinet says: *Blowjob Queen—Candice Crawford*. If there isn't one, there fucking should be.

I bask in her magic mouth for a little while longer, before putting my hands under her arms and dragging her up my body. It's not fair that I'm the one getting all the pleasure.

When her mouth crashes into mine, I flip her over onto her back, covering half of her body with my own. 'It's my turn now.'

'Oh Jax,' she whispers into my mouth, when my fingers trail up her leg and under that sexy little denim skirt she's wearing. I groan when she parts her legs for me, allowing me better access.

I'm still up in the air about what we're doing but I'm losing the battle with every second that passes. The moment my hand runs between her legs and over the soaked fabric of her lace panties, all my indecision vanishes. I need her—more than fucking life itself.

Sliding my hand into her underwear, my fingers glide through her heaven. She's so fucking wet for me. 'I need to taste you,' I say, pulling out of the kiss and making eye contact with her.

'Please,' she whimpers.

'Are you sure?' I ask, hoping she has the sense to stop this, because I sure as hell don't.

My hopes are dashed when she nods before uttering, 'Yes. I've never been surer.' There's no way I can deny her.

Sitting back on my haunches, I glide her pink lace panties down her legs. She lifts her torso away from the mattress, pulling her shirt over her head, and removing her bra while she's at it. Fuck, she's beautiful. Surely she didn't need all those trophies to tell her that. My eyes rake over her luscious body. She literally takes my breath away.

369

I'm so fucking hard my cock aches.

She moans the moment my mouth bears down on her and her fingers grip my hair. Christ, she tastes just as sweet as I knew she would. I love that it only takes me minutes to have her coming undone.

I place my hand over her mouth when she screams out in pleasure. Her mother's downstairs. I don't fancy facing her wrath if she finds out what we're up to in here.

Taking my time, I kiss my way up her body until my mouth covers hers. I know the day will come that I'll regret doing this, but I'm too lost in her to care right now.

My body is still nestled between her legs, and my need to be inside her is so strong.

'Fuck me Jax,' she breathes. Did she just read my mind?

'Candice,' I murmur as I move my cock towards her opening. The moment I slide the tip inside, I throw my head back and groan. She's so tight. She feels ... *amazing*.

My mouth hungrily captures hers as I push my hips forwards, filling her completely. Her pussy feels like a vice. I hear her breath hitch and her body stiffen.

'Shit. Are you okay?' I ask, pulling out of the kiss.

'I'm perfect.'

'Do you want me to stop?' *Please don't say yes.*

'No. Just give me a minute. You're hung like a horse, remember?'

I chuckle at her comment. She has no filter whatsoever. I love that about her.

Stilling, I give her body time to adjust. My mouth meets her again, but this time my kiss is a lot softer. I stay buried inside her for the longest time, while we make out until my need to move becomes too much.

Drawing my hips back slightly, we moan in unison when I slide back in. Within minutes I'm moving at a steady pace, pumping into her little slice of heaven, over and over. Rocking her hips, she meets me stroke for stoke. The sheer enormity of what I'm feeling for her in this moment scares me.

It's like nothing I've ever experienced.

Flipping over onto my back, I bring her with me. 'You've never looked more beautiful than you do right now,' I say as she straddles my hips and sinks down onto my cock.

She rewards me with a smile. 'I've never felt more beautiful.'

My fingers dig into her hips as I slightly lift her before drawing her back down. I watch as her eyes flutter shut and her mouth parts as she sweetly moans. Lowering my gaze, I stare at her pussy tightly wrapped around my dick. It's a perfect fit. Then my heart sinks.

'Fuck,' I grate out, pulling her off me in a panic.

'What?' she asks, confused.

'I forgot to put a rubber on.' I've never gone bareback before. 'Shit,' I say, looking down at my cock. What the hell? Is that blood? 'Fuck.' That's all I damn well need. 'Please don't tell me you're a virgin.'

'Okay, I won't,' she whispers, wrapping her arms around her legs.

'You won't what?'

'Tell you,' she replies, turning her face away from me. In that moment no words are needed, her actions say it all. Christ. How could that be? I never would've let this go so far if I'd known.

The moment I go to stand, Candice grabs for my arm. 'Don't go,' she begs. 'I've mucked around with guys before, but I've never gone all the way. It's no big deal.'

Running my fingers through my hair in frustration, I turn to face her. 'It's a big deal, Candice.'

When I notice the tears pooling in her eyes I reach for her, pulling her to me.

'Why didn't you tell me?'

'Because I know the type of person you are, Jax. You never would've gone through with it.' She's right, I wouldn't have. Too late now, the damage is done.

We're both silent for the longest time, until she finally speaks. 'Please don't leave me.'

I don't reply because truthfully, I don't know what to say. I'm not sure if she's talking about this moment, or me going away to university. The thought of leaving her and not seeing her for God knows how long, is tearing me up inside.

'I need you, Jax,' she says, straddling my lap again. My entire body comes back to life the moment she sinks down onto me. 'I need you,' she repeats. When her lips meet mine again, I'm lost.

I fucking need her too.

'Wait. Let me wrap it,' I say, pulling out of the kiss.

'No. I want to feel all of you, Jax. Just pull out when it's time.'

My common sense screams, 'Don't be a fool, wrap that fucker,' but my heart tells me to give her what she wants. My heart will always win out when it comes to her.

Holding my orgasm back, I drag this out as long as I can. I don't want our time together to end, because I know it will be our last. The second I feel her muscles clench around my shaft, I can no longer stop the inevitable. Quickly pulling out, I stroke my cock a few times until I'm cumming all over her silky soft skin. It's a beautiful sight.

In this moment, I know I'm ruined. I'll never again experience anything remotely close to what I just did with her. *Never.*

*

When I wake, the room is bathed in darkness, and my head hurts like a bitch. I lay there for a few minutes, trying to get my bearings. Then it hits me like a tonne of bricks—Candice.

Please let this be dream.

Turning my head, I see the beautiful profile of her face illuminated by the moonlight shining through her bedroom window. Fuck. It's not a dream.

Throwing my legs over the side of the bed to sit up, I clutch my pounding head in my hands. What have I done? A lump rises in my throat as the enormity of everything I've just risked hits home.

I'm suddenly feeling like I can't breathe. I need to get out of here. Standing, I blindly feel around the floor, searching for my pants. 'Fuck,' I murmur to myself as I slip into my jeans. 'Fuck, fuck, fuck.'

Once I'm dressed, I make the heartwrenching decision to walk away. It's gonna kill me, but it needs to be done. I can't face her in the morning. I just can't.

'I love you,' I whisper as I lean down, gently placing my lips to hers. I've never uttered those words before. My family doesn't do love.

She stirs briefly before releasing a cute snore. Even though my heart is heavy, it brings a smile to my face. I walk towards the door, glancing briefly over my shoulder as I go. This may be the last time I ever see her.

I selfishly put my wants before my needs, and I hate myself right now. I've always wanted her, but more than anything I've needed her. I always will.

I fucked up.

I've ruined everything.

Also by J.L. Perry, author of the #1 bestseller *Bastard*:

LUCKIEST BASTARD: THE NOVELLA

Available now in ebook!

It's been two years since reformed bastard Carter and his treasured wife, Indi, had their happy-ever-after in the #1 bestselling *Bastard* . . .

Contains:
Luckiest Bastard, a novella with a HEA
First White Christmas, a bonus story

Two years and two children after their happy ending in *Bastard*, Carter and Indiana have settled into married life after their tumultuous pasts. But a shocking event will threaten everything they hold dear.

J.L. PERRY

J.L. Perry is a mother and a wife. She was born in Sydney, Australia, in 1972, and has lived there her whole life. Her other titles include *My Destiny*, *My Forever*, *Damaged*, *Against All Odds*, *Bastard* and the novella *Luckiest Bastard*. J.L. Perry is currently writing two novels: *Jax* and *Nineteen Letters*.

For updates and teasers on all her future books,
you can follow or friend her on:

Facebook Profile
www.facebook.com/JLPerryAuthor

Facebook Page
www.facebook.com/pages/J-L-Perry-Author/216320021889204

Goodreads
www.goodreads.com/author/show/7825921.J_L_Perry

Twitter
www.twitter.com/JLPerryAuthor

Amazon Author Page
www.amazon.com/author/jlperry

Destiny's Divas Street Team
www.facebook.com/groups/323178884496533/

JL Perry Fan Page
www.facebook.com/groups/667079023424941/

hachette
AUSTRALIA

If you would like to find out more about
Hachette Australia, our authors, upcoming events
and new releases you can visit our website, Facebook or
follow us on Twitter:

hachette.com.au
facebook.com/HachetteAustralia
twitter.com/HachetteAus